# Re

*Doms of the FBI 2*

Michele Zurlo

www.lostgoddesspublishing.com

Re/Paired (Doms of the FBI 2)
Copyright © June 2015 by Michele Zurlo
Originally published April 2013
ISBN: 978-1-942414-13-1

All rights reserved. This copy is intended for the original purchaser of this e-book ONLY. No part of this e-book may be reproduced, stored in or introduced into a retrieval system, or transmitted, in any form, or by any means (electronic, mechanical, photocopying, recording, or otherwise), without the prior written permission from the copyright owner and Lost Goddess Publishing LLC. Please do not participate in or encourage piracy of copyrighted materials in violation of the author's rights. Purchase only authorized editions.

Editor: Debora M. Ryan
Cover Artist: Anne Kay

Published by
Lost Goddess Publishing LLC
www.lostgoddesspublishing.com

This e-book is a work of fiction. While reference might be made to actual historical events or existing locations, the names, characters, places and incidents are either the product of the author's imagination or are used fictitiously, and any resemblance to actual persons, living or dead, business establishments, events, or locales is entirely coincidental.

Warning: This e-book contains sexually explicit scenes and adult language and may be considered offensive to some readers. It is not meant for underage readers.

---

DISCLAIMER: Education and training are necessary in order to learn safe BDSM practices. Lost Goddess Publishing LLC is not responsible for any loss, harm, injury or death resulting from use of the information contained in any of its titles. This is a work of fiction, and license has been taken with regard to BDSM practices.

# Praise for Re/Paired

A Night Owl Reviews Top Pick: "This is a great read...The relationship was real and honest, and it was fun seeing Malcolm and Darcy! A highly recommended read!"

The Romance Reviews Top Pick: "RE/PAIRED is an awesome read which gave me some sleepless nights, because it was so hard to put down. I wanted to lose myself in the erotic play between Keith and Kat. The way he caressed her body with the flogger, the way he enveloped her in ropes, the endless orgasms she endured from his hands... The storyline is erotic, rich and entertaining. The dialogue is interesting and kept the force of the plot moving along, and I liked that I was able to see their relationship grow and mature into something beautiful."

"Wow. This book was so freaking hot!! [Re/Paired] has great balance....heavy on the romance with enough suspense to keep it interesting and that's how I like it."--Under the Covers Book Blog

5 Stars/Purest Delight from Guilty Pleasures: "This was a great read with a damaged Dom who learns to cherish his sub, a lot of hot BDSM action, suspense, and complex relationships"

"...Great chemistry...emotional highs and lows...There were a couple of secondary characters that I would like to see have their own story."--Literary Nymphs

"Lots of hot sex, kink, and a bit of mystery too. The hero and heroine's journeys are epic, and the goals, motivations and conflicts are all tied up neatly at the end. Zurlo is a good writer, with a huge repertoire of ideas. Please keep them coming!" –Manic Readers

5 Cups/Coffee Time Romance: "A tautly written, sexy, action-packed tale...[Zurlo] employs...the same devastating effect as a flogger in the hands of a skilled Dom. [Zurlo's] descriptions of subspace stand among some of the finest in the genre."

# Chapter One

Shifting into fifth gear, Keith Rossetti lifted his foot from the clutch and punched the gas. He forced the speedometer to seventy before easing the pressure on the pedal. No law against getting to the top speed as quickly as possible. He was frustrated and pissed off at his best friend, and he had no other outlet for his aggression.

Sex might work, but his last submissive had flung his ropes at him, accused him of having a granite heart, and left. And she hadn't been the first one to do it, though most of them had let him down gently, not that he had cared one way or the other. While his heart wasn't stone, it didn't have many soft spots. He didn't need that kind of complication.

Three months ago, he'd made a call that netted a huge bust—they were still mining the data from it and finding a steady trail of evidence and some leads on other cases—but it had put his best friend's girl in danger. While the circumstances were regrettable, the woman had been an asset, and Malcolm wasn't supposed to fall in love. But he had, and only Keith's quick thinking had salvaged the operation. Darcy had been hurt in the melee, and Malcolm had blamed Keith. This was the first time since they'd met that Mal refused to speak to him. He didn't know how to fight to keep a relationship going. When a woman left him, he wished her well and walked her to the door. Now that he was inches from losing his closest friend, his lack of skill just added to his black mood.

He didn't relish the coming barbeque. In fifteen minutes, he'd try to mend the fences, and Malcolm would give him the cold shoulder. They'd likely exchange a few pointed words, keeping it outwardly civil because Malcolm's mother would take off her shoe and bash both of them upside their heads if they didn't.

That was another part of this whole mess he hated. Coming from a family of functioning alcoholics who exchanged nothing but bitter retorts on those rare occasions they saw one another, he'd allowed himself to be adopted by the Legatos. Eleven years ago, he and Malcolm had been home on leave. His parents and two sisters had celebrated by drinking until they passed out, but they did that most nights, so he didn't see a distinction. Of course, he'd traveled that path as well.

Malcolm's parents had welcomed the boys home with a quiet dinner and honest conversation. Keith had liked not having to pretend he hadn't been affected by his experiences in Iraq. When he had come home for good, the Legatos had opened their hearts to him, and he'd become one of them.

Except now that Malcolm wasn't speaking to him, he didn't know where that left him with regard to the rest of the family. Snorting, he told himself to man up. He wasn't even there yet. Besides, Malcolm's mother had called the week before to extract a promise that he'd attend Layla's birthday party, so that had to mean she wasn't taking sides, right?

Not only that, but Kat would be there. He couldn't pass up an opportunity to see the woman whose face and body populated the landscape of his secret fantasies. It would never happen, of course, because he wouldn't allow their relationship to head down that slippery slope. He could handle breaking most hearts without feeling too much remorse. Hurting Kat would kill him.

He parked on the street a few houses down from Layla's. Malcolm's cousin always threw a huge bash in August to celebrate her birthday. He'd been coming to this annual shindig since before Layla had moved out of her parents' house and got her own place.

He lifted the box from the passenger side floor and tucked it under his arm. Two cars passed by, and then he crossed the street. When he arrived at Layla's driveway, he paused. Noises drifted from the backyard. Conversation cadences rose and fell.

Laughter punctuated sentences. Water smacked against concrete, and a high-pitched shriek answered. Keith guessed at water balloons. Cargo shorts and a cotton shirt had been a good fashion call. Layla maintained that a party in August necessitated a beach theme.

"You're tense. Either you haven't gotten laid in a long time, or you're afraid of something."

Keith's heart thumped a little harder, and he had to push it out of his throat before he could answer. Katrina, Malcolm's little sister, always affected him like this. Logic dictated that if Malcolm and his brother MJ were like brothers to Keith, then Katrina should be like a sister. She wasn't. Not by a long shot. Since the first time he set eyes on her eleven years ago, he'd struggled to keep his thoughts clean.

She threaded her arm through his and gave his bicep a hard squeeze. The side of her hot little breast pressed against him as she tightened her hold. "So, which is it? Are you sexually frustrated or a fraidy cat?"

A little of both. Keith sighed. He and Mal had never before had a disagreement that ran this deep. When Malcolm held a grudge, he held it long and hard. The son of a bitch had a stubborn streak that had served both of them well overseas and on many undercover assignments. Keith had one to match. He had no idea how things could ever be the same. He forced a short laugh. "Kitty Kat. Good to know all that lawyer training didn't teach you to mince words."

Her response should have been automatic. The opening he gave was supposed to initiate a scripted, harmless banter. Instead, she'd tensed up for a second, an indication of surprise. He realized he'd inadvertently used the term of endearment that he'd only used before in his fantasies. *Fuck.* It was good to know that when he most needed to be in control, he failed.

Luckily she recovered first. "In case your brain has been fried from spending too much time rotting in tricked out creeper vans, I was valedictorian of my class in law school. Give me a year, and I'll be sitting first chair on your next big bust."

He looked down at her, the first genuine smile of the day on his face. Her deep brown hair was pulled back in a short ponytail. Her dark chocolate eyes gazed at him somberly, belying the light tone in her voice. He could drown in her depths in so many ways. "You'll be a federal judge before we know it, and I'll be knocking on your door at two in the morning to get you to sign emergency warrants."

She tilted her head and looked him up and down. Now that the semi-flirtatious, scripted part of their conversation had ended, there was no telling what she'd say next. "Darcy said she'd make Malcolm play nice. She's on your side with this whole thing, you know."

"Good to know." He glanced up and down the street one more time. "I don't see your car. Did you come with your parents?"

Kat grinned, hugged his arm closer, and batted her eyelashes outrageously. "Say you'll be my hero and take me home later? I might kill my mom if I have to hear her gush over Malcolm and Darcy and the new-grandchild-to-be for another undiluted half hour."

*Be her hero.* He wished for nothing more than to see her staring up at him with stars in her eyes—preferably on her knees and wearing only his collar around her sculpted neck. It would never happen, but he could dream. "Of course. You do know I won't be staying long, don't you?"

"That's okay. We came early to help set up, so I've been here a long time. And you're an hour late." She tugged on his arm. "C'mon, Special Agent Rossetti. I'll be your bodyguard."

He snorted and shook his head, but he allowed her to lead him to the backyard. He'd taught her every defensive move she knew. "I'm the one who does the protecting."

"Ooooh, I hit a nerve. He used the Dom voice. I'm quivering in my flip-flops." She pressed a hand to her forehead and ruined the dramatic effect by laughing. The sound stirred in his chest pleasantly.

Kat often made fun of his dominant side, but she was the single female who regularly benefitted from his need to take care of a woman. Anything she wanted, day or night, whether or not she asked for it, he took care of it. He'd painted her apartment, fixed her plumbing, picked her up from a date that had gone sideways, and let her decorate most of his house. He'd remodeled his kitchen because she didn't like the way it was laid out, and he avoided yellow shirts and ties because she wasn't partial to the color.

Keith chose not to reply because he could only concentrate on the idea of her quivering. Plus, they'd made it to the backyard, which had been transformed into a beach paradise. Blow-up pools of all sizes and shapes were filled with ice. Some held drinks and food while others contained water and people. Colorful tropical flowers littered every surface, wound around table legs, and hung from the two canopies erected for shade.

Donna Legato, Kat's mother, flew at him with arms wide open. She was a beautiful woman, every boy's fantasy mom. Along with a strong sense of loyalty and a love of good food, she'd given her thick, dark hair and expressive eyes to each of her children. "I was afraid you wouldn't come."

He smiled at the woman who had been a surrogate mother to him for the past eleven years. "Mama L, I gave you my word. Plus, I promised Kat I would give her a ride home."

"It's good to see you." Mama L slung a couple of leis around his neck, slapped his cheek affectionately, and headed off to greet more people.

Kat looked up at him and batted her eyelashes. He knew she meant to mock him, but she came off as sultry. "Want me to hold your hand?"

*In the worst way.* Letting his better sense prevail, he shook his head and extracted the gift she'd been holding for him. "I'm fine. Malcolm can't start anything if he won't talk to me. Where is Layla keeping the presents?"

"What did you get her?"

Knowing full well his gift would be met with groans by everybody but Layla, he grinned. "The thing she asks for every year."

Kat narrowed her eyes, years of experience giving her reason to distrust his grin. "Naked men won't fit in that box."

"The other thing."

She closed her eyes and sighed. "Water guns won't win you points with anyone here. We only just got all the water balloons away from her. You might want to reconsider."

Layla had a thing for water fights. She liked water balloons, hoses, and anything else that held water long enough for her to direct it at her target. Because she didn't mind getting wet, meaningful retaliation proved difficult. Every year, a group of relatives took it upon themselves to search her house and remove temptation. Keith liked to fan the flames. This wasn't the first time he had given her the latest in high-tech water guns, and it wouldn't be the last.

He wiggled his eyebrow at Kat. "I have two more in my trunk."

She shook her head in bemusement. Her eyes sparkled. "I think I'm glad you and Malcolm aren't speaking. It's never good for the rest of us when you two team up."

Katrina wanted to be mad at Keith, but she couldn't summon the ire. In the eleven years she'd known him, she'd never before been afraid that one day he'd vanish from their lives. His close friendship with her brother Malcolm had made him a member of the family. She hoped the rift between them wouldn't make Keith drift away.

She watched as he made his way across the yard, stopping every few feet to exchange words with family and friends. Mentally she traced the outline of his broad shoulders and strong back. She spent some time admiring the way his loose cargo shorts draped over his ass so that sometimes she could make out the rounded muscles there, and sometimes she couldn't.

Naughtiness and sin dripped from every facet of his body and made up the bad boy inherent in his handsome face. And it wasn't fake. He looked like one of those men who dated a lot of women and left them hanging, and that was just how he behaved. Malcolm said Keith distrusted women in general and those who showed an interest in him specifically. While he didn't seem as cynical about her or her family members, Katrina hadn't tried to push for more. She dreamed about him, but she kept those wonderful fantasies to herself.

For the next half hour, she watched Keith and Malcolm dance around each other. Darcy, her brother's fiancée, commandeered the seat in the shade next to Katrina. Though they were both about the same height, Darcy had curves Katrina's slender frame would never possess.

She brushed her bangs away from her eyes and smiled at Katrina. "Trina, I'm at a loss as to how to get Malcolm to speak to Keith. I've asked nicely, and I've argued passionately. The most I could get from him was a promise to not say anything nasty."

Katrina laughed. "That explains why Mal hasn't said a word to Keith."

"This isn't his fault, you know. He was doing his job. He made sure the bad guy got caught. I know Malcolm was worried because I was in the middle of it all, but I'm fine. Why can't he let it go?" She frowned at Katrina.

A brief glance at Darcy's stomach revealed a gentle swell. She only recently had begun to show an outward sign of her pregnancy. "It's that protective instinct. And you're carrying his child, which just makes his need to keep you safe more acute."

Darcy snorted. "It's in the past. I'm safe. This makes no sense."

That Darcy wasn't a fragile woman who lacked confidence and a backbone had attracted Katrina's older brother and made her instantly likeable to the rest of the family. "I don't think Malcolm's ever been that afraid before. Give it some time. I bet Keith will have him at least talking before the party's over."

"I hope you're right. Your brother is one stubborn man."

Katrina didn't delve into the reason behind Darcy's smile. She had no desire to know why her brother's stubborn nature appealed to his fiancée. They chatted about other things while Layla opened presents.

She knew the moment Layla opened Keith's gift. Her blonde curls bounced, and her pixie smile turned downright evil. She lifted the super-sized squirt gun from the box and aimed it at Malcolm. "I love that you fill these up before you wrap them."

Malcolm held up his hand and put on his most forbidding expression. "That's not from me, and you should never point a gun at someone you're not planning to shoot."

Layla stood up. "I know it's not from you, and who says I'm not planning to shoot you?" She pulled the trigger as she said "shoot" and let loose a long stream of water that hit Malcolm squarely in the chest.

All hell broke loose. The hidden water balloons suddenly materialized, and more squirt guns appeared from nowhere. Well aware that hiding would prove useless, Katrina dived into the fight. Keith came through with a gun for her, so she was set offensively, but it also painted a big neon target on her body.

By the time things wound down a good hour later, Katrina's light blue shirt, now transparent in some places, clung to her skin, and the denim of her jean shorts chafed uncomfortably. How had she rationalized not bringing a change of clothes? Oh yeah, she'd thought Keith wouldn't want to piss off Malcolm even more.

She found Keith behind the garage. The massive water gun in his hand was raised next to his head, and he pressed his back to the siding as if he were on a raid. Katrina admired his profile for a moment before her discomfort took over. "Hey, half the people have left, and I'm soaked. Are you about ready to go?"

He turned his head at the sound of her voice. His gaze traveled over her body, assessing the damage in a way that made her feel deliciously naked. A flame flickered in the depths of his green eyes. He opened his mouth, but before he could answer, Malcolm charged around the corner and let loose with the full wrath of the garden hose.

Keith shoved her behind his body, which stemmed the worst of the flood, but Katrina was already soaked. His chivalry only mattered because she got to press her front against his back. His heat radiated through the wet fabric separating them, and her nipples pebbled in response.

"Take that, you arrogant son of a bitch!"

If Malcolm's declaration shocked or upset Keith, he didn't show it. "Takes one to know one." He emptied his gun in four long streams, and then he dived for the hose in Malcolm's hands.

They wrestled for control until the hose went slack, and then they just wrestled with each other. Darcy stood over them as they rolled on the ground in Layla's muddy garden. Her yellow sundress molded to her curves. At least it wasn't see-through. "Malcolm, do you want me to get your ropes from the car?"

Both men halted and appeared to consider the idea of ropes. Then Malcolm shook his head. "Those are for you, sweetheart. Keith's more of a masochist."

Keith punched Malcolm in the thigh hard enough to leave a bruise. Katrina sighed at their immaturity, but since Malcolm only pounded on Keith, it meant they'd made progress. They'd exchanged words and made physical contact. They were firmly on the road to mending the rift.

She stuck out a hand and helped Keith to his feet. Luckily he didn't need to use much of the paltry leverage she provided. Cold muck squished between their hands. "Yuck. You're covered in mud."

He grinned. "Guess I'm driving home in my underwear."

The image of him clad only in underwear—dark blue boxer briefs, according to her fantasy—as he navigated the roads to her condo caused her knees to shake. Katrina seriously wanted to lose her shorts too, but she wasn't about to announce that fact. "I find it hard to believe that Agent Rossetti doesn't have a change of clothes in his trunk."

"Laundry day. I did think ahead, though. I brought a couple of towels."

The towels saved his leather seats from the worst of their wetness. Keith had rinsed most of the mud away before getting into the car, but he was still sopping wet, and dirt streaked his clothes. To Katrina, he looked like disheveled heaven. His short, blondish-brown hair was darker in some places, and stray droplets of water glinted in the afternoon light. His sodden shirt delineated every inch of his chiseled physique. In one of the spare bedrooms in his house, he had some hardcore body-conditioning machines.

She wondered if he used any of them for bondage. Though she knew he had a dungeon in his basement, she'd never been inside that locked room, and she'd never broached the subject in a serious manner. Teasing and joking masked her curiosity. She hoped.

The ride from Layla's place to Katrina's condo took less than ten minutes. She shifted in her seat and regarded him with a long look. "It appears that Mal is talking to you again."

Keith's shoulder lifted and fell. "He's not giving me the silent treatment, but he's not going to ask me to come over tomorrow and watch some preseason Lions."

Her heart went out to him at the vulnerability he tried to hide. She reached over and squeezed his wrist. "You can come watch it with me, but I doubt it'll be the same."

"Can we eat junk, yell at the TV, talk about sex, and scratch our balls?" He glanced over briefly, throwing a deviant smile in with the question.

"I don't have balls, but if it'll make you feel better, I could scratch my crotch." She tried to match his smile, but the tingly sensation traveling up and down her spine made her nipples hard and distracted her from doing a good job. Scratching wouldn't salve the itch she had for Keith. "I can even do you one better. I have NFL Network. I bet there's a game on right now."

He pulled into the visitor parking spot across from the carport where her car waited. "If you let me use your shower and loan me something masculine to wear while I throw my clothes in the washer, you got a deal. Oh, and I'm hungry."

She laughed so suddenly that she snorted. "You're so high maintenance."

He pulled the towels from the seats and followed her around to the door that led to her condo. "I said I'd wash my clothes. I didn't say you had to do it. And I'll order pizza. You won't have to make anything for me."

"And I get the first shower." She threw that caveat over her shoulder as she inserted the key to unlock her door. The bolt didn't make a noise to indicate it had disengaged, so she turned the knob and pushed. It opened. "I swear I locked it. I always lock it."

Keith held out his hand for the keys. "May I?"

The question was a formality. He used his Special Agent Voice and wore his Official Frown. Wordlessly she handed over the keys. He closed the door and turned the key to lock and unlock it several times. The frown didn't go away.

"I'll go in first. You stay out here."

He disappeared inside. His demeanor scared Katrina more than anything else. Perhaps she had forgotten to lock it after all. She went through the same routine every time she left her house. It was conceivable that she only thought she'd locked it.

Keith appeared in the doorway. His frown had disappeared. "I want you to look around to make sure, but I think maybe you just forgot to lock up when you left."

Her door opened to a landing. A set of stairs went up to her condo, and the other set, protected by a door, went down to the basement. She jiggled the handle to the basement door and found it locked. Heading up the stairs, she noted nothing different. In her condo, she found nothing out of place. Still, she shivered.

Keith put his arms around her and pulled her close, a concerned, brotherly gesture even though she wished it were more. He rubbed his hands up and down her arms. "I'll stay the night if you want."

*Only if you sleep naked and in my bed.*

"Thanks, but I think it was just a dumb move on my part. My parents were in a rush when they picked me up, but I can't believe I forgot to lock the door. Next thing you know, I'll be leaving the stove turned on or the water faucet running." She shivered again. Though she wanted to stay in his arms, she forced herself to give up that warmth and comfort. "I'm going to jump in and do a quick rinse. Why don't you order the pizza, and then you can take a shower. I have an old pair of M.J.'s sweats around here somewhere."

M.J.'s sweats hung low on his hips, though they weren't meant to sag. Besides being too wide for his slim hips, the elastic in the waist was shot, and the cuffs didn't quite make the trek to his ankles. The doorbell rang. He ran her comb through his short hair and exited the bathroom. The issue with her front door being unlocked had unleashed his protective nature. Kat wasn't usually the kind of woman who forgot basic safety precautions, but his years of training and instinct screamed at him to let it go. She was currently juggling more than her share of cases while trying to distinguish herself enough for the higher-ups to take notice of her skills. People who were tired and overworked sometimes forgot to do habitual things.

Kat came up the stairs leading to the front door as he made it to the kitchen. She'd changed from wet shorts and a transparent tank top to light sweats and one of those T-shirts made for women that showed every curve. The scooped neck highlighted her pert breasts nicely. She wasn't wearing a bra, and he could imagine just how perfectly her breasts would fit in his hands. And the things he wanted to do with her nipples right now—he could bind her arms behind her and torment those wondrous buds until she begged for release.

He swallowed and tamped down the desire tightening low in his abdomen.

She pursed her lips while looking him up and down. "Well, they definitely aren't your sweats. Sorry. Both of my brothers are shorter than you."

He grinned. At six feet even, Malcolm came the closest in height, but Keith still beat his buddy by two inches. "What? No ex-boyfriend gear?"

She set the pizza on the counter separating her tiny kitchen from the equally tiny dining area. "I throw out the gear with the guy. Want to grab a couple of plates?"

At home, he'd just toss the box on the coffee table, turn on the TV, and file slices directly into his mouth. Kat always insisted on plates, and she ate pizza with a fork. He liked those cute little lady touches, so he snagged two plates from the cupboard and handed one across the counter. Then he handed her a fork.

"Thanks." She smiled, a genuine reaction that showed off the sparkle in her dark eyes.

Women showing honest emotion always threw him off for a second. He dated players and schemers because he knew how to handle them. Her smile was a gift and a reality check. A few months with him would wipe any traces of happiness and joy from her life. That reminder quelled his desire.

He piled four huge slices onto his plate and sank down into the soft cushions of her sofa. He'd spent more than one night crashed on the thing. The comfortable furniture felt and smelled like home. She took the seat next to him. Immediately, all residual tension left his body.

Vegging on the sofa with Kat wasn't like sitting with any other woman. She didn't demand conversation or attention. She didn't flirt or make stupid comments that showed she was only watching football to humor his interest. She always cheered and yelled at the screen. She hated the Patriots and let everyone in the room know it. When a team ran a play well or when they screwed it up, she often came out with a comment that opened up a brief discussion of the action.

In short, watching football and sharing pizza with Kat wasn't going to lead to anything else. Nothing he did with Kat was going to lead to anything else. Sure, he picked up on the little signs that showed she'd be amenable to something more happening. But after eleven years spent developing a friendship, he couldn't jeopardize what they had to satisfy his selfish desires.

"I've decided I love the gift you got for Layla. I think that's the best present you've given anyone ever." She bit into her second slice. Cheese strings didn't let her get away, so she wound them around her finger. It looked like she'd abandoned the fork.

"Wow. That's quite a few superlatives. I didn't know you wanted a squirt gun, or I would have got one for you." He folded his third slice and took a hefty bite.

She wiped her fingers on a paper napkin and smiled at him. Humor glittered in her expression. "Oh, I don't want a squirt gun. I meant it was perfect for her. You're pretty good at figuring out gifts in general, but that was brilliant. It got Mal talking to you again, and it was a great way to end the party."

Keith had always possessed a talent for picking out gifts. It wasn't that he put extra time or thought into most of them. He just listened when people talked. They usually said what they wanted sooner or later. Most people preferred gifts that were favors. For Mama L's birthday last April, he'd prepped her flower beds while she was at work. Though he'd promised most of Layla's friends and family that he would stop buying water-fight-related gifts, he knew how much she liked them. That trumped any other obligation.

"So what's your favorite thing that I got for you?" He probably shouldn't have asked such a loaded question, but he was curious to hear her response. He put more time into considering gifts for her than for anyone else.

She slid her gaze away, looked at her half-eaten slice, and then back at the TV. The Ravens had humiliated the Chiefs so badly that watching the game had become painful. When she thought deeply, she scrunched her eyebrows together the tiniest bit. Just now, nothing was scrunched. That worried him.

"Avoidance behavior." Goading her often worked.

She cleared her throat. "The necklace you gave me three years ago for my birthday. I wear it all the time."

The silver dragonfly pendant had diamond and emerald chips. Buying jewelry for women wasn't something he did often, but when he'd seen it, he had known it was the perfect gift. Though her birthday hadn't been imminent, he had purchased it right away and held on to it for seven months. When she'd opened it, the expression on her face had been a priceless reward. He knew she loved it, but he also knew she was lying.

He leaned forward and put his plate on the table. "That's not what you were going to say."

"But it's what I said." She picked up both dishes and headed to the kitchen.

Keith wasn't quite finished with his, and she always asked before she took something that wasn't empty. Her behavior confirmed his instinct. She was hiding something. The part of him that needed to be in control wouldn't let her have this secret, no matter what his better sense said.

He followed her into the kitchen. "Kat, the question shouldn't be so hard to answer."

She set his plate on the island. "Are you not finished with that?"

He took the remaining dish from her and set it down. Then he rested his palms on the counter on either side of her body, effectively caging her. He'd never used his physicality to bully her before, but he couldn't seem to stop himself from doing it now. The sweet scent of her skin and the spiciness of the pizza drew him to her. The upper swell of her breasts strained against the tight fabric of her shirt, and her nipples hardened to points. She dropped her gaze, a subconscious and completely real act of submission.

Leaning down, he captured her attention. Her breath caught. She wet her lips, and his cock noticed the delicate way her tongue darted out.

What in the world had he given her that would make her react like this? Both his curiosity and his libido were piqued. One of them demanded an outlet. Unfortunately, it was the one he couldn't assuage, not without losing everything.

"Kat, what was the first thing that popped into your head?"

She fidgeted, wringing her hands before she seemed to realize what she was doing. As a newer attorney, she had less experience with behaviors and tells than he did. She put her hands behind her, groping for the counter, but she came into contact with his wrists. Immediately, she folded her arms over her chest, hiding her vulnerabilities. "Keith, don't."

He leaned closer, and her breath hitched. Her gaze flickered from his eyes to his lips and stayed there. Ions bounced between them. He really needed to back off, but a perverse streak of self-destructiveness asserted itself. "Don't what?"

She closed her eyes and exhaled a short stream of air. "Do you remember what you gave me for my eighteenth birthday?"

*Hell, yes.* The memory of that kiss haunted him to this day. Her lips had tasted sweet, and that had nothing to do with the cherry lip gloss she had been wearing. It hadn't been a deep kiss or a long kiss, and it had nearly knocked him on his ass. But maybe she meant the other gift, the one she had been able to open in front of everyone. The one he hadn't made her swear to secrecy.

He had to ask. "The shirt or the kiss?"

She opened her eyes, but she didn't meet his gaze. She looked at some point over his shoulder. "The kiss."

"That was your favorite gift?" The part of him that chose collars that would look good around her neck while she lay naked on his bed was absurdly pleased. He ignored the warning bells in his head. Messing with Kat could mean losing the family who had adopted him and saved what was left of his worthless soul.

She shrugged. It wasn't flirty or shy. It was the kind of shrug that communicated uncertainty and discomfort. "It was and it wasn't."

He'd backed her into a corner. If she had been his, he would torment her until she explained. But she wasn't his. She was so much more than something he could possess. He dropped his arms and stepped back far enough to give her space, but close enough that she wouldn't think he was ending the conversation. "Care to explain that?"

Now that he wasn't so close, she relaxed a bit. Her shoulders moved. She drummed her nails against the countertop. "I was... I mean... It wasn't my first kiss, but it was the best kiss. I've spent the last ten years comparing every first kiss to that one, and they all fall short. But I don't know if that's because it was really so good or because I've idealized it in my head. You kinda ruined other men for me."

What the hell was wrong with her? She should have come up with another explanation, something plausible that didn't make him stare at her in shock. Why did she have to be honest with him? Just because she'd never lied to him in the past didn't mean she had to always tell the truth, especially not when the only thing that would come from this was more awkward silence.

He massaged his jaw and regarded her somberly. She couldn't think of anything to say to mitigate the damage. Give her an hour or two without him around, and her brain might remember how to process rational thoughts again.

"Do you want another one?"

Yes, she wanted to kiss him again. No, she didn't want his pity. She shook her head and turned away.

His arm came up, and he rested his hand on the counter, blocking her escape route. She could turn around and go the other way, but if she did that, things would never be normal between them again. No, she needed to face this head-on, downplay the significance of what happened so they could both ignore the topic for another decade. Because if she knew anything about him, it was that he didn't want the same things from a relationship she wanted. He wanted a few nights of companionship where he controlled every aspect.

She wanted a real relationship. The submissive side of her nature clamored for his domination. Though she'd played some games with lovers over the years, she knew there was a huge difference between the slap-and-tickle quality of those interactions and what Keith did. Keith was the real deal. It wasn't a game to him, and she didn't have the experience to know exactly what that entailed.

"To see if the memory is as good as the real thing." He'd lowered his head so that when he spoke, his breath whispered across the place where her neck met her shoulder. "I never meant to ruin anything for you."

She turned to face him, and he backed up to give her space. He'd never behaved like this around her. All those times she'd thought she had caught flickers of lust, desire, or interest in his eyes had resulted in nothing. "So this is a friend thing? A favor?"

Something flashed behind his eyes. His devious smile had long since vanished. "Sure."

Favor or not, she wanted this. Only a fool would turn him down.

"Okay."

He cupped her face in one hand and ran the pad of his thumb over her lower lip. He hadn't done that before, and the move all but guaranteed the impending kiss would rock her world. She felt like groaning, but she lacked the ability to make sounds.

He leaned closer. His lips brushed against hers, the bottom one moving sinfully slow. He spread his fingers and slid them through her hair so that he controlled her head with his palm. She couldn't move unless he allowed it. Tension stiffened her spine, and she became hyperaware of the proximity of his body to hers. She longed to close the distance, but she was terrified he'd break off the kiss if she was too forward.

He teased his tongue along the seam of her lips, and she parted them, granting entry. The warmth of his palm penetrated her sweatpants where he gripped her hip. She didn't know what to do with her hands. With her knees about to buckle, she grabbed for his chest. She met with a solid wall of hot flesh. How had she forgotten he wasn't wearing a shirt?

Her touch seemed to give him permission. He moved the hand he'd parked on her hip and banded his arm around her waist to hold her close. Their thighs molded together, and her breasts pressed against his chest. So many sensations rioted in her body.

The masterful way he controlled the kiss canceled her ability to think. She became a creature of response, grasping at his chest and shoulders in search of an anchor. A frantic noise escaped her throat, a sound that was a cross between a growl and a whimper.

He tightened a fist in her hair and tilted her head back, breaking the kiss violently. She gasped, gulping at air because she'd forgotten how to breathe. Heat smoldered in her core, and he wasn't finished. He trailed firm kisses along her jaw, nipping her skin every few inches. The sharp little bites both stung and sent her nerve endings into overdrive. Mindlessly, she dug her fingernails into his shoulders.

The savage kisses didn't stop there. He licked the column of her throat and sank his teeth into the muscle running along the top ridge of her shoulder. She yelped, not because it hurt, but because it felt so damn good. Sensations she'd never experienced ran unchecked through her body.

He jerked away, ripping from her grip in a manner that left scratches down his shoulders and across his arms. Turning his back to her, he pressed his palms against the counter that divided the small kitchen from the tiny dining area. His shoulders heaved as he took deep breaths.

Every muscle in her body trembled in the aftermath of his onslaught. Was that what she'd missed out on all these years?

Sure, she'd dabbled in bondage and played spanking games, but she'd never let a man take control of her body and soul the way Keith had just done. If a kiss made her feel this way, what would be left of her after a scene?

Suddenly she needed more. She'd always wanted Keith, but she'd held her emotions in check, instinctively understanding that he didn't have anything more to give. The plea tumbled out, surprising her with its desperate quality.

"Train me."

His entire body tensed, not that he'd been the portrait of the relaxed man a moment ago. "You don't know what you're asking." He didn't turn around to look at her as he dismissed her request.

"I do too know what I'm asking." Then she realized her mistake. Submissives didn't demand. They asked. They begged. At least she'd done that last part right. And they knelt, naked, at their Master's feet.

Keith whirled on her, controlled fury glittering from his emerald eyes. Unnerved by an expression she'd never seen on him, Katrina trembled even more.

If she knew anything about Keith, she knew better than to show weakness at a moment like this. He was the ultimate predator, and he regarded her as prey. Rivulets of pleasure ran across her belly. The raw air of danger seeping from his pores excited her like nothing else. She wanted to be naked and kneeling at his feet. She wanted him to show her what it felt like to belong to him.

Moving slowly, she lifted the hem of her shirt.

"What the hell are you doing?"

"Taking off my clothes." She would prove to him that she was serious. "I'm not ignorant, just not trained. You want me to get on my knees and ask properly, right?"

He gripped her hand hard, halting her attempt to undress and hurting her a little. It must have shown on her face because he eased up on the pressure. "Kat, I don't want you to ask at all. I didn't mean to kiss you like that."

Which either supported her point or should hurt really, really badly. He had been overcome with passion, just like she had been. Was it a momentary thing, or did he still feel the pull of passion unsated? She put her other hand over his, holding it lightly. "But you did."

A shadow of pain passed behind his eyes, a haunted look she'd seen before. "You're not cut out for that kind of life. You're too..." He shook his head, a short movement she barely detected.

When he didn't continue, she tried to force the issue. She wouldn't her drop it, no matter how uncomfortable it might be. "Don't you dare call me delicate. I want this. I want to learn about this side of myself."

He took his hand away and leaned down so that his face was the only thing she could see. Though she could read the desperation in his eyes, he spoke through clenched teeth. "I spank my submissives whenever the whim strikes me. They're mine to use however and whenever I want. I make them kneel at my feet and crawl naked across the room. I tie them up and flog them. I hurt them because I get off on their pain. I torture them sexually. Sometimes I tie them up and don't touch them at all. I make them do anything I want, just because I can, and I get off on the power I have over them. You're too good for that."

Standing over her, he was the very essence of intimidation. He might scare anyone else with his growled warning, but not her. She knew him too well to think he would ever hurt her in a way she didn't want to be hurt. Nobody had flogged her before, and she was sure nobody had spanked her the way he would, but nothing he said sounded horrible to her. She'd never fantasized about crawling, but she had considered the other things. It was difficult to imagine submission when she didn't know what it really felt like, what it would really be like.

She lifted a hand and caressed his smooth cheek. "This is what I want, and I trust you."

When he closed his eyes and seemed to luxuriate in her affection, she thought she had him. But then he gently removed her hand from his cheek and dropped it between them. "I know you do. That's why I'm telling you no. I thought the kiss would fail, that it would help you get over me."

The shaking in her knees had its root in her humiliation. "But you felt it too." And now she sounded like a petulant child. Rejection sat heavy on her chest.

"I'm sorry. I really am. But you're one of the few people I care about. You would learn to hate me." Misery etched lines around his mouth. "I just can't take the chance I'd lose your friendship."

This was difficult, as painful for him to say as it was for her to hear. She realized that now. She realized she'd stepped over a boundary he'd put in place long ago, and she knew how much he needed those impenetrable lines.

"I'm sorry." And she was. Sorry she'd asked. Sorry he'd refused. "I shouldn't have asked you. Can we forget about it?"

He nodded. "I'm sorry too, Kat."

## Chapter Two

Monday morning, she woke up singing the chorus of that song about hating Mondays. She didn't know more than a few lines, and they pulsed through her brain to the rhythm of her headache. Normally she looked forward to the workweek. She loved her job as an assistant US attorney, and she very much enjoyed her coworkers.

Though she hadn't done anything much except for the rest of her laundry on Sunday, the day had passed slowly. Each time she found thoughts of Keith occupying her mind, she unearthed another demanding mental task to kick it out, or she played games on her computer that ate up the time.

By the time her head hit the pillow, she'd written three briefs and beat her high score on a game whose primary objective seemed to be the obliteration of little colored balls. Ghosts of the graphics invaded her dreams. Now she was neither rested nor ready to face the day. Her body felt battered. She dragged herself to work and plopped down at her desk. Luckily she wasn't due in court. Only those nearby would be treated to the sight of her bloodshot, puffy eyes.

"Was it that good or that bad?"

She glanced up to find Aaron Buttermore sitting on the corner of her desk, a caramel macchiato, her favorite drink, in his hand. He handed it over. As she sipped, she realized she hadn't unpacked her briefcase, and she wasn't wearing nylons under her knee-length skirt.

With a sigh, she set the cup of heaven next to her keyboard. "Neither. I stayed home all alone. Worked a little. Did a whole lot of nothing. Woke up feeling like my head's full of cotton. Thanks for the coffee. You rock."

He smiled, an expression that lit his friendly face. When he'd first begun working at the US Attorney's office last summer, she'd toyed briefly with the idea of dating him. He was handsome and tall. With his clipped blond hair and mossy green eyes, he seemed a watered-down version of Keith. However, the chemistry between them had fizzled within the first five seconds of actual conversation. They had so much in common, and he behaved more like a girlfriend than boyfriend material. It was just a matter of time before he met the perfect woman and they had a perfect wedding and perfect kids.

"No problem. You should have called me. I would have helped."

Katrina shook her head. She didn't need a witness to her wallowing. With the first smile of the day blooming on her face, she lifted her coffee in a toast to Aaron. "You helped."

He grimaced and looked away.

She realized he had something on his mind, but he was waiting until she could gain her composure. Feeling sorry for herself wasn't going to make anything better, so she took another deep breath and squared her shoulders. "What's going on?"

"I wasn't assigned to the Holbrook case."

The Holbrook case involved a school district superintendent who funneled payments intended to pay for physical therapy for special-needs students into his personal bank account. In the current political climate, nailing anyone in the schools for embezzlement and fraud meant garnering the attention of powerful people. Aaron had been schmoozing Elizabeth Alder, the chief of the White Collar Crimes Unit and their immediate boss, for the past month.

In addition to kissing up, he'd also done a ton of grunt work leading up to the indictment. Katrina squeezed his hand. "I'm sorry. Maybe next time?"

He stared at the place she touched him for a long moment. "Hopefully. I won't stop trying; that's for sure. Alder said I don't have enough experience yet."

Perhaps she shouldn't have let her attention wander, but at that moment, she figured out the real reason Keith had turned her down. His kiss, the one that had knocked both of them senseless, proved he found her attractive. He was reluctant to take her on because her lack of experience increased the likelihood that he'd do something she wouldn't enjoy. Training meant experiencing new things. Some of them she'd like; some of them she wouldn't. Keith didn't want to take the chance he'd wreck their friendship with something she didn't like.

Aaron was still talking, but she only heard the buzzing in her head. Keith couldn't turn her down if she had experience. He wasn't the only Dom she knew. If Keith wouldn't train her, she would find someone else who would. Then she could go back to him with the kind of knowledge and experience he required.

Just before lunch, Special Agent Jordan Monaghan dropped in on her. Though he was a newer agent and younger than them all, he had already struck up a close friendship with her brother and Keith. Jordan didn't seem to have much in common with many of the other agents she knew. He wore his black hair long and loose. Dark stubble perpetually lined his cheeks and jaw. The knot of his tie hung level with the third button of his shirt, which gaped open at the neck. The relaxed, semi-scraggly look worked for him, and he only cleaned up for court. The first time she'd seen his transformation, it had taken her several moments to realize who he was. He'd grinned at her the entire time.

Jordan was also a Dom. A handsome face hid behind his facial hair and the locks falling over his eyes and ears. He wasn't her type, not at all, but he was a Dom. She put him on her list, but not at the top.

He took off his wraparound sunglasses and sank into a chair next to her desk. "Do you have a few minutes? I have some theoretical questions I'd like to discuss." He studied her intently, no smile on his face.

She slid her laptop aside and nodded. "For you? Of course."

He flashed a quick smile, more a dutiful reaction than an indication of emotion. "Let's say there were some discrepancies in the evidence logs."

Katrina knew he was talking to her for a reason. Though they knew each other socially, they weren't close. The details of cases she was currently working zinged through her brain. She needed more from Jordan. "How do you know there are discrepancies?"

Jordan tapped his thigh. "A hunch. Some of that evidence has gone missing, or it has been conveniently misplaced."

Missing evidence could destroy a case. Tampering with the chain of evidence could also destroy a case. Katrina frowned. "The evidence rooms are kept under surveillance."

"Sometimes criminals are smart enough to hide their faces and any identifying features." He stared at her hard, studying her face.

She shifted in her seat, uncomfortable under his scrutiny. "Jordan, what's going on?"

He shook his head. "I wish I knew."

She wanted to ask how much of this theoretical problem involved her, but she knew better than to ask questions whose answers could jeopardize cases. If Jordan had enough to speak in absolutes, he would.

"Sometimes the FBI installs cameras that nobody knows about."

Jordan chuckled, but his laugh wasn't real. "You're confusing us with the CIA."

She wanted to help, but she could only offer insights he already had. "Investigate the cases. Follow the money. Find a motive, find the bad guy."

This time, he snorted and gave her a genuine smile. "It's just like you lawyer types want everything handed to you on a silver platter."

She grinned. "I prefer platinum."

An intern whose name Katrina didn't know came over. She folded her hands demurely in front of her. "Agent Monaghan? Chief Alder will see you now."

Jordan rose with a grace that surprised Katrina. "I'll catch you later, Legato."

———

Keith's office on the fifth floor overlooked Cass Avenue. If he followed that corridor down to Bagley, he'd find the location of the first BDSM club he'd ever attended. He thought about that club now, long since vanquished by the economy and frequent law enforcement raids, and longed to rewind the clock a few years.

The club had featured trained experts who would, for a reasonable fee, whip him into oblivion. Submission was not obligatory, and he always opted to exclude that element. He wasn't submissive, but he did have a masochistic streak that occasionally required nurturing. He could use that kind of anonymous, mind-numbing subspace right about now.

A knock tore his attention from the dark places it had wandered. "Come in." He kept his invitation curt, his way of letting his unscheduled visitor know they were intruding on his valuable brooding time.

Juliette strode into the room, unaffected by his gruff demeanor. Tall and willowy, she had a stately air about her that she'd probably possessed her entire life. She'd been an administrative assistant at the McNamara Building long before he'd arrived on the scene, and she didn't hesitate to let him know it. He might be an agent, but she was in charge.

She smacked a piece of paper down on his desk. "I'm not your personal assistant. It isn't in my job description to field calls from your family."

He glanced down to see that his sister had called six times since Monday. Given that they were only halfway through

Tuesday, that was a lot, even for her. Normally Juliette would forward messages like this electronically. Writing it on paper meant she knew he didn't want evidence of his personal life in the official records, and e-mail was an official record. He appreciated her effort.

"Thanks, Jules. I'll take care of it." He fought the urge to crumple it up and throw it in the trash. There was a reason his parents and sisters didn't have his cell number. He wanted nothing to do with them, but they didn't seem to care about what he wanted. Nothing new about that.

"Hey, Jules."

Keith's day officially became more difficult. Malcolm stood in the threshold, leaning against the jamb. Dressed in a suit, minus his jacket, he managed to look every inch the federal agent he was. The affable smile on his face never failed to put people at ease. He radiated confidence and acceptance. People naturally gravitated to Malcolm. Now that he was in love, his magnetism had increased.

Mal beamed a smile at Juliette, which she returned wholeheartedly. Where Keith had a rather no-nonsense reputation, Malcolm was widely regarded as the more approachable of the duo. That was why Mal often took the "good cop" role when they worked together. People tended to like Malcolm, and they tended to be intimidated by Keith. As a pairing, it worked well.

Getting close to people wasn't easy for Keith. He'd spent too much of his life practicing the art of shutting them out to shift gears and let them in. When they'd first met, Malcolm hadn't seemed to notice Keith's inherent unfriendliness. It had taken some time, but the man had come to occupy a place in Keith's life that few people could ever claim to have held. He had a ton of acquaintances, and being an agent had come with automatic brotherhood, but none of that mattered to him very much without the only person he called a friend.

The state of their relationship for the past two months had cast Keith's world into a hellish state. Juliette slid past Malcolm and squeezed his arm. Even though Keith's actions had netted a huge bust and several breaks on other cases, since Malcolm had been subject to investigation by internal affairs, he got all the sympathy.

She closed the door on her way out, but only after turning to give Keith a warning look.

Malcolm parked his ass in the chair on the other side of Keith's desk. He leaned back and drummed his fingers on the padded armrests. "I forgive you."

If it were anyone else, Keith would have thrown out the sanctimonious bastard. Malcolm's lapse in judgment—who took a time-out from an undercover assignment to argue with the woman he'd knocked up in a house they knew had state-of-the-art security?—had led to Malcolm being shot and put Darcy in danger. People who weren't privy to all the details inevitably blamed Keith's planning for the mess instead of realizing that his quick thinking had salvaged the operation.

However, he knew Malcolm meant what he said. Keith lifted his chin in acknowledgment. "I forgive you too."

Mal chuckled softly. "What'd you do to Jules? She's been muttering under her breath about you since yesterday."

He'd been in the field conducting research. The job of a special agent never ended. "I didn't do anything. Savannah keeps calling here."

"Your sister?" Malcolm frowned thoughtfully. "How long has it been since you talked to her?"

Though he shrugged, he knew the answer. Subtract one month from the number of years it had been since he'd achieved sobriety. He'd given his sisters and his parents an ultimatum. He couldn't have them in his life if they were going to continue to drink. Leaving that life behind meant leaving everything connected to it, including the people who taught him how to be an alcoholic. Of course, that worked better in theory. His mother managed to track him down every six months or so. Sometimes she wanted to know how he was doing, but usually that just meant she was calculating how much money she thought she could shake out of him. He wasn't much of a giver, but that didn't stop her from trying.

"Are you going to call her back?"

"Nope." No hesitation there. He'd meant what he'd said. "I made my position clear a long time ago."

Mal rubbed his chin. "What if she's sober? What if she's calling to tell you that she's turned her life around and she wants to make amends?"

Leave it to Malcolm to poke holes in his logic. It was another reason they worked so well together. The question forced him to reconsider something he'd given up on, compartmentalized with the rest of his shattered hopes, and sealed off. It wasn't that simple.

He knew how to play the logic game. He caught Mal's pass and threw it back. "She's probably calling because she'd been arrested and she wants me to help get her out of jail."

This time, Malcolm shrugged. "You won't know until you call her back."

Returning the call, even just considering the idea, opened up too many wounds. Of the two evils, he'd take his mother over Savannah. Keith shook his head. "I'm done with that. I can't get involved with that stuff again. I can't let it destroy everything I've worked to achieve."

Malcolm studied him for a long moment. Keith's refusal hung in the air, scented with the fear and desolation he kept bottled inside. "People change, buddy. Circumstances change. If you don't learn to forgive and move forward, then you're the one who's losing out. In order to have the love and relationships in your life that you deserve, sometimes you have to take risks, put yourself out there."

Nobody else in the world could have said that and had Keith take them seriously. He didn't come back with a quick or snappy response about how life was so much easier for Malcolm or point out that he'd just practiced the art of forgiveness. Malcolm enjoyed the bonds of a close family and the love of a good woman. Keith had neither of those things, not really. And he desperately wanted them.

While he didn't necessarily want to reconnect with his older sister—she'd been violently abusive to him—he did want something else. An image of Kat, her face tight with the weight of a rejection he hadn't wanted to give, flashed through his mind. He would never be able to live with himself if he hurt her worse than he already had.

He stared at something on his desk, not seeing anything but her pain. "I don't know if it's worth it."

"I'm not saying it's going to be easy, but you'll never know if you don't try."

---

After toying with her options for three days, Katrina decided on Dustin Brandt. She wasn't sure some of the men she'd considered for the task were actually Doms. Confidence and arrogance and a job with the Federal Bureau of Investigation didn't necessarily translate into having a kink. Of the ones she knew about for sure, Dustin seemed safest. He hosted munches the third Wednesday of every month in the private meeting room of an Irish pub not far from her condo. He liked to mentor beginners. She aimed to see if she could persuade him to have more of a hands-on role.

Arriving at the pub at four required a little schedule juggling, and she was still twenty minutes late. She would have to work late on Friday, but that wasn't a new thing. Sunlight streamed through the big front windows of the long, skinny room. She glanced around, but she didn't see Dustin.

A server approached. Katrina must have looked appropriately nervous and lost, because the older woman smiled gently. "Are you here for the munch?"

It sounded innocuous enough. Anyone not familiar with the lifestyle wouldn't understand the term for a meet and greet among kinksters. Katrina nodded, and the woman directed her to the hallway leading back toward the kitchen. "Last door on the left."

She passed the bathrooms, also on the left, and mapped her escape route. The clank of pans and the shout of voices came through a door on the right. A kitchen should have a door that led outside. Should it go horribly wrong, she didn't plan to stick around.

A PRIVATE PARTY sign hung on the door. She wasn't sure whether she should knock. After wrestling with indecision for almost a full minute, she turned away. Just then, the door opened, and a man nearly ran her over.

He caught her arm. "Sorry. I didn't expect anyone to be there. Go on in. Nobody bites without permission."

Heat crept up her neck as she remembered Keith's bites. He hadn't asked permission. She liked that he took what he wanted. It made her feel protected and helpless, safely vulnerable.

"You don't have to keep your eyes lowered here. We don't use protocol at these things. Plus, I'm a sub too."

She had been unaware that her embarrassed reaction could be construed as submission. Looking up, she took in the details of her fellow submissive. He was tall, just under six feet. Wavy blond hair fell to his broad shoulders, and a neatly trimmed beard covered the bottom half of his face. He wore black jeans and a studded belt. A motorcycle emblem graced his dark shirt.

He looked like he could take on an entire gang, and yet he'd identified as a submissive. Interesting. Katrina felt an immediate kinship with the stranger.

She nodded. "I'm Trina."

"Kirk." He grasped her by the shoulders and set her out of his path. "And I'll be back in a few." With that, he disappeared into the bathroom.

Gathering her courage—she'd come this far—she stepped into the room. The conversation died down immediately as they all turned to stare at the newcomer. She felt like a dragonfly pinned to a board, put on display for all.

A quick glance around the table had her suppressing a groan. Not only did she recognize Dustin, but Jordan Monaghan also sat at the huge round table. She hadn't seen Jordan since he'd stopped by to run some theories by her. After his appointment with Chief Alder, he'd returned, moving the discussion to two other cases before he excused himself.

Both big men started for a second before settling back into their usual unflappable mode. She looked from one to the other, desperately wishing she'd chickened out before arriving at the pub.

Dustin wore a white shirt. His blue tie had angled gold stripes, and his jacket hung over the back of his chair. Like her, he'd come directly from work. Though he'd relaxed his posture, she knew his catlike reflexes were poised and ready, and she recognized the curiosity in his dark blue eyes. If Keith looked like a bad boy, Dustin claimed the boy-next-door image. Every strand of his light brown hair fell perfectly into place. He was tan and built, and he looked good in a suit.

Jordan, with his long dark hair and his propensity for wearing denim or leather, bucked the dark-suit archetype that most FBI agents embraced. He seemed to have more in common with Kirk than with other law enforcement types.

"Trina, come on in." Dustin smiled, but the doubt clouding his eyes ruined the effect. He exchanged a nervous glance with Jordan.

Since only six people sat at a table meant for fourteen, plenty of open seats remained. Jordan made the decision for her by pulling out the chair next to him. She sat down and smiled her thanks.

Dustin introduced her to the group. Besides the two men she knew, four women rounded out the crew. Each person there said a little bit about themselves, and then Jordan asked the million-dollar question.

"So Trina, what brings you here tonight?"

She didn't want to be honest with the whole group. Her request could wait until she had a private moment with Dustin. Kirk had returned. She met his friendly gaze and took a breath. "Curiosity, mostly. I think."

Dustin nodded. His expression indicated that he was aware of her evasion, but he let her get away with it. He asked someone else another question, which kick-started things. Conversation flowed until the server brought the bills.

Jordan grabbed Trina's check. Too nervous to eat, she'd had only an iced tea. He flashed a grim smile at her. "We always treat the newbies."

She wasn't sure, but his explanation sounded like a dismissal.

One of the women, Andrea, looked up from where she had been rooting round in her purse. First she frowned at Jordan, her brow furrowed in warning. Then she gentled her expression and regarded Katrina. "We're here the third Wednesday of every month. We hope to see you back next time."

Katrina tried for an uncommitted nod. People left. She lingered. From the way Dustin and Jordan took their time, she knew they wanted a private word with her. When Jordan's cell rang and he got the oh-shit-it's-work expression on his face, Katrina exhaled with relief. She didn't want to proposition them both. Not at the same time, anyway. If Dustin turned her down, Jordan was next on her list. It wasn't a very long list, but it was nice to know she had options.

Jordan and Dustin exchanged meaningful glances, and Jordan left. Two of the other ladies lingered, and Katrina got the feeling they wanted more from Dustin than a friend and mentor. Well, so did she.

Dustin picked up his jacket and slung it over his shoulder. "Trina, stick around for a few, will you? I'll buy you another iced tea."

Disappointment marred the expression of one of the women, while the other looked a little relieved. They said their farewells and left.

Katrina tried to say something. She knew Dustin had questions. This was probably the best time to proposition him. If he'd asked her to hang back because he had questions about a case, it would derail her courage, and she'd waited so long. Though the meeting had opened her eyes a bit, she wasn't really a stranger to this world. She was just inexperienced.

He held the door open and then guided her to a booth toward the back of the restaurant. The server came by immediately. Dustin ordered two iced teas, never once taking his gaze from Katrina. That pinned-dragonfly feeling returned.

He didn't make her wait too long. "Do you want to tell me what you're really doing here tonight?"

This was it. She could put her card on the table and see how he responded. "I wanted to ask you to train me."

Other than the twitch of his eyebrow, he didn't show signs of surprise. "What brought on this sudden interest?" His tone was gentle, and his question lacked judgment.

Not willing to divulge her true goal, she shrugged. "I think I've always been a little interested. Now I'm a little more interested."

He lifted the cardboard coaster and tapped the edge against the table as he thought. "What, exactly, are you interested in?"

She wanted to learn to be the kind of submissive who could make Keith happy. "You've trained submissives before."

"Are you interested in switching, or did you just want to learn the one role?"

There was no way in hell Keith would ever switch. He had constructed his life to have careful control over every tiny detail. "Just subbing, for now."

She sipped her iced tea, belatedly realizing she hadn't noticed the return of the server. Nerves were to blame. This wasn't the easiest conversation in the world to have.

"You're looking for straight D/s, or did you want bondage too?"

"Yes." Heat seared her cheeks. How had she not choked on her drink yet? "And impact play."

He sat back. Those too-knowing eyes seemed to cut through her with laserlike precision. "I'm sorry, Trina. I can't do it. I'm not into casual play."

Disappointment sat heavy in her stomach, a thousand pebbles that didn't belong there. Before she could beg, he continued.

"Plus if I even thought about touching you, your brother and Rossetti would kill me. Dying would seriously damage my career aspirations." He laughed a little, but his attempt to lighten the mood fell flat.

She grabbed the handle of her purse. "I'm sorry. I didn't mean to put you in an awkward position." Tears of humiliation blurred her vision. Dustin said something else, but she didn't stay to hear anything beyond his refusal.

This was why she never asked men out. Rejection sucked. She didn't know where men found the courage. Two strikes and she never wanted to see another man again. She totally preferred when they made the first move.

For the rest of the evening, scenes of her stupidity played in her head. Sound bites of Dustin's refusal mixed with Keith's, and even a punishing workout on the elliptical couldn't chase them away.

---

The next morning, she dragged her ass into work and nearly cried on Aaron's shoulder when he handed her a caramel macchiato.

"It looks like you're having a crappy week too." He pulled a chair closer to her desk. Around them, the office buzzed with the ringing of phones and the bustle of people. Neither of them rated the privacy of an office yet, and the government didn't see fit to waste money on dividers.

"Yeah," she agreed. "Not my best." The details were too painful to say out loud, and she didn't know where Aaron stood on the issue of BDSM. He was the kind of friend with whom she talked about work and casual topics, never sex or anything too personal.

"Good thing tomorrow is Friday." He glanced around before leaning closer. "Can we meet up for lunch? I'm due in court in an hour, and I have some more prep to do, so I can't really talk right now."

She squeezed his knee. "Don't worry about me. I'll be okay. I'm in court all day today too. We could meet at the usual place."

He grinned. "Ice cream and burgers. My favorite meal."

As it happened, she got stuck with a cranky judge and missed lunch. She texted an apology to Aaron and let the matter slip from her mind. If there was anyone in her life who wouldn't hold something like that against her, it was him. After all, the same judge had done the same thing to him before.

Her day ran late, as expected. She didn't make it home until nearly eight. The only thing she wanted more than to get out of her hose and heels was something loaded with carbs to eat. She shucked her clothes and slid into a pair of light sweats. Just because she was so tired, she decided to wash her face now instead of later. She scooped up her pile of discarded clothes and scrunched them into a ball. With practiced ease, she shot over her shoulder to the laundry basket.

The routine motion shouldn't have produced more than a quiet whoosh, so the crash startled her. The end-of-the-day lethargy fled, courtesy of the adrenaline from the shock. She whirled around to find that she'd missed the open basket completely. In fact, the basket wasn't even there. She'd hit a floor lamp that hadn't been there when she'd left for work that morning. The force of her throw had caught the long, skinny pole just right, and it now lay across her doorway with her clothes, still wadded, on top of it.

Thunderstruck, she stared at it for a long time before she recognized the lamp. It had been in her guest bedroom. The thing had a lime-green, metallic shade. It had been a housewarming gift, but it wasn't to her taste, so she'd relegated it to a room she didn't often visit. She couldn't remember who had given it to her, and she wondered why her mind barreled in that direction when it should be trying to figure out how it had come to be in her bedroom. And where was her laundry basket?

Without awareness, she moved backward until the far wall halted her progress. She tried to think, to figure out what she should do. Her brain stuttered and got nowhere. She needed to call someone. Thursday night was her parents' bowling league, so they were busy. Though Malcolm hadn't quite given up his apartment, he pretty much lived with Darcy in Ann Arbor, a full hour away. M.J., her other big brother, would be busy with his wife and kids, plus he'd never struck her as the protector type.

He'd tell her to call the police, but she didn't want a bunch of strangers swarming around her home, especially if she was just going a little crazy from stress.

She swallowed her pride. Keith lived less than ten minutes away, and he wouldn't look at her like she was insane if it turned out to be nothing.

Using extreme caution, she crept to her kitchen, grabbed a huge knife and her cell phone, backed into a corner so nobody could come up behind her, and dialed his number.

He picked up immediately. "Hey, Kat."

"Keith, I...I think someone's been in my condo." A small *pop* drew her attention to the right. It could have been the coils on the refrigerator, but her nerves were too on edge for it not to scare the crap out of her. Beyond that appliance was the hallway to her bedroom and the guest room. Had she left the door to the spare bedroom open or closed the last time she'd been in there? What if the intruder was waiting to attack? She dropped her volume and whispered. "Or they could still be here."

"Where are you?" His voice took on an urgency she'd rarely heard him use.

"In the kitchen. I have a knife."

"Stay in the corner where your counters come together so nothing is behind you. I'm in my car right now, and I'm on my way over. Talk to me, Kat. Tell my why you think someone is in your condo." He spoke a bit harshly, but she needed that to keep her from panicking.

"The lamp from my guest room is now in my bedroom, and I didn't put it there. I went to toss my clothes in the laundry basket and knocked it over. The laundry basket is gone. It...it just had whites in it. I was going to do my whites tonight." That had been her intention when she got up in the morning, but she would have let it slide because she was too tired and there were still several pairs of clean underwear in her drawer.

He blew out a breath. "Any chance your mom might have come over and done your laundry? Maybe she moved the lamp?"

While her mother had done things like that in the past, she hadn't tried to help out unasked in months. "Why would she move that lamp? She didn't like it either. We both thought the color was ugly."

"And here I thought you liked green." He was teasing, trying to set her mind at ease. Not only were they both MSU fans, his eyes were green.

"Not that shade. It doesn't go with anything."

Another noise distracted her. This time it didn't sound so much like the refrigerator. The air-conditioning kicked on, and the soft whirr of the fan filled the silence of her apartment.

"I'm at the door, Kat. It's locked. Come down and let me in."

Keeping the knife raised, she inched around the island counter dividing her kitchen from the dining area and hurried down the stairs. Too afraid to stop and check through the peephole, especially if the intruder was still in her condo, she twisted the dead bolt and opened the door.

Keith stood on her porch in the fading evening light. He wore a pair of camouflage cargo shorts and a washed-out blue cotton shirt. Everything about his attire was casual, which made the gun in his hand stand out even more. He adjusted her grip of the knife, changing it so that the blade pointed upward. "Always stab upward. Aim just under the sternum."

He thrust her back out of the way, closed and locked the front door, and headed up the stairs.

She followed closely. There was no way in hell she was going to let him out of her sight.

He moved carefully and methodically through her rooms, checking any place large enough to hide a person, and all the windows. Nothing seemed out of place, but when they got to her bedroom, her heart stopped cold.

The lamp was gone. Her laundry basket was back in its spot next to the door, and her wadded-up work clothes were on top. She left Keith, rushing to the guest room to see if the lamp was back in that room. It mocked her from the far corner.

"I...I don't understand."

Keith gazed at her with an inscrutable expression. He checked the windows in the guest room, and then he returned to her bedroom and checked the slider that led to the small balcony. It wasn't locked. He looked back at her. "You left it open?"

She shrugged. The balcony overlooked a wooded area. The only thing back there was her neighbor's front door and patio. She sat out there on nice days and read or worked on her cases. But she had been too busy to use it recently. "I don't think so. I don't remember unlocking it."

He slid the bolt into place. "I'm going to go downstairs and talk to your neighbor. What's his name?"

"Her name. Mrs. Hill. I don't think she's home. She has bridge on Thursday nights with her girlfriends." Mrs. Hill was approaching eighty, and she had more of a social life than Katrina did.

She followed Keith back into the living room.

"Stay here." He threw the order over his shoulder as he descended the stairs. "I'll check the basement."

In five minutes he returned. She could tell by the expression on his face that he'd found nothing. She sank down onto her sofa, dumbfounded, and set the knife she'd gripped so tightly on her coffee table. She felt stupid.

"I can talk to your other neighbors, see if anyone saw anything." He gave her a long look. "I want you to lock the door after me. Don't let anyone in until I get back."

Katrina shook her head. She was sincerely losing her mind. She had a few vacation days coming. Aaron would help cover her cases while she took some time off and got her mental house in order. "That's not necessary. I'm sorry I called you over here."

He knelt on the floor and took her hands between his. The soft affection shining from his eyes nearly undid her. "Kat, you don't need a reason to call me. I'm not upset with you."

Jerking her hands free, she jumped to her feet and moved away from him. "You think I made this up to get you over here? I'm not desperate. You're not the only Dom out there, you know. I know what I saw. I know what..." Talking to him was pointless. "Just go. I'll lock the doors and be more careful."

For a second he looked like he was going to say something. He opened and closed his mouth. He scratched at the stubble on his jaw. "I could stay. Or if you don't feel safe, you can pack a bag and stay at my house. I have plenty of room."

"No." No way in hell she was going to take his pity. She would approach Jordan next. He was a little scruffier and younger than she liked, but he was a good man and an experienced Dom.

At last Keith nodded and headed for the stairs. "Follow me down. Lock the door after I leave."

---

Friday dawned stiflingly hot. The still air seemed to ripple with waves of heat. Michigan had a handful of days like this each year. Being outside, just for the walk from the parking garage to her air-conditioned office, made her clothes stick to her body in uncomfortable ways. That irritation joined with her lingering feelings of idiocy from last night. After Keith had left, she'd checked the apartment again. Everything was locked. She ate popcorn for dinner, had ice cream for dessert, and slept with the knife on her bedside table. She briefly considered getting a gun, but then she rejected that idea. What if she came home to find someone in her condo pointing *her* gun at her?

To make matters worse, she had a string of depositions today. The second person on her schedule was Keith. The third was Dustin. Perhaps she should have consulted her work schedule before humiliating herself with two men in one week.

Keith arrived on time, as always. His dark blue suit emphasized the emerald of his eyes, and she melted inside at how handsome he looked. In all her life she'd never seen a more attractive man. It wasn't from lack of searching. She'd even scoured online dating sites.

When he saw her, he smiled warmly, but she wasn't able to muster enough positive feeling to return the sentiment. She strived for polite, and she was relative certain she achieved her goal.

"Interview six is open." She headed in that direction, confident he would follow.

Keith watched her sexy ass sway slightly from side to side as she made her way down the hall. All week he'd been haunted by visions of her, what she'd look like naked, tied with that fine bottom in the air, her legs spread and red handprints all over her luscious flesh. She'd cry out for more and beg him to fuck her hard.

His dick throbbed, and he chastised himself for the slipup. After so many years spent forcing himself not to think of her that way, one kiss had knocked away his control. One kiss and one request. *"Train me."* Her soft voice haunted his dreams.

Nothing would make him happier. But she'd ultimately grow tired of his need for constant and total control, and she would leave. Kat wasn't cut out for that kind of life. Even he questioned whether he could have a real relationship with someone who consented to letting him control every aspect of her life. He didn't need a therapist to tell him he had issues with authority and letting women get close to him emotionally.

No, she was better off not knowing how completely his head was fucked up. He'd already hurt her. And last night... He didn't know what to make of it. Kat wasn't one to play those kinds of manipulative games.

He entered the little room and closed the door. A legal secretary sat at the long table, ready to record every word he uttered. It was better to keep things professional. Eventually their relationship would return to normal. She'd be back to teasing him and treating him like an older brother in no time.

She assumed her seat and regarded him with cool brown eyes. He recognized that she was upset, and it nearly killed him to know he had caused it. The urge to take her in his arms, to kiss her and hold her close, was proving more and more difficult to beat down. It would diminish his acute yearning, but it wouldn't solve the problem. He had yet to figure out how her behavior the night before played into anything.

It was possible someone had climbed onto her balcony and accessed the condo that way. In order not to make a ton of noise, the person would need an extension ladder, and those things were unwieldy. After she'd kicked him out, he'd looked for evidence outside, but he'd found nothing. The entire incident just didn't make sense.

In the hallway by the elevator an hour later, she greeted Dustin Brandt with the same lack of warmth. He watched the pair, his senses attuned to find the smallest tells. The stiffness of her posture. Her plastic smile. His overly solicitous manner. What had happened between them to make Kat so formal and Brandt so apologetic?

They disappeared down the hall and into room six. Keith had other business in the building. No reason he couldn't swing by later and touch base with his buddy.

And find out what else had happened to suck the joy from Kat. Malcolm's words echoed in his head. *"Take risks...put yourself out there... You'll never know if you don't try..."*

She'd said he wasn't the only Dom out there. Did that mean she was going to ask someone else to train her? Did she plan to ask Brandt, or had she already done it? Son of a bitch. He breathed to control his rage.

———

An hour later, the door to interview room six was still closed. It didn't open for ten excruciatingly long minutes. From down the hall, he watched Kat exit the room first. Dustin followed close on her heels. He grabbed her arm. From the way she responded, Keith figured he'd said her name too.

Kat might have turned back to face Dustin, but her gaze remained downcast. Dustin lifted her chin with one finger, an intimate, dominating gesture that set Keith's blood to boiling, and he spoke to her.

The expression on her face softened. Dustin's finger fell away, and a small smile lifted the corners of Kat's mouth. She nodded, and the pair embraced. When they parted, she turned and continued down the hall away from Keith.

Dustin came toward him, lost in thought.

Keith stood directly in his path and forced the man he'd thought was a friend to stop and focus on the moment.

"Rossetti. What are you doing back here?"

"I thought I'd take Kat out to lunch." Though their paths crossed frequently as part of their work duties, Keith had only asked Kat to eat with him a handful of times. His schedule wasn't usually so liquid.

Dustin frowned. "I think she has plans with Buttermore."

Until that second, Keith hadn't formed an opinion about the lawyer. The assistant attorney seemed nice enough, and he knew the man was friends with Kat. Keith took a minute to remind himself that he couldn't go around punching her friends just because he objected to their gender.

Still, he threw a petulant statement at Dustin. "And you're okay with that?"

His buddy shrugged and smirked. That snarky kind of expression seemed to be at complete odds with Dustin's clean-cut appearance, but Keith wasn't fooled. He'd seen Dustin do lots of things that were counter to the boy-next-door image he projected. "I don't see why it's any of my business."

Keith inclined his head down the hall, though Kat was long gone. "I saw you top her a minute ago. How can you say it's none of your business?"

That smirk grew. "I wasn't topping her. I was talking to her about a private matter between the two of us. That doesn't give me the right to dictate who she has lunch with or any other thing she might decide to do. She's an adult, and she has a good head on her shoulders. She can make her own decisions."

"Touch her and I'll kill you." The threat was out before Keith could quell it, and he felt a little sick inside to realize he meant it. He'd kill any Dom who laid a finger on Kat.

Dustin had the sense to drop his smirk, and his entire demeanor changed. The hint of danger that hid so well beneath Brandt's exterior surfaced. He poked a finger at Keith's chest. "It sounds like she made the same request to you that she made to me. My advice? She's determined. If you don't step in and take care of her, somebody else will. I'm not saying it would be me. But she's an attractive woman. Eventually she's going to ask somebody who's outside your reach."

The warning made perfect sense. Somewhere deep down, he'd assumed she wouldn't have the courage to repeat that request to another person. He thought she'd made it because she knew he needed his lover's submission. He hadn't thought she actually craved the submissive experience. The idea of her on her knees, head bowed in subservience, in front of another man, made his vision swim in shades of red. It was one thing for her to have a happily-ever-after with a vanilla man. This was different. This meant they were as compatible as he'd fantasized, at least on some level. He'd never wanted to punch something so badly.

Dustin's firm grip on his arm brought him back to the present. He inhaled and exhaled, using one of the exercises he'd learned in combat training, and got his temper under control once again.

"Come on, buddy. You can't see her like this. She hasn't done anything wrong, and you're about ready to go all primal on her ass. Let's hit the gym. I'll practice kicking some sense into you under controlled circumstances."

———

Katrina threw her briefcase into the backseat and sighed to welcome the end of another draining day. She wanted to go home and curl up with a bowl of her mother's homemade ice cream and a Sandra Bullock movie. If she couldn't be happy, then at least she could watch the evolution of someone else's happiness. As long as it was fictional, it wouldn't compete with the sad state of her life.

She started the engine and turned the air-conditioning to full blast. Her blouse clung to her damp skin, so she pulled it away and leaned forward to let the cool air blow down her shirt as best she could.

A series of chimes from her phone let her know that her mother was calling. Her jacket, which she had shed for the walk to the parking garage, lay on top of her briefcase. The phone was in the pocket. By the time she got to it, the thing had gone to voice mail. It was probably for the best. M.J. and his wife were heading out of town this weekend, and their parents had the grandkids for the weekend. No doubt they wanted Katrina to come over and relieve them from the rambunctious duo. No, thanks. Katrina hadn't yet vacuumed out her car from the last time she'd spent time with her nephews.

While her standards of cleanliness and behavior might be higher than her brother's, she didn't think they were impossible to achieve. She loved her nephews, but she liked them best in small doses.

She shifted the car into reverse and froze. Something wasn't quite right. With a frown, she glanced at her passenger seat. Empty. The cup holder that divided the two front seats held her cell but was otherwise unoccupied. She could have sworn she'd left an empty bottle of iced tea there. A quick survey of the backseat confirmed her suspicions. While nothing had been vacuumed, it had definitely been cleaned up.

It was unsettling to know someone had gone into her car and cleaned it out without her permission or knowledge. This threw last night's scare, which had faded from her mind in the course of the busy day, back into the spotlight.

Nobody else had keys to her car. They'd spent the day with her purse, locked in her desk drawer. The extra set hung on a rack in her kitchen.

An eerie feeling crept up her spine, crawling with agonizing indolence and caramelizing into a bone-chilling fear. Who the hell had cleaned up her car, and why?

Lists of people ran through her mind, but she could think of nobody who would do it. She'd complained to Aaron, but he'd laughed at how uptight she was about those things. Keith knew she didn't like a mess—neither did he—but he didn't know she had one in her car. Did he? No. And he didn't play head games. He wouldn't do that to her, especially not after seeing how freaked out she'd been the night before.

Her phone rang again, startling her out of the fear cage that had enveloped her body. She snatched it up, glad to have the pseudo company. Right now, she'd take a telemarketer, anything not to be alone. The display indicated Keith.

"Hello?"

"Kat? Are you okay?" His voice sounded hesitant, like he'd planned to say something else.

No sense in telling him anything. He would advise her that she was working too hard, or worse—accuse her of manufacturing a reason to see him. She backed out of her parking space. "Fine. You?"

He didn't answer immediately. She heard the radio in the background, so she knew the phone hadn't disconnected. This parking garage had amazingly good reception. At last he exhaled. She wouldn't call it a sigh, exactly. It had too much determination. "We need to talk."

The frosty fear turned to leaden fear, the kind that pooled low in her stomach when she knew she'd displeased somebody. From his tone, she inferred that he'd realized she'd approached Dustin. Or he had more to say about last night.

After the deposition, Dustin had lingered to talk to her. He hadn't reversed his decision, but he did tell her that he admired her courage in pursuing what she wanted, and he'd help her find a suitable Dom. She'd felt nothing but relief—and sadness—for the rest of the day. Finally she was making headway with her quest. One day Keith would find her good enough.

She gritted her teeth. "I think you said everything already." It was too soon. She wasn't trained. She had only a theoretical knowledge of domination and submission. And he still thought she'd lied about last night.

"I'll be at your condo when you get home. Don't be late."

With that order, he ended the call, giving her no chance to tell him off. Did he seriously think he could talk to her like that and get away with it? What the hell had crawled up his ass and died? Malcolm had talked about Keith having his "moods," but she'd always assumed her brother was exaggerating. After all,

Mal wasn't the most easygoing guy in the world. Look at how long he'd held a grudge against Keith for doing his job.

The drive home seemed to drag on forever. She hit traffic coming out of the city that made her want to bang her head on the steering wheel or shout insults out of her window at the top of her lungs. She settled for swearing at her fellow drivers with her windows safely up.

Keith's car was parked in the visitor's space outside her condo, and it suddenly seemed like her drive hadn't taken nearly as long as it should have. She grabbed her courage and her briefcase. When she rounded the corner of her building and spotted him sitting on her stoop next to her potted flowers, wearing the same suit he'd had on earlier, she wondered if she'd jumped to the wrong conclusions. After all, he might be here because he wanted help with Malcolm. Or perhaps he wanted to apologize for last night.

He rose and held out his hand. She looked at it uncertainly. Did he expect her to hand over the house keys or her briefcase? The problem was solved when he took her jacket and the leather bag. The steel in his eyes matched his grim expression. "If you have plans this weekend, you have five minutes to cancel them."

She honestly didn't know how to react to that. Nobody had ever said something like that to her before. "Why would I cancel my plans?" Other than Sunday brunch with her mother, Layla, and Aunt Cindy, she didn't have anything big planned. Saturday was for errands.

He leaned close, stopping with his face so nearby that her eyes wouldn't focus. "Because your Master told you to. You asked to be trained. Apparently I failed to understand how serious you were. Your training begins now."

She trembled, anticipation mixing with outrage. This wasn't the Keith she knew. That man didn't threaten or bully. He might coerce every now and again, but his intentions didn't vacillate wildly from one day to the next. It took courage she didn't have to push him back, so she sidled out of his way and tried to fit her key into her dead bolt. Lining up the key with the hole took more dexterity than she had right then. Her heart pounded, and blood roared in her ears. She'd asked for this, but she wasn't ready for it. Was his goal to scare her off? If so, he was doing a damn good job. She'd never seen him like this.

As her heart beat the rhythm of her fear, heat rushed between her thighs—just as it had when he'd kissed her last weekend. She felt him press against her back, crowding her to the wall.

"Kitty Kat, bad slaves are punished. Turning your back on your Master and refusing to obey a direct order is definitely grounds for punishment." His breath spread warmth behind her ear and down her neck. More heat radiated through her abdomen. He'd called her by that name once before, the same day he'd kissed her. The way he said it made her sound wicked, completely decadent, something she'd never been.

"I didn't agree to let you be my Master." Her voice came out husky and a little hoarse, as if she'd been doing a lot of screaming. If she went along with what he asked, she probably would be doing a lot of screaming.

"'Red,' my sweet slave, is the word you're looking for. Say that, and I'll stop whatever we're doing and we'll talk. 'Yellow' pauses the action. We talk and decide where we want to go from there. 'Green' is the all-clear signal." He didn't move an inch.

The pulse in her neck ticked hard against her skin. She had the sense he was waiting for her response. "You said we had to talk. This isn't talking. You're scaring me, Keith. I've never seen you like this."

"*This* is what you asked for, Kitty Kat." He took the keys from her shaking hand, moved her to the side, and disengaged the lock. "And you asked it from more than just me, didn't you?"

He released her and motioned to the opened door.

She looked at the portal, knowing it led to either an escape from this strange encounter or entry into a foreign world. "You weren't supposed to know that. Dustin said he'd keep it between us."

"He did. I'm just fucking awesome at putting together the little clues." He looked her up and down, never altering the impassive expression on his face. "Like the fact that you're incredibly turned on right now. Yes, you're afraid. I see that too. You're a smart woman. You should be afraid."

A bead of sweat trickled between her breasts. Sometime between his deposition and now, she'd loosened the top three buttons on her blouse. Cool air came through the open door, but she made no move to enter. She regarded him warily. Perhaps she thought that if they went inside, the negotiation portion of the evening was over. He wasn't much for negotiating anyway. Generally a sub either consented to doing things his way or he moved on.

Or maybe she was rethinking the entire dynamic. Part of the reason he'd walked away last weekend was because he knew she didn't understand the scope of her request. Maybe tonight she would realize that she was better off not knowing this side of him.

He hooked his arm around her waist and pulled her over the threshold. "We're letting the air out, Kitty Kat. We'll talk over dinner. I brought food." After giving back her briefcase and coat, he grabbed a grocery sack and his gym bag from where he'd set them on her porch. Then he closed the door and locked it.

She stared at the gym bag, no doubt wondering at the caliber of torture equipment hidden inside. "What's for dinner?"

This wasn't the time to let her change the subject. He inclined his head toward the stairs. "Up you go. I think we'll discuss expectations, and then punishments. You're racking them up."

Without further protest, she turned. He wished she'd protest. If she refused a punishment, he could call the whole thing off. Nevertheless he enjoyed the view as they headed up the stairs, and he counted the minutes until he could have her naked and over his lap.

The stairs terminated in a large area that served as the living room, the kitchen, and the dining room. It wasn't as private as his house—he had a dungeon; she had a downstairs neighbor—but it would suffice for tonight.

He set his bag down on the living-room side and carried the grocery sack to the kitchen. "What plans will you be canceling?"

"None. I have plans to meet my mom, Layla, and Aunt Cindy for brunch on Sunday. I'm not canceling on my mother. Her wrath scares me more than yours."

She'd delivered her refusal with the appropriate gravity. He nodded. "I'll allow that"

He unloaded fixings for a spinach salad and a béchamel sauce that would go over penne.

"I didn't have any other plans. I was going to get some work done."

Shaking his head, he rounded the counter and took her briefcase. "Work will wait until Monday. Don't worry. When you get to the office, more will be waiting for you."

She didn't move, but she did look down the hall anxiously. He remembered the fear in her voice when she'd called the night before, and he frowned. What if the call hadn't been designed to get him over here? What if something had actually happened?

Abandoning the food prep, he did a visual sweep of her apartment. He checked every room. She didn't follow him, but she appeared vastly relieved when he returned with no news to report.

"Keith, I...I... You said..." She trailed off and licked her lips.

He put her briefcase in the hall closet and closed the door. "Get undressed. You can put your clothes in the laundry."

She didn't move, but he expected that. The first time a submissive must present herself naked to her Master was, in some ways, the most difficult step. He set a pot under the tap and turned the faucet on.

"I...I... You want me to eat dinner with no clothes on?"

Now he gave her all his attention. There could be no mistake in her mind about the way things would be. "Yes. You will be naked until I tell you to put on clothes. Should someone come to the door, I will allow you a bathrobe, and you may tell them you just got out of the shower. Or, if you're sweaty, you can tell them you were about to get into the shower."

Her eyes widened, her mouth formed a cute little circle, and a blush crept up her neck. "But you're keeping your clothes on?"

He grinned. "Yes, Kitty Kat. I am the Master, and you are the slave. You exist to please me. It pleases me to have you naked. Now."

The steel in his eyes thrilled Katrina to no end, as did the wicked way he said her name and the iniquity of what he'd told her to do. She'd known he required his submissives to be naked, so why did his order shock her so much?

*Because I thought he would be different with me.* And didn't they need to talk first? At the munch, Kirk and one of the other submissives had talked a great deal about negotiating, debating how much say a sub should have in what could or couldn't happen in a scene.

But she didn't know what, exactly, any of that looked like, and Keith wasn't really flexible on a lot of things. This probably was no different. If she refused to undress, then he'd probably go back to being just a friend, which she didn't want. She reached for the remaining buttons on her blouse, intent on giving him an erotic eyeful. He watched for a moment, approval registering in his eyes, and then he turned away to attend to the pot filling with water behind him.

His apparent lack of excitement left her more than a little discomfited. Didn't he want to see her undress for him this first time? Since he wasn't paying attention, she sped up the process, stripping away her clothes with neat efficiency.

With equal efficiency, he extracted a cutting board from her cupboard and put it next to the sink. "Slice some squash and zucchini for the pasta." He glanced her way, lifting a brow to ask for her response, but he didn't seem to notice her nudity.

She nodded, her movement tight, and obeyed his order. Cutting food while wearing nothing had never been on her top-ten list of erotic fantasies. The man had no clue about the times when he should be romantic or appreciative.

He caught her arm as she slid past him. "Yes, Master."

Surprised, she glanced up, momentarily forgetting her pique and her lack of clothing. "What?"

"When you answer me, you will reply with 'Yes, Master.' Failure to address me respectfully will result in punishment."

She remembered that she'd already earned a punishment for turning her back to him in a display of willful disobedience. Not even his submissive for ten minutes, and she'd already earned two punishments and nothing approaching sex. Dropping her gaze, she strove for a respectful attitude. "Yes, Master."

He released her arm. "Thin slices. You know how I like them."

Yes, she did know those little things about him. They'd done this ritual before, only then the silence had been broken by more than the sound of water washing vegetables or the rhythmic *shick* of the knife shaping dinner. And she hadn't been naked.

She didn't know if this new development was a good thing or a bad thing. Right now, it didn't seem to be any sort of thing at all.

## Chapter Three

A deep red cloth, a housewarming gift she rarely used, set the backdrop for the candlelit meal waiting on her dining room table. Keith had directed her to put together this romantic tableau, but nothing he'd said or done had acknowledged the changed circumstances of their relationship since he'd told her to undress. If he were the one walking around naked, she'd definitely have a problem keeping her eyes and her hands to herself.

How could he not notice?

From her position kneeling on the floor next to the table, she double-checked the details. Silver candleholders with red tapers. Knives, forks, spoons. Water and wineglasses, though he'd brought sparkling cider. She knew he never touched alcohol. His parents and his sisters were alcoholics. He wouldn't take the chance he'd end up like them. Her best plates were piled high with steaming food that smelled sinfully delicious. Lunch had been a long time ago.

She heard him returning from down the hall and dropped her gaze, hoping she hadn't noticeably altered her position. The idea of a third punishment didn't appeal to her, mostly because she didn't know what it entailed. Ignorance was not bliss. She preferred to know what was coming so she could be mentally prepared.

He spread a towel on the cushioned seat of her chair. She watched as the powerful muscles in his thighs strained against the fabric of his pants.

Then he turned back to her suddenly, no doubt catching her not looking where he'd told her to look. He held out his hands. "Stand up."

Accepting his help, she placed her hands in his and followed his order. Automatically her gaze lifted to meet his. As it had been the entire time they'd prepared the meal, his mouth was set in a tight slash, and his eyes glittered hard. She shivered at the repressed emotion there. Keith had always been intense, but he'd never been mean. She wasn't sure what to expect.

"I can see I definitely have my work cut out for me, Kitty Kat. I wasn't gone a full minute, and you failed to follow a simple order."

Katrina wouldn't pretend she didn't know what he was talking about. He'd been clear when he'd put her into position and told her exactly where to keep her gaze to avoid moving a muscle. "I'm sorry, Master."

He released her hands. Tangling one hand in the hair at her nape, he urged her head back. She didn't know what to expect, but his gentle kiss took her by surprise. He moved his lips over hers, massaging and caressing, letting her know without words that he wasn't disappointed. Katrina instinctively understood that he wasn't comfortable saying tender things, but demonstrating affection was a different thing altogether.

When he ended it, he rested his forehead against hers. "Apology accepted." He closed his eyes, squeezing them tight and exhaling hard. She waited for him to say something more, but he only pressed a kiss to the tip of her nose and released her. "Sit. We'll eat and talk. After dinner, I'll ask you to reevaluate your request."

Starving, she slid into her chair and dug in. Keith had cooked for her several times before, and she'd loved his food each time. He definitely had a culinary arts gift. Growing up in an Italian household, Katrina was well versed in those kinds of dishes, but Keith seemed to know a little bit about everything.

"It's delicious, Master. Thank you." She congratulated herself on remembering to use his title. It wasn't easy, and it didn't come naturally.

"You're welcome. Tell me what you're expecting from this relationship."

His direct question kept her on edge, which was probably his intent. She stalled, not sure how to answer. Finally, she settled on an honest assessment. "I don't really know. I know about D/s and bondage, but my understanding is largely theoretical. I thought you would show me what to expect."

"Did you expect to be naked, eating dinner with me?" He inserted that question smoothly between bites of food.

Katrina shook her head. "I thought you'd wait until we were in the bedroom doing a scene." She'd been to his house before when he'd been in a relationship. None of his girlfriends had ever been naked, and none of them had looked like they'd hastily dressed. Her knowledge about that preference came from her brother and from random comments some of Keith's exes had made.

"I won't keep you naked all the time." Another forkful disappeared into his mouth. His eyebrows drew together. "Just most of the time. If we're expecting company, you will be instructed to dress. I won't pick out your clothing unless it's lingerie or an outfit for a scene. I sometimes like to role-play in the dungeon."

With her mind reeling at the way her life was going to change, she didn't answer immediately. She thought while eating. It seemed to her that he hadn't exerted overt dominance over any of his submissives in front of other people. If he wanted to pick out her lingerie, she had no problem with that. But she had no idea what he meant by role-playing. Did he have Princess Leia and Han Solo fantasies? "Tell me about this role-play thing. I didn't think you were into LARPing."

He laughed. "It's a sort of live-action role-play. Most of the time, you'll end up bound or tied to something. You'll inevitably end up as a sex slave."

The fact of her nudity had slipped her mind, but now awareness returned. She sipped her cider and studied him over the rim of the glass. He'd shed his jacket, loosened his tie, and unbuttoned the top two buttons on his shirt. His shirtsleeves were rolled up as well. Despite the casual nature suggested by his attire, he exuded strength and confidence.

At last, she mustered enough courage to be direct. "As long as I'm the only sex slave there. I understand that training me doesn't mean you'll stop seeing your other submissives." Though she wished it did. "I mostly have tame fantasies, I guess. Honestly, I don't know what I'll like. I think about being overpowered and held down. Spanked. Having my hair pulled." In her fantasies, he was always the one topping her. "I've messed around, but I've never done any of those things with a Dom, so I don't know if I'll like the reality of it."

He nodded thoughtfully. "So you're asking me to show you different things to see what you'll like and what you won't?"

"Yes. I'd like that. Master."

He grinned to acknowledge her belated use of his title, and she realized he didn't mean for her to constantly use it, not in conversation. As a response to an order, especially when she was on her knees, but not all the time.

"Let's start with the fact that I don't deal with more than one submissive at a time. Then we'll discuss punishment."

Her heart beat faster at that admission, and his mention of punishment nearly sent her over the edge. She knew she had a couple coming, but that didn't mean she relished them. It seemed she wasn't one of those women who enjoyed the idea of being punished. Mostly she hated that she'd let him down with her rude behavior.

"Generally," he continued as if he hadn't noticed the heightening of her anxiety, "I want an apology, an admission of your mistake."

That got her attention. She'd expected him to start with something a little violent, like a spanking, or something humiliating, like forcing her to lick his shoes. She'd have to draw a line before they got to that point. There was no way in hell she'd lick his shoes. That just wasn't sanitary. She waited for him to continue, to drop the bomb, but he didn't.

*An apology from a submissive should be delivered on her knees.* She slid from her chair and knelt next to him, her head bowed because she didn't know if she could just apologize or if she had to wait for him to recognize her. She opted for the latter choice.

The silence weighed heavily on her nerves, and she struggled to keep her spine straight. From the corner of her eye, she saw his hand move closer. He touched her hair, smoothing it back from her face.

"Yes?"

"I'm sorry for turning my back on you and for hesitating when you gave an order. Please forgive me, Master." The apology was heartfelt. Katrina absolutely hated when anyone was upset with her. While she thrived on debate and argument in her professional life, she detested any kind of disagreement in her personal life.

"You're forgiven. Now finish your dinner. After we clean this mess, we're going to play."

Anticipation tingled between her thighs. She'd wanted him to play with her for so long, and his lack of response didn't exactly make her feel sexy or desirable. However, a quick glance at his lap as she shifted to return to her chair revealed that his nonchalant demeanor was a false front.

They finished eating, and then they split the cleanup duties in the kitchen. As she dried her hands on a dish towel, she heard the chimes that indicated the buttons being pushed to start her dishwasher. And then he caged her against the counter with her back to him.

Warmth radiated from his body, and the strength of his presence put every nerve ending on alert. She'd always responded to his physicality, to the authority he commanded with his every look, his every move. She felt the flutter of his lips on the back of her shoulder, and she closed her eyes to luxuriate in his attention.

"Tonight you're going to practice following directions. It won't be easy. You're going to have to trust me."

She trusted Keith. It was Master she didn't know so well. "Yes, Master."

He smoothed his hand over the length of her hair, down her back, and stopped on her hip. "You'll find some things painful or uncomfortable, perhaps embarrassing or humiliating. I want you to take as much as you can. I'll help you. Only call yellow or red when it gets to be too much. Do you understand?"

The hand on her hip didn't mitigate the unease he caused with his warning. She kept reminding herself that she wanted this. She wanted this with Keith. Thank goodness he'd agreed to initiate her into this world. She didn't think she would have been able to go through with it if she'd been with Dustin. "Yes, Master."

He placed his hands on the fronts of her thighs, a light touch full of energy that zapped the strength from her knees. She leaned against him, and he didn't stop her. Slowly he moved up her body, exploring her skin. Pausing long enough to glide his fingertips over the short, trimmed hair at her pubic mound, he left her wanting a more thorough investigation.

The journey continued over her stomach and ribs. At last he cupped her breasts. She wanted to reach behind her to wrap her arms around his neck, but he hadn't instructed her to move, so she gripped the dish towel tightly. Her nipples had pebbled an hour ago, standing at attention to beg for his touch. Her breasts were small but sensitive. He flicked his thumbs over her nipples, and she felt it all the way to her core. A whimpering sound purred in the back of her throat, and she fought the urge to lean all her weight against him.

For several long moments, he teased the rocklike peaks. Then he pinched them lightly between his thumbs and forefingers. "Have you ever worn clamps?"

Katrina shook her head. Sometimes she didn't even like to have her breasts touched for too long. "I think they're too sensitive."

Behind her, his laugh rumbled against her back. "Oh, my precious Kitty Kat, that's what makes it fun. We'll start light and work our way to something with more bite."

Then he pinched them viciously, squeezing hard. She cried out and arched, trying to relieve the pressure, but it didn't work. He kept up the torment, ignoring—or perhaps delighting in—evidence of her pain.

"Breathe, Kat. Inhale. Exhale."

She forced herself to follow his orders. Concentrating on her breathing did make it easier to bear, but she stopped fighting it.

"Beautiful. Now let go of that dish towel before you tear it in half."

She looked down at the soft, absorbent fabric twisted in her hands. It took some effort, which further took her mind away from the pain he caused, but she managed to release it.

"Keep breathing. Relax against me. Perfect. Now tell me what you feel."

She took her time in analyzing the sensation. Something about this kind of agony slowed her mental processes. "It doesn't hurt as bad when I breathe."

"I know. Tell me what you feel, not what you don't feel." His voice sounded low in her consciousness, and she had no choice but to follow the hypnotic quality of it.

Another deep breath. His hands moved with her chest. "It's starting to feel good. Weird good. It's traveling down my arms."

"What else?"

She wanted to shake her head, to refuse to tell him about the heat it sent straight to her core. It was like her nipple had a direct link to her pussy, only she'd never pushed the button hard enough to make the connection.

He squeezed harder, sending fresh waves throbbing through her system. She gasped loudly. "Answer me."

"My...my... Between my legs." A week ago, she never would have thought she'd be talking to him about anything happening between her legs while he tormented her nipples.

"Is your cunt wet, Kitty Kat? Just from this?"

She hated that word, but she forced herself to get over it. "Yes, Master."

"Say it. Tell me your cunt is wet."

Katrina licked her lips. The rapidity of her breathing had more to do with the things he wanted her to say than the things he was doing. When she at last forced it out, she could barely hear what she said. "My cunt is wet, Master."

"Is your cunt wet for me?"

*More often than you could possibly know.* "Yes, Master."

He increased the pressure, which she found amazing. She was sure her nipples were flattened by now. "Say it, slave."

"My cunt is wet for you, Master."

He eased the pressure until she was free, and she sighed. Some of her energy drained away, yet a new sense of liquidity and acquiescence suffused her limbs. She thought he might explore her pussy next, but he turned her around with a gentle tug on her hip.

She faced him, and heat crept up her neck. For some reason, she could take his attention when she wasn't looking at him, but facing him was different. Looking at him forced her to remember that she'd fantasized about this man for years, and he'd never once indicated reciprocal feelings. Even all those years ago when he'd kissed her, she'd been stunned to her toes, but he had only looked amused.

He drew his fingertips along her cheeks, and then he feathered them into her hair at her temples. The firm set of his lips softened, as did the steel in his eyes. That small evidence of affection did pleasant things to her stomach. "Last chance to back out before we start."

She didn't want an escape, not after all she'd gone through for this chance. "I've been naked for the past hour, Master. We've already begun."

He closed his eyes. That pleasant feeling turned a little cold. He'd better not be having second thoughts. If he walked out her door, she didn't know if she would recover.

"I don't want to hurt you."

She half snorted and half laughed at his admission. "Yes, you do. You want to tie me up too. You get off on it."

His answering laugh contained no mirth. Leaning forward, he pressed his forehead to hers. "I'm a bastard, Kat. I'll ask for everything from you, but I won't give much in return. I want you to understand that I'll never be the kind of man you deserve to have. Eyes wide open. I am who I am. You can't change me."

Though he hadn't instructed her to move, she couldn't resist cupping his face. He seemed so lost and vulnerable. It tugged at her heart and brought out her need to provide comfort, to salve the wounds with her embrace, her kisses, and her submission. She'd caught glimpses of this side of him, of his deep unhappiness, and she knew where it originated. He was a better man than he gave himself credit for being.

"I don't want to change you."

He slid his hands back and tightened them in her hair. At the same time, he captured her lips in a punishing kiss, mashing his mouth against hers. He stabbed his tongue inside, and she was lost. This wasn't a kiss in which she could participate. He filled her senses, mastering her, turning her into a receptacle for his harsh affection. With a heartfelt moan, she softened into him, accepting what he needed to give.

She liked this far more than she'd thought she would. Now she knew she wasn't doing this just to show Keith she could be the woman he wanted. Submission was in her heart where he was concerned. She liked his roughness, and she looked forward to learning all the ways he would introduce her to more wicked and wanton activities.

Abruptly he broke the kiss and stepped back. She teetered to maintain her balance, groping for the counter to aid her attempt. He steadied her with a quick hand on her rib cage. The heat of his palm left an indelible print on her skin, a promise that warmed her inside and out.

"Hands and knees. Crawl to the chair across from the sofa."

Katrina had never crawled in her life. Even as a child, she'd learned to walk first. Though he'd warned her, she still found his command shocking. Lowering to her knees, she realized exactly how undignified this would appear.

She wondered if he liked the power inherent in making her do something unseemly, or if he just liked the unobstructed view of her pussy. Either way, the bit of submission he'd coaxed from her with that kiss hadn't subsided. She felt like she belonged to him, and that acceptance overrode her reservations. Acutely aware of his gaze, she sank to all fours and crawled to the chair.

"Stand up."

Facing the empty chair, she stood.

"Hands behind your neck. Link your fingers together."

She felt the magnetism of his proximity and swayed back in response. He halted her movement with a hand on her back. Wordlessly he adjusted her posture, pushing at her shoulders and pulling her elbows until they were at right angles to her head. Then, with the toe of his shoe on her instep, he nudged her feet apart. Moisture rushed to her pussy as she complied.

The position exposed her like nothing else. With her breasts thrust forward and her legs spread wide, she could think of nothing but belonging to him. At long last, she was his possession.

"Memorize how this feels, slave. When I tell you to stand, I want you in this exact position. When it's time to kneel, you'll put your arms behind your neck like this, and your knees will be spread wider than your shoulders. You are allowed to hide nothing from me. This body belongs to me alone. Say it."

"This body belongs to you, Master." Her voice sounded rusty, as though she hadn't spoken in a long time. In truth, she hadn't. The woman standing in her living room was the woman she hadn't yet met.

He ran his palms over every inch from her ankles to her neck. The caress made her acutely conscious of the wetness soaking the insides of her thighs, the only place he neglected to touch. When he came to stand in front of her, he ended his forays by washing his hands over her face. There was nothing tentative or reverent in his demeanor. His expression and his rough caress were strictly proprietary.

"Keep your eyes open."

She hadn't realized she'd closed them. She popped them open to find him regarding her fiercely. For the first time, she recognized his fear. He wanted her to enjoy this, and he was afraid she wouldn't. She'd always known that being dominant was an integral part of who he was. She'd never known how much of his soul he showed with that stoic mask, just as she'd never understood how much of himself he'd hidden from them all.

"Yes, Master."

He disappeared from her field of vision. A *thunk* sounded on her oak coffee table. Though she didn't dare turn around to look, she guessed that he'd retrieved the bag she'd noticed next to the stairs earlier. Rummaging sounds set her nerves on edge. She knew he would want to engage in impact play, but she didn't think he would leap right in and use a crop on a novice. The waiting made her short of breath.

When he again stood in front of her, he held a small chain that terminated in modified tweezers. Rubber covered the ends. He dipped his head and sucked her left nipple into his mouth. Pain from his sudden, violent onslaught mingled with the inferno of his mouth. Tears gathered in the corners of her eyes, and she cried out. It took all her strength not to pull away.

After a few moments, the sensation morphed, as it had before, and bloomed. Her cry turned to a moan, and she thrust her breast closer in offering. A sharp *crack* rent the air, and a hot sting on her backside brought her out of the cloud of ecstasy that had enveloped her mind. He'd smacked her ass. Not hard, just loud enough to get her attention.

"Don't move. Breathe through it. Maintain control. I guarantee you won't like the lessons on controlling your responses." His hot breath brushed against her wet flesh.

"I'm sorry, Master." Not too sorry, though. She heard the pleasure in his voice. He liked her reaction, even if he didn't approve of the way she expressed her enjoyment. She was also hyperaware of the warmth spreading through the skin on her ass.

He pinched her nipple and pulled it until she gasped. Then he slid the tweezer around it. Nipple clamps. She'd heard of them, but she'd never seen them. She hadn't thought they'd look or feel so benign. As he adjusted a screw and the thing squeezed her tender flesh, she adjusted her opinion. She opened her mouth with the intention of telling him that it hurt, but he beat her to the punch. "Breathe. You can take it."

It had worked before, so she concentrated on inhaling and exhaling. Simple steps, but it required her full concentration, especially when he subjected her right nipple to the same torture. When he finished, he stepped back.

She looked down to check out his handiwork, and what she saw definitely made her pause. Her nipples were distended and engorged. They tingled and throbbed. The clamps cut into her flesh, but the pain was receding. Or she was just getting used to the sensation.

Lust darkened his eyes, and his gaze moved over her body, stopping again and again at her breasts. She thought he might close the short distance between their bodies, drag her to him for a ravaging kiss, but he took a step back and sank into her armchair. She stood before him, panting with desire and fighting the urge to rip his clothes off.

"Straddle me." His voice came out strong and steady, almost fierce.

Katrina did as she was told, but she didn't get her hopes up. The smooth fabric of his pants skimmed against the sensitive flesh on the insides of her knees and her inner thighs as she positioned herself on top of his fully clothed body.

Beginning at her bent knees, he slid his hands up her thighs. He altered his angle when he made it to her hips, and he gripped her ass briefly before continuing up her body. Though she enjoyed the sensations evoked by his touch, she watched him. She watched how the steel in his eyes softened as he looked at her. For the first time, she saw flickers of peace and hope replace the perpetual remoteness.

She gasped when his thumbs came into contact with her nipples. Fire flared and singed a path to her core. Molten cream wet her pussy, and she smelled her arousal. Keith's nostrils flared, and that fragile bit of vulnerability disappeared, supplanted by satisfaction.

"Nice. Very responsive. Master likes when his slave hides nothing." He winced at something. It was a slight movement, something she would have missed if she hadn't been watching him so intently.

"What else do you like, Master?" She knew the protocol for the third-person formal-communication pattern he was attempting, but she felt it put artificial distance between them, so she opted not to follow that lead. Plus, she was pretty sure Keith didn't want things that way either. If she let him set that tone now, they'd never get away from it. Though it wasn't the most submissive thought or reaction, she didn't temper it or pretend she didn't know what she was refusing. She would give him her submission, yes, but not at the price of emotional distance.

He looked into her eyes as he moved the pads of his thumbs over her nipples. Finally he dropped his hands and gripped her hips firmly. "I want to see you come. Touch that pretty pussy for me."

Given his lack of nakedness, she'd expected something like this, only she'd hoped he would do the honors. Masturbation wasn't something she'd ever tried with an audience. She debated asking him to finger her, but then she reasoned that he'd refuse. This was a test of her obedience. He wanted to know that she could follow his directions. Questioning them wouldn't go over well tonight. She'd save that for later, when he was more comfortable in their relationship.

She started with her breasts, running her hands up her rib cage to barely cup them. She had a little less than a handful, and she wasn't about to call his attention to her lack by proving she could barely fill her own hands. He'd already figured out she couldn't fill his.

Lifting them jiggled the clamps a bit. Without touching them directly—that area seemed to belong strictly to Keith—she experimented with the way the movement sent a bit of pain through her system. There was definitely a fine line between pain and pleasure. The heated expression on Keith's face tipped the scales toward pleasure.

Then he reached forward and tugged the chain linking the clamps together. For a second as the sharpness knifed through her system, she forgot how to breathe. Tears wet her eyes, but she fought them. She was afraid he'd change his mind if she cried. She grappled for control and won.

"Don't stop."

Until he spoke up, she hadn't been aware she'd frozen in place. She met his gaze, noted the cocky tilt to his lips, and slid one hand between her legs. A few tears, shed or unshed, wouldn't be enough to end the fun. As long as she didn't use her safe word, he wouldn't halt the scene.

Her pussy was sopping wet. She slid her fingers easily between her labia to find her clit. Keith's grip tightened on her hips, so she used her free hand to open her lips a little more. He wanted her to hide nothing, and so she exposed herself that way.

With a groan, he took over, pulling her wide open. The move decreased the sensitivity in her clit, so she deserted the little nub. She leaned back, bracing one hand on his knee behind her, and worked two of her fingers into her opening. Abandoning any kind of seductive intent, she threw her head back, closed her eyes, and gave herself over to the act.

That sweet tension built inside. She felt his touch on her clit and on her breasts. Seconds before the wave crashed over her, he loosened the clamps on her nipples. The heated pain of them being put on had nothing on the fire that rocked her when he removed them. She cried out, and the orgasm ricocheted through her body. Pins and needles poked at her toes, fingers, and her breasts, and her vision grayed out for a moment.

When the sensory overload lessened and she could once again feel her extremities, she found her head on his shoulder and his arms around her. Keith feathered caresses at the base of her spine. His clean, masculine scent filled her consciousness. She took a deep breath, basking in it. She'd always loved the way he smelled.

Her small movement must have cued him to her returned consciousness. He tilted her head back and kissed her, his lips gliding soothingly over hers. "That was a wonderful effort, slave, but we're just getting started. Sit up."

Pushing against his chest, she struggled to right herself. Because he'd pulled her closer to his torso, she felt rocklike evidence of his arousal beneath the juncture of her thighs. She reached for his belt, but he clamped his hand over hers before she could loosen it.

"Never undress your Master without permission."

In all the times she'd reached for a man's belt, not once had she met with resistance. She froze in place, stunned that he would deny access. Then she recovered her wits. "Master, may I undress you?"

He shook his head. "Not yet, my sweet slave."

She struggled to hide her disappointment. Here she was, naked on the lap of the man of her dreams, and he'd really only taken things to second base. She'd masturbated in front of him, but he hadn't participated. Doubts plagued her. What if he was doing this to prove a point, not because he actually wanted to train her?

"Don't do that." He gripped her arms loosely and ran a rough caress up and down them. "Don't hide your feelings from me."

"I'm sorry, Master." Those reservations wouldn't subside. She couldn't meet his gaze.

He grasped her chin and forced her to look at him. "Tell me what's wrong."

She decided to be blunt. "I don't want you doing this because you feel obligated. If you don't want me, then I wish you'd just tell me."

By way of responding, he took her hand and put it on his cock. The hard length stirred, throbbing through the layers of fabric separating their skin. "I want you. I will have you, but I refuse to rush things. We do this on my schedule. I'm in charge, remember?"

She flexed her fingers in anticipation, involuntarily squeezing his cock. He closed his eyes for a moment. When he opened them again, he removed her hand and set it on her thigh. Their eyes met, and she realized just how close he was to throwing her to the floor and fucking her senseless. She marveled at how quickly he vacillated between seeming to have no passion and appearing to be barely in control.

"Crawl to the bedroom. Bow your back to lift your ass high. Hide nothing that belongs to me."

Scrambling from his lap, she tried to land on the floor with as much grace as she could manage, but on her best day, she wasn't all that graceful. Add the semidegrading nature of the position into the situation, and she wasn't sure she could even manage sexy.

Keith kept his gaze on Kat's naked ass. He'd made women crawl before, but his goal had always been to subjugate them. While his original intention with Kat had been the same, the move had backfired. One glimpse of her sculpted little ass and those glistening nether lips and he'd been tempted to jump on her and rut like a tiger in heat.

Before he caught up to her in the hall, he snagged his bag of tricks from where he'd stashed it next to the landing. If she had been a little more used to him, he would have extracted a crop from it and peppered her ass and cunt with taps and pokes as she crawled.

He shouldn't be here with her, not like this. Screw the promise he'd made all those years ago to Malcolm to keep his hands off Katrina. Keith knew full well why he had no business touching her the way he'd only ever dreamed about. *It's just training*, he reminded himself. He could justify training her. After all, this was really his one talent where women were concerned. He knew how to blow their minds with sex. It was afterward, when they wanted to do relationship-type things, that it all went to hell.

But Kat didn't want that. She wanted to maintain their friendship, and she wanted him to train her. They were two completely separate things. He'd just make damn sure this fantasy went on for as long as he could drag it out, and then he'd live on these blissful memories for the rest of his life. It would have to be enough, and it was far more than he deserved.

She stopped in the middle of her bedroom floor and sat back on her heels. Her posture was good, but he didn't like the placement of her hands. She'd kept them on her thighs, palms up.

"Link your hands together behind your neck."

That position made her small, high breasts stick out a little more. Her nipples were still swollen and red from the clamps and from his rough play. She trembled the tiniest bit. He knew putting herself on display made her uncomfortable, and it thrilled him that she didn't hesitate or try to hide her nudity.

He set the bag on a chair next to her dresser and pulled out a flogger made from the softest deerskin. While tonight's goal was pleasure, he also wanted to see how sensitive she was. They both needed to learn to read her body's signals. She needed to know what she could and couldn't handle; he needed to know how far he could push her limits.

"Hold out your hand."

She accepted the flogger from him. First she stared at it, and then she lifted her gaze to ask a silent question.

"Touch it, Kitty Kat. Run your hands along the falls. Drag the tips over your thighs. Get to know this flogger, because I'm going to turn your skin pink with it. I'm going to tie you up and whip your ass, back, thighs, and calves. Then I'm going to turn you around and give that same treatment to your breasts, stomach, and pussy."

A bit of color drained from her face at his frank description. Her eyes widened, and her puzzled expression altered to show her trepidation.

# Chapter Four

"What's your color, Kitty Kat?"

Katrina didn't know. The falls were soft in her hands, but even soft leather would have a bite when it was divided into strips about half an inch wide and slapped against naked flesh. Using the technique he'd taught her, she breathed to steady the emotions rioting inside.

When she'd asked him to show her a variety of experiences, she'd known she wouldn't clamor for them all. But if she didn't do this, her training would end, and she would spend the rest of her life wondering if she'd bailed too soon.

"Green, Master."

He didn't smile. Other than to turn back to his black gym bag, he didn't react at all. While he rummaged around, she studied the flogger closely. The black-and-purple braided handle was half the length of the falls, which she estimated to be a foot and a half long. She didn't count the falls, which continued the color scheme from the grip, but she figured there were between thirty and forty. It felt nice in her hand, strong and sturdy, yet soft and pliant. She wondered what it would be like to wield it.

"Stand, slave."

She stumbled to her feet, not sure whether they'd fallen asleep or she was just that nervous. Keith held out a hand to steady her. Lifting her gaze, she attempted to smile. Her effort fell short, and she cleared her throat, mostly as a distraction. "Thank you, Master."

He grinned the same cocky, shit-eating grin he'd used when he'd instigated the water fight at Layla's party, and he took the flogger. He tossed it on the foot of her bed. She watched it arc the short distance and land with a soft *thud*, the same way it would no doubt land on her back.

What was she thinking? Maybe she did like some rough nipple play, but that didn't mean she wanted to have her body tenderized by a huge whip. A moment of panic stole her focus. She worked to stabilize her emotions. When she had herself under control, she looked up to find Keith studying her in that intensely silent way he had about him. He waited. Everything about him exuded dominance and confidence, but she felt no pressure to proceed.

"I'm ready, Master."

He held out his hand, and she put her wrist in it. In seconds, he had wrapped soft cuffs—she guessed neoprene—around her wrists and secured them with Velcro. Then he knelt in front of her and wrapped matching cuffs just above her knees.

"Spread your legs."

Belatedly she remembered that she should have been standing with her legs shoulder-width apart this whole time. But when she complied, he tapped her inner thigh to coax her to widen even more. By the time he was satisfied, she had to bend at the knee to remain standing. Her muscles strained after only several moments, damning her for not doing lunges.

From his bag, he produced a metal bar that he threaded through loops attached to the cuffs on her legs. She'd heard of a spreader bar, but she hadn't seen one before. It kept her spread wide, completely exposed and at his mercy.

He helped her waddle to her bed, which wasn't very far away. Her condo was small, and the room size followed suit. He bent her over the side of the mattress and adjusted her position until she was exactly where he wanted her.

"Put your arms above your head. I like strict restraint, but I'm going easy on you tonight."

Like his other comments, this one did nothing to set her at ease. Now she would have to figure out what the hell he meant by strict restraint. She would ask, but right now she had other things on her mind. She stretched her arms above her head to find him already standing on the other side of the bed, waiting for her compliance.

He snapped her cuffs together, attached a rope, and bent down. From his movements, she deduced he'd tied the other end to the bed frame. An experimental tug proved her correct. When he stood, he dug into his pocket and came out with a piece of black fabric. "A blindfold will heighten the experience."

Dread twisted in her stomach. She didn't necessarily want the experience heightened. She just wanted to get through it. A fast-forward button would be helpful right about now. "Do I have to?"

His eyebrows knit together in mild reproof. "Kitty Kat, do you honestly think I'd put you through more than you can bear?"

She wasn't convinced. It must have shown, because he got on his knees, putting his face level with hers.

"Isn't that the point of doing all of this? Experience new things? Push your boundaries? Kat, I know what I'm doing. I need you to trust me. Try the blindfold. You can do this." Using the powers of persuasion inherent in those startlingly sincere eyes worked wonders on her confidence. What Keith wanted, Keith invariably got. He'd done this to her before, and she'd caved just like she was doing now.

"Okay. I'll try it."

"Master." He'd kept his tone gentle, but she didn't make the mistake of thinking she had an option.

"I'm sorry. I'll try it, Master."

He brushed a kiss across her cheek, and she began to grasp the extent of his power. With just the tone of his voice, he could elicit a heartfelt apology from her.

The world went dark.

"Rest your head on the bed, slave. If you don't relax, you'll strain your neck."

Nothing happened for far too long. She could hear him moving around the room. The floor creaked in two distinct places. Though she'd rested her cheek against the comforter, she couldn't relax. He was going to beat her, and she'd given consent.

Then she felt his legs press next to hers. His hips pressed into her ass, and the weight of his hands pushed into the bed near her head. He didn't say anything, but she felt the light caress of his finger as he moved her hair away from her neck, and then the softest kisses fluttered along her spine. Heat from his body radiated into hers. He'd removed his shirt.

"Beautiful Kitty Kat. You're so fucking gorgeous. Spread out here like this, waiting for the kiss of my flogger. Offering your sweet secrets up to me." His vehement whispers rumbled through her skin via his roving lips.

He explored her upper back, sending gooseflesh streaming in all directions. She gasped when his teeth sank into the fleshy part of her shoulder. The man bit like a god. Tingling sensations joined the gooseflesh. Now she shook for a different reason. Rekindled desire had replaced her trepidation.

His weight shifted as he climbed off the bed. She tensed a bit, knowing what was coming next. But something soft brushed the places he'd just kissed. It took her several seconds before she recognized that he was trailing the falls over her skin. It felt good. This puzzled Katrina. As with the clamps earlier, she'd expected some kind of pain that would morph into pleasure, and so this unexpected gentleness knocked her completely off balance.

The length of his passes increased. Soon she felt the caress run from her calves to her shoulders and back to her feet. The rhythm lulled her into a relaxed state.

The first slap of the whip was far less dramatic than she'd imagined. It didn't whistle through the air. It didn't hurt at all. The small stings were so light the impact felt like a massage. Keith kept a steady rhythm, but he moved up and down her body. Soon a weightless feeling came over her. She felt a little as if she were floating and a little as if she were flying. Why did this instrument have such a notorious reputation?

All too soon, he stopped. The pleasant, disoriented feeling didn't. She sighed and settled into this curious consequence of the flogging. Vaguely she registered that he'd flipped her over and moved her so that she was more fully on the bed.

"Master." She murmured his title reverently. At this moment, she'd do anything he wanted.

He subjected her front side to the same delicious treatment. She didn't know how long it lasted, only that she could lie here forever and let him do this. She could see why submissives begged their Masters for this bliss. Before long, the massage ceased. When he freed her arms and repositioned her so that her arms were wrapped under her knees, drawing them up as high as she could hold them, she didn't wonder at his intent.

"Are you still with me, slave?"

He'd spoken directly below her ear, and then he caught her lobe between his teeth. She shivered and tried to release her leg so she could pull him closer. That was when she noticed he'd snapped her wrist cuffs to the spreader bar.

Her eyes flew open. She didn't remember when he'd removed the blindfold, but it was gone. The soft lights from her twin lamps combined with the buzzing in her head to make everything seem surreal. "What have you done to me?" Her question could have been heated, but she couldn't seem to find the energy to want to protest her circumstance.

He chuckled. "I made you my slave, Kitty Kat. I've given you a precious gift. Now I'm going to take my reward. I'm going to fuck you however I want as long as I want, and there's nothing you can do but lie there and take it."

She had pictured their first coming together as fiery and passionate. He'd hold her down and kiss her hard as he rocked his body against hers. But in all her fantasies, she'd fully participated in the lovemaking.

From the triumph glittering in his eyes, she knew he hadn't considered similar scenarios. Deep down, she was glad he'd bound her like this, and she liked the way he claimed her. She liked being at his mercy, his to use as he wanted.

She nodded. "All right, Master."

As if he'd been waiting for her agreement, he swept his tongue inside her mouth and ravaged her with all the fire and passion she'd originally imagined. He gripped her face between his thumb and forefinger, holding her in place as he fucked his tongue into her mouth. She felt owned, mastered, and she loved it.

He broke the kiss and knelt up, swiftly discarding his pants. She wanted more time to look, and she badly wanted to touch him, but he didn't seem inclined to give her the opportunity. Keith didn't have her restrictions. He touched her everywhere, never pausing as he explored her body with his hands, and his kisses trailed closely behind. He made his way down her sensitized flesh and sucked her clit into his mouth.

She writhed beneath the onslaught, trying both to get closer and to escape. He kissed her pussy the same way he'd kissed her mouth and sucked at her nipples. She wanted to cry out, to beg him to stop, but the sharp pain converted into liquid heat, and she came in his mouth.

Between her legs, he moaned and lapped even faster. "Fuck, yes. Give it to me. That's my orgasm, slave. You may thank me."

The buzzing in her head nearly drowned him out, but she had enough of her wits about her to understand that not thanking him would be a serious offense. "Thank you, Master." She had the feeling she would be thanking him a few more times before the night was over.

Keith rose to his knees and took in the gorgeous sight before him. Kat lay on her back. The spreader bar kept her knees far apart, and the way he'd attached her wrist cuffs forced her to hold her knees high and wide. Juices, proof of her recent orgasm, glistened in the lamplight. She'd tasted every bit as delicious as he'd imagined, and she'd responded beautifully to his brutal style, first fighting the onslaught and then surrendering to it.

Her dark brown hair streamed over the emerald comforter and highlighted the dreamy, sated expression on her face. She was at his mercy, and he couldn't imagine a more perfect moment.

Dragging two fingers through her cream, he snagged a little of that lubrication. A bit of languor faded from her expression, and she watched him intently. This was what he desperately wanted and most feared—a slave who made him the focus of her attention because she was interested in him, not just the things he could do to her. For his entire life, he'd avoided these kinds of emotional entanglements. Kat was a heap of trouble he couldn't resist.

He rubbed her essence on his cock and pumped his hand up and down his shaft. Gaze fastened to his cock, she licked her lips, and her chest rose and fell a little more rapidly.

"Want this, slave?" Her lips parted, and her breaths came even faster. If he didn't watch it, he'd shoot his wad before he got inside her. On second thought, that sounded like a better option. If he wanted to follow through on his plan to drive her insane with need, he had to relieve some of the tension that had been building ever since she had unbuttoned her shirt in the kitchen. "Don't worry. I'm going to fuck that sweet, soft cunt eventually. Right now I'm going to make you watch."

Her eyes flared wide. He watched shades of desire and curiosity cross her face. He wanted to ask if she'd ever watched a man touch himself before, but he was afraid she'd answer in the positive. He'd rather not know. Besides, what he was doing now drove her crazy. He could tell she wanted to be the one touching him, pleasuring him. Evidence of her longing sent him over the edge. His balls drew up, and he aimed for her stomach, spilling his ejaculate on her smooth flesh.

Waves of need washed through him. The small climax had only whetted his appetite. His cock began to harden again before it went completely soft. He visually traced the trail of his semen up her abdomen. If he were going to be nice, he'd wipe it away. But it pleased him to have her wear the mark of his dominion, and she didn't seem bothered by it.

Leaning forward, he brushed his lips over hers, teasing but not delivering. They'd skipped an important part of the prescene discussion. "I'm going to use a condom, Kitty Kat, but I still need to know whether you're on birth control."

She nodded. "I am, but I do prefer the added protection. You can never be too careful."

Keith grinned at her warning. Malcolm had knocked up his girlfriend while using protection. Kat had a life plan, he knew, that didn't include an unplanned pregnancy. No matter. Since he planned to never reproduce, he'd elected to have a vasectomy years ago, a fact he'd never shared with anyone.

He kissed her hard, and she responded in kind. The effects of her orgasm and the deerskin whip had vanished. That was the problem with such a light implement. When she was ready, he'd introduce her to something with a lasting bite.

She licked and bit the inside of his lower lip. The sharp pain quickly faded to pleasure, and he moaned involuntarily. The little minx would soon figure out he was as much a masochist as he was a sadist. He usually hid that detail because he didn't trust his subs enough. Most were manipulative and would use that fact to try to top him. Nothing killed his hard-on faster than a sub topping from the bottom.

To distract her, he circled her clit with his thumb and slid his finger into her hot sheath. She moaned and tried to cant her hips to take more. She was tight, and the position into which he'd bound her meant she would be extra snug.

He broke the kiss and let her catch her breath as much as she could with his finger pumping into her. She moaned when he added another. Passion lightened her eyes to cinnamon, a color he had never seen before on her. Ordinarily her irises were like dark chocolate. They lit when she was happy and darkened to nearly black when she was upset.

"What a tight, hot cunt you have for me, slave."

A shudder rocked her shoulders, and she flexed around his fingers. It seemed graphic talk turned her on.

He extracted his fingers and moved to tease the tight ring of muscle around her back entrance. "Have you ever been fucked here?" Without waiting for her response, he eased one finger inside. They hadn't discussed this topic, so he technically should have asked first.

She stopped breathing, and her eyes rolled back. "Yes. I can take more. Please, Master. Please give me more."

Shocked at the huskiness of her unexpected request, he added two more fingers when he should have only added one. He wasn't sure if he'd stumbled upon something she was just discovering or if she had answered in the affirmative. He rocked in and out, fucking her ass with his fingers. "Like that, slave? Do you want your Master to fuck your ass?"

"Yes. Oh God, yes!" She bowed and writhed, finding the strength to move despite her position. "Harder. You don't have to be gentle. I like it rough."

He withdrew his fingers and wiped them on a moist towelette he'd stowed in his bag of tricks. His cock wanted to be in her ass, pounding its way to oblivion. It would get there eventually, but he wanted her pussy first.

"You're very cruel, Master."

She sounded pleased, so he took her observation as a compliment. He knelt between her legs and grinned as he rolled a condom over his cock. "Just wait."

She watched him anxiously, her muscles taut with need. He loved the wanton way she responded to him. Shifting on his knees to get the right angle, he positioned his cockhead at her opening. This first time, he'd take her slowly, let her become accustomed to the way he felt.

He eased into her velvet warmth. She trembled with the effort it took to hold still. While she couldn't move much, she could wiggle and buck if she really wanted. He'd restricted her movements instead of outright restraining her.

Another inch, and she sucked in a breath, but she didn't close her eyes.

"That's it, Kitty Kat. Keep your eyes on me. Hide nothing."

Her hot walls fluttered around his cock, and she whimpered as he buried himself deep. "Master." She gasped his title, a plea and an exclamation.

To answer, he withdrew and thrust again. The spreader bar and the way he'd positioned her arms meant he couldn't lean forward to hold himself over her while he fucked her. No, this position dictated a leisurely pace, if only because he had to sit up.

It afforded him the opportunity to see how playing with her nipples and clit affected her responses. He reached up and tweaked one nipple. The redness from their earlier play had faded, but they were still a bit swollen. She tossed her head and arched her back, offering more.

He alternated breasts, pinching lightly with each thrust. She whimpered and writhed beneath him. He felt her frustration building, and he reveled in it. He abandoned her breasts, lifted her hips a little higher, and ruined the rhythm. This wasn't supposed to get either of them anywhere. He wanted to see how far he could push her before she misbehaved.

Her eyebrows drew together, and her lips pressed in a thin line. Her breathing normalized. At last she snapped, "I never knew you were such a pussy tease."

Just to madden her further, he slowed his pace. "It's my absolute favorite thing, Kitty Kat."

She closed her eyes, so he slapped her exposed clit. Her lids flew open, but she didn't yelp or gasp. She regarded him with wonder and expectation. This development interested him. She'd been exceptionally nervous about being flogged, but she didn't seem to have the same reservations about pain play on her breasts or pussy.

He slapped her three more times, and her pussy squeezed around his cock. It hurt just enough for him to quicken his pace. If she kept tightening on him, he wasn't going to remain in control for much longer. She thrashed her head from side to side.

Pressing his fingers hard against her clit, he rubbed. If she liked the stinging sensation, she should find this annoying. His goal was to distract her from the urge to climax, but it backfired. Her pussy convulsed wildly, and she cried out. He slowed his movements to draw out her moment of enjoyment. It helped stave off his need to orgasm as well.

"Thank you, Master." Passion blurred her eyes and slurred her words.

"It's time you learned to ask before your take what belongs to me. No more orgasms without permission. Understood?"

Her gaze focused, and a pleased smile lifted the corners of her mouth. "Yes, Master. I understand."

He withdrew and flipped her over. This forced her to kneel with her ass straight up in the air, her arms still wrapped around her legs, and her weight resting on her right shoulder and the side of her face. She was helpless now, and he planned to show her what that meant.

Gripping her hips hard to hold her in place, he plunged into her, not stopping until his balls hit her exposed pussy. Then he fucked her with quick, rough thrusts. He kept the rhythm even when he reached underneath to twist her nipples. Immediately, she emitted a low moan. Within seconds, another followed. Each time he touched her breasts, she lost control a little more. Her pussy fluttered, a preorgasmic sign he was coming to know well.

"Don't come, slave. You don't have permission." With that warning, he gave her nipple a particularly vicious pinch. She buried her face in the bedcover and screamed, doing exactly what he'd told her not to do.

He gritted his teeth against the need to follow her over that cliff and fucked her faster. Impossibly, her body bowed, and the convulsions came harder. She gasped and sobbed, losing herself in the sensations he knew overwhelmed her mind and body. Her reaction combined with the delicious heat inside him. He wanted more, so much more, but he couldn't withstand the demands of her pussy. Muttering a low oath, he gave in and came.

The edges of his vision turned white. He forced his consciousness back from the brink. He couldn't leave her bound like this much longer. With clumsy, lethargic hands, he released the strips holding her cuffs in place. It was easier than removing them from the spreader bar.

Then he attended to the mechanics of the situation, laying her down on the bed with her head on a pillow and the sheet covering her cooling body. He disposed of the condom in her bathroom and brought back a damp cloth to clean away her juices and the still-slick trail of semen on her stomach. Checking her skin wasn't a priority. He hadn't done anything lasting. She might still be a bit sensitized, but no trace of the flogging remained.

When he finished, he found himself at a loss. He wasn't the kind of Dom who cuddled with his subs. That was part of the reason his subs left. He had no tenderness or affection to give.

He liked them, and he appreciated their submission, but he didn't particularly want to be close to them. If she were anyone else, he could have parked himself in the chair across the room and waited for her to recover.

Kat deserved more. They all did, but Kat was the first woman for whom he considered changing his routine. Normally he would wait a few more minutes and continue the scene.

However, he didn't want Kat to learn to expect less from a Dom. If he was honest, he knew he was training her for someone who would cherish the gift of her submission, someone who knew how to love a woman. Therefore he could rationalize and justify his next action. He slid into bed next to her and took her in his arms, holding her stiffly. She nestled her head against his shoulder and rested her hand on his chest.

He remained in place for the longest time. Ticking noises announced when her air conditioner kicked on and off. Gradually he felt his body relax as it acclimated to this foreign stimulation. Her hand moved over his bare chest, tracing small patterns on his skin in an intimate caress he'd never before allowed. Something deep inside cracked, and he panicked, but he covered it well.

Closing his hand over hers, he halted her exploration. "You didn't fall asleep. Good. We're not finished with the scene."

She smiled. He felt the small movement against his shoulder a second before she pressed a kiss there. "You're an insatiable Master."

More than she could possibly know. There was a void inside him he'd tried to fill his entire life, but nothing had yet done the trick. Exercising his dominance brought him the closest to fulfillment, but even that only provided temporary relief.

Bringing up the arm he used to hold her against his side, he palmed her breast. She shifted, brushing her leg over his and arching to give him more access. Everything in him protested the sensuality of her action. It tapped his vast reserves of self-loathing and bitterness. He didn't deserve someone like Kat. He hated himself for taking so much from her, but he couldn't be someone he wasn't. He had warned her. Like the others, she had ignored it.

Like the others, she would learn the hard way.

Twisting his hand in the hair at the base of her head, he urged her to tilt her face toward his. Then he captured her lips with a punishing kiss. Who he was punishing was open for debate.

"Remember when I told you that I enjoy causing pain?"

Katrina nodded. Some of Keith's actions puzzled her. He seemed to vacillate between tender and rough, almost as if he couldn't decide which course to take. At times she caught glimpses of the man she knew, the friend who would do anything for her. Then a stranger would take his place. His expression would harden, and his eyes would grow cold and remote.

She knew he wrestled demons of several varieties, but she had no idea how much he normally kept under wraps. She wasn't surprised when he took care of her after the first part of the scene ended, but she had been a little shocked when he pulled her into his arms voluntarily. In the past, he'd rarely initiated physical contact—that was her forte.

She had no trouble remembering his reasons for turning her down a week ago. He was afraid she'd see his dark side and she'd run screaming. Some of it might be difficult or painful to face, but she wasn't going anywhere.

"I remember. Are you going to spank me now?" She deserved it. In the back of her mind, she felt guilty for coming without permission right after he'd warned her against it. Though he had said he didn't dole out physical punishments, she could see where what she would consider retribution, he might consider discipline or teaching. Keith's entire life operated according to his own rules.

"No." He pushed her hair back from her face and traced a caress along her temple. "I will take a moment to remind you that using your safeword is the only way to stop me. Protesting, begging, pleading—none of these will have any effect on my actions. I'm going to tie you up and fuck your ass. Since you're so experienced that way, I won't go easy on you."

She sincerely doubted his plans were as simple as bondage and sex. He'd said he wanted to hurt her, which meant he had something else up in that torture bag, and he meant it to be a surprise. Part of her wanted to protest, to safeword and plead tiredness. The braver part of her, the part determined to show him that she could be the woman he needed, kicked the sissy out of her head.

The analytical piece of her personality threw out her next question. This often helped her at work, so she didn't keep a tight rein on that impulse. "Do you like to hear protesting and begging and pleading?" She felt she could do those things and be quite sincere. It would be an outlet for her fears.

His hand stilled on her arm. "I don't like acting, especially bad acting. If it's an honest reaction, then I like it. If not, I'd prefer not to hear it. I did bring a gag."

She heard that warning loud and clear. He wanted to drive her to desperation. He didn't want her to arrive there through artificial channels. "No acting. Good to know."

The world tilted suddenly as he rolled her onto her back and pinned her to the mattress with the length of his body. Because his move had been so unexpected, she wrapped her arms around his neck. He pried them loose and pressed them down beside her head. She felt protected and powerless, completely engulfed by his presence. Even the air she breathed was heavy with his masculine scent. It all combined to make her wet and ready.

The edge of impatience tightened in the lines around his mouth. "Master."

For some reason, probably his relaxed demeanor and the fact that he was taking the time to explain things to her, she'd thought they'd suspended protocol. "I'm sorry, Master. I appreciate your patience."

The line, something they'd joked about as being a snarky way for companies who kept customers on hold to remind them who was really in charge, elicited a raised brow from him. She'd meant it, but there was no way to say it without sounding a little condescending.

When his expression didn't change, she scrambled to do some damage control. "Seriously, Master. I meant that. You are very patient. And a little scary."

He lowered his face to hers and nipped her lower lip. "Scary means you don't trust me. I'd never do anything I didn't think you could handle."

She knew that. She also knew he probably had some pretty insidious plans. While she might be able to handle whatever he threw her way, that didn't mean she didn't fear it. "I do trust you, Master. But I know you too well to think you didn't mean it when you said you got off on causing pain. That's a little scary to me, but not enough to make me chicken out."

The raw desire on his face when he'd put those clamps on her had only underlined his sadistic tendencies. And she'd really liked being on the receiving end.

Instead of responding or letting her study his nonverbal reaction, he closed the distance and kissed her. It was a long, thorough kiss, the kind that possessed and controlled without being violent.

When he changed the tempo, fucking his tongue into her mouth and then trailing a series of sucking bites down her neck, she responded on a primal level. Writhing under his slow attack, she sought both to escape the stinging points of contact and to bring him closer. She couldn't help but notice how her desperate movements solidified his hard-on.

"Don't ever hide or fake your reactions." He sucked her nipple into his mouth, trapping it between his teeth and tongue before letting it go. "I need to be able to read you at all times. If you hide things, it makes it difficult to read you, which can lead to some unintended consequences." Back and forth, he tortured her breasts until she cried out.

He regarded her expectantly. She stared back, uncertain what he wanted. At last she said, "Yes, Master."

That seemed to satisfy him. It dawned on her that he'd asked her to bare herself to him. He'd warned her that he'd ask for everything from her and give nothing in return. She wondered if he considered this request a step in that direction. The irony nearly made her laugh. He wanted to know her reactions so he could make sure the scenes were good for them both. While he didn't say as much, he had already taken steps to get to know her body in a way no other man had. He'd spent the evening studying her reactions, planning his next move based on what he thought she wanted.

And he presented it as a selfish thing. Only Keith would see it that way.

He knelt up and hauled her with him. "On your knees. Face the headboard. I'm going to bind your arms and legs first, and then I'm going to make you scream and possibly beg." He said it in the same matter-of-fact tone he used during depositions. No emotion, just facts. Somehow that made it all the more sinister, which caused another rush of desire to tingle through her system.

The headboard of her bed consisted of a series of slats. He took the padded cuffs from the spreader bar and put them back around her wrists. Instead of using the snaps to attach them, he threaded a few feet of rope through the snap on one, around a center slat, and through the other snap. When he finished, she had enough leeway to wrap her hands around the long, rectangular top piece, which meant she could only move them inches away from where he'd tied her.

He grabbed the pillows from the bed and tossed them on the chair next to her door. Then he pulled her back so that she had to bend forward and rest her weight on the headboard to stay upright. When she was in the perfect, exposed position, he guided her legs farther apart.

From his bag of tricks, he extracted a length of rope that was at least an inch in diameter. He wrapped it around the middle of her left thigh and secured it to the bed frame beneath the mattress. With a second line, he secured her other leg in the same fashion.

Though she was only bound at three points, she found it surprisingly difficult to move. The position of her arms meant she couldn't rest back on her heels, and her body was effectively held in place by the ropes on her legs, so she couldn't scoot forward to find a different balance. She was stuck, legs spread wide apart, exactly how he wanted. He moved around her, checking and rechecking the places where things wrapped around her body. "If you experience numbness or tingling in your hands, wrists, legs, or feet, call yellow and tell me what's going on. Got it?"

"Yes, Master." Right now her pussy was the only thing tingling, and he hadn't indicated that he had plans for it.

He held up a strip of black leather studded with metal loops and rivets, and she recognized it as a bondage collar. Without asking permission, he buckled it into place and checked the fit. As he stared at her, a bit of peace settled into his eyes. He nodded, a quick action heavy with finality. "This means you're mine."

Katrina swallowed, and the weight of the collar shifted with the movement. It was odd, heavy and bulky, almost alien. At the same time, a place deep inside responded to this show of possession. For the first time, she felt like they weren't just playing a game. This was for real. She would grow accustomed to the collar.

He hadn't asked a question, so she didn't respond. Not that it mattered. He'd already turned back to his bag and was fishing around inside for something else.

She gasped when he dumped a bag of stainless steel clothespins on the bed next to her knee. Several slid into the indent she made and bumped into her skin. They were cool to the touch. She'd only ever seen clothespins made from wood or plastic. She'd clamped them on her skin before. Sometimes they hurt, especially when they were pulled off. Something about these being metal lent them a menacing quality. She shivered, half in fear and half in anticipation.

Keith climbed onto the bed and knelt so that he was facing her, yet his entire consideration went to her chest. Tied to the bed, bound into position, she had become his plaything, just as he'd warned her. Excitement curled low in her belly, but she wasn't sure she should embrace it. If she consented to being objectified like this, did she have to turn in her feminist card?

He plumped one breast, squeezing and kneading the tenderized flesh.

Unable to help it, she hazarded a glance at those menacing steel torture tools. That was when she noticed he was wearing pants.

"You got dressed?" That came out sounding a little more upset than she'd intended. She tried to make amends with the way she added his title. "Master."

His lips curled in that sinfully sexy smile that stopped her heart every time she saw it. He didn't otherwise answer. Thinking about it, she realized it was another way to emphasize the power shift. She was naked and powerless. He was clothed and dominant. When she considered that perspective, she was less upset.

While she was distracted by her need to rationalize everything, he clipped the first clothespin onto her nipple. It exerted less pressure than the clamp, but it still pinched. When she'd experimented with clothespins before, she hadn't tried them on areas that were this tender. Her mistake.

He pinched the skin on her breast just below the nipple, pulling at the area he'd already pinned and making it burn a little. Then he attached another clothespin. Circling her breast, he attached two more. Now she had four total, each working against the other to simultaneously pull and pinch. Every breath she took aided the nefarious configuration. It stimulated, but it hurt too.

By the time he started on her other breast, the pain had grown disproportionately to the pleasure she derived from the pinch. Using the breathing technique he taught didn't help, because the rise and fall of her chest exacerbated the situation. She wanted him to remove the clothespins. Frustration built, and she snapped at him.

"What is it with you and breasts? Do you have a boob fetish?"

He glanced up, clinical curiosity his only apparent reaction. He studied her, no doubt noting the way her lips trembled. "Not really. I do prefer smaller sizes. Too big and it's difficult to find the right combination to produce the pleasure/pain sensations I'm after."

He wasn't finding the right combination now. Her breasts felt like they were on fire. She only felt the pain. Clothespins on her nipples wouldn't have caused this distress. Earlier, with the clamps, Keith had established her love of that kind of stimulation. These additions just hurt.

She had no problem remembering her place. He'd seen to that when he bound her like this. "Master, this hurts. It doesn't feel good at all."

He finished and leaned back to survey his work. A satisfied smile settled on his mouth. "Perfect."

He flickered his gaze between her face and her chest. Then he brought his hand up and brushed his thumb across her cheekbone. She felt the wetness of a tear. She hadn't been aware it had fallen.

"Beautiful." He kissed her lightly, reverently, and she realized exactly how much he loved seeing her like this. "Just wait. It's going to get worse before it gets better."

It was a hollow assurance. A glance down showed a mountain of desire tenting his pants. She hoped he lost control of it before she started sobbing like a baby.

He disappeared behind her only to reappear as he shouldered his way between her legs. Leaning up on his elbows, he buried his face in her cunt. He licked her wetness, fucked her hole with his tongue, and circled her clit with his thumb. She liked the way he dived right in and set about his task with urgency and passion. The rush of pleasure took her mind away from the pain in her breasts. It was still there, but it mattered less.

Taking a chance, she rocked against his face. The bindings had left her with a little wiggle room there, and she used it to her advantage. He moaned and matched her rhythm. The vibration triggered a small orgasm, and her vagina convulsed around nothing. She'd had no idea she was that close. Air hissed through her teeth, the only outward sign that she'd inadvertently gained completion without permission.

He dropped down and rested on his back between her legs. She thought he was waiting for her to come down from her climax, but he reached for a clothespin and closed it on one edge of her labia. It hurt in a different way than on her breasts, maybe because she was more sensitive there. Tears immediately welled and fell from her eyes.

"Son of a bitch." She hissed the oath. There was no way he could think she was calling him names, though it might come to that before they were through.

But if he heard, he didn't show it. Slowly, methodically, he clipped two more clothespins to that side of her labia. Each ratcheted up the pain factor. Then he evened out the torture by attaching three to the opposite side. She couldn't stand it. He might think she was capable of withstanding—or even enjoying—this kind of agony, but he was wrong.

Trying to escape the burning pain on her chest and between her legs, she jerked against her bonds. "Master, please take them off. They hurt too much."

He wiggled out from between her legs and put the rest of the pins into their bag. "No. You can handle this, Kitty Kat. You're brave and strong. Breathe through it."

Breathing through it made it hurt even more. She lost her temper. "Son of a bitch. Take them off." Now she was calling him names, and he took it that way.

He leaned against her bedpost and crossed his arms. "That's no way to talk to your Master. I just gave you an orgasm, and I didn't even make you ask for it."

And he'd given her loads of fiery pain. She choked on a combination of tears and rage. All week she'd been upset and more than a little pissed at him for turning her down and forcing her to have a conversation with Dustin she'd never wanted to have. For over a decade, she'd lusted after Keith and loved him from afar. And then last night when she'd called him to tell him someone had been in her apartment, he'd treated her like she'd fabricated the whole experience. Now he was calmly persecuting her just for the fun of it.

Those feelings came barreling out. She called him every combination of horrible names she could think up, and then she accused him of lacking any kind of compassion. "You're inhuman. That's what you are."

He leaned close and licked the trail of tears on her cheek. "Yes, Kat. I am. It's important you understand that about me. I'm not the kind of man you think I am. Call red, and I'll stop everything. I'll take off the clothespins. I'll untie you. I'll wrap you in a blanket and hold you until you feel better."

His quiet acceptance caught her off guard, and she realized the danger inherent in his game. If she cried off, she would confirm that his initial reaction had been the correct decision. They weren't compatible. She couldn't let him win that way. Perhaps she didn't particularly like this, but there were plenty of other ways he could pleasantly torture her.

"No." She shook her head to emphasize her point. "I can take this. I don't have to like it." *A submissive endures pain for the pleasure of her Master.* She repeated that to herself silently.

He gave her that same sinful grin, and she melted a lot. Then he smacked a powerful kiss on her lips. "Slave, would it help to know the pleasure is always greater than the pain?"

Without waiting for her answer, he moved away. She didn't turn her head to follow his path, but it wasn't long before she felt him slide into position behind her.

It did help to know that. She was fast realizing that he liked the mental game as much as or more than he liked the physical game. This shouldn't have been a big revelation for her, having participated in countless heated discussions with him, but it was. He wasn't into sex for the romantic aspects; that much was for certain.

She felt his fingers at her anus, smearing lubrication on the tight muscle here. He inserted two fingers to stretch and pull. A wave of pleasure washed through her body. She'd always loved this kind of stimulation. She didn't question it. She just went with it.

He fingered her that way until she moaned. The pain of the clothespins had once again become minor. "That's it. That's my beautiful, strong slave."

The tip of his cock nudged against her sphincter. Taking a deep breath, she let him know she was ready. Even though she exhaled and relaxed, she still found herself stunned and frozen when he entered her. He'd reamed her. She hadn't expected him to be gentle, but she'd thought he would at least enter her the first time with a little more care and caution. He didn't know what she was used to.

"Son of a bitch." She gasped when she finally recovered the ability to breathe.

He withdrew and thrust again. "I think I'm going to ask you to choose a new term of endearment."

Her vision narrowed. The hot-and-cold, prickly feeling that preceded a huge orgasm was running up her spine. "Master." She wanted to warn him, but the word came out too reverently to be anything but a verbal caress.

"That'll do."

He set a fast pace. She shoved back, bearing down to ensure that he took her hard. The sense of losing control spread, and the feeling she was flying settled over her. She'd kissed this bliss when he'd whipped her with the deerskin flogger, but this was so much better. "God, yes. Master, please!"

"No, Kitty Kat. No orgasm yet. Hold it back. Breathe."

It was too much. She closed her eyes and leaned her forehead on her arms. "I...I can't. Please, Master. Please let me come."

He reached around to her front, and she sobbed. The tears tonight seemed to have no end, but now she was crying for a different reason. Just when she thought to beg him not to touch her clit, he ripped away two pins. She cried out, and he pulled the rest of them off.

Blood rushed to her vulva. The smoldering fire burst into flame, and so did her orgasm. She came hard and fast. From far away, she heard screaming. A hand clapped over her mouth and blotted the sound.

It went on and on. He pumped his cock into her, and he removed the pins from her breasts. Each sharp jerk—he didn't bother to open them when he pulled them off—made her orgasm pulse faster. Every cell on her body stood at attention. Individual follicles of hair prickled on her scalp. The world went black, but she still felt every one of the tumultuous sensations rioting through her body.

Another shout, this one deeper and shorter, joined the high-pitched one keening in her ears.

When full awareness returned, she found herself wrapped in her sheet and curled up on Keith's lap. The last vestiges of her tears finished falling as he smoothed her hair away from her face and whispered praise and assurances. Her entire body trembled, inside and out.

"I c-can't s-stop sh-shaking." Her teeth chattered too.

She felt him smile as he kissed her forehead. "It's all right. I got you. I won't let you go."

They sat in silence and let the minutes pass. Her heart slowed back to a normal rate, but she seemed to be getting all her body heat from him. Still, the quivering wound down as well. She knew it had a lot to do with the fact that he held her as if she were the most precious thing in the world.

"Talk to me, Kat."

"Seriously? Men never want to have conversation after sex." She meant it as a joke, because she needed time to think of something to say. What, exactly, could she say to the man who'd just put her through hell to show her a new level of orgasm she'd never believed existed?

He kissed her forehead again. "Real men do. If a Dom doesn't talk to a sub after a scene, then he's not fulfilling his responsibilities."

While she didn't want to be thought of as a responsibility, she wasn't willing or able to have that discussion right then. "Thank you, Master. I didn't know orgasms came that large."

His laugh rumbled against her shoulder and chest. "Pain turns into pleasure. That's the reward you get for trusting me. But I need you to be honest with me, Kat. I need you to tell me what you liked and what you hated."

So much had happened in just a few hours. He wanted her to process it all now? "Keith, my mind isn't really working right now. Can we talk about this tomorrow?"

He eased her up so that she sat on the bed next to him. She wanted to protest the loss of his protective embrace, but she could see by the firm set of his jaw that he was going to demand answers. He'd probably also reached his limit on cuddling, and this topic of conversation couldn't be all that comfortable for him. Shifting to cross her legs, she noted that the ropes were still wrapped around her thighs and the cuffs were still on her wrists.

She scrambled for something to say. "I liked pretty much everything. You almost put me to sleep with that flogger. I really thought they were supposed to sting."

"Some do. It depends on the material and the force of the swing. We'll get to that eventually." He regarded her cautiously, and she noticed that although he'd disposed of the condom, he hadn't put his clothes back on. They were equals for this discussion.

"The clothespins hurt. Seriously hurt. I think I'm going to have bruises."

He nodded as if that were no big deal. "Bruising is pretty normal. I won't cut you. I'm not into blood play, but bruising happens. Welts too. You're going to be sore tomorrow, but that's nothing compared to how you'll feel after this weekend is over."

She wasn't sure she wanted welts or bruises, but she figured she'd reserve judgment for now. "I liked the lighter stuff, but..."

The first part of the scene had been light BDSM, and the second part had been a heavier practice. She understood what he'd done. He'd given her a comparison, and now he wanted to know which product she'd chosen.

She looked up at him and realized he'd never once let his gaze wander from her face. And he was waiting patiently while she gathered her thoughts. "The clothespins are a bit of a sticking point. I think I'm okay with them on my nipples and pussy, but I didn't like them on my breasts. That was too much."

He regarded her solemnly. "So that's a hard limit, then?"

"Yes." She knew the terminology, but she'd forgotten to use it. "That's a hard limit. Also I don't think I could do the harder play all the time. I liked it, and I loved the payout, but it was draining, physically and emotionally."

Not to mention he'd played head games with her. She definitely didn't like that.

"Kat? You have that look on your face."

"What look?" She'd been inside her head, so she hadn't been aware of her expression.

"The one you get right before you lay into someone." He held steady, his gaze locked to hers, but he clenched his jaw as if he expected her to say something horrible.

She couldn't recall ever saying anything cruel to him. Even when she'd cursed him out during the scene, she hadn't been malicious. Sure, she'd snapped at him when he'd annoyed or teased her too much, but that was when he'd treated her like a sister. Of course, he'd seen her eviscerate a dishonest witness before, so he knew how her tongue could cut.

"I don't like the head games. I don't like when you pretend to be a jerk. Keith, I know you like to pretend you don't care, but I know you better than that." She placed her hand over his heart and soaked up the warmth radiating from his chest. "You've walled it up pretty well, but I know it's there."

Color drained from his cheeks. She didn't know if he was going to vomit or run, but she had enough sense to figure out he hadn't wanted to talk about feelings. He'd wanted to analyze the scene. Always an agent.

"I'm not going to hurt you or try to tear down anything. This is temporary. You're just training me, and then you'll turn me loose." She rushed to assure him that her intentions were good. "I just want you to know you can be yourself with me. I like you."

He stared at her for the longest time. Blood returned to his face. He shook his head in disbelief. "Kat, you don't know all the sides of me. When I told you earlier that I was a bastard, I wasn't lying."

With a start, she realized he really believed that. Lucky for him, she didn't.

## Chapter Five

A shaft of light focused on Keith's left eye, turning the inside view bright red. He turned his face the other way. The scent of the pillow cradling his head was both familiar and unfamiliar, and the air smelled faintly of sex and sweat. *Kat.*

All at once, he was fully awake, and so was his cock. She'd rocked his world, and then she'd laid down the law. She was not a compliant submissive. In fact, unless he had her bound or in pain, familiarity intruded and she forgot her manners. Normally he wouldn't put up with a submissive who took him to task the way she had or who continually crossed the lines he set.

Training someone who mattered to him was new territory. Kat unsettled him. She pushed his emotional boundaries, and he felt himself responding in alien and unexpected ways. As yet, he had no regrets about opening this door, and he had definite plans for them today.

Part of that plan was to keep her on edge. Today, she was going to learn to control her orgasms. Or rather, she was going to recognize they belonged to him. They'd happen when and if he wanted. He planned to introduce her to the concepts of orgasm denial and forced climax.

He snagged a condom from the bedside table and covered his cock. Never having slept next to her before, he didn't know whether she woke slow or fast. It would be fun finding out.

In her sleep, she'd rolled onto her side, facing away and curled up into a ball. He pulled her toward him, turning her onto her back, and pushed her legs out of the way. With a series of smooth, practiced moves, he had her in position, and he slid into her warmth. The condom was lubricated, so she didn't have to be ready for this. She only had to be willing.

He thrust twice before her eyes opened. She stared at him in shocked silence laced with speculation, but she didn't safeword. At last she opened her mouth to say something. He wasn't in the mood for conversation, so he pressed his finger to her lips. "Shhh. I'll just be a minute, slave. Don't talk. It's distracting."

She closed her mouth and drew her knees up to allow deeper access. When she met his thrusts, he knew she was seeking her own completion. He couldn't let that happen. It would spoil his plans. Two more, and he climaxed.

Before she could initiate more action, he withdrew and rolled away. "You hungry? I was going to run out and get some breakfast."

Silence greeted his question. He let her have a moment to come to terms with the fact he'd just used her body without seeing to her pleasure. It could be a difficult idea to assimilate after he'd so thoroughly seen to her pleasure the night before.

He felt a slight shift in the mattress as she sat up. "Yeah. Don't forget coffee."

She didn't sound upset or angry, only tired, so he hazarded a look over his shoulder. She blinked and swayed a little, clearly still not quite awake.

"You can go back to sleep if you want."

Gravity took over. She flopped back and closed her eyes.

———

The warm spray washed over her skin, soothing some of her sore muscles. So many places hurt, but her thighs seemed to have borne the brunt of the strain. The positions into which he put her certainly required stamina.

She wasn't sure whether she was pissed at Keith for the stunt he'd pulled earlier. It was one thing to have a quickie. She knew the score when it came to that kind of thing, and she wasn't upset that he hadn't discussed it with her first. He'd asked for her limits, and she had merely shrugged. This wouldn't be one of them. She didn't mind being awakened that way. She didn't even mind that he hadn't made her climax.

The way he told her not to talk took the cake. It hadn't registered until later, but that kind of treatment crossed a line. Before last night, she hadn't been sure if she would draw any kind of lines with Keith. From the bottom of her soul, she wanted to please him. She wanted to give him the gift of her submission. But there was definitely a line, and it was becoming easier to see. She wouldn't tolerate being spoken to in such a disrespectful manner.

She shoved that thought aside for now. He'd left her unfulfilled, and she didn't have a problem taking care of herself. Actually, the shower was her favorite place to masturbate. She lifted the showerhead away from its holder and brought it closer to her body. Over her shoulders, down her breasts, she directed the warm spray lower and followed with her free hand. She pinched her right nipple. All these years with this body, and she had never appreciated the sensitivity in those nubs. She'd spent her time cursing the fact she couldn't wear lacy bras because she inevitably ended up with headlights, and that just drew attention to the area in which genetics had skimped. At least Keith didn't seem to mind.

Pinching harder brought forth a moan she couldn't suppress. She took her time, playing awhile before she continued. Turning the water to the pulse setting, she aimed it at her clit and eased two fingers into her opening. From the periphery of her vision, she saw a shadow and realized Keith was in the bathroom, watching as she touched herself.

Though she couldn't see more than just his outline through the smoky glass door, and she reasoned he could only see hers, she exaggerated her movements and put on a show for him. The remembered heat in his eyes from the night before, when she'd straddled his lap and masturbated, drove her now. She pumped her fingers harder, jabbing at her G-spot in exactly the right way. Warm water pulsed over her clit. She moaned. Her knees weakened, and the climax took her harder than it normally did when she pleasured herself.

She rested her forehead against the tiled wall while she recovered. Then she finished her shower and opened the glass door.

Keith held out a towel and wrapped her in its softness and his embrace. He pressed his body to her length and massaged her lips with a tender kiss. She closed her eyes and surrendered to his masterful touch.

"I see I have my work cut out for me."

Still feeling the effects of her climax and his kiss, she blinked uncomprehendingly. "Your work?"

"Yes. You came without permission. I don't mind if you want to touch yourself, Kitty Kat. I do mind when you steal an orgasm. I'm going to have to teach you some restraint, but that'll keep. Right now, you need a punishment, and not the usual kind." He caressed her temple with his lips and fluttered tiny kisses against her eyelids. "Turn and face the counter. Bend over and brace yourself."

Katrina let her towel drop to the floor as she assumed the position. In the foggy mirror, she could see the fuzzy, distorted image of two people. The sense of foreboding clenching its fist in her stomach wasn't apparent in the shadowy figure of her reflection. The edge of the counter dug into her palms, and she prepared for the worst. He'd said he only wanted an apology for any infraction, but it became clear to her that he wasn't following his rules. This had to be new territory for him. Knowing he was changing his routine for her was a balm to her fraying nerves.

"This is going to hurt. Feel free to cry out."

The fog in the mirror cleared a bit, enough to see that he had her brush in his hand. She wasn't under the illusion that he wanted to brush her hair. She waited for instructions to count out a specific number, but he seemed to have skipped that part in the romance novels she'd read.

She watched his arm come back and swing down in a wide arc. The hard plastic stung her ass far worse than the deerskin flogger. She exhaled afterward, forgoing the scream for now. Hot pain radiated in short bursts. She'd barely begun to acclimate to the sensation when he struck again and again.

What happened to instructing the submissive to count out the progress of the punishment? Counting made the slave breathe out, better absorbing the force of the blow. It hurt less that way, right? Should she tell him how it was supposed to happen?

He picked up the pace. The heat blended together. Her butt felt like it was on fire, but he kept up the steady pace. Tears wetted her eyes, and she gritted her teeth. All capacity for thought fled her brain. At last she could stand it no longer. She gave in, surrendering to the will of her Master, and she cried out.

The spanking stopped. He traced a random pattern on her ass. She flinched and whimpered. "I'm sorry, Master. I promise I'll ask next time." And she was genuinely contrite. Last night, he'd been clear about wanting her to ask beforehand, and she'd ignored his wishes. Never again.

He lifted her and folded her in his arms until her sniffling subsided. Lesson learned. She wouldn't come again without permission, even if he wasn't there to ask.

"Get on your knees." He released her so she could follow his order.

The discarded towel and the spongy bath mat cushioned her knees and provided relief that the tile floor wouldn't have. She sank down, knees wide as he'd shown her yesterday. Water dripped from her hair and from her body, and the cooling air gave her gooseflesh. It prickled the sensitized skin on her buttocks, increasing the burn and the reminder of her transgression.

He'd dressed in cargo shorts and a thin cotton shirt. With the flick of his wrist, he unbuttoned the shorts. They fell to his ankles, and he wasn't wearing underwear. His cock sprang from its nest of dark golden curls. She knew what he wanted.

"Open your mouth, slave."

She'd fantasized about sucking his cock, but in her imaginings, it had always happened on her terms. He'd stand there and just enjoy her gift. This, she knew, would be different. He was going to take what he wanted, and she was merely a vessel for his pleasure.

She opened her mouth. He eased the tip inside, letting her wet him with her tongue. She took the opportunity to explore him, dipping her tongue into the drop of precum beading at his tip and running it along his sensitive ridge. When she completed the preliminaries, he grasped her head in his large hands, and she gripped his hips.

"Relax your jaw. Cradle my cock with your tongue."

He pushed deep, almost to the back of her throat. She choked, but he didn't seem to notice. Or perhaps that was part of the discipline? At any rate, he fucked her mouth with quick, deep thrusts. She fondled his sac to increase his pleasure, and so she felt his balls draw up, signaling his imminent climax.

Instead of thrusting deep to come in the back of her throat, he pulled out. Ejaculate shot all over her lips, cheeks, and chin. She closed her eyes against the splatters and the complex feelings arising as the result of his unexpected action.

Had he come on her face as part of the punishment because she'd climaxed without permission, or had he done it because he was a Dom and he enjoyed the look of semen on his slave's face? Either way, she didn't like it. Spanking, she could appreciate. Coming on her face, she could not.

She felt for her towel, and then she wiped her face. As she rocked back to rise to her feet, she nailed him with a look. She wasn't sure what the look conveyed, because her emotions were too jumbled to be clear. Instead of saying anything to him—

because she didn't know what to say—she turned to the sink and washed her face.

In the mirror, she saw him pull up his shorts and fasten them.

She scrubbed her face furiously. Keith watched with mixed emotions. He'd come on his subs' faces so often that he no longer stopped to consider whether they'd enjoy it. The practice marked a sub, literally and figuratively, as property. He'd held her head and forced her to watch as he ejaculated on her face. The marks on her ass were already fading. But no matter how vigorously she washed, the image, the feel of his hot spunk, and the strong emotions he elicited left an indelible tattoo that could never be removed.

Clearly, he'd pissed her off. He'd warned her that he was a bastard. Though he'd made a deliberate decision to hold her after sex, that didn't change his general philosophy or practice as a Dom. The subs who liked humiliation lasted longer with him, but not much longer.

Face dripping with water, she straightened and turned. The towel where she'd initially wiped the mess lay wadded on the floor. She cast a hateful look at it before pushing him out of her way to access the linen closet. She patted her face dry, and then she used the new towel to squeeze some excess moisture from her hair and to finish drying her body.

Keith watched, his face purposely devoid of any expression. He had to wait her out, to see how she would react. Would she accept what he'd done, or would she add that to her list of hard limits?

She stalked from the bathroom and grabbed her bathrobe from her bedroom closet. He hadn't told her to dress, and her move to cover herself made his impassive mask difficult to hold.

When he'd returned with her requested coffee, he had expected to find her still asleep. He'd used her hard, and he knew she had been exhausted by the time he finally let her go to sleep. When he found her in the shower, her hands gliding over her slick skin as she lowered the showerhead to point the spray at her pussy, he'd become instantly hard. He could—and fully intended to—watch her masturbate often. But she needed to learn to ask before she climaxed.

And the blowjob hadn't been a punishment. She'd turned him on, and it was her job to satisfy his needs, especially the ones she created. Coming on her face had been part habit and part primal need. Her stunned reaction had given him pause, which was why he let her tie her bathrobe closed when every inclination he had screamed at him to rip away her clothes and paddle her ass again. Not for punishment; just for fun.

"I feel an almost overwhelming urge to slap your face."

He leaned a shoulder against the frame of the door separating her bedroom from her bathroom and crossed his arms. "It's good you refrained." He liked to be on the receiving end of impact play, but not on his face.

Five steps, and she closed the distance between them. She poked a finger at his chest, letting loose some of that bottled fury. "What the hell was that?"

Closing his hand around her finger, he eased some of the pressure of her jab and exerted some of his own. "The blowjob? You started it. You know I like watching when you masturbate. You saw me watching you. It made it hotter for you, didn't it? You got off on the fact that it turns me on to watch you."

"That is so not the issue!" She jerked her hand from his grasp. "I know what kind of women you tend toward. Maybe they like it, but I doubt it. That's probably why they kick you to the curb so quickly. Never, ever do that again."

He narrowed his eyes, knowing full well how frightening his glare could be. "It wasn't punishment, though I see I'm going to have to spend some time teaching you to control your orgasms.

As I said, I don't mind if you touch yourself, but you are not to come without my permission."

This time she smacked the palm of her hand full on his chest. She packed quite a wallop, but she failed to move him. "Damn it! Stop trying to change the subject. I'm not into humiliation. I don't mind crawling or sucking your dick or even the fact that you got yourself off this morning when I was barely even awake. I will not countenance you treating me with such disrespect. I'm the same person I was yesterday, and I expect you to treat me with the same dignity and respect."

"You're upset that I came on your face?" He asked to clarify. Though she'd said she was okay with blowing him, he wasn't sure whether she was upset over the rough treatment or the way he'd finished.

Fury flared brighter in her eyes, lending a hellish darkness to them. "Don't play games with me. You know exactly why I'm upset. Everything was fine until you pulled that stunt."

As a child, Keith had always been the one to push until someone retaliated. He had instigated more than his share of fights because he looked at the boundaries people set and barreled through them. Telling him to stop was like waving a figurative red flag.

One swift move, and he had her pinned between the wall and his body. "Let me get this right. You're okay with me shooting my junk all over your stomach, but not your face?"

She wiggled her hands between them and pushed, but he had the advantage in weight and height. "I also don't appreciate being told to shut up. You want to fuck me in the morning, fine. Don't you ever tell me to be quiet in such a condescending way again. I won't put up with it, Keith. Maybe your other subs were doormats, but I'm not."

"Chest?"

She shoved harder. "Move. You don't get to intimidate me when we're not in a scene."

He knew he wasn't intimidating her. Despite his best effort, or perhaps because of it, she was about three seconds from nailing him in the balls. He thrust a knee between her legs to block that move. "Answer the question. Are you okay with me coming on your chest?"

Her bathrobe had come loose, and he had a clear view of the softly rounded tops of her breasts. Blood rushed to his cock.

She stopped struggling and shifted to lean against the wall. "Yes. That's kind of hot. I did like when you came on me yesterday. Watching you masturbate was definitely a turn-on. I even liked the way you woke me up this morning. It made me feel powerful and important. Like I belonged to you. Like I mattered. But the other things were not cool."

Her admission eviscerated any doubts he had about her submissiveness. Though she sounded every bit as pissed off, her voice had softened, and so had her expression. At least until she got to the last part. He pushed back a strand of wet hair that had fallen over her forehead. "That's the kind of Dom I am, Kitty Kat."

"No. It's not."

With a sigh, he stepped back and gave her some space. "It is. I've been trying to tell you this since last weekend, but you don't want to believe it. The evidence is staring you in the face, but you don't want to face facts. Since you just want me to train you, I've actually been nicer and more considerate with you than I've ever been with a woman. Still, it's less than you deserve."

Lines scrunched between her eyebrows as she adjusted her robe. "That's a nice piece of bullshit, but I'm not buying. Maybe it's the kind of Dom you've been, but it's not who you are. I know you, Keith. I know the sides of yourself that you hide from your lovers. You can't pretend to be someone you're not with me. You don't get a free pass to be an asshole."

He backed away and sank down on the edge of her mattress, more than a little defeated. He should have known she wouldn't be able to accept this side of him. "You want someone who can be gentle, who can look at you with affection and touch you with reverence. That's not me."

She shook her head. "You're selling yourself short. I won't let you do that."

Her faith in him was tremendously misplaced. He couldn't win this argument, and he wasn't sure he wanted to try to convince her to settle for him. He'd been a fool to entertain the possibility that he could have a piece of this dream. At the end of the day, he was only howling at the moon. "This was a mistake. I shouldn't have come here last night."

Little by little, her eyes widened and her lips parted as she realized he was breaking it off. "You're afraid. You're ending this because you're scared."

Afraid of losing her friendship? *Hell, yes.* "I can't take the chance I'll cause more damage than I already have."

She covered her eyes with her hand. He couldn't tell if she was holding back tears or anger. "Fine. I can't force you to do something you don't want to do. I'll ask Jordan to train me."

It killed him to imagine Jordan anywhere near her, but she deserved someone who could cherish her body and soul. Jordan Monaghan could do that. He might look a little rough around the edges, but he knew how to treat a woman—and he had a huge nurturing side to him. "That's probably for the best."

She turned her back to him, though not before he saw the moisture gathering in her eyes, and yanked open a drawer in her dresser.

Katrina snatched at the stack of panties that was supposed to be on the left side of her top drawer, but she came up empty. The tears blurring her vision brimmed over and burned hot on her cheeks. She'd been stupid to think he wanted this as much as she did. Malcolm had told her several times that Keith was emotionally damaged, that he'd probably never settle down because he didn't believe he deserved happiness. She'd rolled her eyes at her brother's dire prediction, but now she saw the truth of his statement. Keith went out of his way to alienate anyone who got too close.

Well, she couldn't let him do that to her. She whirled around to give him a further piece of her mind, only to find him standing right behind her. He wrapped his arms around her and held her so tight she thought he might crack her ribs.

"I'm sorry. I never wanted this to happen."

She tilted her face up, though it took some doing to get him to ease his hold enough for her to move. "Keith, just because we disagree doesn't mean it has to end. I want you to train me, not somebody else."

The relief in his expression was immeasurable. "I'm not used to such a feisty sub."

She thought he probably selected subs who capitulated to his every demand because he thought that was the kind of woman he craved. While she knew he wanted a submissive, she also knew he needed someone who wouldn't let him get away with being a jerk. He needed to be with someone he liked and respected. If she could just keep him around long enough, she could get him to see that.

However, she wasn't naive enough to give voice to her analysis. "Yeah, well, you needed to spice things up anyway."

He kissed her thoroughly. It was a comforting clash of tongues and lips, a reacquainting of what they'd almost ended and a confirmation that they hadn't. When he pulled away, she rested her cheek against his chest. "I need coffee and food before we have any more drama. I'm not cut out for this kind of precaffeine excitement."

He smoothed a hand down her back. "I have a caramel macchiato waiting for you in the kitchen that's probably cool enough for you to chug it."

That sounded good. "Okay. Let me get dressed. You and I have some negotiation to do before we do another scene." She was sure he would prefer to talk while she was naked, but that wasn't going to happen. Part of her wondered if being naked last night had short-circuited her brain. The litigator in her needed clothes to function—at least around Keith.

He let go slowly, and she sensed his reluctance. They were leaving his comfort zone, but he wasn't protesting. He got points for that.

Behind her, the drawer was open. Now that her tears were gone, she could clearly see that it was empty. Her socks and stockings were still there, but her bras and underwear were all missing.

He headed toward the door. "I picked up some more of that Greek yogurt you like. Do you want it with cereal or fruit?"

She whirled and regarded him, hands on hips so he knew she meant business. "What did you do with my underthings?"

He paused in the doorway and looked back over his shoulder. His brows were drawn together, a severe look that only accented the dangerous air he liked to affect. "What?"

"My bras? My underwear?" She exhaled hard through her nose. "I'm not in the mood for games. My blood sugar is getting low, and I really need to eat. Just tell me where you put them."

The expression on his face changed, melting to that inscrutable special-agent-in-charge look. He swept the room visually. A cold chill raced down her spine.

"I didn't touch your clothes. I never opened your drawers." He inspected her bed and bathroom before he slid completely into work mode. "Stay here."

While he did his thing, she mentally recounted her activities from the time he'd left Thursday night. She'd wallowed for about ten minutes before anger took over. She'd double-checked her doors and windows. Then she'd done her laundry, folding everything neatly and putting it away, a kind of thumbing her nose at both Keith and the stress causing her to go a little crazy. Plus the thought of someone touching her possessions kept nagging at the back of her mind. She hadn't been able to go to sleep until she'd washed her clothes.

A weight lifted as she realized she wasn't losing her mind. Somebody had indeed been inside her apartment. Though terrified, she felt a bit vindicated.

Waiting wore on her nerves. She checked all the drawers and her closet, looking to see if anything else was missing. With dread coiling low in her tummy, she dumped her laundry basket. The only items inside should have been the clothes she'd worn to bed Thursday night and a towel from her Friday-morning shower.

Her panties were missing from the hamper as well.

Keith returned and let her know with the shake of his head that he'd found nothing. "Everything's the same. Your clothes from yesterday are still folded on the kitchen counter. Including your underwear and bra."

She gestured to the pile at her feet. "My panties are missing from the dirty laundry as well. Why on earth would someone break in and steal my underwear?"

The expression on his face said too much. She'd worked a few cases in Violent Crimes, enough to recognize the beginning stages of having a stalker.

"I'm calling Malcolm." He already had his cell in hand.

She leaped for it and caught his wrist. "Not Malcolm. How can we explain you being here?"

Keith lifted a brow. "You want to keep us a secret?"

Since he seemed surprised, she wondered whether his sense of survival was still intact. "Yes. Malcolm will kill you if he finds out you're training me. I know he made you promise to stay away from me."

Jaw set in a mutinous slant, he studied his phone. "That was a long time ago. Things have changed since then."

"He's still my brother and your best friend. I just think, on top of everything else, you shouldn't rock that boat." It had taken her brother a long time to forgive Keith, and she didn't want to be the one responsible for straining those bonds.

Keith's stiff shoulders let her know he wasn't happy about keeping things under wraps. "Dustin, then. We need to keep this in-house. It could be related to a case you're working on."

She swallowed. Dustin was the best choice. He knew how and when to keep his mouth shut, and he would know this could be related to one of Keith's or Malcolm's cases as well. Sometimes criminals targeted family members of agents.

By the time she agreed, he had already dialed Dustin's number. She paired leggings with a longer shirt so that nobody would be able to see whether she was wearing panties. Her only pair wasn't clean. Wearing yesterday's bra wasn't a big deal, and she didn't really have a choice about that. Just being near Keith made her nipples pointy.

Though they both wanted to maintain the crime scene, Katrina insisted they put away all the bondage toys and stow his bag in a closet. Dustin might figure out what was going on, but he didn't need to see something she considered private.

Thirty long minutes later, she sat on her sofa, drinking the cold coffee Keith had brought, and haltingly answered Dustin's probing questions.

"When did you first notice the items were missing?"

She appreciated that he didn't smirk or smile at the item description. "This morning. I went to get dressed after showering. I opened the drawer, and that's when I realized they were missing. Everything was here when I left for work yesterday morning."

"How many?"

She shrugged. Who counted their bras and panties? "At least twenty pairs of underwear and six bras."

"What kind? Regular or lingerie?" He looked at his notepad, but she knew he was studying her every reaction.

"Do you really need to know that?" The prosecutor in her searched for a way that information could be used to prove guilt beyond a reasonable doubt.

He regarded her calmly. "Taking your underthings can indicate a desire for control. On the plus side, they weren't shredded or destroyed, so whoever did this hasn't reached a violent stage. Knowing what he or she has taken is helpful in profiling."

"A mixture. They even took a pair from the laundry hamper."

"Nobody was here yesterday when you arrived home?"

Katrina flicked her gaze to Keith, who stood as a sentinel behind the chair where she'd first discovered the joys of nipple clamps while straddling his lap. From there, he had a sweeping view of the common areas of her condo and the windows overlooking the parking lot. "Keith was waiting outside."

Dustin didn't miss a beat. "Does he have a key?"

She shook her head. "My parents have a key, but that's all."

"Do you keep one outside for emergencies?"

"No."

"Are your keys ever out of your sight?" He looked around as he asked the question, no doubt searching for where she kept her keys when she was home.

She helped him out by pointing to her key rack. "When I'm at work, they're either in my briefcase or locked in a drawer in my desk." She ran her hand over her eyes. "Yesterday I had the feeling someone had been in my car while it was parked downtown."

Keith perked up. "You didn't tell me that."

A little residual anger stirred. "You didn't really give me a chance. Plus you didn't actually believe me when I said someone had been in here Thursday night."

Dustin touched her wrist, bringing her back to the moment. She focused on his kind eyes. "What happened Thursday night? Was that the first incident?"

Thinking back, she realized it wasn't. "Last weekend, when I got home from my cousin's house, my front door was unlocked. I was sure I'd locked it, but Keith said I probably forgot, and I let it go."

She described the incident, relating only the relevant details. He didn't need to hear anything about her relationship with Keith. Then she told him about her car.

Keith wandered across the room to the kitchen. He sipped coffee and stood at her counter. He set down his cup at the mention of her car. The sharpness of ceramic against granite clanged through the air.

It wasn't like there had been time to tell him about the weirdness of somebody cleaning out her car. She hadn't thought about it after he'd told her to undress. Dodging the suggestion of anger in Keith's gesture, she adjusted an outside seam on her leggings. "I find it odd that someone would want to break into my condo just to move around a lamp or take my clothes or clean my backseat. It doesn't seem like a normal stalker thing to do."

"No," Dustin agreed. "But stalkers aren't normal. I'm going to need access to your cases. I'll file formal requests Monday morning, but if you have anything on you, I'd like to get a jump on it."

Katrina nodded. Keith hadn't planned to let her work this weekend anyway. "My briefcase is in the closet."

"One last thing before the team gets here to sweep your place." He leaned forward, keeping his tone low. "Have you asked anyone else to train you?"

Surprised at his question, she considered the implications. Since she'd only asked Keith and Dustin, she didn't see where that information was relevant. "What does that have to do with anything?"

He shrugged. "You ask someone, or if you're overheard by someone you didn't ask, you're automatically a target. It could explain the disappearance of your underwear, though most pervs prefer used clothing to freshly laundered."

"No, I haven't." She glanced over at Keith, but he was busy with his phone.

Dustin lifted a brow, and his gaze sidled to Keith and back. "It's just a coincidence that you've had Rossetti over that many times in one week?"

Heat crept up her neck, and she felt her cheeks flame. "Dustin, don't go there."

"You have about ten seconds to finish that line of questioning." Keith's quiet warning sounded loud in the tenseness of the room. "Malcolm just pulled into the parking lot."

Katrina started. "I told you to keep him out of this."

"Sweep team is here too." He pocketed his phone and regarded her with a firm look. "It's ludicrous to think he won't hear about this, and that he wouldn't be pissed if it came from someone other than me or you. Now answer Dustin's question so he can move forward."

As usual, he had a point, and he hadn't actually agreed to keep Malcolm in the dark. She turned back to Dustin. "Mostly coincidence, yeah. On Saturday he gave me a ride home from Layla's, and we watched a game. Thursday is my parents' bowling night, so they weren't home. I was afraid. I called Keith because he lives the closest now that Mal is all the way in Ann Arbor."

She trailed off, thinking of the way he'd dismissed her fears and accused her of fabricating an excuse to get him over here. Her doorbell chimed. She jumped, and her heart raced. It took her a moment to remember to breathe. An intruder wouldn't ring the doorbell or knock. He'd just let himself in. She hated feeling so vulnerable and helpless. With Keith, feeling that way had been empowering. This was vastly different.

Dustin gripped her chin, something a Dom would do, not an agent questioning her. "Yesterday? Trina, don't be vague. I need to know."

She swallowed her fears. With Dustin and Keith here, nothing would happen to her. "Keith agreed to train me. But Dustin, you need to keep that private. Mal can't know."

Keith jogged down the stairs and pretended that rage and fear weren't doing a tango in his stomach. He felt like an ass for ignoring her concerns. Of course Kat wouldn't make up an intruder just to lure him to her place. She'd come right out and asked him to train her. When he'd refused, she'd asked Dustin. That rankled, but it proved she wasn't being manipulative. He had to stop letting his distrust of all women tarnish his view of Kat.

Just because she wanted to change the terms of their association didn't mean he could categorize her with the rest of the conniving females in his life. Though she hadn't said it yet, she wanted more from him, and foreign parts of him were voting to let her have it. Other parts were firmly entrenched in horror at the idea of having an emotional attachment to a woman. If he didn't watch it, he would begin treating her with the same callous passive-aggressiveness with which he usually approached a woman. He'd already slipped up a couple times, and she hadn't let those incidents pass without comment.

The way her face had paled when the doorbell rang clutched at his dormant heart, evidence that organ wasn't cold and dead. He wanted to kill the bastard who was doing this to her.

He disengaged the dead bolt and opened the door to find Malcolm and Darcy standing on the other side. Her hasty ponytail and the fact they both wore sweats told him they'd jumped out of bed and rushed over when he'd called.

Mal's scruffy face couldn't camouflage the hard glint in his eyes or the firm set of his jaw. "Where's Trina? Is she okay?"

"Upstairs. Living room. Brandt's questioning her now. She's shaken, but she's holding up." It had been hell listening to her answer questions, watching her try to keep it together, and not being able to do anything. Now that Malcolm was here, that would change. "Did you bring the equipment?"

"It's in the car. We'll install as soon as the sweep team is done."

Keith didn't hold out much hope they'd find anything. He'd already searched the place. In the parking lot beyond the small front yard, an FBI van ignored the NO PARKING signs. Three agents emerged, more than the FBI would normally send. This was a sensitive case. Who knew what criminal had set his sights on her and for what reason?

"They're here. It won't be long," Keith said.

"Good." Darcy regarded them coolly. "The last thing she needs after being violated is to endure this. Malcolm, go up there and hug your sister. Hold her hand and let her know you're there for her. Believe me, it makes a difference."

Darcy viewed law enforcement the same way Keith regarded pretty much anyone who wanted more than a professional relationship. He didn't judge her for that. Malcolm ushered Darcy up the stairs, and Keith stepped outside to brief the forensics crew.

It had never occurred to Keith that he should hold Kat's hand or sit close to her for moral support. Darcy's directive had illustrated just how bad it would be for Kat if he tried to have more than a Master/slave relationship. Nowhere in his past had anyone taught him what it meant to be empathetic or caring. He could identify those behaviors. He knew what they looked like, but he didn't know when or how to apply them. Now that Darcy had said something, the signs stood out with neon clarity. Kat deserved a man who didn't have to be told she needed a hug.

Without letting his personal failings get in the way more than they had, he briefed the analytic team and set them to work.

# Chapter Six

Katrina shaded her eyes as she peered up the ladder. "Darcy and I are going to go pick up something for dinner."

Malcolm adjusted one of the night-vision, motion-activated cameras he and Keith had installed. This one covered the area leading up to her front walk and a portion of the parking lot.

"She's been craving Chinese." Malcolm finished something off with his power screwdriver. "I could go for something Mandarin, extra spicy."

For as long as she could remember, she'd regarded her brother with a sort of hero worship. Though he was only two years older, he'd always looked out for her. Growing up, they'd almost never fought about anything. She felt a little guilty for sleeping with his best friend behind his back, but she could rationalize it by telling herself she was keeping the secret to protect their friendship.

"You're not leaving."

Katrina whirled around to find Keith standing a few feet behind her. A spot of grease smeared the corner of his shirt, and his face sported a day-old beard. The coarse stubble only made him look that much more foreboding.

The entire day, he'd been close, but he hadn't said much, and he hadn't touched her once. This wasn't how she'd imagined this weekend unfolding.

A soft wind blew hair into her face. She swiped it away with one hand. "Why not?"

"It's not safe. Because I said so. Pick whichever works for you."

This wasn't the first time he'd leveled an order at her like this, but it was the first time she realized he'd topped her in small ways the entire time she'd known him. Now that she recognized what he was doing, she wasn't sure she liked it. In the bedroom, she could accept it. Outside of that context, it rubbed her the wrong way.

"Neither of them works for me. I refuse to let fear rule my life. I'm hungry, and so is Darcy. I'm sure you are as well. None of us has had much to eat today." After the agents had left, she and Darcy had cleaned the fingerprint chemicals from everything and straightened up the general mess. Keith and Malcolm had scoped out locations for cameras and set about installing them. "Besides, whoever did this isn't after me. They want something I have."

Those emerald eyes bored into her like lasers, cutting through any sense of security she'd gained from having a house full of agents invested in making sure she was safe. "He took your underwear. It's personal. He's after you."

That thought shook her far more than she cared to admit. All week, she'd been sweeping her concerns under the carpet. Now that pile of crap moaned and groaned. She stomped it back down. "Regardless, I refuse to live like a prisoner. I'll be in public. With Darcy. I can kick ass if I need to."

Behind them, Malcolm cleared his throat. "As much as I love watching you two go at it, I have to side with Trina. She can't let this son of a bitch control her life."

Keith glared at Malcolm over her shoulder. Katrina opted to stay out of their silent war. She went around Keith and entered her condo. She needed to grab her purse and see if Darcy was finished in the bathroom. Pregnant people spent a lot of time in that particular room. Or perhaps Darcy had used it to escape the presence of so many federal agents. While she loved Malcolm and seemed to have accepted Keith, she wasn't overly comfortable around them in groups.

Katrina dug an older clutch from her closet. Dustin had advised her to use something smaller so she could put it in her briefcase instead of locking it in her desk at work. While he hadn't indicated he thought anything was happening there—it was such a public and well-monitored place—he wanted her to take every precaution.

Downsizing meant evaluating the junk inside to separate what she really needed from those items she liked to have in case she needed them. The nail file made the cut, as did the tiny vial of hand cream, but the pocket mirror didn't.

She didn't look up when her door closed. Keith's presence announced itself without visual confirmation. Every nerve ending tingled pleasantly, responding to his proximity. She wanted him to pin her down and remind her what it was like when not being in control brought feelings of safety and comfort.

"Kat, wait a half hour. I know you're hungry. You had coffee for breakfast, and you barely ate anything for lunch. We're almost finished. Then we'll all go out and get something. Or have it delivered."

His quiet tone didn't plead. It laid out her alternatives in a calm, orderly manner. She liked that about him, but she wasn't going to pick either of his options.

Stuffing her things in her newer, smaller purse, she rose to her feet. "I need to get out of here. I need a change of scenery."

He caught her in his arms and held her close. It was the first time he'd shown a tender feeling all day. She rested her cheek on his chest and let her body relax against his hard length.

He stroked his hand over her hair and pressed a kiss to the top of her head. "I'm going to kill the bastard who did this."

She didn't doubt it.

"Wait a half hour."

In a half hour, they could have the food, she could have a break from being in her condo, and they could be back with dinner. Katrina didn't really want to eat in public. This trip was as much a test of her nerves as it was an excuse to get away. "We'll have dinner here by the time you guys finish."

It was all the compromise she was willing to make, not that it was really a concession.

"I wasn't asking, slave. If you go against my wishes and put yourself in needless danger, I will paddle your ass as punishment. I went light on you this morning. You won't sit for a week this time."

The gravity of his declaration scared her, especially since he seemed to have reversed his earlier stance on having an apology as the punishment. She wiggled, trying to break his tight hold. "Keith, let go."

"No."

Just like that, his dictates were nonnegotiable. She'd never seen this side of him. Well, she'd certainly asked for it.

That didn't mean she accepted it. "We're not in a scene, and you don't get to control where I go, when, or with whom."

He released her suddenly. She stumbled back a few steps and fell against the bed. More than a little shocked by this personality shift, she stared up with wide eyes. He met her gaze with pure steel.

"That's where you're wrong. You asked me to train you. You wanted to know what it was like to be a slave. This is it, Kitty Kat. I forbid you from leaving here without me."

She straightened up and composed herself. "But you won't stop me from walking out the door." It was a hunch. She didn't think he'd do something that would tip Malcolm off as to their changed relationship.

He shook his head. "I'll never stop you from walking out on me. That's your choice. It's the coming back that you have to worry about."

A weird feeling seized the pit of her stomach. It wasn't quite fear. More like anticipation. She went with the curious feeling. In her whole life, she'd never pushed for anything. Even when she'd asked Keith to train her, she hadn't forced the issue. Now that she was knee-deep in his world, she realized she had to be her own advocate. If she let him, Keith would railroad over her, just as he'd warned her.

"Do you have a preference for food? If not, I can just pick something out for you from wherever Darcy's cravings take us."

Keith pressed his lips together in a grim line. He parked his hands on his hips and waited, never altering his hard gaze or his firm expression.

She nodded. "So that's how it's going to be. Fine. You get what you get, and you don't throw a fit."

Surprise flickered deep within those emerald depths. Katrina didn't wait to see what else was going to happen. She turned on her heel and left.

Outside, Malcolm kissed Darcy good-bye and grabbed Katrina's arm before she and Darcy could walk away. "Trina, don't be mad at Keith. This isn't easy for him. It's not easy for either of us. We want to catch this bastard and fix the problem. We will do it, but it'll take time. If we didn't love you so much, the wait wouldn't be so bad."

She touched a palm to his scruffy cheek. "It's not easy for me either. I love you, big brother. I'm going with Darcy to get dinner, and Keith's going to have to get over it."

Mal's lips parted, but he didn't say anything for the longest second, almost as if he was trying to make an important decision. Then the moment passed, and the choice was made. He pulled her closer and lowered his volume. "In this whole world, there are only two women Keith loves. Mom and you. With Mom, he can put her up on a pedestal as the perfect mother, and she'll never disappoint him because she's pretty awesome. But he doesn't know what to do with you half the time. You don't quite fit the image of a sister for him. You're friends. I don't know if you noticed this, but he doesn't have any other female friends."

She hadn't noticed it. Keith seemed to have no problem gathering women. His fellow agents liked him, and the US attorneys he worked with—male and female—loved working cases with him. He was meticulous and thoughtful. Everything he touched turned out well. Justice was always served.

But Malcolm wasn't finished sharing his insights. "Women serve one function for him, and as soon as they serve it, he loses respect for them and moves on. I'm not saying that's right. He doesn't know how to trust, not really, and he doesn't know how to love or what to do with any fierce emotions he feels. He didn't have good role models growing up. His childhood was a nightmare. You're a different animal, though. He trusts you, and that confuses the hell out of him. He was coping until today. He just wants to keep you safe. I think if anything happened to you, he'd never forgive himself. That's where he's coming from."

"What about Layla?" As far as Katrina could tell, Keith didn't seem to have an issue with Layla.

Malcolm grinned. "She's just one of the guys. I'm not sure he's noticed that she's a woman yet."

Katrina didn't know what to say, but Mal's take explained why Keith treated her so differently now that they were sleeping together. She nodded. "I'll keep that in mind the next time we have an argument. Which might be when we get back."

Malcolm looked over her shoulder at Darcy. "I told you it wasn't personal, sweetheart. You have to give him time. He still can't always figure out what to do with Trina and Mom."

Darcy nodded thoughtfully, but she was grinning. "So you say. I'm the one who pushed you to forgive him. I think he already likes me."

He kissed her again, and then Katrina and Darcy headed out.

"Thai." Darcy buckled her seat belt. "I have a craving for something in peanut sauce. This kid better appreciate my sacrifices. That stuff gives me indigestion. Good thing I now carry antacid."

Katrina knew a good Thai place nearby. She turned in that direction. "Did you guys find out the gender? And are you even sharing that information? I won't be offended if you don't want to say anything."

Since she'd known Darcy only a few short months, they'd established a foundation for a friendship, but Katrina sometimes didn't know what kinds of topics or questions were okay and which weren't.

Darcy laughed. "I found out. Malcolm wants to be surprised. He said he wants to decorate everything in shades of green and yellow. Those are the colors of paint he bought for the nursery. So I'm keeping it to myself."

She put her hand over the small bump in her abdomen and beamed. Katrina was happy for her brother and sister-in-law-to-be, but she was also a little jealous. While she didn't want kids just yet—maybe not ever—she did want to have the kind of warmth and affection with Keith that these two had with each other.

"Okay, subject change." Katrina flashed a grin to show that her feelings weren't hurt. "Can I ask you a theoretical question about dominance and submission?"

If Darcy was surprised, she didn't show it. "Sure. Are you thinking of trying it?"

Katrina decided she could reveal her intentions as long as she didn't put a name to her Dom. Lawyer that she was, she kept her answer ambiguous. "I am."

"Okay. What do you want to know?"

"I had questions about punishment." Katrina realized she was chewing on her cuticle, a nervous habit she thought she'd kicked. Not only was she nervous about Darcy's response—and her reaction to the question—but she worried about why Keith would suddenly change his policy on punishments. "Spanking, in particular."

"Okay. I'll warn you that I'm a masochist. I don't consider the normal punishments as punishments."

*What does that mean?*

She didn't have to voice her question, because Darcy had forged ahead.

"A punishment is earned when a submissive violates an agreed-upon rule. That means it's unique to the individual. I'll be the first to admit there's a difference between a punishment spanking and an erotic one, but for me, I'll take either one any day. Malcolm has found either prohibiting or forcing orgasm to be a better bet." A dreamy smile softened Darcy's mouth and reflected in her eyes.

"What if no rules were agreed upon?" Keith had asked her to discuss limits and things like that, but she'd declined.

Darcy's smile vanished. "Never play with a Dom if you haven't agreed upon protocols and punishable behavior. If he's inexperienced, then you'll need to have that conversation a lot. When Scott and I first started out, we did a lot of trial and error. Open communication is the key. You have to be honest, even if it's something that might hurt his feelings or offend him."

Scott had been Darcy's Master for years. Investigating his murder had brought Darcy and Malcolm together.

Katrina blushed. Keith had tried to steer her in this direction. "What if I just said I wanted to learn his rules and his preferences, but I didn't tell him any of mine because I'm not sure what they are?"

This was maybe a little more revealing than she had intended, but Darcy seemed so willing to talk. She turned and studied Katrina, who tried not to squirm under the scrutiny. "Do you trust him?"

More than she'd ever trusted a lover. "With my life."

Darcy seemed to accept that. "Still talk about everything. After a scene, talk about what you liked and didn't like. Tell him what worked for you and offer suggestions. It's not topping from the bottom to ask for what you want. You just can't necessarily expect to get it on your terms or your timetable."

While she found a parking space, Katrina took some time to digest Darcy's advice. She shot her brother's fiancée a glance. "You won't tell Malcolm we talked about this, will you? He'll flip out."

"I don't think he'll flip out. I just don't think he wants to know the details of your sex life." Darcy laughed. "Besides, you didn't really tell me anything."

On the way back, Darcy put her hand on Katrina's arm. "Is your Dom upset because you were supposed to scene today and that fucking stalker ruined everything? Because that's not your fault."

Katrina shook her head. "It's something else. One of those if-you-do-this-I'll-paddle-your-ass things. And I went ahead and did it anyway. I don't know that I'm okay with him trying to control my behavior outside the bedroom."

"Then set that boundary." Darcy squeezed her arm. "I know you said you agreed to go by his rules, but maybe you need to have a conversation about how your limits will evolve as your relationship grows. Nothing is static. With Malcolm, we both started off with some hard limits that have become flexible, and we've put other limits in place where there didn't used to be a rule. It's a relationship, Trina. Things change. Communication and flexibility are key."

Beginning that dialogue wasn't going to be easy. Katrina had thought she could approach this like a fling, whether or not she intended for it to last longer, and that she could put up with little things she didn't like. Not having a plan for dealing with those things long-term was already proving to be a problem.

"One more thing." They'd arrived back at the condo. Darcy undid her seat belt and turned to regard Katrina regretfully. "You did misbehave. If he told you not to do something, whether or not you agree with him, you're the submissive. You willfully disobeyed, and you do have a punishment coming. Take it with grace and dignity. Don't hide your emotions, even if you're not comfortable showing them. He needs to see your tears, your guilt, your misery. Otherwise he won't know if the punishment has been effective."

Though she didn't agree with Keith, she did feel guilty for defying him and flouting it in his face. He had given that order out of concern for her safety, and he'd offered alternatives to her plan. In retrospect, she realized he'd been very flexible. She was the one who hadn't reacted responsibly or respectfully. For so long, she'd called the shots in all her relationships. Assuming a submissive role was going to be a tough transition. Now she understood a little better why Keith had originally refused to train her.

What if she wasn't cut out for this lifestyle? She'd lose her chance to be with Keith. Over the course of dinner, as the four of them sat at her small dining room table and chatted while they ate, Katrina renewed her internal commitment to exploring her submissive side. It was there. She'd found the majority of their scene the night before intensely enjoyable, and part of that came from the fact that Keith was calling the shots. It had made her feel more *herself.*

After dinner, Darcy yawned and stretched. "Trina, I'm sorry. I missed my nap, and it looks like I'm in for an early bedtime. If you don't feel comfortable staying here tonight, you're more than welcome to stay with us. I have a very nice guest room."

Malcolm seconded the invitation. Keith watched the exchange silently.

Katrina declined. "Thanks, but I'm not going to let this jerk scare me away from my life. I'll be fine."

Malcolm pursed his lips together, but one glance at Keith had him relaxing. Keith stood and took his plate to the sink. "I'll stay with Kat tonight. Fucker comes near her, and he won't know what hit him."

Keith walked Malcolm and Darcy to the door. Kat had stayed upstairs to tidy the kitchen. He liked that she never left the dishes for the next day. A dirty sink bothered him first thing in the morning. It went against his need for order. *Kat* went against his need for order. He was going to need to adjust his expectations, because she wasn't his usual submissive. He wasn't sure she had it in her to be as submissive as he required, and that could seriously derail his plan to keep distance between them.

Last night and this morning, he'd caught glimpses of submissiveness. He'd tapped into it, but he didn't know how to keep her there. He didn't know if it was possible, only that he needed his submissive to behave.

Mal stopped just outside the door. Darcy paused a few feet away, her gaze demurely averted to give them some privacy. He liked Darcy. He thought she was good for Mal. But that didn't mean he knew what role she could play in his life. In the past, Mal's girlfriends had been inconsequential to Keith. He'd known those relationships wouldn't last. Darcy, he knew, was permanent. She was The One. He was going to have to figure out how to integrate her into his tiny inner circle.

Malcolm stifled a yawn. "Thanks for staying with her. Call me tomorrow before you leave. Trina will blow her top if we're all hovering around, but we can't leave her alone for long. We have to catch this bastard, and soon."

Keith shook his head. "I'm not leaving her alone. I'll call to check in with you tomorrow, but I can guarantee she won't be alone for a second." Whether she liked it or not.

They hugged, a macho, manly display of affection that involved pounding each other on the back. Without waiting for permission, Darcy rose to her toes and kissed Keith's prickly cheek, and then the couple left. There went another woman who didn't find him intimidating.

Keith ascended the stairs slowly, not sure what he'd find at the top. Kat had already been upset with him before this whole mess. As the stress of the day wore on them both, she'd become increasingly obstinate.

Silence greeted him. A quick sweep of the place nearly stopped his heart. She knelt on the floor in the middle of the living room, naked, with her hands linked behind her neck in the pose he'd required the night before.

He approached, but she never lifted her gaze. Last night she hadn't been nearly this disciplined. Her eyes had darted anywhere she detected movement. That was a natural reaction. Good submissives had a tight rein on those impulses. They were controlled when they needed to be, and they ceded control when their Dominant required it.

Right now, he was both relieved and proud of her. He stopped at her side and ran his hand over her hair. He'd never grow tired of touching her silky dark tresses. Her eyelids fell to half-mast, and she swayed slightly, but she corrected her position without being told.

"Permission to speak, Master?"

He wanted to laugh at her military tone, but he schooled his features. Normally he would begin the conversation. Not answering immediately allowed his unspoken point to penetrate. While she could ask questions, she needed to learn to wait until he gave her permission to speak. She held her position, not fidgeting, though he knew she was growing anxious.

After almost a full minute, he relented. "Slave, I know you have something to say. Given everything that's happened today and the expression on your face, I'd have to be an idiot to miss that. In the future, you must wait for me to verbally acknowledge you first. Only then can you ask to speak."

Her eyes flicked up quickly before she remembered to keep her gaze on the floor. She opened her mouth to apologize but closed it without speaking. He read the contrition in every line of her body, and the shell around his heart cracked a little more.

He gave her time to put this information together, and then he grazed his fingertips along her cheek, urging her to look up at him. "What's on your mind, Kitty Kat?"

A brilliant smile curved her lips and lit her eyes. The smile vanished, a concession to the serious nature of what she had to say, but the light in her eyes didn't dim. "I'm sorry, Master. I'll try to do better next time."

He nodded, a gesture of his benevolence and a signal of his forgiveness for her slight transgression.

"Earlier today, I disobeyed you. More than that, I thought only about myself, and I failed to take into account your concerns for my safety. I didn't like the dictatorial way you told me I couldn't leave the condo. I should have told you that, but instead I got mad and openly defied you. Even after you explained yourself and offered alternatives, I refused to listen. I'm sorry for all of that, not just because you're my Master, but because you're my friend. I dismissed your concerns and I disrespected you. I accept my punishment."

In all the years he'd known Kat, she never failed to impress him.

"I accept your apology." He spoke softly, but he had no intention of forgoing her punishment. In the past, he'd made his submissives apologize because he didn't care enough to take the time and energy to physically punish them, and he liked to practice humiliation. He didn't need a psychiatrist to know why it appealed to him.

For the first time in his life, he felt the need to physically punish his slave, and it had nothing to do with humiliation. This had become about Kat and earning her respect, not about him. The desire to do right by her burned deep, a foreign feeling that unsettled him more than a little. She made him believe he could expect more from a woman than a warm body and a place to park his dick. He would never find lasting happiness with anyone, but she offered the only respite he knew he'd ever find.

She inhaled, a sign of relief, and her shoulders relaxed. "Thank you, Master."

He sank down in the center of the sofa. "Lie down across my lap."

She crawled the short distance to him and draped herself elegantly over his lap. Voluntarily getting into position was a wonderful act of submission, and it really turned him on. Kat had a great ass, and he was definitely an ass man. While she would find little about this experience to like, he hoped to introduce her to an erotic spanking soon.

Submission aside, he needed to deal with the mechanics of the situation. "Scoot up a little bit, Kitty Kat. Arms above you." Reaching up forced a slight curve to her lower back, which fully exposed her vulva. "Turn your face to the back of the couch. Good. Now spread your legs a little wider."

She responded to his instructions beautifully. Now that she was in the perfect position, he spent some time caressing her ass. Not only did he enjoy spending the time touching her, but it increased anticipation.

The scent of her arousal reached his nose. "Are you turned on, Kitty Kat?"

She cleared her throat twice. "Yes, Master."

"Tell me what turns you on about this situation." He kept his tone gentle. It was an honest query, not an attempt to find something about which to deliver a reprimand.

"I like... I like when you touch me. I like being completely in your hands, knowing that nothing that happens tonight is up to me." Her voice came out soft, with a hint of breathlessness.

In that, she was wrong. Everything that happened was up to her. She could stop it with a single word. "Remind us of your colors."

"Red, yellow, green."

"Excellent. I'm not going to lie to you. This is going to hurt." With that, he cupped his hand and delivered a firm swat to her left cheek.

She sucked in a breath and held it.

"Breathe, Kitty Kat. You're going to count for me. That was one." Forcing her to count would force her to breathe. He hadn't made her count before because he hadn't hit her very hard. The spanking he'd delivered that morning had been a punishment, yes, but it had mostly been for his pleasure, not because she'd climaxed in the shower without permission.

"One." She barely croaked the word, but the air in her lungs whooshed out. "That really hurt, Master."

He chuckled at the wryness of her tone. "The proper response is 'One. Thank you, Master.'" He smoothed his palm over the red handprint blooming on her ass.

She inhaled again. "One. Thank you, Master."

In a perfect world, he would tell her how many she could expect. But this wasn't a perfect world, and he didn't know what she could take. Three might break her. Fifteen might elicit nothing more than a grunt or two.

He smacked again, this time aiming for her right cheek. She flinched, but the movement was concentrated mostly in her shoulders.

"Two. Thank you, Master." The tone of her voice had changed, softened a bit. She'd resigned herself to this punishment.

He delivered two more in quick succession, centering them on the same places he'd hit before. She counted them out, her voice steady and accepting. Three more introduced the first tenuous note to her tone. He watched her face and the lines of her body to see how much more she could take. It wouldn't be long now.

"Three more, Kitty Kat."

The sound of his palm meeting her flesh echoed from the room's high ceilings. A sob escaped on the ninth one. He centered the tenth over her glistening pussy, and she cried out, a high-pitched protest.

Carefully he turned her around to cradle her in his lap. He grabbed a soft throw she kept on the back of the sofa and draped it over her body. Tears wet her eyes, but none had fallen. He pushed her head down to rest on his shoulder.

"Never worry me like that again."

Keith held her in the solid cocoon of his arms. Every now and again, he turned her face up and kissed her temples and cheeks. Though she'd honestly thought he would enjoy punishing her, she didn't get the sense that he had. He'd punished her because he needed to, not because he wanted to, exactly the opposite of what had happened in the bathroom that morning.

She drew her finger up his sternum and along his collarbone, exploring solid evidence of his innate strength. "Keith?"

"Hmmm?"

"We need to talk."

He was silent for a long while, and then he heaved a sigh. "I know."

"I think I have more of an idea about what I want out of this." She didn't mean to sound so solemn, but that was how it came out, in a breakup tone. Beneath her, she felt his whole body tense.

"Fewer spankings?" He grinned, a valiant attempt to lighten the somber atmosphere that had descended over the room.

Planting both hands against his chest, she pushed away until she sat up on his lap. After a second, she rethought that move. Her ass burned pleasantly when nothing touched it. He'd held her so that her thigh and hip bore most of her weight. Now that she was sitting on it, she realized exactly how thoroughly he'd spanked her. She probably wouldn't be sitting comfortably for a few hours.

Aside from the physical aftereffects, a well of peace had formed inside. She basked in the discovery of something so significant. How had she not known this capacity was hidden away? "Not necessarily, no."

He shifted, and she cringed at his trepidation. Maybe he knew they needed to talk, but he wasn't overly comfortable doing it. He'd released her when she sat up. Now he splayed one hand over her lower back. She felt his heat through the blanket still covering her body. It gaped open in the front.

To Keith's credit, he kept his gaze on her face, not once letting it stray to catch glimpses of her breasts. "Are you upset because I changed the rules?"

She shook her head. Honestly, kneeling and apologizing seemed like an okay punishment for minor infractions, but they turned a larger issue into a joke. "I know I wasn't supposed to enjoy the spanking, but I didn't not enjoy it. If that makes sense."

The skin of her ass radiated heat, but the abused muscle there seemed to communicate to her clit that something wonderful was about to happen. She was slippery with her own juices.

He slid a hand under the blanket and rested it on her bare thigh. Some of the tension drained from his shoulders. "It makes sense. You'll probably enjoy an erotic spanking very much."

Silently, she agreed. But that wasn't what she wanted to talk about. "Keith, did you deliberately do things to me you knew I wouldn't like because you don't want to do this? I don't want you to train me if that's not what you want." It was slightly better than outright telling him that she wanted him to want her. Desperation wasn't a fragrance she liked.

He exhaled a ragged breath and leaned his head back against the top of the couch. "No. Truthfully, I've been nicer to you than I have been to any of my subs. I've never held one before, not for comfort or closeness. As restraint, yes." His leg moved under her knee, wiggling from side to side in a physical display of his discomfort with the topic. "I'm not a cuddler. Sometimes I handcuff them to the bed so I don't have to worry that they'll try to touch me while I sleep. Mostly I don't let them sleep in the same room with me."

A hint of ruddiness colored his cheeks, and she knew he'd never revealed that piece of information to anyone before. The night before, he'd curled his body around hers. Right now, he wasn't holding her close, but he still touched her in an intimate way that provided a sense of comfort and closeness.

"Why?" Normally she didn't want to hear about a man's exes. With Keith, it was different. When he ended a relationship, those women never popped back up in his life again.

"Kat." Her name was his plea for leniency. He didn't want to delve into a painful subject. "Why don't you just tell me what you've realized about the things you want or don't want from me? So far, I have a list of your hard limits that includes no clothespins on your breasts and no ejaculating on your face."

Mention of the second limit made her flinch, but she couldn't let him derail the conversation. He might be the Dom in the relationship, but that didn't mean he got to control the discussion. She had too much experience keeping people on track to fall prey to his authoritative suggestion.

"Keith, it's important for me to know why you're treating me differently. I have to know you're not doing this to humor me." She felt the pull of his body like a magnet, urging her to sink back against him and let him do or say whatever he wanted. The impulse wasn't easy to resist, but she did it.

As he had the night before, he took her hand and placed it over the bulge in his cargo shorts. "I told you that I'm not doing this to humor you. I'm doing this mostly for selfish reasons. I know this is only training. It's temporary. But I've wanted you on your knees for a long, long time."

The vehement, almost bitter confession startled her. While she didn't lift her hand from his hard cock, she nearly toppled from the surprise. She braced her hand against the back of the sofa to provide the needed support. "You're an opportunist."

She meant it to lighten his mood, which had gone decidedly dark. But he used the opening to take things to an even darker place. "Yes. I am. I use women, Kat. I've never had feelings for a single one of my subs. I pretended to care, but I truly didn't give a shit about any of them. Some saw through my act and left, but most tried to change me. Those women, I dumped, and I wasn't nice about it either. I can't change. I'm warning you now. I've been this way for too long."

He'd lost her. She drew her eyebrows together as she tried to fit his skewed perception of himself with how she saw him. Finally, she shook her head. It didn't work to jumble the pieces into clarity. "What way?"

In one easy, fluid motion, he lifted her from his lap and set her on the sofa as far away as he could get her. She leaned against the back and the arm, facing him, and pulled her blanket closed around her to replace the security she'd lost along with his embrace. The sensations in her ass were muted now that her attention was firmly elsewhere.

He leaned forward, resting his elbows on his knees and his chin on his clenched fists. "I held you last night because that's what you should expect from your Master after a scene. You should expect to be pampered and cherished. You should expect affection and praise. It was the first time I've ever attempted something like that. I had to talk myself into it, and I had to force myself to follow through. You deserve that much consideration, Kat. You have the right to expect those things."

His confession hit her like a slap in the face. She flinched, but he wasn't looking at her, and he plowed forward.

"I've never spanked a sub for disobeying me. If they piss me off, I just get rid of them. They weren't worth it to me. I didn't care enough to punish them. But you..." He clenched his fists and laughed ruefully. "You're different. I've never topped anyone who knew me as anything but a Dom. This is new territory for me. You may not have liked some of the things I did or the way I've treated you, but let me tell you, it's a damn sight better than the way I've treated women since I figured out what use they were to me."

Malcolm had told her repeatedly over the years that Keith had a very utilitarian view of women. The full weight of that truth was just beginning to dawn on Katrina. She put a hand on his shoulder, an attempt to comfort him, but he slipped out of her grasp, standing to escape her touch. That stung a lot more than a slap on her ass.

He paced away to stand across the room. Looking out the window with a clear line to the parking lot, he clasped his hands behind his back. "I'm trying to do right by you."

She didn't want him to do right by her. She wanted him to want to be with her, which he did, but not in the ways she expected. Visions of the ways in which he'd pampered his girlfriends floated through her memory. Her mind played memories of him bringing various women a plate of food at a cookout, or a glass of water, or a jacket when it grew cold. For the first time, she saw the interactions through a new lens.

First, he hadn't let them talk very much. Katrina had thought perhaps he liked shy women, which knocked her out of the running, because she wasn't timid. Now she understood it wasn't shyness. They'd been prohibited from speaking unless spoken to.

Second, he had controlled everything about their experience, choosing what they ate and drank, where they sat, and with whom they talked.

Third, he had never actually had a conversation with one of his girlfriends in her presence. He'd talked to other people, including her, about a variety of topics, but never his dates. In most instances, her attempts to draw them in had been met with short answers, murmured after they'd looked to him for approval. Most of them had appeared once and never again. Katrina had always assumed a mismatch, but now she accepted that he'd been treating those women as arm candy.

All at once she comprehended his struggle. He was trying to show her what she should expect from a Dom who loved her. He didn't want her to settle for someone who treated her the way he treated his submissives.

If she was going to have a chance at a future with Keith, she had to help him. The best strategy for changing a habit was to remove triggers that propagated it. The courage that had prompted her to proposition him in the first place returned. "I don't want to call you 'Master.' I don't want you to call me 'slave.' I don't want to use titles at all."

He turned his head, staring at her over his shoulder with a deep frown on his face. "That's not how it's done. I've never known anyone who didn't use titles."

She drew her legs closer and tucked her feet under the blanket. The air was warm enough, but his demeanor lent a chill to the room. "That doesn't mean we can't do it. I prefer to use your name, and I like when you call me Kitty Kat."

"Titles show respect." His eyes glittered hard as granite.

Katrina shook her head. "Actions and tone of voice show respect. You've used titles for years, and you have no respect for a single woman you've been with."

He barked out a short, bitter laugh. "You sound like your brother."

The comparison didn't rankle. Katrina admired both of her brothers. She recognized Keith's defense mechanism, and she realized he was very close to kicking her to the curb. She put "fear of intimacy" at the top of his list of phobias.

The ruthless prosecutor in her came out, which wasn't always a good thing. "What do you want out of life, Keith? What do you see when you look into your future? Marriage? A loving wife? Children? What?"

"Exactly like your brother." A dull thud sounded as he leaned his forehead against the window with a little too much force. "No, Kat. I don't see any of those things. I have no intention of ever getting married, and I sure as hell don't want kids. I have no desire to deal with that kind of crap. Ever."

Again, his words hit her like a slap in the face. Though she'd said she didn't want to change him, in the back of her mind, she'd assumed he wanted the same things she did. Well, she wasn't sure about the having-kids part. Truthfully, she'd never felt the need to parent anyone. She liked being an aunt. Knowing she was going to give them back made it enjoyable to spend time with her nephews. Right now she didn't want that chaos.

But she did want to fall in love and get married. She did want a life partner. Best to rip off the scab quickly. "Why?"

"You wouldn't understand."

She was close to turning him over her knee. "Try me."

Rocking back, he straightened up and turned to face her. "You grew up with a nice family. You always had something to eat when you got hungry, and you didn't get the shit beat out of you on a daily basis."

Katrina's heart squeezed painfully. She knew the outline, the barest details about his upbringing, so what he said wasn't news to her, but it was vague. Malcolm kept Keith's confidences to himself, as a good friend should.

Now wasn't the time to push him on that issue. She stood and let the blanket fall to the floor. "Just because you grew up in a house like that doesn't mean you have to live in one. It doesn't mean you have to be alone your whole life."

Taking a chance, she crossed the room and stopped in front of him. He yanked the cord to the drapes and let them slide into place. It was probably best not to flash the neighbors or give her stalker ideas. She shivered in fear. Being with Keith made her feel safe, so considerations like that slipped from her consciousness.

Keith folded his arms over his chest. "Don't get ideas, Kat. I'm only good for one thing. Keep that in mind, and I won't break your heart."

Too late for that. For far too many years, she'd nursed romantic intentions toward him. Those dreams didn't go away easily, especially not when she had him within reach. Nonetheless, she rushed to assure him of the thing he needed to hear. The subtext of his concern brained her over the head, loud and clear. "I don't have an endgame in mind."

It wasn't a lie, because she didn't want this to ever end.

"I do." He grabbed her hips and pulled her closer. "I'll train you. You'll figure out what you want from a D/s relationship, and then you'll find someone who can give you what you need and treat you the way you deserve to be treated."

Then he devoured her lips, plunging his tongue between them to take possession of her mouth. The passion he unleashed was completely at odds with the coolness of his stated intention. She lifted her knee and wrapped one leg around him in an attempt to get even closer. She wanted him inside her, their skin slapping together as he held her down and found solace in her body.

But he tore himself away, reining in his baser instinct to regard her with icy eyes. "Get dressed. Pack an overnight bag. You're staying at my place tonight."

Keith fumed at himself as he shifted into third and passed someone about to turn right into one of the many businesses lining the highway. He'd never meant to reveal so much about himself. He knew Kat too well to think he hadn't whetted her appetite for making him her next project. She possessed a generous nature and a warm heart. If anyone she cared about was in need, she was the first one there to help them out.

He didn't want to be one of her fucking charity cases. He'd long ago come to terms with the way his life had to be.

"Limits." He growled the word at her.

She whipped her head around and regarded him curiously, but she didn't say anything.

"You said you had a better idea about what you want from this training. I can't give it to you if you don't tell me what that is."

In the glare of lights from the multitude of parking lots, he saw her scrunch her nose as if she smelled something bad. "I guess when I said I wanted you to train me, I was asking you, Keith, not you, the Dom. I really didn't think there would be a difference."

But there was. He put on a good face for her. With her, he could relax and be the person he wished he was. Dominating women tapped directly into his dark side. It was an outlet for the ugliness and bitter hate he harbored. She couldn't have known that when she asked him to train her.

He gritted his teeth. "Now you know there's a difference."

She seemed unaffected by his grouchiness. He could hear the sound of gears churning in her brain, and he knew she was searching for a diplomatic way to make her point.

"Don't take this the wrong way, but I don't like when you act like an asshole." She paused, gauging his reaction.

He didn't react. He couldn't. She didn't usually describe him using terms like that. When she'd called him out on his behavior that morning, it was the first time she'd hurled names. Of course, beginning last night was the first time she'd seen what a bastard he could be.

"I want to be treated as a person, a woman worthy of respect. You can tie me up and fuck me however you want, but you need to remember that I'm a person with thoughts and feelings. Sometimes I get the sense that you aren't in your body when you're with me. The look on your face just before you came on mine was cold and remote, almost hateful. You had the same thing going on last night when you wouldn't take some of the clothespins off."

They'd already discussed this issue. He didn't see a reason to make the connection between his behavior and his description of the kind of Dom he was. She was a bright woman. Eventually she'd figure out he hadn't lied.

"I only want you to be a Dom during a scene."

He snorted. "You're sure you want to be trained as a submissive? Because right now you're about the farthest thing from submissive."

"Asking for things doesn't make me not submissive. Being silent about what I want makes me a doormat. I refuse to let you wipe your feet on me." She sounded confident, even a little derisive, but the way she twisted her finger in the fabric of her shirt told a different story.

Keith had never once allowed a submissive to ask for anything. When he'd originally asked her what she wanted and she threw the ball back to him, he'd mentally categorized her with other submissives he'd kept. That had been a mistake, and he was only now realizing the magnitude of it.

Kat represented so many firsts in his life. He'd known from the start that she wasn't a 24/7 kind of submissive. Dominating her was proving to be more problematic than he'd thought. Never once had he considered that she'd lay down the law. He thought she'd put up with him until she reached a breaking point, and then she'd never speak to him again. He'd live on memories and fantasies.

"No feet wiping. Noted."

He hit the button on the garage door opener and pulled his SUV inside. Normally he'd make her undress before he let her in the house, but he had a feeling Kat would rebel. He reached into the backseat for her bag, but she stopped him with a hand on his arm.

"Keith, I meant what I said about the title thing. I can submit to you just as well using your name instead of a title I'm just not comfortable using. Maybe one day I'll feel differently. Right now I feel like it puts an artificial barrier between us."

Bullshit, she wasn't comfortable calling him "Master." She'd cried out his title and whispered it on a reverent breath. This was something else. He focused on her comment about the barriers. Using titles had always been a way to keep women at arm's length. Kat had started out already close to him. No, it wasn't the title that made her uncomfortable; it was the distance.

Moving slowly, he retrieved her bag and set it on his lap. Old dog, new tricks. He could handle this learning curve. "No titles. For now."

She leaped on him, simultaneously pulling the bag from between them and tossing it into the seat she'd vacated. In the space of two seconds, she straddled him. He had a momentary glimpse of her smile before she peppered his face with kisses.

Nobody had ever done something like this to him. Keith stiffened under the force of her onslaught. He sought to control her with his hands on her hips, but she only rolled her pelvis forward in a sultry move that made his cock stand up and take notice.

A light feeling suffused his limbs. The strange sensation traveled up his body. "Happy you got your way, Kitty Kat?"

She stopped, her hands resting on his shoulders and her forearms draped against his chest, and regarded him thoughtfully. "I'm happy you're open to negotiation. I looked up all these protocols, you know, and I talked to Darcy. Negotiation and communication are vitally important to the success of a D/s relationship."

That light feeling took flight, replaced with a leaden sense of dread. A successful relationship didn't end. This thing between them would eventually end, and Kat was going to get hurt. "You talked about this with Darcy? She's going to tell Malcolm. A good submissive never keeps secrets from her Master."

Kat shrugged. He couldn't tell if she'd changed her mind about not wanting Malcolm to know, or if she didn't think Darcy would say anything. "It was a theoretical discussion. Neither your name nor penis size was mentioned."

Speaking of his penis, he shifted her back a little to ease the pressure there. "As long as you're truthful, I don't mind you bragging about my size."

She giggled. "I can't imagine how to do that without sounding like a bad porno film. And then we'd have to show it off. There would probably be a tape measure involved."

Keith shook his head, but he was glad to see her in such a good mood. He'd been afraid that she might fixate on the idea of her stalker and remain tense the entire night. "Never going to happen."

He slid one hand from her hip to her breast and gave it a playful squeeze. She closed her eyes, and her breaths came a little faster. Damn, but she did love breast play. Perhaps he would introduce her to his set of suction cups.

In the midst of his musings, she'd gone silent and still. When he lifted his gaze, he found her studying him again. She'd better not choose to use this moment to make him a project. He'd rip her clothes off, tie her to his spanking table, and stuff every hole in her body until she forgot about anything but the pleasure rioting through her system.

"Let's go inside." He tapped her hip, an indication she needed to move.

"Wait. One more thing."

*Christ. Here it comes.* He steeled his nerves. "Spit it out."

"I prefer to swallow." She grinned briefly. "Seriously, though. This isn't all about me, or it shouldn't be. You have fantasies too. I'm willing to role-play. Actually, I'm kind of excited about it."

For all he'd fantasized, tantalized, or threatened, Keith had never once actually role-played with anyone. They'd all been down-and-dirty scenes. Plans for how to make it work played out in his head, not much differently from how he choreographed a raid.

"Okay. I'm not set up for what I'd like right now. How about I figure it out and give you the details later?"

She nodded. The self-satisfied smile on her face made his heart beat a little faster. She really wanted to do this.

# Chapter Seven

*"Tonight is all about pleasure."*

That was what he'd said just before he'd excused himself to the basement. Katrina checked the digital clock on his chest of drawers. Twenty-two minutes had elapsed, and now she heard the sound of his footsteps echoing up the wooden basement steps and vibrating against the closed door.

She felt safe here, in his house. Anxiety drained from her shoulders. Every second alone in his bedroom was a step toward a different kind of tension. Keith's decision to bring her here was a good one. She hadn't realized how on edge she was. She wouldn't have been able to enjoy his company or the upcoming scene if they'd stayed at her condo.

The basement door rattled and opened. Then he started on the second set of stairs, this one carpeted, muffling the sound of his approach. She knew he could move stealthily when the situation warranted. That meant he wanted to be heard coming up from his dungeon.

He appeared in his bedroom door, a playful smile highlighting the sin in his eyes. Having just unpacked her toiletries bag, she stood in the opening leading from the bathroom, her hands clasped together in a false display of calm.

He grabbed her by the waist, lifted her in the air, twirled around, and pinned her against the wall.

Her crotch rested on his thigh, the only thing holding her off the floor, and he imprisoned her wrists by pressing them to the wall. Focusing on his eyes made it easier to regain her bearings. Her chest heaved with excitement as she tried to slow her breathing. His wicked grin let her know he liked knocking her off balance.

"Tonight I'm going to use strict restraint and a TENS unit on you. I'll let you choose the flogger."

The pressure of his thigh against her pussy made it throb in anticipation. Cream soaked through her thin leggings, a consequence of not wearing panties. She now understood the concept of strict restraint—she'd be bound so that she wouldn't be able to move a muscle—but she had no idea what a TENS unit was. And she didn't know enough about floggers to select anything.

She tore her attention from his lips. They hovered so close she could almost feel them. They were bait, a promise, incentive. "What's a TENS unit?"

He kissed her, devouring her lips with tender possession. He ground his pelvis forward, dry fucking with small movements that made her lust for him even more. Heat bloomed, and she wanted their clothes out of the way. Just before she crossed the line from arousal to madness, he stopped.

"You'll find out."

The topic of conversation had fled her mind. *Find out what? Oh, the TENS unit.* "Will it hurt?"

"It could, but I won't go that far. You should find it stimulating. Frustrating. Relaxing."

Those descriptors didn't seem to go together. "Frustrating and relaxing are diametrically opposed ideas."

He grinned, a sloppy, lopsided look that highlighted his evil charm. "Frustrating you relaxes me. Eventually. The journey is positively orgasmic."

And she'd be tied down, unable to move while he teased her body. "Are you going to gag me?"

"With my dick. Maybe. If you earn it."

Her knees grew weak, and she felt every fiber of her being yield to him. She knew he'd make her cry again, but this time, she was looking forward to it. She didn't know why, exactly, but she wanted to turn her every thought, her reason for being, over to him. "I don't know how to choose a flogger. I don't want one that hurts too bad, but that last one almost put me to sleep. I liked the floaty feeling."

"Floaty with a little bit of bite coming up." With that, he sank his teeth into her shoulder.

The heat of his mouth and the unforgiving pressure of his bite sent her fragile control into a tailspin. Her nerve endings short-circuited, and her legs liquefied. If he weren't holding her up, she'd slide down the wall. She moaned, a low primal noise she'd never heard before.

He nipped a path up her throat, using his tongue to soothe away the hot sting. Then he devoured her mouth once more with his kiss.

The hands holding her arms dropped. She felt liquid, malleable and free. Unable to control the trajectory, she let her arms dangle at her sides. This lack of control only seemed to fuel the voraciousness of his exploration. Small bites stung her lower lip, and he sucked it into his mouth, easing the pressure and letting her know that she was completely at his mercy.

And she was. No thoughts of resistance or worry about logistics or the real world crossed her mind. She didn't remind herself to call him by his title instead of his name, or think about the fact that he'd agreed to forgo that protocol. At her core, she accepted his dominance and reveled in her submission.

He enveloped her breast with his hot hand and kneaded the small mound. She marveled at how in tune with her body he was. Most men she'd been with hadn't taken the time to discover how sensitive her breasts were. Keith had realized right off how much she enjoyed his touch there, and he used that pleasure to control her even more.

In a sudden spurt of controlled violence, he ripped her shirt away, pulling it over her head and tossing it to the floor. That, too, was uncharacteristic behavior. According to Keith, clothing didn't belong on the floor. Ever.

Taking a chance, she did the same with his shirt. He stared at her for a long moment, his well-defined chest heaving, and a spark of tenderness glinted wildly from his eyes. She ran her fingertips over his solid abs and upward. His heart thundered a furious rhythm beneath his thick chest muscles. She paused there, fascinated by her effect on him.

Pinning her hips to the wall, he fell to his knees and pressed his lips to her stomach. Small stings punctuated the path of his affection as he made his way along the waist of her leggings. Inch by agonizing inch, he eased the thin fabric down.

She alternately rested her hands on his shoulders and ran her fingers through his short hair. Looking down, she watched his progress and admired the view. The taut muscles in his broad shoulders shifted and bulged as he fed her passion. For the first time, she noticed the smattering of freckles sprinkled across his skin. They were light and only appeared closer to his neck. Though she felt like she was moving through gelatin, she traced her finger from one small dot to the next.

He lifted her feet, one at a time, and removed her leggings. Now she stood before him, naked. He was the one on his knees. She accepted his sovereign right, and she felt power surge through her body. This gorgeous man desired her.

Wordlessly, he lifted one of her legs and brought it to rest on his strong shoulder. He eyed her pussy hungrily and licked his lips. She trembled with anticipation.

Last night he'd been rough, but she'd been primed so well that she'd climaxed quickly. Tonight he teased her with long, slow laps of his tongue. He paused frequently to draw his fingers through her wetness.

She arched her hips, trying to establish a rhythm or to encourage him to penetrate her vagina. Even one finger would bring welcome relief.

"You have the most beautiful pussy I've ever seen, Kitty Kat. Tomorrow we're going to make it even better." He pressed a kiss to her clit, rocked back on his heels, and stood in one smooth motion.

Leaning forward, he fucked his tongue between her lips, and she tasted the musky flavor of her juices. She didn't know what he meant by making it better, and she really didn't care. Right now, she wanted him to grab a condom and make good on the promises he insinuated.

"And you taste like heaven. I could lick you for hours. Tie you down and not let you move until I've satisfied this craving." He spoke against her lips, breathing the words as smooth taunts, more promises. "Soon. You won't be able to escape."

Escape was the last thing on her mind.

"I'm going to take you to the dungeon now. Say your safewords."

After two false starts, she cleared her throat of the passion clogging her airways. "Red, yellow, green."

He backed away, giving her some space. "When do you use them?"

"When I need you to stop, adjust something, or let you know everything is all right." She noticed there were no words to signal wanting more. Acutely aware of her nudity and her need, she lifted her gaze. "Keith, what about if I want more of something?"

His chuckle held a hint of devilry. "You can beg. I like hearing you beg. But that doesn't mean you'll get what you want. You're not in a position to demand anything. You're mine. Pleasure or pain, you take what I give, and you thank me for it."

The inherent unfairness of this struck her wrong just then. At the same time, it thrilled her to no end. She was in his hands. *His.* Just like she'd always wanted.

He inclined his head toward the door. "Let's go to the dungeon. When we get inside, I'm going to show you where to kneel. Whenever we enter the dungeon, whether or not we intend to do a scene, you'll follow the same protocol. Kneeling tells us both you cede complete control to me, that you trust your body to me. It also tells me that you accept my rule in the dungeon."

She nodded, knowing words weren't necessary. She had yet to find a room that wasn't his dominion, even at her place.

The door to the dungeon was the same as the interior doors in the rest of his house. Katrina had thought it would be heavier and soundproof. Only the lock on the handle marked it as different. The other doors didn't have them.

"This only locks from the outside." He inserted the key and rotated it clockwise. "I'll never leave you alone inside this room, but the inside knob will open whether or not the outside is secured, so you won't have to worry about getting stuck."

He pushed the door open and stepped forward. She followed him to the center of the room and knelt in the place he indicated. She was dying to look around, but she fastened her gaze to a point just in front of her knees, the way he'd taught her. Luckily she didn't have to wait for long.

"Rise, Kat. You may look around."

She sprang to her feet and scanned the room. Most the equipment looked familiar or was easy to figure out. She recognized sawhorses, a Saint Andrew's cross, a spanking bench, a Y-table, and a table that looked a lot like the one in her gynecologist's office, maybe a little more comfortable. A closer look revealed that most of the equipment had been bolted into the cement floor. Above them, the ceiling had been left unfinished, and the high trusses had been reinforced with two-by-tens. Holes had been drilled into the additional support beams at regular intervals. In several places, chains had been attached, and they dangled from the ceiling.

"What do you think?"

She glanced at Keith, noting that his arms were folded across his chest. He was nervous about her reaction? She struggled for words that were honest and would set him at ease. "Parts of it are what I expected, but I'm wondering about a few things."

He nodded, a curt movement, and his shoulders remained tense. "Ask."

She looked up at the nearest chain. "What are the chains for?"

"Suspension, mostly. There will be times when I want to tie you up and suspend you from the ceiling."

Heat pooled between her thighs at the thought. She knew he would make sure they both enjoyed the experience. She turned to him and lifted a brow. "I have no plans Tuesday and Thursday nights."

The look in his eyes guaranteed that she now had plans.

She gestured to the far corner. "What's the exam table for?"

"Playing doctor." He kissed the top of her head. "My way."

The thick leather straps attached to the table promised that she'd find her body secured to the table and her legs tied to the stirrups. "You do realize that no women have fantasies about the gynecologist's office?"

His shrugged as if saying he knew something she didn't. "Go lie facedown on the Y-table."

It wasn't difficult to figure out that the split part was for her legs. Katrina went to that end.

"No, the other end."

She studied the table, trying to figure out why he gave that order, then remembered she wasn't in a position to be analytical. When Keith gave an order, it was her job to comply. Immediately and without question. She lowered her body to the narrow, padded strip and prayed he wouldn't torment her for much longer. The bench part was wide enough to hold her securely, but narrow enough to provide access to her breasts. Her feet dangled off the end she'd originally thought was for her head.

He opened the nearest cupboard and grabbed a few things. She couldn't quite make out what he held. One looked like a blood glucose monitor. He set them on her back, and she gave up trying to figure it out. He went back to the cupboard, but this time she recognized the rope in his hands.

"Stretch your arms above your head."

The table wasn't wide enough to support her shoulders or arms, so she'd let them hang from the sides. Stretching her arms above her head was ungainly for the same reason. She clasped her hands together to keep them from slipping to the sides. Staying like that wouldn't be possible. In this instance, the ropes would help her stay where he wanted.

But he apparently didn't want her to remain that way. He took one arm and bent it so that her elbow dropped below the bench and her wrist was above it. "Stay like that."

Katrina worked out when she could, which translated to about four or five times each month. Or two. She couldn't maintain that position for very long. Still, she knew better than to argue.

He arranged her other arm the same way on the other side of the bench. If she were standing or lying on her back, she could hold this position with no problem. But she was on her stomach and fighting gravity. Thank goodness he was going to tie her in place.

He wound rope around one elbow, looped it under the table below her head, and secured it to her other elbow. Then he tied her wrists together above the table, forcing her hands to stay at the top of her head. It solved the problem of resting her arms, but the position proved awkward. He played around with the ropes, tugging on them and slipping his fingers beneath to test the give.

When everything was satisfactory, he stood next to her and fiddled with the things on her back. With her head turned and her inability to move, she found herself staring at his crotch. This table was the perfect level for him to slip his cock into her mouth. Saliva pooled on her tongue at the thought, and she swallowed.

Keith said nothing. He put sticky things on her back. From what she could feel, two were just under her shoulder blades on each side, and two were on the muscles she most liked massaged after a long day of research and paperwork.

"I'm going to turn it on. Tell me when it becomes uncomfortable."

At first, she felt nothing. After several moments, she became aware of a light tapping underneath the sticky things. The tapping sped up and became sharper. It didn't hurt, but the sensation surprised an unplanned exclamation from her.

"Kat? Does it hurt?"

"It doesn't. It's...different. I can't quite decide if it feels good or just weird. Is this the TENS unit?"

"Yes." As he said that, the distinction between each tap vanished. Underneath the pads, her muscles bunched and relaxed. The sensation traveled a counterclockwise path around her back, a weird kind of massage. "Oh, now that feels good."

"I'll leave it here for now. Close your eyes and relax."

She gladly complied. Within a minute or so, the physical manifestation of her stress melted away. Her mind drifted on a tide of tranquility. Even when he slid her down the table so that her legs and hips were no longer supported, she clung to that place, stubbornly refusing to leave.

He closed his hand around her ankle and guided her to stand with her legs apart. Ropes wound around her flesh, fastening her to cold metal poles.

Then he turned off the device. She groaned in protest, but she did remember her manners. "Thank you, Keith. That felt nice." It didn't do anything for the fire he'd lit in the bedroom, but it did release the tension from deep within her muscles.

More rope encircled her legs just above her knees. He buckled a thick belt over her lower back, further binding her to the table. She couldn't move any part of her body, and she took a moment to admire his strategic placement of the ropes. He stood behind her. She could detect no movement, so she deduced he was just looking at her. He was definitely big on the visual aspects of sex.

He caressed her ass, brushing the soft back of his hand over her skin. Since it was still sore from earlier, that touch was magnified a thousand times. She felt the soft, sticky pads as he repositioned two of them low on her ass, only inches from her pussy. The other two ended up high on her thighs, equally close to her vaginal lips. She wasn't sure about this part of his plan, but she trusted him, so she tabled her reservations. She'd liked the kneading feeling on the places in her back where stress lived. A massage around her pussy couldn't be anything but pleasurable. Right?

"You have permission to come tonight as often as you can. Don't temper your reactions. I want to see you and hear you."

He stated his instructions firmly and with as much devious passion as he'd used the night before when he told her he got off on her pain. Though she'd liked some of the kinds of pain he'd issued, she worried a little.

Tingling under the pads drew her attention away from her fretting thoughts. As the sensation picked up the pace, traveling from pad to pad, it began to feel like she was being slowly fucked. She liked the feeling, but she would rather it was closer to her pussy.

"Keith? Could you maybe put one of those pads on my clit?" Her voice came out thin and flat. Thin because she was a prisoner of the electricity pulsing through her ass. Flat because her cheek was pressed against the bench.

"It's not safe to do that, Kitty Kat. Dry skin only." He slapped a flogger lightly against her ass. The falls landed together, but they fell down her behind by themselves, scraping against her tender skin. "Don't worry. We have all night."

As the last of the falls slithered down her flesh, he lifted them. He ran them up her back and down her legs, sensitizing her skin to what was about to happen. Her heart beat faster, because she knew he would deliver on his promises.

"Relax. Breathe into it. This is going to hurt at first. I'm going to cover this lovely tanned skin with red stripes. You can scream as loud as you want, Kitty Kat, and I won't stop until you look exactly the way I want you to look."

A response wasn't necessary. Because his will was her will, her permission was assumed. She wanted this because he wanted to give it to her. It was as simple as that.

The first series of lashes lacked serious bite. It awakened her nerve endings, not that they needed all that much help. Her muscles tensed, and she had to work to keep them soft. In a purely theoretical way, she knew tightening them up would make it hurt worse.

Through it all, the pads that were almost between her legs pulsed in a sensuous rhythm. The muscles of her lower ass and inner thighs danced to it. They were helpless in the face of the electrical onslaught.

The next stroke of the flogger snapped loudly, the sound startling her more than the feel. Only when the tips of the falls pulled away did the searing pain register, eliciting a cry of protest. He'd said he would go for a light sting to give her a floating feeling. This wasn't light by any means.

She opened her mouth to call yellow so she could remind him about what he'd agreed to do, but the snapping sound came again, high on her left shoulder. He was careful to hit the fleshy parts, she noticed, but it still hurt like hell.

*You can do this.*

The voice came from somewhere inside her head, a cheerleader urging her on when the coward inside argued for a reprieve. She breathed into the sting, winning her internal battle. She would be strong, and she would do this for her Master. And she called him by that title because he was a Master. Her Master.

But she still didn't want to utter the word. For some men the title was a mark of respect. For Keith it was a wall she wouldn't let him build between them.

As she rationalized her decision yet again, Keith picked up the pace. The snaps came at regular intervals, ringing through the air to become her consciousness, and the lag time between them seemed to have disappeared. Just as the searing sting from one blow registered, he was already delivering the next. The sensations ran together. The agony throbbed through the skin of her back, ass, and upper thighs. He even targeted the curves of muscle along the backs of her calves.

She cried out. She struggled against her bonds. Desperate pleas fell from her lips, but she wasn't cognizant of anything she said. She wanted out. She wanted it to stop. At the same time, she felt as if she would die if he didn't continue.

Sobs heaved from deep in her chest, and at last her body relaxed. She submitted to this torture, accepting this pain because it had obliterated everything else, and she needed to erase the stress of the past week. With that decision came peace. She floated in a vast sea of calm, riding the ripples of pain that had transformed into the sweetest pleasure.

The snapping sounds of the flogger came from far away. Vaguely, she registered that it was falling with even more force that before. Instead of hurting, it served to keep her anchored to this refuge where no worries, no pain, nothing bad could penetrate.

Some time passed before she became cognizant of the fact that he'd stopped, but she had no idea how much. Her entire body buzzed, tingling with awareness and the remnant sting of the flogger. Keith sat on a low stool next to her and smoothed her hair away from her face. He murmured quiet praises of both her performance and her beauty.

Her eyes had been half-open. She blinked, clearing away the heaviest of the cobwebs, and focused on his handsome face. The lines around his mouth had softened. His entire demeanor had softened, as if he'd found relief the same way she had. For the first time ever, she saw the tentative beginnings of tranquil peace through the windows to his soul.

"Thank you, Keith." She said his name as reverently and respectfully as if it were his title. In her heart, she wanted to call him Master, but her heart didn't overrule her better sense. She didn't want to use his title until he could feel the true weight of that word.

"You were made to be flogged, Kitty Kat. Your fight and your surrender were beautiful to witness." He leaned forward and kissed her wrist.

She wondered if he was going to untie her.

Seeming to read her mind, he shook his head. "Wiggle your hands and feet. They weren't cold when I last checked, but you need to make sure you still have feeling. We're not even close to being finished tonight."

Nothing was amiss, though she noted that her shoulders were going to be sore. She voiced that concern, but he just chuckled.

"Most of your body will be sore in the morning. It just means you were well and thoroughly used. That should be a point of pride."

Or at least cause for a sated grin. Though he hadn't actually given her an orgasm yet, she knew that was on the menu.

He stood and made his way to stand behind her. She felt the coolness of his palm sliding over her hot skin, moving down her shoulder blade, over the belt binding her to the table, to the smoking flesh of her ass. The light caress burned like wildfire. She tried to buck his hand away from that tenderized flesh. It had been twice abused in only a few hours.

But Keith knew his way around restraints, and she was only able to flex her muscles.

"I love your ass, Kitty Kat. I've spent years stealing glances at it."

All went silent, and she knew he was taking time to look his fill. Never once had she caught him checking out her ass or sporting a guilty expression. As the utter stillness continued, she became acutely aware of how wet she was. Being bound in this position and the impact play had certainly turned her on. Even the spanking, discipline though it was, had whetted her appetite to have Keith inside her. His simplest touch had the ability to send her senses reeling.

Now she was finding out that he didn't even need to touch her. The power of his inspection melted her insides and made juices rush to her pussy.

"Like what you see?" In all the years she'd known him, she'd never censored her sense of humor. It might get her into trouble, or he might remember how much he liked her wit.

"Most definitely."

She heard his amusement, but he didn't touch her. He didn't do anything. This was almost worse than physical torture. At least when he was flogging her or spanking her, she knew exactly where his attention was centered. She wanted to squirm, but she couldn't. She tried to lift her head to look over her shoulder, but his ropes were doing their job.

After an eternity, she heard the sounds of things moving. Small noises told her that he was doing something to the table directly underneath her pussy, and that made her realize he'd removed those sticky pads sometime during or after her flogging. The long, slow trek of his tongue from her clit to her rosebud startled a strangled cry from her.

He returned for a second pass, then a third, almost as if he couldn't help himself. His tongue became more insistent. He moaned and added his fingers to the mix, circling her clit, alternating light and heavy pressure. The heat of his tongue teased her hole before plunging in. She moaned and struggled to push back against his face.

He played her body expertly, and she could only lie there and take it. Heat suffused her core, highlighting the job the flogger had done on her skin. It came from everywhere and blanketed her mind. The force of her climax shattered any illusion of control she thought she had.

Waves of delicious warmth lapped over her in time to the rhythm of his tongue. He licked away her cream and prolonged the orgasm. When her clit tried to hide, he pinched it to draw it out of its protective hood. Tremors shook the insides of her thighs as the stimulation reached the point where it was too much.

Just as she opened her mouth to beg, he stopped. Sort of.

Something settled against her clit. It was large and round, squishing against the tip of her nub and extending almost to her vaginal opening. Cold jelly covered it.

Keith appeared near her face. Her juices glistened from his lips and chin, and the scent of her musk permeated the small amount of air between them. He planted a kiss on her cheek.

"A little-known fact, Kitty Kat. A woman's clit is a larger, ovoid structure. What we think of as the clit is actually the tip. The rest of the muscle stretches down in two strips around the urethra, meeting up again just above the opening of the vagina. The best orgasms come from remembering to stimulate the entire area."

No wonder he was such a good lover. He knew more about her body than she did. What he said made sense. When she masturbated, she concentrated on the areas that felt good, and she didn't limit her forays to her clit or her vagina.

"This pretty pink vibrator is the size of a baseball. It's fitted to a mount that's welded to the crossbars of the table. It's not going anywhere, my sweet, sweet Kat. There's no escape." The cocky smile accompanying his speech sent a thrill of helplessness down her spine. Every nerve ending prickled to life, and gooseflesh traveled up her neck and down her legs.

He leaned over her. She heard a *click*, the flick of a switch, and the thing between her legs hummed to life. It pulsed, simulating fucking her differently from the way the TENS pads had. This device came into direct contact with her pussy, and it was mercilessly automated. She whimpered at the intensity as it pummeled her clit, forcing it back into the game.

Keith sat back and watched her, his hungry gaze roaming her body and coming to rest frequently on her face. She realized he planned to watch her climax, so she rested her head back down on the bench and gave herself over to enjoying the sensations her voyeuristic Master wanted her to feel.

The languor of her last orgasm hadn't quite faded. The gentle whisper of pleasure grew, fed by the special vibrating machine. She wanted to grind against it, to control the buildup and release. At most, she managed to flex the muscles of her inner thighs a few times.

When she had acclimated to the pulse setting, he switched it to a steady vibration strong enough that she felt it in her ass and thighs. That steady upward climb took on a new urgency, and the need to rock against it became almost unbearable. Energy she would have expended that way became trapped in her pussy, and she cried out as another climax broke.

This time, she didn't labor under the delusion that he would remove the device once it had delivered. He wanted to torture her with orgasms. He wouldn't free her until she'd had as many as he wanted her to have. She took comfort from the brutal honesty of the pleasure he took in watching her submission.

As the next orgasm loomed on the horizon, he stroked his hand over the bulge in his shorts. "I can't tell you how many times today I wanted to take you into your bedroom and make you come. Watching you masturbate in the shower this morning was one of the most erotic things I think I've ever seen. However, my sweet Kitty Kat, your orgasms belong to me. You will have them at my discretion. Tonight you'll learn what happens when you fail to secure permission."

Katrina didn't know whether his words, his tone, or the steady pass of his hand over his cock drove her need the most. She craved his touch. Not only did he deny it, he taunted her with the velvet of his voice and the sight of his cock, so close yet completely out of reach. She whimpered, begging for it.

He unzipped his shorts and eased them down to draw out his erection. She wanted him to remove his shirt again, but he didn't seem so inclined. Another denial.

His wonderful hands with their strong, tapered fingers wrapped around his cock, pumping up and down. He lifted his hips, thrusting into his palm, again tormenting her by performing an action she desperately wanted to do.

"Please." The word creaked forth from her dry lips. "You already punished me for coming without permission."

Those gorgeous green eyes fell to half-mast, and he lifted one side of his mouth in a sinful grin. "This, my dear, is discipline, not punishment."

As that tidbit dropped into place, she realized he wasn't giving her a free pass because the day had been so stressful. In a way, she was grateful that he wasn't treating her differently from the way he'd intended. She'd asked to be trained, and he was following through with his promise.

He stood, and his shorts fell to the floor. With one graceful motion, he shucked his shirt to stand before her with nothing on his wickedly handsome body. "Beg, Kitty Kat. Tell me what you most desire."

She wanted so much. How could he possibly take her in every orifice at once? "I want you, Keith. I want to feel you sliding in and out of my pussy, my ass, and my mouth. I want you to take me hard and soft, fast and slow, all at the same time.

I want to feel you on every part of me, to know every inch of my body belongs to you."

When he didn't immediately reply, not even to laugh at her impossible demands, she craned her neck to look up at him. The shuttered expression he'd adopted more often than not had slipped away. He regarded her with open appreciation and unadulterated reverence.

Another climax loomed. She tried to fight it, but her struggle was deliciously futile. As it pummeled her, the low growl of his tone reached her ears. "You belong to me."

"Yes." She repeated the affirmation over and over, a response to his statement and to the bliss suffusing her limbs, making them heavy and useless, not that she could move them anyway.

He reached down, and she felt the hard pinch of his fingers on her nipples. The waves of her orgasm grew, sweeping her up the sheer face of another cliff before she could completely fall from the previous one.

Leaning over her, he reached around and plucked at the other one, subjecting both stiff peaks to the same mercilessness. That invisible connection sprang to life. She tried to squirm, only to be reminded once again of her situation. The ropes on her arms and wrists dug into her skin, another piece in the complicated pain puzzle falling into place.

She screamed. Tears leaked from her eyes, a reaction to the maelstrom inside and the vulnerability inherent in her surrender. The smoothness of the ropes scraping against her skin helped anchor her as the rest of her body drifted away.

For several moments, she felt as if she were outside her body, looking down on the bound and sated woman below. She observed Keith's satisfied expression and how it morphed into ruthlessness as he rounded the table to stand behind her once more.

He swiped at the juices running in rivers down the insides of her thighs and rubbed the natural lubricant into the tight ring of muscle guarding her ass. Soon he positioned his cockhead at her back entrance. Now she understood the full reason he had tied her at this end of the table. It afforded access to anything he wanted.

Her body was becoming acclimated to the steady vibrations rocking her most intimate tissues. She would have to concentrate hard to have another orgasm, and the inert pressure of the tip of Keith's cock at her anus distracted her in a big way. Would he take it slow, tease her by withholding more of what she wanted, or would he ream her like last time?

Just when she thought she might go insane from not knowing, he pressed forward. She exhaled, relaxing those muscles to admit the pleasure he brought.

"Tighten around me, Kitty Kat."

Though reluctant to hurt him, she did as he asked. As she clenched, it changed the tenor of the vibrating ball curving against the flesh of her pussy. New life breathed into her tired, overstimulated clit, and she felt the stirrings of yet another climax. This one she wasn't sure she wanted to have. She didn't know what else he had planned, but if he kept this up, she wouldn't be awake for it. Already her serotonin levels were high, combating the endorphin rush from the flogging.

He set a leisurely pace. She experimented with how tight to hold him, noting when his moans and grunts changed to indicate lessening or increasing enjoyment. She wanted to pleasure him, to show him how much she appreciated what he'd done for her. That meant learning his tells, like how he gripped her hips harder when he lost himself in the bliss or how he went completely silent when he was about to explode.

Sharp tingles rocketed up her spine, and the vibrator seemed to slow down to pulse in time to Keith's rhythm. Heat, both frozen and liquid, flooded her body, and she lost the ability to control any of her muscles. With another loud cry, she came.

*Re/Paired*

The climax went on and on, throbbing and pounding. She lost track of where she was and even who she was. The world shrank, and she only knew the point where she and Keith came together.

She woke up on a massage table. Keith had a cloth pressed between her legs. It was soft and cool, exactly what her overused pussy needed. Bits of orgasm pulsed every now and again, a pleasant reminder of her first time in his dungeon.

The soft lights illuminated enough for her to know they were in a different room. It was small, barely large enough to be a utility room. Other than the massage table, cabinets occupying two corners were the only furniture. Two closed doors told her nothing, but the absence of windows told her they were still in the basement.

A spitting sound let her know he'd squirted something from a bottle. Then his hands were on the abused skin of her ass, anointing the tenderized flesh with something soothing. As he worked his way up her body, the pressure of his caresses increased until he was massaging her muscles. She groaned when he got to her shoulders. After having spent who knew how long in a raised and bent position, her muscles screamed in protest.

"I know, Kitty Kat. The more we do this, the easier it will be to hold those positions for longer and longer periods of time."

Longer? She'd been stuck that way for at least an hour. She wasn't complaining—not by a long shot—but she wasn't looking forward to finding out what he meant by a longer period of time. The massage felt wonderful, though. By the time he'd finished pampering her arms and legs, she felt like jelly. Put her in any container, and she'd assume that shape.

"Thank you, Keith. I'm so glad you changed your mind. I can't imagine being with anyone else like this." Not only could she not imagine it, she didn't want to try.

He lifted her into his arms and carried her to one of the doors. In lieu of a response, he kissed her forehead and bent his knees to reach the doorknob.

Emotion choked Keith's throat, closing it so tightly that he couldn't utter a single word. He hugged her closer to his body. In all the years he'd been a man, he'd never once taken care of a sub the way he'd just pampered Kat. Sure, he washed them down and put arnica or something similar on their skin to make sure it healed without problems, but it had always been a clinical thing, like cleaning the dishes when he finished eating.

This was different. He'd thoroughly enjoyed every second of aftercare. He loved the soft glide of her skin under his hands, feeling the tightness in her shoulders yield to his ministrations. Those muted sounds of contentment she'd made winnowed a path directly into his core and made him want things he knew better than to want.

He carried her up two flights of stairs and set her gently in his bed. Her olive skin popped against the pale blue sheets. She gazed up at him with no small amount of wonder and adoration in her eyes. At that precise moment, his life changed. He accepted the inevitable. There was no way in hell he would ever let her go. The foreign feelings she generated terrified him, but he no longer wanted to fight them.

Lost to emotion and completely powerless to do anything else, he turned off the lights, crawled into bed, and made love to her. No restraints, no domination or submission, just reverent caresses and quiet, whispered praises.

# Chapter Eight

Keith wasn't there when she woke the next morning. Sunlight peeked around the edges of the blinds, and the digital clock across the room indicated that she'd slept for almost ten hours.

The scene had been incredible. Though she was sore, her skin didn't chafe or burn the way she thought it might after having been so thoroughly flogged. She rolled and stretched. Keith's scent suffused the bedding. It was in her pillow, on the sheets, and in the comforter. She indulged herself for a few seconds by burying her face in his pillow and inhaling his purely male scent.

Then she made the bed and headed for the shower. She had to meet her mother, cousin, and aunt for brunch in a little over an hour. She didn't know where Keith was, but she reasoned that he wouldn't let her go there alone. For better or worse, he'd taken the job of being her personal bodyguard.

It didn't escape her notice that he'd dropped the parts of his dominant attitude to which she'd objected. He'd stepped up to embody the man she both liked and admired. This was the man who'd fed her morning shower fantasies for a decade.

Halfway through her shower, while she was rinsing conditioner from her hair, she noted his silhouette on the other side of the beveled glass shower door. Because she knew how much he liked to watch, she slid her hand down her body, over her breasts, and across her stomach, ending between her legs.

The effects of the vibrator hadn't lasted long after he'd stopped the device. Her pussy wasn't as sore this morning as she'd thought it would be. He'd been decidedly gentle and loving when he'd taken her in his bed.

He neither moved nor said a word, and she was loath to break the silence. It seemed naughtier to know he was there without acknowledging the fact he was watching her masturbate.

Tendrils of heat coiled, ready to spring loose. It wasn't close to the caliber of orgasm he gave her, but it was an orgasm, one of those things good at any size. This time she remembered to ask. "May I come, Keith? Please?"

"Yes." His strong voice carried the assurance that he thoroughly enjoyed witnessing her completion.

She gave in to the delicious release. When she stepped from the shower, she found him waiting with a soft, oversize towel held wide open.

He wrapped it around her and held her in his arms. "Good morning, Kitty Kat."

Reluctant to lean her wet head against his chest, she settled for planting a kiss on his neck and inhaling his heated scent. He smelled like coffee and fabric softener and something distinctly Keith. She was addicted to that last fragrance. Maybe the first one too. It was awfully strong.

He reached back with one hand and produced a steaming mug. "I brought you coffee, but I didn't bother with breakfast. Your mother called to make sure you were still coming today. I told her I would have you there on time."

Katrina lifted her head to regard him with a questioning gaze. "My mother called you to ask about me?"

He nodded stiffly. "I already talked to Malcolm this morning. We've analyzed the footage from last night and found nothing suspicious. Mal told your parents what happened. They're worried. He assured them that neither he nor I will be leaving you unprotected until that bastard is behind bars."

Now it was her turn to stiffen. It was one thing for them to all know she'd stayed the night with Keith. He had two guest bedrooms, and she'd stayed here before. "Malcolm is here?"

Keith shook his head. "We're streaming the footage on a secure line."

"So Malcolm saw me leave with you." The leaving together part didn't worry her. The parts where Keith kept a proprietary hand on her lower back did. He wasn't the kind of person who went out of his way to have physical contact with anyone, which magnified the significance of the gesture. And had his hand strayed down to squeeze her recently disciplined ass?

His mouth tightened. He released and stepped back. "He's not stupid, Kat. He's going to figure it out eventually. If he asks, I won't lie to him."

A cool breeze, generated by his swift change in demeanor, rushed at her. She didn't expect him to lie outright, though she fully acknowledged omission as a form of lying. Rubbing the towel over her body, she dried herself with quick efficiency. Then she squeezed excess water from her hair. "I just don't want to be the cause of him getting mad at you again. He's spent years warning me away from you."

Keith chuckled, but it was the unhappy kind. "And he's forbidden me to date you. I don't blame him. I have serious reservations about you seeing someone like me."

Training and dating were two completely different animals. She paused in her drying ritual to look at him. "So now we're dating?"

His nod was brief and curt. Because she recognized the anxiety behind his stoic mask, she wasn't offended by his brusqueness. It explained the tenderness of his lovemaking the night before. She was making headway faster than she'd expected.

Knowing he wouldn't want her to make a big deal out of it, she put on her bra and a sundress before throwing her arms and legs around him. As if he expected her attack, he was ready, and he caught her with ease.

"I always wanted to date you."

He gazed deep into her eyes, the gravity of his seriousness no match for the brief smile her confession elicited. "I'm not going to hide it, Kat. Your brother might get mad at us both, but I'm not going to pretend you mean nothing to me."

A stone formed in the pit of her stomach. He might think he could ride out Malcolm's ire, but Katrina feared her brother would see it as a betrayal. All along, she had thought Keith could and would keep their changed relationship a secret. He tended not to be forthcoming with details about his romantic involvements. It wasn't that he hid anything, just that he didn't talk about it.

She appreciated his position on the issue and what it meant. He was in this for the long haul, and she knew he'd never opened himself to anyone like this before. She had to honor that.

"Okay, but let me tell my mom first. Not today, though. I have to get her alone. If she's on our side, then nobody else will have a choice but to be supportive." Her mother would also be the easier sell. She already loved Keith and treated him like a son. However, if he broke her heart, as he was apt to do with women, her mother would never forgive him. "But Keith, if this doesn't work out between us, and the reason won't matter, nothing will ever be the same again."

Instead of answering, he kissed her. It was a sweet kiss, almost passionless except that it communicated a whole host of things he couldn't seem to say out loud. This expression of love stole her breath. He'd stolen her heart years before, so that matter was already resolved.

When it ended, he set her back on her feet and rested his forehead against hers. "So not working out is not an option. Got it."

---

*Re/Paired*

The restaurant Aunt Cindy had chosen for brunch bustled with people. Not only was the food sinfully addictive, it was located near the busy downtown shopping district in Madison Heights.

Keith had walked her inside, but he'd been too preoccupied with visually sweeping the area to do more than press a kiss to her cheek and admonish her to behave. Since he also kissed her mother's cheek, the small act didn't make a statement.

Her mother had refrained from peppering her with questions until Keith left. Though he'd said he had errands to run, Katrina knew he hadn't gone far.

"I want to know everything, Katrina Marie. Malcolm said the first incident was last weekend. Why didn't you tell anyone?" Worry lines creased her mother's brow, adding ten years to her pretty face.

Katrina hated that she'd caused her mother's distress. Having Keith by her side yesterday had made the situation easier to bear. Last night, he'd purged the unpleasant events from her mind and done incredible things to her body that made sitting still in a chair today a little challenging.

Before she could answer, Aunt Cindy intervened. "Donna, leave her alone. Malcolm already told you what's going on. I'm sure Trina just wants to relax and not think about that horrible man."

"Yeah." Layla's blue eyes sparkled. "But now you have an excuse to buy all new underwear. And if Keith is your bodyguard today, you can drag him with you. I'd love to see him try to not have an expression while he's watching you pick out sexy panties." Then she inhaled sharply, and her sparkle turned a little wicked. "You're not wearing anything under that dress, are you?"

Katrina was sure her blush answered the question satisfactorily.

Donna squeezed Katrina's hand. "Baby, I'll go shopping with you. That way Keith can keep his distance. Or I can bring your father. He's used to watching us shop, and Keith can have the afternoon off."

Certain that nothing would induce Keith to leave her side today, Katrina shook her head. "I'm fine. It's fine. I already told Keith what I have planned for today."

And he'd lifted his lips in that cocky grin, but he hadn't promised to take her shopping. She was sure he had some plans of his own. She smiled and spent the next hour enjoying the company and the food.

When they left the restaurant, Layla linked her arm through Katrina's and rested her head on Trina's shoulder. Though they'd always been close, Layla was physical with practically everyone. Katrina leaned her head against Layla's, returning the gesture with equal affection.

"I'm worried about you, Trina. This is some serious shit."

"I know." She pushed away the feelings of violation and insecurity. She might be a target, but she refused to be a victim. "Malcolm and Keith put infrared, motion-detecting cameras all around my condo. They're watching everyone who comes and goes. And I haven't been alone all weekend."

"You can come stay with me. Or I can come stay with you. It's probably safer at your place now that the dynamic duo are playing spy games."

Enveloped in the love of family, Katrina felt safe and secure. She was lucky to have them. "I'll keep that in mind for when Keith needs a day off. Right now, nothing's going to make him leave my side."

Layla squeezed her arm tighter, but the line of conversation was forgotten as they both spotted Keith standing next to his SUV, waiting for her. His arms were crossed over his chest, and he exuded barely suppressed fury. The woman standing in front of him had to be a foot shorter. She had one hand on her hip, and the other poked dangerously close to his chest. Keith's demeanor gave Katrina the chills.

"Yikes," Layla said, giving voice to Katrina's reaction. "I've never seen him look so pissed off before. And cold. I can see how he makes the bad guys pee their pants with just a look. All this time, I thought he only stood there looking dangerous and handsome. But right now he's deadly scary."

Hate. That was the emotion they were both having trouble identifying. They'd both seen him upset, annoyed, even mad. But in all the years Katrina had known him, she'd never seen him show pure, unadulterated hate for anyone or anything.

Her heart went out to him, breaking a little. Hate was a strong emotion. In order for him to feel it, this woman must have meant a great deal to him at one point.

With her back to them, Katrina couldn't see her face or tell much about the woman. She wore cutoff jeans that were ripped up at the bottom and a yellow, short-sleeved shirt. Her blonde hair was clipped up in the back of her head. Though she wasn't large, her flesh definitely strained against the confines of her clothes.

"She looks trashy." Layla whispered her unkind observation. Silently, Katrina agreed.

"I think that's his mother."

Katrina and Layla whirled around. They'd forgotten the presence of their moms. Donna had her eyes narrowed, and her gaze pointed at the woman standing in front of Keith. She nodded and added to her guess.

"Yeah. I met her once years ago. That woman is a piece of work. It's a wonder he managed to escape and make something of himself." Donna didn't bother to hide her disdain or her disapproval.

Instinctively Katrina knew Keith wouldn't want her mother to witness this exchange. He had a lot of pride, and part of it was wrapped in his ability to keep his cool under any circumstance. Katrina hugged her mom and aunt.

"I'll see you guys later."

She tried to walk away, but her mother grabbed her arm. "Trina, leave him be. He won't want to introduce you to that woman."

Strains of conversation replayed in her head. That woman had beaten him when he was a child. It didn't matter how old he grew; he was still a defenseless little boy against that woman. "Mom, I can't let him face her alone."

From the periphery of his vision, he watched Mama L try to stop Kat from coming closer. He appreciated her effort. There was no way he wanted his precious Kat close to the monster in front of him.

"Your sister has been calling you for months."

He was well aware of his sister's attempts to contact him. Jules had read him the riot act, but then she'd become curiously silent on the matter. He figured Malcolm must have used his charm to get her to lay off. The messages hadn't stopped coming, but now they were shuffled to the bottom of the stack.

When he didn't answer, his mother poked at the air in front of his chest, as if she knew the slightest physical contact would send him over the edge. "You're her brother, and she needs you. For once, you could stop being such a selfish little bastard and be there for your sister."

Kat sidled up to him. She put her hand on his arm, her skin still cool from the air-conditioning in the restaurant. Though she said nothing, she freely lent him the strength of her presence. Suddenly it wasn't such a struggle to keep a leash on his temper.

"She's in prison. Second-degree murder. I looked it up."

"It wasn't her fault." His mother waved her hand dismissively while glaring at Kat. "Tell your whore to get lost. This is family business."

Kat's hand tightened on his arm, and she placed the other against his chest to hold him back. While she couldn't hope to have the physical strength to stop him, she provided a different kind of restraint.

Though he should defend Kat, anything he said would only be breath wasted on this woman. He put some more ice in his glare. "You are not and have never been my family. Don't contact me again. If you see me on the street, keep walking."

When doing surveillance, especially when he was with the target, both socially and emotionally, he had to go about his business as if he weren't constantly scanning for the slightest clue that someone might be watching them. In keeping with that cover, he'd run a few errands and window-shopped while his girlfriend had brunch with her relatives.

Dustin wasn't finished working up a profile of who might stalk Kat, but Keith figured the person was most likely male and between the ages of twenty-five and forty. While he hadn't been dismissing them, he also hadn't looked too closely at the women. When this one had approached, he'd stepped out of the way to let her pass.

She'd come at him with a nasty comment. The years had not been kind to the bitch who brought him into this world. She looked tired and used, far older than her fifty-six years. Mama L had just turned sixty-seven, and she could pass for his mother's daughter.

Putting one arm protectively around Kat's shoulders, he steered her away from the situation. He didn't say a word as he opened the passenger door and saw her safely loaded into his car. She watched him thoughtfully, but she didn't say anything until they were on the road.

"So that was your mother."

He didn't want to admit it, but he couldn't very well lie. "Yes."

"What's her name?"

"Starr. Two r's."

She nodded, but he had the sense it wasn't any kind of acknowledgment. "What did she want?"

He shook his head. It didn't matter what she wanted. "Don't know. Don't care."

"You're not even a little bit curious?"

"My sister's been calling. I looked her up in the system. She's been part of it since she was fifteen. Of course, those records are sealed. She's been in and out of jail for the past seven years. Three DUIs. Possession. Solicitation. Things like that." He let out a mirthless chuckle. "She used to be so much better at eluding the law."

Kat made a knowing sound. "Starr thinks you might be able to pull some strings."

"Probably. I won't, though. She gets what she deserves." He didn't bother to hide his bitterness. Of his two older sisters, one had ignored him, and one had taken pleasure in beating him up every single day. Some of his earliest memories were of searching for places to sleep where Savannah wouldn't think to look. Even now he couldn't stand to be touched while he was asleep.

One glance at Kat softened him a bit. Her touch didn't bring him the same sense of dread. She comforted him with her presence and brought peace with her embrace.

Determined to change the subject, he smiled as he reached into the backseat. "I got you something." He fumbled around until he found the right bag, and then he deposited it on her lap.

She gave him a glance ripe with cynical understanding that let him know he wasn't off the hook, but that she'd let him wiggle away for now. Her expression morphed when she peered into the bag. "Ohhh. You bought me underwear." She lifted out a pair of light blue lacy panties. "These are pretty. Way better than what I had before."

And they'd look incredible on her. He loved lighter, brighter colors that contrasted with her olive complexion.

"Matching bras. Wow. They're so soft and sexy. I didn't know you liked lace this much." She oohed and aahed some more as she went through his selections.

Her approval pleased him inordinately. Before Kat, he hadn't cared for lace on a woman. He'd preferred anything that came off easily. It hadn't been about being sexy. It had been about convenience and control. Kat had asked him to leave that part of him behind. Shedding the false front felt good, like he could finally be himself. No way it could happen with anybody but Kat.

The short drive ended as he pulled into his garage and shifted into park. "You're a beautiful woman. You should have beautiful things."

She leaped from her seat and landed straddling his lap. He was less surprised this time, but he was pleased at her excitement. He grinned and pulled the key from the ignition, fully intending to luxuriate in whatever way she wanted to thank him.

She cupped his face between her hands and held it steady. He threw his keys in the console and settled his grip on her hips. She wasn't wearing panties under that sundress. It would be an easy matter to unzip his pants and slip his cock into her velvety warmth.

But she didn't lean in for a kiss. A close look at her expression made him groan. His effort to redirect her attention really hadn't been successful.

"You're a beautiful man. Inside and out. Nobody can take that away from you."

He closed his eyes, a feeble attempt at escape. He wanted to be the man she saw when she looked at him, but he wasn't. The run-in with his mother had underscored the facts. The apple didn't fall far from the tree. A part of him would always be an addict. He could pretend to be the perfect man for Kat, and he would keep her close until she discovered that he had some serious shortcomings she couldn't fix. And then it would all go to hell. She would move on, and he wouldn't bother fighting the demons of addiction anymore.

"I know it's not easy to face the woman who was supposed to love and protect you, but who hurt you instead. No mother who loves her children could ever beat them. I'm proud of you, Keith. You didn't let her destroy your life."

What the hell had Malcolm told her? His eyes flew open, and he pinched his brows together. "What are you talking about? My mother didn't beat me."

Now her brows drew together, matching his. "But you said she beat you every day."

He shook his head. "She got drunk and passed out every day. So did my dad. My sister beat me. She's eight years older. I didn't stand a chance. I was half-starved most of the time, scrawny as all hell. I didn't know what it was like to eat regular meals until I joined the military. My mother didn't lift a finger to stop the beatings, and my father thought it was funny. He'd sit there with a forty in his hand and laugh his ass off. He only got mad if I bled too much."

Color left her face, turning her skin a startling shade of gray. He'd never talked about his past to her in anything but general terms. She knew his parents were alcoholics and that he'd had to fend for himself, but he'd sheltered her from the true horror of it. He had no idea why he told her those things now.

It was his turn to grip her face. "Breathe, Kat. Inhale. Exhale. Slow breaths, honey."

Huge tears brightened her dark eyes, and his gut clenched at her raw pain. She held in her tears, not wanting to upset him further.

"It's in the past, Kitty Kat. Savannah went to jail when she was seventeen, and by the time she got out, I was big enough to fight back. The house was peaceful without her. My parents and my other sister, Leanna, were lazy drunks. It got really quiet once everyone passed out." He didn't add that he'd joined them too many nights to count.

He didn't actually recall signing the papers to join the Marines, and as a teen, he'd learned to function drunk well enough to hide his problem from almost everyone.

She seemed to pull herself together. The wet sheen disappeared from her eyes, and she gave him a sad smile. "My heart breaks for that little boy, but I have no sympathy for the man."

Now it was his turn at confusion. While he hadn't wanted sympathy, he'd still thought she would give some. "None?"

"None. You're a wonderful man. I meant what I said. Maybe your parents didn't beat you, but they abused you just the same. Neglect is the most insidious form of child abuse there is. And you not only survived, but you've managed to thrive. You have a great career, the respect and admiration of pretty much everyone you meet, and an awesome girlfriend. Really, you've done pretty well."

He slid his hands under the hem of her dress and caressed her thighs, pushing the fabric up as he went. "I'm so glad you're here to count my blessings."

Truly, he was. He tended to spend time wallowing in the negative. Kat was a bright ray of sunshine on her cloudiest day. He needed her to save him from the darkness. He massaged his way to the apex of her thighs.

With her dress out of the way, he could see the deep rose of her pussy. It was barely damp, but after the topic they'd spent time discussing, he hadn't expected otherwise.

"I stopped by your house and picked up your briefcase and some clothes for work. I didn't get my full weekend with you, so you'll be staying the night." He didn't think twice about his high-handedness in making this decision for her, but for the first time it occurred to him that he'd always done things like this to Kat and she'd never once protested.

She'd been his submissive all along.

"Take the bag upstairs. Choose one lingerie combination. When you come down, I expect you to be wearing that and nothing else."

With a pleased smile lighting her eyes, she darted forward and kissed his cheek. "Yes, Keith."

She'd replaced his title with his name, but she infused it with the same respect and reverence, so there wasn't a real distinction. As he watched her disappear through the door to the house, he wondered if she truly objected to the title or if she'd refused to use it in order to protest his treatment of her their first night together. Now that he was behaving toward her with the same consideration he'd always shown, she seemed much happier.

For years he'd fantasized about being able to hang out with her, talk to her about anything and everything, and then tell her to get naked. In a way, she'd insisted on making his dream a reality. He owed her a reward.

He hauled her things from the back and brought them inside. She wouldn't need her work clothes until the next day, so he hung them in the spare bathroom upstairs. From the sounds of water running in the master bath, he figured she was freshening up.

He liked that she took time with the details, and he didn't want to disturb her while she was seeing to them. Women could be weird about those things. Watch her masturbate in the shower? No problem. Watch her pluck or shave? Major disaster. As her Master—whether or not she used the title—it was his right to interrupt her at any time. As a man, he knew better than to tempt fate.

By the time he saw her again, almost half an hour had passed. The fourth step creaked as she came down, alerting him to her progress.

"In here," he called from the living room. Sunday meant football, and he had to at least check out how the preseason prospects were shaping up.

However good the new Denver lineup looked, Kat took precedence. He watched the opening that led to the kitchen, the only way into the room. With all the dramatic flair of a supermodel, she paused in the entryway, one hand on the wall and one hip thrust forward. Straight tendrils of hair brushed her shoulders. It would feel like silk when he ran his fingers through those luxurious tresses. He was glad she'd left it down. Next her long, shapely legs invited his thorough visual caress. The light blue satin made her skin seem to glow. Or was that extreme happiness? He could wish, couldn't he?

The lacy scraps barely covered her breasts, while at the same time emphasizing their graceful swell. The vividness of her areolas formed circles beneath the pale bra. Matching panties hung low on her hips, just catching her jutting hip bones. A tiny bit of lace covered her mound, drawing his attention to what it hid.

"Simply beautiful. I could spend hours just looking at you." Smooth words flowed easily, but he meant it. She presented an incredibly lovely vision. He'd chosen her clothes well.

Color rushed to her cheeks, and he was amazed to find her still nervous around him. How could she doubt his desire after the last two days?

He motioned to the large throw pillow he'd positioned at his feet. Her laptop and briefcase were on the low table in front of the sofa. "I know you have work to do. I'll give you time to research and write your briefs. And then you're all mine, Kitty Kat."

"I'm already yours." She smiled, and he could tell she was pleased that he remembered her need to get some work done before Monday. If he didn't provide the time, she'd spend the whole night stressing over the things she hadn't accomplished. She knelt on the floor and dug into her briefcase.

The scene sent a pleasant tingle zipping through his bloodstream. She settled into the position he'd chosen with a contentment that couldn't be faked. It bothered him that he still looked for evidence she was doing this because it was what he wanted, not what she wanted. He needed to move past his insecurities and trust her a little more.

"Oh, you got my things back from Dustin." She threw a brilliant smile over her shoulder. "Thanks. You really were busy while I was having brunch. Good. I was afraid you'd spent the whole time watching me."

Dustin had stopped by while she was still sleeping to drop off her stuff and debrief Keith. He hadn't made headway in the case, but he was still gathering information, so that wasn't a surprise.

They'd decided not to tell her that she was under constant, though unofficial, surveillance. The bureau didn't have the resources to keep tabs on her, so Dustin, Malcolm, and Keith had decided to take that matter into their own hands. While Keith had been shopping, Dustin had been keeping an eye on Kat. They had a plan for most contingencies, and Jordan had offered his services as a backup plan.

She set to work. He flipped through three different games and watched the time-lapse video feed from her condo on his laptop. He looked over some case files, trying to fit together the puzzle pieces on cases he believed to be connected. Proving the links existed would enable them to streamline several investigations. Of course, life was never simple.

Eventually the steady tap of Kat's fingertips on her keyboard came to a halt. She put it in sleep mode and rested her head just above his knee.

Wanting her to take some time to get comfortable with the position, he refrained from touching her at first. Then he gave in to the urge to stroke her hair.

She sighed, and he felt her eyelashes flutter against his skin. "I like this."

A month ago, he would have punished a slave for speaking without permission. Now he wanted to hear her speak whenever she had something to say. Marveling at how much he'd changed in such a short time, he smiled contentedly and continued toying with her hair. "What do you like, Kitty Kat?"

"This. Being here with you. Sitting on the floor at your feet. You playing with my hair. I've fantasized about it. I'm not sure what that says about me, but I feel so peaceful and calm, like everything is right with the world." She planted a tiny kiss on his leg and smoothed a caress across his ankle.

Though he knew she couldn't see it, he smiled gently at her awed tone. "It says you're submissive. How do you feel about that?"

The finger exploring his ankle moved higher. It wasn't an evasion so much as an indication that she was processing the question. "I am fine with it. I don't think I would bring it up in casual conversation, because people would judge me. But I can't pretend I don't want this—that I don't need it. I don't feel like you put me here to show that I'm lesser than you. It's more like it's symbolic of our relationship. That you'll take care of me. That I'm yours."

Another piece of his soul came to life, dropping down to join the rest of what she owned. Perhaps she belonged to him, but he belonged to her just as much. "You are mine, Kitty Kat. And I'll always take care of you, no matter what." Even if she suddenly decided she couldn't be with him like this. "Now come sit on my lap. I want to play with your pussy."

In stark contrast to the way she'd moved in his car, she rose with lazy grace. He guided her across his lap with his hands on her hips and arranged her so that she lay with her head against his shoulder, one leg bent up and out of the way on the sofa, and the other leg dangling off the side.

This gave him a clear path to her pussy with both his eyes and his hand. Her breathing sped up as she anticipated his touch. Of course, he had no plans to make it easy on her.

He spent time caressing her legs, especially the sensitive places behind her knees and near the junctures where each leg met her pelvis. Then he meandered upward to knead and pluck at her amazingly responsive breasts. The scent of her arousal saturated the air, and she whimpered. He liked that she accepted his will, made it her own, especially when her desires were driving her to the brink.

Flipping aside the soaked scrap of lace covering her pussy, he admired her handiwork for several minutes, stroking her outer lips with the barest of caresses as she shivered in his arms. "I like it, Kitty Kat. Have you ever shaved completely like this before?"

She shook her head. "I know you didn't tell me to, but it seemed like something you'd want."

Though many of his fellow Doms had strong views on the topic, Keith didn't. A woman's pussy was an expression of her personality. It functioned as an early warning system. Wild women had wild pussies. Neat women had neat pussies. There were tons of shades in between, and piercings presented even more options. Kat had laid herself bare for him. He wasn't about to dismiss the implication of her offering.

"I want you every way I can get you." With that, he captured her lips in a searing kiss and pressed her clit. She surged in his arms, crying out in surprise and ecstasy as she climaxed. He rubbed lightly, widening his forays to prolong her pleasure.

"I'm sorry, Keith." She panted her apology and grasped at his arm and knee with trembling hands. "I didn't see that coming. You're very good at this."

He chuckled at her attempt to turn her misbehavior into a compliment. "Thanks. But you still stole an orgasm, my sweet Kat. Stand up with your back to me."

When she'd spent such a long time changing earlier, he'd stowed some gear in the small cabinet in one of his end tables. He extracted a few things. They weren't for punishment, not really, but she did need some discipline. He had the sense that disciplining Kat was going to consume significant quantities of time. Though she was a natural submissive, she wasn't naturally obedient. He liked that about her. It made things more interesting.

He pulled her wrists together behind her back. Beginning with the middle of a medium-gauge line, he wound it around her wrists, leaving about a six-inch gap. Then he brought the lines together in the space between her wrists and twisted the rope once. A few inches higher on her arms, he wound the line again. He continued up her arms, braiding them into his rope design until she was bound from wrist to shoulder, an elegant web of twisted rope running parallel to her arms between them. It was both decorative and functional.

The position thrust her breasts forward and put a nice arch in her spine. He turned her around to face him. Her lips parted, waiting for him to stake his claim. Her pupils were dilated, wide with wonder, and her chest heaved, bringing those pebbled nipples closer.

She'd just come, and now she looked almost ready to do it again. He couldn't totally resist her siren's song, so he leaned down and brushed his lips against hers. She moaned and opened farther to offer more, but he refused the bait. If he got sucked in, he would lose himself in her generosity and beauty, in the headiness of loving the perfect woman in his arms.

Next he extracted a collar from his hiding spot. She trembled as he placed it around her neck.

"Nervous?"

She licked her lips. All that panting was drying them out. "No. I trust you."

"You're shaking like a leaf in a heavy wind."

"Because I know you're about to blow me away. But I also know you'll hold me up and bring me down at the right time. It's desire. Want. Not nerves."

As he'd thought, but he liked hearing her say the words.

Bending down, he took her nipple in his mouth, lace and all. She sucked in a sharp breath, and her shoulders twitched hard, and he knew she'd tried to bring her hands to grip his head. He banded an arm behind her, lacing it between her bound arms and her back to hold her upright. She arched into his mouth, braced her pelvis against his, and sagged her weight onto his arm, surrendering completely.

She whispered his name, the reverent tone giving way to pleading when he switched to her other nipple. He played for a long time, taking turns torturing her sensitive buds with his teeth, lips, and tongue.

By the time he settled himself back on the sofa and had her straddle him, thick cream smeared over the insides of her thighs and dripped onto his shorts, enough lubrication for him to take her ass if he was so inclined. He'd get to it eventually. She had an exceptionally lovely rear end.

The last accessory he had for her was a pair of clamps on a chain. She hadn't liked the clothespins on her flesh, but she'd loved having something on her nipples. Now that he'd prepared them, it was just a matter of slipping the clamps over her swollen nubs and tightening them down.

He slid the cold metal under the panel of her bra. This way the clamp would make her nipples stand out, and the wet lace would provide a constant friction as she moved her body.

She whimpered, begging wordlessly for more, as it squeezed her flesh. Then he threaded the thin chain through a link on her collar before he treated her other nipple to the same stimulation. Now whenever she moved her neck, it would give them a tug. She could exercise limited control over this sensation, invoking it when she wanted a little extra stimulation. It also presented an opportunity for an unexpected sharp reminder if she forgot about the connection and tossed her head with passion.

Then he set her back and reached for a condom.

"No," she said. "I know we said to use them, but you didn't last night, and I really like the way you felt inside me. I'm on birth control, and we're both clean. How about we just use them for anal sex?"

He stared at her as he tried to recount their activities from the night before, and he realized she was right. When he'd taken her in the bedroom that last time, he hadn't even thought to use a condom.

Though he probably owed her an apology, he couldn't bring himself to be sorry. And she didn't seem to want his contrition.

He nodded. "Lift up."

She rose to her knees, and he pushed his shorts down to allow access. She canted her hips forward, trying to line him up at her opening. He helped.

"Slowly, Kitty Kat. Sink down slowly." Her dripping heat felt like heaven on his cock. "You're going to fuck me. Then you're going to kneel on the floor and lick me clean. You'll lick me until I'm ready again, and then I'm going to fuck you again. If you come without permission, I will stop, and I will beat your ass." And then he'd fuck it, but he didn't add that. She seemed incapable of controlling her orgasms when he took her anally. Part of him didn't want to see her learn to control them. He liked that he could drive her beyond her ability to command her body.

She sank down until he was fully sheathed. Her hot, velvety warmth gripped him like an enclosure made just for his cock.

The expression on her face morphed from need to an almost painful bliss, and he understood the enormity of what she felt, because he felt it too.

After a few seconds, she began to move. She tried to set a fast, grinding rhythm, but with her arms bound, she lacked some of the necessary maneuverability. He wasn't inclined to help her, because she had him nearly there a lot faster than he had wanted to arrive.

Then she clamped down on him, her pussy tightening around his cock. His Kat had figured out that he liked the pain with his pleasure, and she used it now to heighten his experience.

"Vixen."

She smiled in triumph until he was forced to grip her hair and ruin her attempt at control with a punishing kiss. Her juices dribbled from her pussy, drenching his balls. If possible, she squeezed him even harder. His balls drew up, and he came, a torrent of hot semen bursting from his cock to mark its territory.

Immediately, he lifted her from him and placed her on the floor between his legs. The cushion wasn't there. He'd placed it to his right side so she could work on her briefs uninhibited by the placement of his limbs. No matter. The room was carpeted, so she had some padding.

She regarded his softened cock cautiously.

He smoothed her hair back from her face. "Have you never tasted yourself, Kitty Kat?"

She shook her head, but her expression remained uncertain. "But this isn't just me. It's you and me combined."

That seemed to solidify her resolve. She bent down, and her pink tongue darted out, taking a swipe at the sensitive tip of his cock. She paused for a second as though considering the flavor, and then she went at him like he was covered in chocolate and whipped cream.

She moaned and slurped, two of the sexiest sounds he'd ever heard her make. His cock didn't take long to rouse. It stirred to life, seeking the heat of her mouth.

Abruptly she lifted and captured his mouth for a searing, short kiss, and then she returned to his cock. He understood that she'd shared the treat, but in reality all she'd done was strip away his patience.

He tore her mouth away from his clean cock, pushing her back so abruptly she nearly toppled. In seconds, he had her splayed out on the sofa with his face buried between her legs.

She wiggled and shouted. The sudden movement had caused her some additional pain in her breasts. With her arms still tightly bound, her hands ended up under her ass, which had the added benefit of lifting her into the air.

Not bothering with niceties, he licked and sucked, thrusting his tongue into her hole to gather the cream hiding there. The extra saltiness, he knew, was his contribution to their passion.

She sobbed and screamed, pleading with him. "Please, Keith. May I come? Please, oh please, Master. Let me come."

That last part might have been a slip of the tongue, but it showed her true attitude toward him. His heart soared, and he mumbled permission against her quivering flesh.

And then she came, climaxing with such force that her juices rushed out, bathing his face in her fragrance. Damn, but he could die here.

No, he couldn't. His cock wanted more, and it was finally fully ready. He flipped her over to relieve the stress on her arms and shoulders, and he positioned her ass high in the air, exposing her swollen pussy. It still pulsed from the aftershocks of her orgasm.

He plunged inside, fucking her hard to an impossibly fast rhythm. The sane part of his brain remembered her nipple clamps. Taking them off too soon would chase away her orgasm. He waited until she begged once again for permission. As he consented, he released both clamps.

She buried her scream in the sofa cushion, her vaginal muscles sucking him deeper as they spasmed around his aching cock, and he pounded into her until he fell over that precipice too.

# Chapter Nine

What a change one week could make. When Aaron set a cup of coffee on her desk Monday morning, Katrina felt worlds better than the last time he'd opened the workweek with a caffeinated gift.

Keith had used his powers of persuasion to make her stay the night, and in the morning he'd ordered her to masturbate in the shower. This time he joined her, watching at first and then treating her to the sight of his fist pumping along his shaft.

They came together, by the power of their hands, in each other's arms.

She gave Aaron a brilliant smile. "Good morning, counselor. How was your weekend?"

He lifted a pale brow. "Okay. This is weird. I heard you picked up a stalker, and here you are, beaming like you just won the lottery."

And giggling like an idiot because she'd just come from a weekend-long sexual marathon. It took a few seconds for her to regain her composure. "Unfortunately, I did pick up one of those nasty things. But I'm surrounded by family and friends, and that can make all the difference."

A look of admiration came into his eyes, and he returned her smile. "Good for you, not being intimidated. You can't let this chase you away from your home or work, or make you afraid to live your life."

Keith hadn't left her alone all weekend, so technically she wasn't being all that brave. She shrugged. "The FBI is on it. Malcolm and Keith set cameras up all over, and they haven't left me alone yet. It's easy to be brave when I have such strong support."

Aaron nodded slowly, almost as if his head was already inside his next case. "Well, if you need anything, I'm here for you too."

She squeezed his hand. "Thanks. Your friendship means a lot to me."

"Really?" He looked down at her hand. Then he put his other hand over it and squeezed back. "Do you maybe have a minute to read over a brief for me before I file it?" A teasing grin accompanied his request.

She swallowed her groan. As much as she loved Aaron, his briefs were often a mess, frequently with incorrect citations and faulty logic. But he was her friend, always there for her when she needed him. "I've got about fifteen minutes. I'll look it over, but I can't guarantee I'll be as thorough as I usually am."

Sitting in lingerie with Keith inches away hadn't been conducive to work. While she had been able to get some things done, she had a lot left to do.

Leaning down, he brushed a kiss on her cheek. "You're the best, Katrina. Thanks."

Five minutes later, she sipped her coffee and shook her head at the mess of words on the computer in front of her. The names of both the judge and the defense attorney were spelled wrong, and those were the small issues. Aaron would never earn a seat on a prominent case until he learned to take more time with things. She sent it back to him with a note to have him recheck some of his facts.

The day flew by, but reality intruded when she went to her car after work to find Keith standing next to it in the parking garage. She wanted to sprint the distance between them and throw her arms around him, but he wore his special-agent look. It sent her stomach plummeting.

"What's wrong?"

He frowned and shook his head. "I wanted to make sure it was safe for you to get into your car."

They could have driven to work together. He worked two blocks away, and they'd both come from his house. However, Katrina knew how unlikely it would be for them to both leave at the same time. She often had to go to court or visit a witness or suspect. He drove all over the east side of the state during the course of his regular duties. One of them would have ended up stranded, so he'd taken her home to retrieve her car this morning.

She swallowed and nodded. The fear she'd denied all day came to the fore. While she'd been stuck in the office, her stalker could have broken into her car.

He handed her a set of keys. "I had the locks on your condo changed. You have a set, I have a set, and I've already delivered a set to your parents. I made an appointment to take your car in tomorrow to get those locks changed. I need you to go with me and sign off on it."

Feelings lodged in her throat. She might call them words, but she couldn't think of anything to say. Malcolm and Keith installing cameras had made her feel secure, but she recognized now that the cameras weren't an early warning system. They might or might not act as a deterrent. If her stalker came for her when she was alone, the cameras would only offer evidence after the fact.

Keith closed the distance. His strong arms provided physical support for her emotional upheaval. "Breathe, Kat. I've got you. I'm going to follow you home. I've already been to your place today, and I've reviewed the tapes. Nothing's happened."

He was, she realized, just as terrified of leaving her alone as she was of being alone. He sought to reassure her and to convince himself that she would be safe there without him. Because his schedule wasn't regular, he'd eventually have to work late, which would leave her on her own for the evening.

"I'm okay." She mumbled the reassurance into his shirt. "What time tomorrow?"

"We'll go on the way home from work. Can you pop your trunk?" He released her enough that she could fumble with her keys and push the right button.

He lifted the lid, revealing the industrial-sized first-aid kit her father insisted she always carry. Ever the thorough agent, he also checked inside the zippered case. "Looks good." He slammed the trunk of her sedan shut. "Okay, go ahead and get in. I'll meet you at your house. There's a one-hundred-percent chance that your parents are going to be stopping by for dinner and an eighty-percent chance that your mother made orange marmalade ice cream."

That was a new flavor for her mother, but the woman constantly added to her repertoire. "Where did she come up with that one?"

Keith grinned. Most men would have come off as smug, but he managed to look sinfully handsome. "We might have discussed it earlier today."

From his tone, she assumed they'd be the ones cooking dinner and her parents were bringing dessert. "I'm not cooking naked tonight."

That grin didn't diminish.

---

Keith managed to meet her at her car every day after work that week. Tuesday, after taking her to have her car rekeyed, he ran her through a review of basic kickboxing moves at the FBI's indoor training facility. In college, she'd dutifully learned how to kickbox and how to use a variety of firearms as an excuse to get closer to Keith. All those lessons, and he'd never once tried anything. That, and Malcolm had frequently joined them.

This time proved no different, at least until they arrived back at her place.

Wednesday night at his house, she spent the majority of the time naked. They played in the dungeon. He sent her to subspace and let her stay there for a little while before he took her to his bedroom and made love to her.

Thursday she was scheduled at the courthouse. After an exhausting day arguing motions and going through the motions to hear pleas, she was ready to spend some serious downtime kneeling at Keith's feet. In all the years she'd lusted after his body and pined for his affection, she never thought she'd look forward to being naked—or nearly so—and on her knees. She didn't even particularly like feet.

She did like the way it made her feel. When she sat on that oversize pillow and rested her cheek just above his knee, she felt protected, cherished, appreciated, and even loved. She felt whole and happy. He gave her permission not to think about anything but being there with him.

Exiting the building at five always proved to be a slow process. It seemed like a million people were trying to get out at the same time. She knew about half the people flowing in her direction, so she didn't lack for company or conversation.

As freedom came closer, she ran through her mental checklist to make sure she had everything. Now that she was keeping her purse and keys in her briefcase—and her briefcase was in her possession at all times—she was developing a habit of forgetting other things. The day before, she'd forgotten several important files on her desk. She'd left them lying out in the open, which wasn't the custom. Files were supposed to be kept under lock and key. If she wasn't going to take them home, she needed to return them to the records room.

Aaron had shaken his head at her mistake, but he hadn't commented on it as she returned them the next morning. She liked that he wasn't the kind of person to rib her for it or make a big deal out of the lapse.

Once she made it outside, the August heat hit her like a brick wall in the face. Her colleagues scattered in all directions, and someone tapped on her shoulder.

She turned on the wide sidewalk to find a rough-looking woman with her face twisted in a half sneer. The odor of stale cigarettes hung in the vicinity like a disgusting cloud. The woman pointed her finger at Katrina. "I thought you looked familiar. You're my boy's girlfriend?"

Recognition wafted into Katrina's brain on a nicotine courier. "Mrs. Rossetti?"

The sneer melted, and the woman nodded. "You can call me Starr. I knew you was special when he got pissed about me calling you a whore. He don't usually care. Didn't think Keith would ever settle down with one woman. But you're classy, ain'tcha? A lawyer. Not the type he usually dates." Her voice was deep and throaty with the kind of huskiness that came from years of smoking.

Katrina had no idea how to respond to that. She opted for offering a friendly smile. "It's nice to meet you, Starr. I'm Katrina Legato."

Her face scrunched up again. "You related to Malcolm?"

"He's my brother." She didn't know what Starr Rossetti was doing at the courthouse. And then she wondered if Keith's sister, Savannah, was inside one of the holding cells in the basement.

"Look, I know Keith don't want nothin' to do with me. He always wanted a different kind of mother, probably one that liked kids. I don't apologize, cuz it seems to me he turned out just fine. Those other two, though." She shook her head. Strands of pink and gray gleamed from her brassy hair. The ponytail in the back showed evidence the ends had recently been dipped in red. "The one's a lazy, good-for-nothin' drunk. The other just got eight years. Manslaughter, I think. Something like that."

Katrina wondered how in the world Savannah's mother could fail to even know what the charges had been, but she knew better than to ask. "I'm sorry to hear that."

"Keith don't talk about us none, does he?" Her tone was neither angry nor regretful. It was a fact she had already accepted.

That didn't stop Katrina from feeling sympathetic toward the woman. Despite what she said, she was his mother. "No. I'm sorry."

Starr batted her hand as if waving away a bad odor. The stench of cigarettes stirred, but it didn't diminish. "Whatever. You tell him those kids are in the system. I think they go up for adoption next week. I don't want 'em, and Savannah knows she ain't gonna be any good for those kids. Anyway, the state won't let her keep 'em. If he don't want 'em, I guess they can just as well find a new family. He wouldn't listen to me. I'm only telling you because I thought he should know."

With that, Starr Rossetti turned around to leave.

Katrina reached out and snagged Starr by her shoulder. "Wait. What kids? I don't know what you're talking about."

She sighed as if to say she'd washed her hands of the topic and didn't care to revisit it. "Savannah had two kids. I think they're something like four and two, or maybe four and one, or three and one. I don't know. They're little, and the one don't use the toilet. I don't do diapers. Keith's dad dealt with the crap." She paused to laugh at her joke. "But he don't want no kids around neither. We raised ours. We ain't raisin' more."

If Savannah couldn't find a place for them, the state would put them into the foster care system, but it couldn't force her to relinquish her rights. That was a voluntary action.

Katrina played a hunch. "Were they taken away? Has the state terminated her parental rights?"

"I lose track of all her trials. They're living with some family in Roseville, but it's just supposed to be temporary. I don't know. I don't go visit. You gotta ask the social worker." She stabbed a final finger at Katrina. "You tell Keith."

Starr jerked her shoulder from Katrina's grasp and walked away, setting a fast pace that signaled the end of the conversation. Something in the stiffness of her back warned Katrina not to follow.

Keith was likely waiting at her car. She texted him a quick message to let him know she'd been held up, and then she headed back into the courthouse. He might be unwilling to listen to his mother, but Katrina understood the woman's underlying concern. Though Starr wasn't prepared to take them on, she didn't want to see her grandchildren end up with strangers.

The least Katrina could do was look into the matter.

A brief foray into records turned up nothing, mostly because everyone was heading home for the day. Savannah Rossetti's name wasn't in the system. Downstairs in the jail, she searched the sign-in sheets to see who Starr had visited. She'd just found the name Savannah Shaw when she felt the prickle of eyes boring into the back of her head.

Whirling to face the threat, she found Dustin leaning against the far wall. Though it was the end of what had to have been a long day for him too, he managed to look fresh. He smiled and waved.

She lifted a brow. "Are you babysitting me?"

Dustin pushed away from the wall and came closer. "Terrible reception down here. Rossetti tried calling, but he couldn't get through."

In her text, she hadn't reassured him or told him where she'd be or what she was doing. Guilt sat heavy in her chest. "Sorry. I had some last-minute things to do."

Inclining his head at the direction of the papers she'd just returned to the uniformed clerk, he said, "Finished?"

She nodded. Though she had a lot more digging to do, she was reluctant to air Keith's laundry, especially when he didn't know it was hanging out the window. "Is he terribly worried?"

"Yeah." Dustin put his hand on the small of her back and guided her toward the door. It was a subtle alteration of the way he'd always interacted with her, as if the Dom in him acknowledged the sub in her. "I was in the building, so when he called me, I came looking for you."

As soon as they got upstairs, Dustin fired up his cell. "This is Brandt. We're heading your way."

Startled at his officious tone, Katrina angled her body toward him. "Please tell me there's not a whole team watching me."

"There's not a whole team watching you."

His delivery left Katrina feeling unconvinced. "Really?"

He shrugged. "We take care of our own, Trina. You're Legato's sister and Rossetti's sub. That makes you doubly ours."

Did that mean her interaction with Starr had been witnessed? She wasn't ready for Keith to know that, not until she had all the details behind his sister's case.

Before she could say anything more, she heard someone calling to her. Aaron hailed her from across the lobby. He hustled toward her, a stack of files tucked under his arm.

"Katrina. Glad I caught you. I was packing up for the day when I noticed you'd left some files on your desk again." He handed over a stack of folders.

She hadn't left them on her desk—she'd made it a point to check—and they weren't the kinds of things she would normally take home anyway. For the most part, she kept everything she needed on her laptop because it was much easier to transport and access. But she didn't want to rain on Aaron's inept thoughtfulness.

"Thanks." She took the files and shoved them into her already bulging briefcase. As she did, she noticed that many of them weren't relevant to her current caseload. The situation was puzzling, but a waiting Keith came first. "Got any big plans this weekend?"

Aaron usually packed his weekends full of activities. He was an avid hiker. He also liked to camp, and he was known to travel great distances just for a concert or two. He grimaced. "I promised I'd help my mom clean out her basement. She's calling in the favor, so I'm going to be trapped in a hoarder's paradise for two days. Actually, I'm going to get a head start tonight. As long as she doesn't throw a fit when I try to toss out garbage, it shouldn't be too bad."

Katrina laid a sympathetic hand on his arm. "Rent a Dumpster. They haul it away for you."

He laughed, the pathetic sound of a man who knew he was about to embark on a useless endeavor, and then he greeted Dustin. "Agent Brandt, how are you?"

Dustin nodded a polite greeting. "Can't complain, especially not now that I know what you're doing this weekend. Good luck with that."

A few stragglers rushed through the lobby, confirming the lateness of the afternoon. The strange pull in her gut signaled a need for Keith. It had been too long since she'd seen him.

Aaron scratched at a spot on his forehead. "Thanks. I need to get going. I'd offer to walk you to the parking garage, but I can see you're already well guarded."

As he walked away, she debated steering Dustin toward the elevators so she could return the files, but she reasoned that Aaron would notice that she wasn't bringing them back the next morning, and that might hurt his feelings. He'd gone out of his way to bring them to her. "Are you finished for the day?" Dustin's question held no judgment or warning to hurry. "Did you get what you needed from downstairs?"

Across the empty lobby, she spied Jordan speaking on his cell phone. He nodded at her and Dustin but made no move to join them. After several seconds, the elevators opened. He ended his call and stepped inside. Katrina didn't envy him or whomever he had to meet after the end of a long workday.

She didn't want to be the cause of Dustin having to pull a later night at work. "Yes and sort of. I can dig a little deeper tomorrow."

They turned toward the exit nearest the parking garage. As she did, her heavier briefcase slipped from her hand. It hit the floor with a dull thud, and the files fanned out across the shiny terrazzo tiles.

"Crap." The last thing she needed was another delay. Keith was probably waiting for her at home.

Dustin knelt down and helped her gather the files. He read the name of the nearest one. "Snyder. I didn't think you were still on that case."

Katrina shook her head. She'd been removed from that case months ago. Chief Alder had cited the personal nature of her association with several witnesses. She'd meant that her relationships with Malcolm and Darcy could present a conflict of interest. "Aaron means well, but most of these aren't even tangentially related to cases I'm working. I worry for him."

Picking up the next file, Dustin frowned. "Friedman. I thought that case was eyes-only right now. It's an active investigation."

As far as Katrina knew, Dustin was correct. It was on the tip of her tongue to suggest returning the files, but visions of Keith beckoned. "I'll keep hold of them and return them in the morning."

She needed to seriously consider whether to inform the chief of this development. It could mean grave repercussions for somebody, and that gave her pause. What if they'd ended up on her desk as part of an honest mistake? She had no idea how that might have happened, but at least they were safe in her custody.

Dustin made small talk with her until they reached the row where her car was parked. Though she could only make out his outline in the dim structure, she knew it was Keith leaning against her car with one foot propped on the rear bumper.

"He looks angry."

If Dustin heard the worry in her tone, he didn't react to it. "You made him wait."

That knot of longing drawing her to him turned into apprehension. The text she'd sent him hadn't been detailed, nor had it included a time that he should expect her. "He didn't have to wait."

Dustin snorted. "Seriously, Trina? You think he'd just leave you here?"

"You're here." According to him, she'd had a tail the whole day. It wasn't like Keith was part of the detail assigned to her case. Nobody was. As she went through the arguments in her head, she knew none of them would hold up.

So did Dustin. He didn't bother to reply.

They stopped behind her car. Keith's hard stare had her dropping her gaze to fasten it on the concrete floor.

"She had her face buried in the visitor sheets at the county jail."

From the periphery of her vision, she saw Keith nod. He held out his hand, and the two men shook. "Thanks. I'll take it from here."

She felt a little like a prisoner being transferred from state to federal custody. Should she thank Dustin for the escort, or would that only get her in trouble for speaking when she wasn't supposed to? She glanced up, looking to Keith for any kind of signal as to what she should do.

Dustin took care of the problem. He pulled her in for a big hug and a brotherly kiss on the cheek. "Take care, Trina. Hopefully tomorrow isn't a day where you have to spend a lot of time sitting."

With that inspiring comment, Dustin left her alone with Keith.

She returned her gaze to the floor and tried to remain as still as possible. Defensive arguments ran through her head. Arming herself intellectually against anything he might say only made her tenser.

*Re/Paired*

Finally she could stand it no longer. "I'm sorry. I should have let you know how long I'd be."

He crushed her in his arms, holding her so tight she thought she'd suffocate. "I know there are days when you'll have to work late, and there will be plenty of times I won't be able to meet you like this to make sure you're safe."

It was amazing that he'd been able to do it four days in a row. Malcolm was never this consistent, and his lateness was always due to work. Keith must have pulled a lot of strings to be able to watch her this closely.

"But I could at least let you know where I am and when I expect to be done." She wasn't sure how much he understood with her face buried in his chest. The white shirt he wore would likely bear some imprint of what was left of her makeup after this long day.

"That would be thoughtful." He released her a little. She inhaled fresh, oxygenated air.

"Have I earned a punishment?"

The pensiveness of his stare made her feel funny. She was afraid he would refuse to punish her and nervous that he would. Sometime in the past week, she'd come to need that certainty. A simple spanking had the ability to turn her on and chase away her guilt.

For so many years, she'd carried around guilt for deeds great and small. When she said something that somebody took wrong, even though she apologized, she would feel bad about it for weeks afterward. If she disappointed someone or if she passed up a chance to do something thoughtful for another person, the moment would replay in her mind, haunting her at those times when she was most vulnerable, like when she was about to fall asleep.

Certainly she'd messed up with Keith. It wasn't possible to know every single expectation or custom until they'd been together for a while. They'd been friends for years, but not like this.

He shook his head. "No, but now that we've established guidelines for when one of us is going to be late, you will earn a punishment if you ever do this again."

His explanation made the lack of punishment easier to bear. She nodded her understanding of the rule and realized he was holding himself to the same standard. Such a tight manifestation of his morals reflected the man she had always loved.

"It won't happen again."

And she refused to feel guilty for not telling him that his mother had contacted her. Once she knew more about the situation, she would tell him everything. There was no point in rubbing salt in one of his childhood wounds if she didn't have to.

He kissed her forehead and released her. "I'll meet you at your place. We can stay there tonight, but I want you to pack a bag, because you'll be staying with me this weekend."

She tossed the extra files into her trunk, but she stowed her briefcase in the passenger seat of her car.

On the way home, she reflected on the strangeness of the week. If this were a normal relationship for either of them, she wouldn't have spent every night with him. She would have communicated with him in some way—a phone call, a text, or an e-mail—but she probably wouldn't have consented to seeing him more than once or twice during the workweek.

Keith, she knew, had maintained complete control over his girlfriends, though he hadn't been in the habit of seeing them more than a couple days each week. That must have been part of his game, forcing them to await his whim. If he pulled that crap with her, she would boot him to the curb, her years of fantasies be damned. While she truly liked having him assume control of certain aspects of her life, she didn't want to play games with anybody.

She wondered if his level of involvement was due more to the presence of her stalker or because he wanted to see her so much. She muted her radio, put her phone on speaker, and dialed Keith. His car was right behind hers. In retrospect, not carpooling this week was turning out to be a tremendous waste of gas.

"What's wrong, Kitty Kat?" As if he could tell she was growing upset, he purred his greeting.

There was no point in mincing words. "Are you spending so much time with me because you want to or because you're so dedicated to keeping watch over me?"

"Both." He followed her lead and didn't hesitate. "Does it bother you that I'm over so much? Honey, if you need some time alone or a night out with your girlfriends, just tell me. I'm not trying to keep you prisoner or alienate you from your friends."

She didn't think he had been, and given the hours she normally worked, her career was the only thing suffering from lack of attention right now. Her friends were equally busy, so she didn't see them frequently, though she did keep up electronically. "No, that's not it. I just don't want you to feel like you have to spend all your time with me."

# Chapter Ten

Keith was more than a little relieved that Kat wasn't in the car with him. He'd never been one of those Doms who demanded his submissive give up or alter her connections to her family and friends. Those were the things that anchored a person, and they were an integral part of who a person was. And while he hadn't cared much about who his subs were as people, he had always respected their right to nurture other relationships. In fact, he insisted on it, if only to give himself some nights off.

Especially with Kat, he didn't want to impede her life. He wanted to give her more, to make sure somebody took care of her while she was busy taking care of everyone else. He was shocked by her question even though he knew that he had been monopolizing her time. Even when she'd dined with her parents on Monday, he'd been by her side.

"Honey, I don't feel obligated to spend all my time with you." He needed to spend as much time as possible with her. That was completely different. The role reversal—the idea of him being the needy one—was something he hadn't expected. In many ways, he was still acclimating to the fact that he needed her at all, much less that he needed her more than she needed him.

As he pulled into the designated parking slot next to hers, he looked through the glass, caught her eye, and ended the call without another word. She looked shaken, more so than she had when Dustin had delivered her to him and she'd comprehended just how worried they'd all been due to her cryptic text.

He made it to her car door before she could gather her things, and he opened it. Closing it provided an opportunity to cage her against the car. "Want to tell me what's going on in that beautiful, intelligent brain of yours? Are you getting tired of me or tired of being under surveillance?"

"Neither." She focused on his tie and didn't meet his eyes. "I don't like having to be under surveillance, but I understand why it's necessary. I just know how much you hate being tied down."

In the past, he'd used his submissives and tossed them aside if they became clingy. The suffocating feeling set his nerves on edge and reminded him of waking up more than once with his sister pressing a pillow over his face. It was different with Kat. He tried for a lighter tone to put her at ease. "I do prefer to be the one tying *you* down. You look damn sexy wearing nothing but a few ropes."

The rate of her breathing increased as tension fled from her shoulders. She parted her lips and traced her tongue along the inside of the bottom one. Before his eyes, her breasts seemed to swell. He watched the rapid rise and fall of her chest, and he appreciated how well she responded to his dominance and the promise of bondage.

A collar, he decided, and nipple clamps. She was wearing entirely too many clothes. He needed to get her inside before he shoved up her skirt and took her in the parking lot. He wound his fingers around her upper arm. "Come on, Kitty Kat. It seems you need another lesson in how much I want you."

Ever the vigilant agent, he made her wait in the kitchen while he scoped out her condo. Detecting no threats, he had her check things a little more closely. When she returned to the kitchen shaking her head, he noted there had been no incidents since her locks and been changed and security cameras had been installed. Had her stalker been watching, or did he have another way of knowing about the new safety precautions?

Dustin was running checks on all the neighbors, especially those with windows that offered a direct view of Kat's place. It was routine, starting with the closest and most obvious, but Keith didn't think that avenue would yield anything, especially since Dustin was essentially attending to the investigation on his off time. Their immediate boss had approved a preliminary investigation, but she hadn't allocated other resources.

Taking her hand, he tugged her close and fitted her body to his. The tight rein he'd kept on his cock since she'd dropped her gaze in the parking garage eased, and he let her feel the evidence of his desire.

She pressed her hips closer, cradling him with her body, and rested her hands on his chest. She moved them around until she found his nipples. They responded to the light flick of her thumbs, and he wondered at the calculating look in her eyes. But not for long. She pinched them through his shirt.

An unexpectedly sharp pain radiated up his pecs and down to his abs. He struggled to conceal his gasp. No woman had ever dared something like that.

"You like pain." She loosened his tie and unbuttoned his shirt for more access, and he didn't stop her. He wasn't sure whether this counted as topping from the bottom, but he wanted to know if her foray had been a fluke. Yes, he liked pain. But he'd never considered his nipples as sexual organs before.

And he'd only let her get so far before he took over.

She raked her nails down his chest, returning to twist both nipples at the same time. He didn't know how she managed to grasp them, but as the pain throbbed through his system, he gave thanks for her dexterity.

He let her play for a few minutes more, her touch driving him to the brink. Once he got there, he snatched her wrists and imprisoned them behind her back. She gasped at his sudden violence, but her body softened, as did the expression on her face.

"Yes," he said. "I like pain." He'd never admitted that to a submissive before. It proved how in tune she was with him, to have picked up on that tiny detail. Malcolm had mentioned it before, but in a way that everyone could assume was facetious.

He devoured her with his kiss, pouring his need to possess her into that one act. Waves of heat, generated by her mouth and her pussy, called to him. He plunged his tongue between her lips, taking her so violently that she couldn't hope to participate in the kiss. She softened even more, yielding heart and soul.

Then he broke it off suddenly. "Turn around and bend over. Brace your hands on the floor."

The need to possess her drove him. She needed this reassurance that she belonged to him, that he wanted nothing but what she could give to him. And she needed to be reminded of her place. She might not want to use titles, and she was new to being a submissive in practice, but he couldn't be too lenient. It marked how much he cared about her that he took the time to remind her of her role. In the past, a woman who took the liberties Kat had would have been shown the door.

The position made her skirt stretch tightly over her fine ass. He lifted the dove-gray material to find those delectable cheeks split by the electric-blue thong he'd purchased. His cock, already hard, reared up and surged forward. It wanted freedom.

He nudged the inside of her high heel. "Spread your legs a little wider, Kitty Kat. And turn your toes inward a bit." It would help her balance. He had no intention of being gentle.

With one finger, he drew away the string of her thong. Heat and silken softness gripped the head of his cock and pulled him deeper. Immediately she clenched her vaginal muscles. White edged his vision, pleasure mixed with pain. Even in this physically demanding position, she was seeing to his needs.

He held her hips, anchoring her where he wanted her, and fucked her with everything he had. The creamy slurp of her arousal was answered with the smack of his hips against her ass. This was hard and wet, meant to confirm her submissiveness, not to give her an orgasm.

In another turnaround, he refused to come until she did. Gone was his need to deny her an orgasm just because he didn't want to hold off long enough to see to her pleasure. She could experience the affirmation and ride the sweet endorphin rush that, according to the way her walls sucked at him, was imminent.

She made desperate, guttural noises that threatened to drive him over the edge.

"That's it, Kitty Kat. Come for me." Drawing on the last of his reserves, he increased his pace. "For me."

She shouted his name, screaming loud enough to alert anyone near the condo that she was having an orgasm. He pounded into her four more times before he couldn't hold off his climax any longer.

He lifted her up and into his arms, not bothering to fix his pants first. Collapsing against the counter that divided her kitchen and dining areas, he held her tightly against him. She trembled and clung to him, and a single sob escaped her throat.

"I've got you, honey. You're safe."

If possible, her grip intensified. "I know I'm safe with you. I think it's all the time I spend away from you that gets to me. I...I've never been a needy person, and needing you like this scares me a little."

The weight of the worry pressing down on his shoulders threatened to topple him. "We'll find that bastard, Kat."

She shook her head, but because she refused to lift her face away from his shirt, it ended up being a tiny movement he felt rather than saw. He was also sure he was now wearing her mascara on his white dress shirt, but he didn't mind that so much.

"He doesn't even matter in all this." She sniffled and looked up at last, but she kept her eyes downcast. The remnants of tears glinted from her eyelashes. "You make me feel such extreme emotions, and I've developed a powerful attachment to you. I like knowing I belong to you, that you'll take care of me, that you'll take pleasure in my body and then I can spend some time with my head against your knee and your hand moving through my hair."

Kat was a capable, independent woman. There was no disputing facts. However, she harbored the sweet soul of a submissive. All these years, she'd spent enormous amounts of time and energy trying to please everyone in her life. Now she could concentrate those intentions on him, and she was finding the comfort in being needed. Happiness soared through him.

He hooked his finger under her chin and forced her to look him in the eye. "There's nothing wrong with any of that, honey. I promise I'll always cherish you and the gift of your submission. There is nothing on this earth more precious to me than you."

Not one for tender words or loving declarations, he expected the reassurance to lodge in his throat, but it didn't. His pride thoroughly approved, and some of the scars on his heart softened. For the first time in his life, love filled his chest, and it didn't hurt. He meant to tell her. He even opened his mouth, but the doorbell rang, cutting him off and putting him on high alert. They weren't expecting visitors.

He fixed his pants and pulled a small piece from the holster in his jacket, checked the chamber, and handed it to her. "If I don't call out that it's all clear, you shoot whoever comes up those stairs. Got it?"

She had good aim. He or Malcolm took her and her mother to the gun range regularly to keep their skills sharp. He didn't worry about the actuality of her having to shoot someone. The pervert would have to go through him first.

Kat studied him, the passion dimming slowly from her eyes, replaced with concern. "Do you really think my stalker would knock?"

They hadn't experienced activity in five days. Stalkers tended to lie low after a larger event to lull their victim into a false sense of security. People took chances when they didn't have their guard up. Neither he nor Malcolm would allow Kat to take risks. They were both too protective of the ones they loved. "Don't know," he said. "As time passes and nobody catches him, he'll become more confident. His actions will escalate. He might even become bold enough to knock at your door, pretending to be lost or something."

She pressed her lips together, girding herself for whatever happened, and nodded her understanding. By the time he'd crossed her small eating area, she'd smoothed out her clothes.

Her door didn't have a peephole. The only window down at her entryway was above the door. It let in light, but the angle of the steps coming down didn't allow for a preview of the visitor, and the cameras they'd aimed at the door weren't set up to record faces. Another flaw of the building design. Kat was going to need to sell her unit. Even after they caught her stalker, there was no way he was going to let her stay in a place so difficult to secure. In the meantime, Malcolm had to build a better camera, and Keith would pay a visit to a home improvement store to get a peephole. They weren't difficult to install.

Throwing open the door, he centered his gun on the figure standing there.

Darcy's jaw dropped open, but she froze instead of clutching her chest. Or the little bump showing on her abdomen. That would have been worse.

Keith holstered his weapon. "Sorry. You didn't call, and we don't have a live feed set up to show who's at the door."

She closed her mouth and smiled, completely composed despite the circumstances of his greeting, and he was reminded of how well she'd kept it together during the bust that had nearly cost him his friendship with Malcolm. "Now I really, really have to use the bathroom." Her blue eyes sparkled, and he was relieved to realize she hadn't taken it personally.

He stepped out of her way, pivoting to call up the stairs. "All clear, Kat. It's Darcy."

Darcy squeezed his arm as she swept past him. She almost never passed up the opportunity to touch him in some reassuring or friendly way. He wondered if Malcolm had told her about Keith's aversion to uninvited touching.

Few people who attempted casual contact didn't set off Keith's internal alarms. While Darcy didn't trip any warning wires, he still wasn't sure exactly how to treat her. The friendly, welcoming manner in which she always treated him was at odds with the wariness to which submissives instinctively reverted around him. Even many people who didn't consciously identify as submissive bowed to his authority. No doubt about it: his best friend had netted a singular woman.

Since he was at the door, he did a visual sweep of the area before returning to the main floor. Kat waited for him in the kitchen, her eyes wild and questioning. He felt a tightening in his chest, because he knew she was worried that Malcolm would find out about them. Though he knew Malcolm would be pissed initially, he preferred to be open about their relationship. If he wasn't concerned, why should she be?

Kat handed the gun back to him and smoothed her hands over her clothes. Her attempts at fixing her appearance only made him want to tear her clothes off so he could watch her hands run over her naked flesh. "Where is Mal?"

Keith shook his head. "I didn't see his car."

"He's picking up some Thai food." Darcy breezed into the kitchen, a bright smile lighting her face. "I asked him to drop me off first so I could use the bathroom. He was supposed to call."

Kat extracted her phone from her purse. "Yep. He called about thirty seconds ago. It went right to voice mail. I hate when it does that."

"So anyway, unless you guys want to explain to Malcolm why you both look like you just had sex, I'd go clean up." She leveled a firm look at Kat. "Wash your face. Maybe change into something less wrinkled. I'll call him and let him know you're safe so he doesn't come zooming back without food. I'm too hungry to wait for him to process all this before I eat."

Keith used the guest bathroom. He didn't have much to fix. His dishabille was the result of hastily pulling his pants into place and a misbuttoned shirt. He had been chasing bad guys today, so a few stains on his shirt would go unremarked. Kat did look like she'd been well and truly loved. Her lips were a bit swollen, and her makeup had run when she'd cried.

He returned to find Darcy relaxing on a chair in the living room, the remote in her hand. She'd turned on a home improvement show. Seeing him, she blushed. "I can't seem to stop watching these shows. Malcolm is going to kill me if I ask him about redecorating or remodeling another thing. I've already changed my mind about the baby's room a dozen times and told him I didn't like his living room furniture. That black leather sofa needs to die."

Keith grimaced. Malcolm had searched for almost six months before he found a couch he liked. It was a distinctly masculine sectional, and Darcy's home decor walked a fine line between classical and modern.

He sat on the sofa and leaned forward. "You sent Malcolm out for food because you didn't want him to catch us. How did you know?"

She seemed to chew on that one for a while. Thoughts marched through the shifting frowns on her face until she settled on something. "I didn't know. I suspected. She said a few things last weekend when we were alone that made me think she was seeing somebody, and then I noticed the way you were looking at her. You've always looked at her like you were half in love, but this was different. More possessive. You looked at her the way a Dom looks at his sub, and that was new. She responds to you differently now. And just a few minutes ago, she looked like a well-satisfied sub. It's a great feeling, though it does sometimes leave your face a mess. I'll have to give her some makeup tips."

"Why would you keep this from Malcolm?" He had a list of questions, and that meant their conversation was going to come off sounding more like an interrogation. He knew he had to be careful—Darcy wasn't fond of being questioned like this—but he needed answers. Plus he was baffled that she would keep this from her Master.

"I won't for long." Her ice-blue gaze chilled him, and he understood that she didn't like deceiving Mal. "However, I recognize that it's your place to tell him, so I'll give you one week. He isn't going to be happy about it, especially if it comes from me. At least if you tell him, you can explain. Assure him that your intentions are pure."

His intentions were anything but pure. Honorable, maybe, but also carnal and primal. "Kat doesn't want him to know."

"No, I don't expect she does. She'll go to any length to protect the people in her life, won't she?" Darcy muted the TV and turned to face him fully. "I bet she's struggling with lots of guilt, though. Lying doesn't sit well with her. That's a good thing. Lies ruin relationships."

Yes, his Kitty Kat went out of her way to avoid hurting people's feelings. He loved that about her. But guilt was definitely becoming a factor. It did eat at her from the inside. He nodded at Darcy in agreement. "I'll talk to her about it."

With that, Darcy took one step closer to becoming one of the few women he trusted. The rest of his questions sidled away, of lesser importance now that he understood her position.

"Have you called your sister?"

Though her volume dropped, Keith jumped visibly. Of course Malcolm told her everything. After lying to her the way he had when they met, he probably went out of his way to make it up to her by telling her more than she had a right to know.

"Why would I do that?"

She seemed taken aback by the derision in his voice. He watched her struggle to find the right response.

He strived for a gentler tone. "Whatever Malcolm has told you, it can't be the whole story if you think I would contact any of those people." Of course, Mal thought he should contact his sister, so Darcy probably shared his opinion.

Kat emerged from the hallway. She'd exchanged her power skirt for a pair of white shorts and a fitted blue cotton shirt. The cut of the shorts emphasized the sexy length of her legs, and the brightness of the white highlighted her olive complexion. Keith shifted to ease the growing discomfort in his pants.

"What people?" She sat down next to him, though he noticed the longing look she cast at the spot on the floor near his feet. The ache in his balls grew.

He sighed and braced to hear the same speech from Kat that Malcolm had given him last week. "My sister has been calling, leaving messages for me at work."

Her eyes didn't widen with surprise or sympathy. "And your mother was trying to talk to you Sunday."

"Malcolm is under the impression that you were going to at least call. He thought he'd convinced you to take a chance on your sister." Darcy's eyes widened as she made the connection. Then she laughed. "But you decided to take a chance with his sister. Oh, he's going to love the irony. Eventually."

Keith wasn't sure about that, but he didn't get a chance to respond. Kat clasped her hands together, worrying them in her lap. "He's not going to get the chance. I'm not ready for him to know." She cast an apologetic look at him. "I'm not ready to face his anger, and I haven't even told my parents yet."

He wanted to reassure her, but he also knew he needed to push her on this issue. This was an ideal area for him to assert his dominance. "Darcy's promised us one week to get ready. She's a good sub, and we're putting her in a bad position by asking her to keep this from Mal."

Darcy's phone trilled. "That's Malcolm. I called to let him know that I was right and you guys were fine." She picked up the phone and motioned to the front door, mouthing the words *He's here.*

The promise of a week's reprieve seemed to have relaxed Kat, but Keith wasn't similarly comforted. Malcolm was far from stupid, and if Darcy had noticed the way he looked at Kat, then it was only a matter of time before Malcolm noticed as well.

He decided to let Kat spend some more time in her bubble before he was forced to pop it. Perhaps giving her a deadline would help her mentally prepare for the coming-out process. Darcy coming over had turned out to be a good thing.

Malcolm had brought more carryout than four people could possibly eat at one sitting. Kat surveyed the number of paper sacks brimming with hot deliciousness that Malcolm managed to carry inside.

"Jesus, Mal. How many more people are coming?"

Malcolm grinned and kissed his sister on the cheek. "The way Darcy's craving any kind of Asian food out there, I'm going to need these leftovers. She'll go through them in a day or two."

Halfway through dinner, many of the cartons of food had ended up untouched. It wasn't due to lack of trying, though. Once they all slowed down—even Darcy, who had packed away an impressive amount—conversation began to flow.

"The Holbrook case is going to break wide open this weekend." Malcolm stabbed a fork into his rice as he spoke.

Kat regarded her brother with her eyebrows drawn together. "I thought the investigative portion of that case was finished. It's set to go to trial in two months."

This didn't come as much of a surprise to Keith. He'd heard rumblings before he'd left the office, but he'd been too intent on getting to Kat to stay to hear the details.

"So did I, but an informant in another case gave up some juicy intel. Jordan had a hush-hush meeting with Elizabeth Alder today." Malcolm lifted his gaze and regarded Kat with a somber expression.

Keith understood the implication of Mal's look. A meeting with her boss meant that warrants had been requested or a battle strategy had been hatched, or both. With her safety in question, the risk factor had officially increased, especially since a large break like this could pull dozens of people from other, less important cases. Like hers.

Malcolm continued. "Keith and I are both active in this case. We have to be there this weekend, which means you can either stay with Darcy or stay with Mom and Dad."

Kat sidled a troubled glance in his direction that he interpreted to indicate she didn't want to be away from him at all, but she understood what it was like to be with an agent. Then she grinned at Darcy. "Sounds like a girls' night out to me."

"In," Keith corrected. "Girls' night *in*. You guys can paint your toenails and watch chick flicks."

Both Kat and Darcy cast affronted looks in his direction. He didn't understand what he'd said wrong.

Kat licked her lips. He followed the tantalizing move and vowed to kick Malcolm out as soon as possible. He wanted to see her pink tongue wrapped around his dick, her naked pussy perched over his face. "You have no idea what women do when men aren't around, do you?"

The visions that leaped into his head probably weren't the visions she'd intended.

Across the table, Malcolm frowned. "I'm not sure we want to know."

But Darcy had already moved on. "We can invite Layla and my sister Amy. It'll be fun."

The two women exchanged smiles. Malcolm looked exceptionally pleased that his fiancée and his sister were bonding. He'd only begun bringing Darcy around a few months ago, and it was important to him that she become friends with those closest to him.

For the first time, Keith's apprehension fled, and he regarded Darcy as a full member of his family.

But he noticed that Kat never fully relaxed.

―――――

Keith closed the door behind Malcolm and Darcy. The sharp click of the dead bolt echoed up the stairwell. Kat jumped at the sound. Her nerves had been on edge throughout dinner, growing markedly shakier as time passed. She knew Darcy didn't plan to say anything to Malcolm until her deadline elapsed, so he didn't understand why she seemed to be unraveling before his eyes. Did the possible fallout from revealing their relationship to her brother really cause her so much emotional pain? It distressed him to see her upset like this. He had to do something about it.

"I want to see you kneeling naked on your bedroom floor in five minutes."

Her chocolate gaze rose when he began speaking, but then it dropped off and fastened on the steps to her left. "Keith, I'm really not in the mood for—"

Pressing his finger to her lips, he cut the flow of her weak protest. "Your wishes are inconsequential right now. Time's ticking. Four and a half minutes left."

He kept his tone gentle. The countdown wasn't fair or accurate, but that mattered little. She needed this. Her emotions were rioting out of control, and it fell to him to help her deal with them. It was less a matter of her wishes being inconsequential than it was that he understood what she needed.

She didn't say anything more as she turned away and climbed the stairs to the main floor. His order hadn't calmed her one bit. It would take time and experience for her to realize he had her best interests at heart. This was new territory for him. In the past when he'd given an order like that, he really hadn't cared what his submissive wanted. Guilt washed over him at the thought of the callous way he'd treated the women who'd given themselves to him. To a certain extent, he'd drowned in them the same way he'd once escaped into the bottom of a bottle. No more of that. He bid a final farewell to that hollow existence. Kat had opened his heart, and he was discovering the depths of caring and generosity he'd long ago locked away.

Slowly he followed the melancholy shadows of her recent path. The kitchen and dining areas were clean. Darcy and Malcolm had helped with that before they left. He liked that Darcy didn't hesitate to pitch in and help with dishes. Malcolm and Kat had been raised that way. Keith's parents hadn't cared about cleaning one way or the other. His nearly obsessive fastidiousness was a reaction to the chaos and filth of his youth.

He checked all the windows, as he did every night, closed the living room curtains, and shut off the light. Then he freshened up in the guest bathroom. His bag of tricks was in the hall closet. He extracted a coiled length of rope, but he didn't need anything else from there. Tonight Kat needed to know she belonged to him more than she needed the escape a bit of prolonged pain might offer.

Though he was early, he found her kneeling obediently as he'd ordered. A visual sweep of the room confirmed that she'd closed the curtains to ensure their privacy. He crossed over to her slider to check that the door leading to the balcony was locked behind those heavy drapes. Then he checked the single window.

After turning around, he paused to study her. She faced a little to his right, so he had a three-quarter view of her body. She sat with her bottom resting on her heels, knees spread, and her hands were clasped behind her back. Her steady gaze didn't waver from a point on the floor just in front of her body. She trembled, and he figured it was equal parts nerves and the effort of holding that position.

When he felt her nerves had stretched nearly to the breaking point, which didn't take long, he strolled across the room. He stopped and stood with one foot on either side of her leg. She quivered from the effect of his nearness, but she didn't move. Wordlessly he reached out and ran his fingers through her hair. He shifted, putting his leg in closer proximity to her head, and urged her to rest her cheek against his thigh. She exhaled and relaxed, immediately surrendering to his will. The sweetness of her body heat radiated through the material of his pants. He'd never seen such beauty in submission, such grace and trust, as he saw right now. She stole his breath.

And so he sat there for a few minutes and let the simple essence of their combined existence wash through him, cleansing away the accumulated cynicism and filth that came from a lifetime of living in the dark. He ached to tell her that he loved her, but the words stuck like sand in his throat. *Baby steps.* He couldn't let his insufficiencies affect her. Right now, she needed his strength.

"Submission isn't just about power or possession. It's the ultimate show of trust." A confidence he'd falsely held until now. "It's also about having the security of knowing you can and will rely on me to see to your needs. Do you know what you need, my Kitty Kat?"

She didn't tense a muscle or otherwise shift, and when she spoke, her voice was laced with sadness. "No."

He stroked his hand down her hair again and again, tucking stray strands behind her ear. "You need to stop pretending this isn't upsetting you. Being watched by an anonymous person who wishes you harm, being tailed by federal agents, being forced to be with me all the time—all these things are wearing on you. It's okay to be afraid, and it's okay to expect me to support you through this. Through everything, Kat. I mean that."

Her jaw flexed. He wasn't sure if she had something to say or if she was grinding her teeth.

"You have permission to speak."

"I only wanted to say that I don't mind spending all this time with you, though I suppose it's wearing on you. I know how much you need alone time to regroup." She pressed her face harder against his thigh, her shoulders taut.

Yes, he was known for having little patience with most people. He continued caressing her hair until she relaxed again. "Being with you isn't like being with anyone else. You're an essential part of me. I want to take care of you. I *need* to take care of you."

Abruptly he released his hold on her and stepped back. Her gaze didn't waver, and he felt a sense of pride at how far she'd come in just one week. He knew she was curious, but this proved she trusted him to see to her needs.

Kneeling in front of her, he cupped her face in his hands. She lifted her gaze then, meeting his with unspoken meaning. All defenses were stripped away, and he could see the depth of her fear and vulnerability. Now that they'd acknowledged these feelings, he could work on helping her deal with them.

Her lush lips quivered and parted, inviting him closer. He took careful advantage of her plea, kissing her with gentle possessiveness. She moaned, and he felt her whole body sway closer. Her arms didn't move. It was imperfect obedience, a lack of control as she surrendered even more.

Keith wasn't intent on making her demonstrate control or master anything tonight. He wanted to show her that he was her rock, and he was made of sturdy stuff. He ended the kiss and dotted smaller smooches along her temples and cheekbones, ending with a barely-there trace of lips over her eyelids.

She sighed contentedly.

He allowed her to bask in the tenderness. Then he stood, lifting her so that she got to her feet with him. He took a moment to make sure she was steady before releasing her from his hold.

The coiled rope he'd tossed on her bed waited for the next part of his plan. He measured off several feet before he wrapped it around her lower arm. This extra would be used to finish the design.

Next he crossed her arm under her breasts, looping and tying the line to ensure she couldn't move her arm. Then he did the same thing to her other arm. When he finished, her arms were bound to her torso in a forced hug. This pose exemplified her vulnerabilities, plumped her breasts in offering, and provided a bit of comfort at the same time.

He circled her body, checking the tightness and fit. "How does it feel?"

"Confining." She sounded breathless. "I feel so helpless, but I know you'll take care of me."

Tying a sub with her body spread exposed them. Bindings like this sometimes triggered claustrophobic sensations. It forced her to touch herself, to acknowledge the truth of her position.

He feathered another few kisses over her eyelids, cheeks, and lips. "Always, Kitty Kat. I'll always take care of you, no matter what."

Taking three steps back, he put some distance between them. This wasn't intended to make her feel lonely, though her shiver and the way she dropped her gaze indicated that she thought so.

"Look at me."

He waited until she complied before he continued with his plan. First he went for his tie, loosening it slowly. He pulled it away and let it fall to the floor. She watched, the line of her gaze following it down briefly before snapping back to his face. He waited, and she didn't disappoint. Realization dawned in her expression. While the outward evidence of her vulnerability didn't disappear, it lessened, morphing to desire as she figured out that he was stripping for her.

Next he removed his belt and tossed it aside. Her lips parted as she inhaled a shaky breath. He loved how much he affected her, and he treasured the fact that she didn't hide it.

By the time he'd opened his shirt, she was regarding him with a hungry expression, and the faint scent of her arousal tickled his senses. His muscles were hard and long, cording his arms and legs and defining his abs. He worked out regularly, punishing bouts of exercise that happened mostly in the training gym at work, and so he knew how good he looked.

When he was fully naked, he stood motionless before her and gave her a visual feast. He drew out the moments, savoring the desperate heat radiating from her very being. Then he turned away, smiling at her whimper of protest, and settled himself on the center of her bed.

"Come here, Kitty Kat."

She scurried over, climbing onto the mattress with a graceful agility difficult to achieve without the use of arms to aid in balance. He was impressed.

"Straddle me."

This order was followed to the letter. His cock was up for the job, but it wouldn't be easy for her to do it alone. He dipped the tip into her juices and slid it around, teasing a pleading cry from the back of her throat.

At last he gave her what she wanted. She sank down on him eagerly, moving her hips to find the right rhythm and still keep her balance. Keith luxuriated in the silken heat of her tight sheath, but when she increased her pace, he slowed her with an authoritative hand on her hip.

"Slow, Kitty Kat. There's no hurry. We've got all night." Though if she kept clenching around him as she'd developed a habit of doing, he wasn't going to last nearly as long as he wanted. She was gifted at delivering just the right amount of pain to ratchet up the intensity of his orgasm. "Relax. No squeezing."

She opened her mouth to protest. He hadn't made a secret of how much he loved when she exerted extra pressure.

Pressing one finger to her lips, he said, "I hope you aren't thinking of arguing with me."

That effectively squelched anything she might have said. With that concern out of the way, she could concentrate on her own pleasure. Soon tiny moans and squeaks poured from her, and he felt small flutters as her vaginal walls contracted around him.

He tightened his hands on her hips and forced her to stop.

"Master?"

Her question nearly undid him, not because she questioned his actions, but because she only called him by that name when she felt the comfort and safety of her submission.

"Lift up and turn around. You're going to ride reverse-cowboy-style."

She'd been close to climaxing, but it wasn't going to be enough to take her to the level she needed tonight. A huge helping of orgasm denial would do far more to help her deal with the complex coil of emotions knocking around inside her.

This time, she wasn't so graceful. He helped her turn around and get into position, taking advantage of the opportunity to run his hands all over her body. She arched her breasts into his palms. He kneaded the small mounds and pinched her nipples until she threw her head back and murmured, "Yes."

Then he positioned his cock at her entrance and grasped her hips as she sank down once again. With her arms bound, it would be even more difficult for her to balance this way. She would have to concentrate harder, another thing that would help deny her the chance to climax. "Slow, Kitty Kat. I want to savor the way you feel around me."

At first her movements were sporadic and lacked rhythm. After about a minute, she found a pace that worked. The whole time, he kept his hands on her hips to help her stay upright, and he talked to her, speaking reverent words of praise and encouragement.

When something wet fell on his thigh, he immediately recognized it as a tear. Moving with the utmost care, he shifted under her until he sat up with his legs tucked underneath his ass. He pulled her back until she rested against his chest. This position forced his cock to press hard against her abdomen. The small bit of sharp pain nearly finished him. Through sheer strength of will, he refrained from ejaculating.

He wrapped his arms over hers, fortifying the self-hug he'd forced on her. Another tear landed on his arm, but he made no move to wipe them away or quiet her.

"Am I hurting you?" He didn't think he was, but he had to make sure.

She shook her head.

"Talk to me, then. Tell me what's wrong."

She shook her head again. "Nothing's wrong. Everything is right. It's just that when I'm not with you, like this, after you've checked all the doors and windows, this feeling goes away. I hate looking over my shoulder all the time. I hate the way my heart races for a few seconds when I'm in court and I get the feeling somebody's watching me. I never used to notice the other people in the courtroom, the ones waiting for their cases to be called. Now I can't stop."

He'd known she was trying to put a positive spin on her circumstances. Denial was going to eat her alive if he let her go on much longer without letting it out. Another tear splattered on his wrist.

"I've always gone out of my way to be nice to people, even if that just meant asking about their day. But now I find myself looking at everyone and wondering if they're the one who broke into my bedroom and stole my underwear. I feel bad about not being so friendly. I feel guilty for suspecting my friends. And I feel so completely helpless. I hate it."

She really broke down now. He held her in his arms as she sobbed. Inside her, his cock softened a little. The sight of her tears only turned him on when they were shed from pleasurable pain or sexual frustration. This cut him to the quick. He'd driven her here because she needed to deal with these emotions, but that didn't mean he liked it. He turned her in his arms and untied the rope. Then he scooted back until he could lie against the pillows and hold her as she cried.

Kat clung to him, and for the first time in his life, he felt peace instead of revulsion when a woman looked to him for emotional support, and he understood what it truly meant to be a Dom.

When her tears subsided, he wet a cloth and wiped her face. Then he kissed her, telling her without words all the tender things he felt for her but couldn't give voice to just yet. There would be time enough for that later.

She kissed him back, and he slipped into her silky warmth and made love to the woman he'd dreamed about for so long.

# Chapter Eleven

Catching sight of Aaron through the open door of the file room as she searched for the right drawers, Katrina cringed at his appearance. He looked as if he hadn't slept at all the night before. From her vantage point, she could make out the dark circles under his eyes and the wrinkles in his clothes. If she wasn't mistaken, he was wearing the same suit from yesterday. It didn't look like cleaning out his mother's basement had gone well.

Her night hadn't started out much better, even though she usually loved when a family member dropped by to visit, but Keith's dominance had made a difference. He'd forced her to break down and face her fears. Things hadn't improved. It still sucked to have a stalker, but now she knew that he was there for her in all the ways she needed to be supported.

She finished putting away the files Aaron had been so thoughtful about bringing to her and rose to her feet. "Hey, you. Feeling okay?"

He exhaled loudly and flopped down on the chair at his desk. "I'm okay. I lost track of time and worked all night. No coffee for you today. Sorry."

"That's okay. I don't expect you to bring me coffee." She really didn't. Though she liked a strong cup or two in the morning, she rarely drank it during the day. Still, she appreciated his thoughtfulness. "I have to run out in a few minutes. I should be back in time for lunch. Did you want to meet? My treat."

A bit of life sparkled through his eyes, and he managed a smile that seemed to cost him a great deal of effort. "I think I'm going to clear my schedule this afternoon and go home. Now that I'm sitting down, last night is starting to catch up to me."

While she could offer to take on some of his duties, it would mean using up the part of her day she'd set aside to investigate the situation with Keith's sister. Choosing presented no contest. Keith was her priority.

Aaron ran a hand through his hair, further beating down the tracks that were already there. "Hey, I think I accidentally gave you some of my files yesterday. Do you have those handy?"

She shook her head. "I wondered about that. None of them were mine. I just finished refiling them. You'd better be careful, Aaron. You had some files that shouldn't leave the office. I know you have a lot going on, but that kind of mistake can ruin a career."

He pressed his lips into a thin line and peered at her strangely. Then he dropped his gaze to focus on his computer screen. "Thanks for the advice."

Snatches of her conversation with Jordan came back to her. He'd mentioned evidence logs, but they had to sign out files as well. She had a brief sense of uneasiness, and then she shook away that feeling. A bad night spent cleaning out his mother's basement didn't change who he was. Having a stalker was definitely fraying her sensibilities.

Her first deposition of the day was scheduled to begin in a few minutes. She gathered her paperwork and patted him on the shoulder. "Get some rest. I'll bring the coffee tomorrow."

Looking up, he gave her a curious frown, but then he shook his head, and the expression disappeared. "Sure. I'll be here."

Katrina had a half hour of free time after scarfing her lunch. She used that time to search the DOJ database for Savannah Shaw. It didn't take long to find out that Keith's sister had been convicted of three counts of vehicular manslaughter. That, coupled with charges of possession, theft, vandalism, and the more serious DUI charges, had netted her the maximum. She'd be lucky to see daylight in twenty years.

Other than a notation about an upcoming appearance in family court, Katrina couldn't find specifics on the kids. It made sense. Records concerning minors were sealed, and that wasn't limited to criminal charges. She would need to make a trip to

Child and Family Services to find the right caseworker, though that guaranteed nothing.

She tapped her fingernail on her desk three times before she made the decision. The Women's Huron Valley Correctional Facility was in Ypsilanti. It was out of her way, so she rearranged her schedule, informed Dustin of her whereabouts, and headed west.

The prison didn't look like much from the outside, but Katrina figured that was the point. It wasn't supposed to be a desirable place to visit. Because visits were only allowed on Sundays, Katrina walked an ethical line and used her credentials to get an audience.

Fifteen minutes later, Savannah Shaw plopped down in a chair on the opposite side of the table. A guard handcuffed her to a bar welded to the top. Katrina looked over Keith's sister.

Dark blonde roots were slowly replacing the dull platinum dye job with something that looked far better. In addition to hair color, she shared Keith's emerald-green eyes and general face structure. Savannah Shaw was the feminine version of her brother. The woman was about the same height as Katrina, but that was the only similarity. Savannah had generous curves that made her orange jumpsuit tight across the hips and breasts.

She blinked at Katrina twice, a scowl forming almost instantly. "Who're you?"

Katrina extended her hand. "I'm Katrina Legato, a friend of your brother."

In one contemptuous gesture, Savannah looked at and dismissed the proffered hand. "You're a lawyer."

Lowering her hand to the table, Katrina nodded. "I am. But that's not why I'm here. Your mother visited me yesterday. She's concerned about your children."

Savannah rolled her eyes. "I told her to leave them be. What's she doing now?"

"Nothing." Katrina wondered how Savannah felt about not being able to raise her kids, or the fact that her mother had no

*Re/Paired*

plans to step up and take care of them. "She wanted me to tell Keith they were in the system and that they might be adopted soon. I wanted to meet you, to have the whole story before I said anything to Keith."

A tinge of bitterness twitched across Savannah's face. "So why do you care? Don't tell me Keith sent you, cuz I know that'd be a lie. I bet he don't even know you're here."

Katrina regarded her solemnly. "You'd win that bet. Your mother tried talking to him, but he wouldn't listen. He doesn't want anything to do with you guys."

Her husky chuckle turned into a coughing fit. "Sounds right. He was an asshole from day one. I had to share a room with him and my sister. Fucker cried all the time. Probably still a whiny brat." She sat forward, folding her hands on the table. Her nails were chewed to the quick, and her hands were lined and worn years before their time. "So what's your story? You think if you agree to play Mommy to my bastards, he'll stay with you? I got news for you, darlin'. You're just another one of his pretty whores. He's gonna make you do all sorts of degrading and humiliating things. Then he's gonna toss you aside with the rest of his bitches. That boy is fucked in the head."

Hearing his sister talk about him that way rankled, but Katrina wasn't here to defend Keith's kinky side. She brushed away Savannah's poisonous words with a dismissive wave of her hand. "Do you have custody of the children, or does the state?"

Savannah studied her with an intensity that would have disarmed her if she hadn't already been on the receiving end of that kind of stare. She knew better than to flinch. Several long minutes of silence passed. Finally, Savannah sat back in her chair and looking as casual as she could with her hands cuffed in front of her.

"Court date is a week from next Thursday. I'm going to voluntarily give them over. I'm doing a minimum of twenty years. I asked my mom to take them, but my bastard of a father don't want them. He's always hated kids. Don't know why he had any." She picked at the edge of the table, and there was a fragile helplessness in the firm set of her mouth.

Katrina felt a little sorry for her. "How old are they?"

Savannah's expression softened. Her entire demeanor changed, and cracks of vulnerability showed for the first time. "Angelina is three, and Corey is eleven months. They're good kids. They should have a good home. Lord knows I never did anything much for them." She shook her head, a wealth of regret in the action. "About ten years ago? No. Maybe eight or nine, whenever Keith got sober, he came around and told us that if we didn't all stop drinking, he wouldn't have no more to do with us. I been sober for three months now. It sucks, but I guess I woulda done it sooner if I'd known I'd lose my kids."

It took Katrina a minute to digest all that. She'd known Keith for eleven years, and she'd never once seen him take a drink. True, he'd been in the military then, and she'd only seen him when he was home on leave, but he'd never seemed intoxicated.

She couldn't go into any of that now. Though she wasn't sure what her next steps should be, she regarded Savannah steadily. "I'm not making any promises." Keith hated his sister, and he wasn't big on kids. He tolerated her nephews pretty well, but like her, he was relieved to leave them with their parents.

Savannah let loose that husky chuckle again. "You lawyer types never do. Look, don't ask Keith to take them. He don't owe me. But you seem like a decent person. Can't you just make sure they end up with a good family? That's all I want."

Katrina could do that for the sake of two innocent kids. "I'll do what I can. Thank you for meeting with me."

As she drove back to Detroit, she wrestled with the paths unfolding before her. If she told Keith about the situation, he would get mad at her for sticking her nose into his business. That was a given. She didn't think he would want to punish her for it, and for that she was a little regretful. She'd rather face a spanking than his displeasure.

Was this something he really wanted to know about? His mother had tried to talk to him, and she was obviously trying to manipulate Katrina. Katrina didn't know how much Keith's mother had been able to say before Keith cut her off. He wouldn't do anything for his sister's sake. This was the woman who had made his childhood a living hell. He had been clear that he wanted nothing to do with those people.

Even so, she would follow through on her promise and ensure those kids ended up in a good home. Now that she had their names, it would be easier to track down their caseworker.

And she needed more time to think about the other thing his sister had revealed. Why hadn't anyone ever told her that Keith was an alcoholic? Surely Malcolm knew. Did her parents? Though she could understand why Mal would keep this to himself, why had Keith never said a word? Was he ashamed, or did he want to forget he'd ever been ruled by addiction?

She couldn't ask him about it without revealing how she'd come by the information. She simply didn't possess the guile to mislead him like that, and moreover, she didn't want to.

By the time she finished, most of her afternoon was gone, and she'd convinced herself to take the weekend to think about what she'd learned. She headed for home. It was his secret to tell her. She didn't know how long she could wait, though. His lack of confidence in her stung more than any whip.

―――

Saturday afternoon, she spurned Keith's efforts to drive her to Darcy's house. Not only was it out of his way, having him do so would strand her there unnecessarily. If this operation went like most of them, she might not see Keith for a few days. While he intended to see her tomorrow, criminals weren't always that obliging. They committed their crimes and revealed evidence on their timetables, not the FBI's.

Darcy greeted her at the door, wearing a sky-blue sundress, a rosy glow, and a huge smile. "I have some great news."

Katrina entered the house and set her overnight bag in the living room. "Don't tell me Malcolm put security cameras all over the place here too."

Darcy glanced around the large, open foyer. Then she went outside and surveyed the obvious places—anything with a view of the front door or driveway. "Doesn't look like it. I guess what happens here stays here." She waggled her eyebrows suggestively. "No, this is better news. I'm over Chinese food. I've moved on to key lime pie and barbecued anything. I still have to chase it with antacid, but it's worth it. Malcolm slow-roasted an entire brisket. And your mom sent over key lime pie ice cream. It has chunks of lime-soaked piecrust in it."

With a laugh, Katrina followed Darcy to the kitchen. "She's just happy to have more grandkids on the way. I don't remember her doting on us that much. It was always, 'Clean your room,' and 'Take it outside.' She never tells my nephews to be quiet. I think she was born to be a grandmother."

The moment she entered the kitchen, the smell of barbecued meat hit her hard, reminding her that Keith had kept her busy well past lunchtime. Her mouth watered.

Darcy pulled a roasting pan from her double oven. "Some people are. My parents greeted the news by putting their house up for sale and buying a condo in Florida. They like Malcolm, mostly because he cleared my name and they don't know he's a Dom."

"You're not going to tell them?" This surprised Katrina. Darcy's first fiancé had been her Dom, and that information was common knowledge.

Darcy shrugged. "They never understood my relationship with Scott. I figure this is a fresh start, so I'm going to just not ever mention it. That way they'll always like Malcolm, and I won't have to beat my head against the wall trying to explain why their daughter needs to be whipped and spanked."

The smell stole Katrina's attention. She heard what Darcy said, and she understood why Darcy wouldn't want to deal with that mess again, but she could only think about the food. Her brother was a decent cook.

"Not to change the subject, but do we have to wait for Layla and Amy before we eat that?"

Darcy laughed. "Nope. Baby is hungry, so that means dinner is served." She set it on the counter and handed Katrina a plate. "I say we dive in and forget manners."

The meat was so succulent it fell off the bone. Katrina stabbed chunks with her fork to load up her plate.

"I have potatoes baking in the lower oven. They should be ready by the time we're on seconds or thirds." Darcy grinned. "I've always had a healthy appetite, but I've seen Mal's jaw drop several times at the amount of food I've been eating. I'm just so hungry. I'm warning you now not to eat every time I do. I don't want to be the reason your pants no longer fit."

Katrina had always been on the slender side. She'd never worried about gaining weight. In her teen years, she used to pray for weight gain just so she'd develop curvy hips and breasts. But it had never happened. Her genes dictated a flat chest.

"I'll be okay. I skipped lunch, so I'm starving." She settled into a place at the kitchen table and dived into the pile of meat. After she'd taken the edge off her hunger, she sat back in her chair and slowed down her intake rate. "So besides painting our toenails and watching chick flicks, what are we doing tonight?"

Darcy picked a string of meat from her plate and licked it off her finger. "I want to know how you and Keith got together. He's so hot, and a bit of a badass if you like that kind of thing, which you apparently do. Malcolm is of the firm belief that Keith will never be serious about a woman, and it makes him sad to think his best friend in the whole world will never find love and happiness."

Keith hadn't mentioned loving her. He was happy, she knew, and he did love her, but she wasn't certain he'd begun to love her as a woman yet. It wasn't an issue she wanted to push. "You don't consider Malcolm a badass?" Katrina's brother might be a few inches shorter than Keith, but he bulged with muscle every bit as much as his best friend.

Darcy cocked her head to one side. "Not really. He's kind of a geek, which I find endearing and sexy as hell. Keith seems so ruthless with everything, including protecting the people he loves. I'm very glad he never had occasion to interrogate me. That could have gotten bloody."

Having read through the file on Darcy's case, Katrina was familiar enough with the details to know that Darcy had been questioned about Scott's disappearance more than sixteen times in six months. Malcolm had confided to her that Darcy hated cops, and Katrina had witnessed Darcy's unease around Malcolm's friends from the bureau.

She'd also watched video of Keith tearing down a suspect. He could be very intimidating when he wanted, but she couldn't imagine Darcy taking shit from anybody. No, it probably wouldn't have been a fun experience for either of them. "Well, it's a good thing that case is closed with regard to you."

Darcy frowned. "The trial is next month. I'm scheduled to testify."

"I meant that they charged Snyder and Halter." Discussing this wasn't ethical. Katrina smiled and tried to change the subject. "So if I tell you how Keith and I got together, are you going to tell Malcolm? Because there are things a brother should not know about his sister."

Darcy's mouth tipped up at the corners. She nodded, acknowledging that they couldn't discuss the case. Though Katrina wasn't directly involved, many of her colleagues were.

Darcy dragged her finger through the leftover sauce. "Your brother makes the best barbecue. It could possibly be a reason I'm marrying him. That, and he knocked me up. Another good reason is that he recognizes boundaries. Keeping the fact that you're dating Keith from him violates my moral code concerning what I need to share with my Master, but the details of how you got together or any other things that fall under the heading of 'girl talk' are strictly confidential."

"I don't want to get you into trouble." Katrina finished her brisket and pushed the plate away.

Darcy lifted her brows, her blue eyes wide with shock. "There is a difference between dominating and controlling. Malcolm is dominant, yes, but he's not controlling. Men control women—our associations, friendships, actions, conversation—when they don't trust them. At least that's my interpretation. I could never be with a man who was controlling. I'm too independent and opinionated."

All her life, Katrina had relied on others. Her opinions had never been important to her, not when faced with a strong opinion from somebody she loved. Part of what she liked about being submissive was that she didn't have to be so independent. It was a relief to lay her worries and fears at Keith's feet.

Then she remembered that she was keeping information about his niece and nephew from him. Surely that fell under this discretionary heading that meant it was okay to keep it to herself until she was sure about what she wanted to share.

Katrina chewed her lip. She knew her brother better than to think he would limit the kinds of conversations Darcy could have. "Sorry. I just... Keith said if Malcolm found out you knew about us and didn't tell him that you could get into trouble."

"I wish." Darcy's expression softened for a moment. Then she refocused on Katrina. "Trina, anybody in a relationship would feel betrayed if their significant other kept important information from them. You're his sister, and Keith is his closest friend. You're both very important to him."

Katrina felt bad about her cowardice. Darcy said the same thing Keith had, but she phrased it in a much more sympathetic light. She saw how keeping this from Malcolm wouldn't preserve his friendship with Keith. It might even damage the trust between them, and that possibility hit Katrina hard.

And Darcy wasn't finished. "He would be mad at me because I hurt him. This upsets me because I hate the idea of him being hurt, especially by me. I'd rather face a year of not being flogged than hurt him. That's why you have a deadline."

Katrina didn't want to cause problems between Darcy and Malcolm. She nodded her understanding. "I'll tell him. He's going to flip out."

Darcy squeezed Katrina's wrist. "I'll be there if you want. I'm pretty good at calming him down and getting him to listen."

"Hello!" A voice called from the front hall. Katrina didn't recognize it, so she figured Darcy's sister had arrived. She'd interrupted an emotional exchange, and Katrina had to tamp down annoyance at the intrusion. Darcy didn't release Katrina's wrist.

"In the kitchen!" Darcy grinned in the direction of the door to the hall. She lowered her volume to say one last thing to Katrina. "We'll talk about this later. I know you won't want this getting out just yet. Our secret for now."

Amy was Darcy's older sister, the kind who was opinionated and protective of her little sister. Katrina had met Amy only once before. She'd been solicitous and polite. Malcolm spoke highly of her, and that was enough for Katrina.

Her hair framed her face in a way that made her large blue eyes stand out. Katrina knew Amy was thirty-two and a party planner, but that was about all. Amy set a bottle of wine on the table and gave Darcy a huge hug.

Behind Amy, Layla frowned at Katrina and shook her finger. "Hey, you never called me back."

"Called you back?" Katrina had been unaware that Layla had called. Her week had centered around Keith and work and that other issue, and nothing else had fit into her head. She felt guilty about that. Once upon a time, Layla had been her closest friend in the world. Now that she thought about it, she realized that she and Layla had been drifting apart for years, since about the time Layla had dated a Dom most of the family had disliked. With a pang, Katrina recognized how much she missed her cousin. "When did you call?"

"I didn't. But you knew I wanted you to dish on that whole thing with Keith's mom." Layla hugged Darcy, grabbed a plate, and helped herself to some of the cooling brisket. "Damn, this stuff smells good. I need a man who can cook."

Amy pulled the cookie sheet full of foil-wrapped baked potatoes from the oven. "I just need a man. At this point, I don't care if he cooks or not. I don't even want him in the kitchen."

Darcy sat down in the chair next to Katrina. "Just the bedroom, then? You know, there are lots of places in a kitchen to tie somebody up, Amy."

Wrinkling her nose, Amy opened the foil on a potato. "I don't want to get my hopes up."

Layla snagged a potato and sat down across from Darcy. "You should try one of those online dating sites. I can see it now: 'Seeking single male for bondage and sex. No cooking required.' You'll get lots of calls."

"Yeah. No, thanks. My luck I would end up with some biker freak." Amy set down her plate next to Layla, and then she went to the refrigerator to grab fixings. She added butter, sour cream, and shredded cheddar to the mix. The sights and aromas made Katrina hungry again, so she availed herself of the food.

"Ohh, wine. Yum." Layla got three glasses from the cupboard. "Just what I need." She poured for Katrina and Amy without asking if they wanted any. Katrina didn't mind. She sipped the wine, ate her potato, and let herself get caught up in the conversation and company.

Two hours later, the bottle was empty, as was another one that Amy had pilfered from Darcy's cupboard, noting that Darcy wouldn't be drinking it anytime soon. The topic turned to flogging.

"I just don't get it," Amy said, her brow furrowing severely. "Why would you want to let somebody hit you with one of those things? How is that a turn-on?"

Darcy smiled serenely, but she didn't say a word.

Layla rolled her eyes, evidence she'd been through this with Amy before. "It feels good. Really good. You should try it."

"It doesn't always hurt." Katrina added her caveat quietly, thinking of the soft kiss of that deerskin flogger. It could have hurt if he'd used more force in his delivery, but Keith had chosen to initiate her gently. "A lighter hit can feel like a massage."

Layla lifted a brow at Katrina. "Sounds like somebody popped her S and M cherry. Congratulations, honey. Who's the lucky guy?"

Katrina didn't want to answer that. Thankfully Darcy intervened. "You know, Amy, it's mostly all about the scene and the skill of the Dom. I mean, sure, I do like to be flogged or whipped or whatever just because I enjoy the pain, but a lot of people who don't particularly enjoy it still like it as part of a scene."

From Amy's expression, it was clear her sister's explanation puzzled her. "I just don't understand where you stick it into a romantic night. Movie, dinner, conversation, making out, beat me, have sex?"

Layla burst into laughter, pressing her hand to her chest as she rocked back. "Damn, girl. You don't have to have sex."

"I do," Darcy said. She sipped her herbal tea. "It's a punishment if I don't."

With her amusement dying down, Layla shook her head at Darcy. "You've only been flogged by people you want to have sex with. If I flogged you, you'd feel differently. Sometimes it's nice to have a relaxing session, then curl up on the sofa and watch a movie that doesn't make you think too hard." She sounded wistful.

With her gaze fixed on her teacup, Darcy appeared to consider Layla's assertion. It made Katrina think as well. Last weekend Keith had flogged her as a form of relaxation. Inherent in that was an underlying trust that Katrina didn't think she could muster with another person. She gathered Darcy felt the same way.

Then Darcy surprised her. "Okay. I'm willing to try it." Then she turned to Amy. "You should try it too. I know how to be gentle. Scott didn't like the stinging sensations, so I learned to be good with a light thud. But I might be out of practice. Malcolm won't even consider switching, not that I want to. I like things how they are."

"I'm not out of practice." Layla finished off her wine. "Though I think we should wait an hour for this light buzz to wear off. And you need to get permission from Malcolm first. I'm not touching you without his consent."

"Of course." Darcy already had her cell on the table. She tapped out a text message.

Katrina felt left out, though she didn't want to be flogged by anyone who wasn't Keith. However, she recognized an opportunity when it stared her in the face. "I'd like to learn how to use the flogger."

Layla arched one blonde brow. "If you got yourself a switch, then your mystery man isn't who I assumed it was. I can't believe you're keeping secrets from me. We've been friends our whole lives."

While Amy merely looked curious, Layla was hurt. Being the same age and the daughters of close sisters, Katrina and Layla had been close since birth. When they were younger, they used to buy matching outfits so they could dress like twins. They'd even lobbied their parents to move to the same school district so they could take classes together. It hadn't worked, but that hadn't dampened their friendship.

Katrina bit her lip. "You have to promise to keep it a secret for a week."

"A week?" Layla frowned.

"Just until Thursday night," Darcy said. Her tight smile reminded Katrina of the deadline and just how serious Darcy was about it.

Reluctantly Katrina nodded. In her mind, she scheduled that evening as the night it would happen. She'd invite Mal and Darcy to dinner, where she and Keith would reveal the truth. "Thursday night. You have to promise."

"Okay, I'll keep it to myself until Thursday night. Don't Amy and Darcy have to promise too?" Layla's cutting tone was one she rarely used. For the first time, Katrina realized how difficult it was going to be to date someone who was so close with her family.

Katrina already had Darcy's promise. She looked to Amy, who shrugged. "I can't think of anyone I'd tell anyway."

Taking a deep breath to delay the inevitable, Katrina sort of wished Darcy would do it for her. But then she shook off the thought. She needed to have the courage to do this herself. "Keith. I'm dating Keith, and Malcolm doesn't know yet."

Layla whistled. "It *is* who I thought it was. Damn, girl. You're playing with fire. Keith dated a friend of a friend of mine. She said he was seriously intense, and not always in a good way. She had some less-than-flattering things to say about him."

Katrina shrugged. Keith had admitted that he wasn't in the habit of treating his submissives all that well. "He's different with me."

"I hope so, because Malcolm will kill him if he isn't." Layla sat back and considered something. "So, you're not seriously thinking Keith will let you flog him?"

Actually, she did think he would let her. It might take some convincing, but she had the impression he would want her to have that skill. "Flog him, yes. Switch, no. I'm not sure how that'll work, exactly. I just know it will."

"I think I struck a nerve with Mal. He said 'no' to Layla and 'practice on a pillow' to Trina." Darcy bit her lip as she stared at the text message on her phone. "Yes, I remember now. Scott spent a lot of time abusing our pillows. I don't have any velour, but Malcolm has some suede throw pillows that go with his leather couch."

Amy giggled. "You hate that couch. I'm surprised you don't practice on it with a bull whip."

Katrina and Keith had been with Malcolm when he'd purchased his black leather sectional. She remembered how he'd fallen immediately for it. Three weeks ago, Malcolm, M.J., and their father had remodeled the living room, putting in an eight-foot sliding glass door where there used to be a window. The maligned sofa dominated that room. Katrina thought it looked nice in there with the mahogany flooring and monster-sized television set. It was essentially a man cave. "What do you have against it?"

Darcy rolled her lips inward, obviously thinking of a way to make her criticism diplomatic. "It just isn't my taste."

"Darcy hates leather furniture." Amy laughed at her sister's discomfort. "She always has, but this is a little worse. Now the smell of leather makes her nauseated. She can't go in that room at all anymore."

Katrina's heart went out to Darcy. "Does Mal know that?"

Darcy waved her hand dismissively, and Katrina had the feeling she was more uncomfortable airing her grievance than she was having the offending furniture in her house. "I'll get my way eventually. Now, I say we head down to the dungeon. Layla and I will walk you two newbies through Floggers 101. Trina, can you grab the suede throws?"

Just to show Darcy that she wasn't the kind of person who would choose sides in a disagreement between her brother and his fiancée, Katrina fetched three of the pillows from Malcolm's man cave. Malcolm and Darcy's dungeon was bright and airy, enjoying the benefits of three large daylight windows. The glass was heavily frosted to let in light and preserve privacy.

A black lacquered Saint Andrew's cross filled one corner. Other equipment was folded up and pushed against the walls, so Katrina couldn't get a real sense of the setup, which was fine with her. She didn't need to see those kinds of details with regard to her brother.

Darcy led them to a wall that was covered in hanging floggers, canes, crops, and things Katrina didn't know the names for. She thought they'd get right to work, but Layla and Darcy insisted on talking through the way a flogger was made and the mechanics of a swing.

"You want to look for rounded edges and tips. If they're sharp, especially the tips, they could cut the skin. Unless you're into blood play, avoid the cheaper floggers." Layla pointed out the features as she talked.

It took Katrina a moment to figure out what she meant. The falls were flat, and the tips were cut on a diagonal. If she looked closely, she could see that the flat edges weren't squared off; they were rounded. The tips did come to a point, but that point was rounded as well.

Amy shivered. "It still looks scary."

"It's not," Katrina assured her. "The first time Keith flogged me, he nearly put me to sleep. He said he used deerskin."

Darcy wrinkled her nose. "It can give a light sting. Malcolm has deerskin down here somewhere. He hasn't figured out yet that I'd consider that thing a punishment. It wouldn't do the trick for me. I prefer elk or rubber."

"I like the deerskin," Layla said. "You can get a lot of mileage out of it, and it's good for beginners. Not everybody is in it for the pain."

Amy looked confused, which was becoming a common expression on her face now that the conversation had turned firmly to impact play. "What else is there?"

Layla pushed her bangs back from her eyes. "Relaxation. Trina told you that it can feel like a massage, and there's this endorphin rush that takes you to a place where stress doesn't exist." She handed the whip to Amy. "Touch it. Brush it over your arms and legs."

Amy ran her hand down the length of the falls, and her eyes widened in surprise. "They're soft." She gazed at the flogger with wonder as she experimented with the sensations it caused on the insides of her wrists.

Katrina thought about the way Keith liked to start off gently. When he flogged her, he varied the intensity so that she didn't know what to expect next. He took her beyond the ability to think. If it weren't for him, she didn't think she'd be able to deal with the stress of having a fucking stalker.

A tap on her arm brought her back to the present. "You okay?" Layla's brow wrinkled with concern. "You don't have to do this if you don't want to. Or is something else on your mind?"

Katrina didn't want to bring up that topic. "I want to do this. But I want to learn more than just the flogger. I want to learn to use the cane and the crop and—" Because she didn't know the name of it, she broke off and pointed to a very thick-handled whip that tapered to almost nothing.

Darcy, who had been hanging back while Layla took charge, laughed loudly. "You don't waste time, do you?" She came forward and fingered the coiled length lovingly. "This is my absolute favorite thing in this room right now. But I will admit I don't know how to use it. If you want training on that, you'll have to buy one of your own, and you'll have to ask Malcolm or Keith to train you."

"Hey! You're assuming I don't know how to use a single-tail." Layla put her hands on her hips in a show of mock umbrage.

Darcy shook her head, a small grin playing at the corners of her mouth. "I know you don't." She turned her attention back to Katrina. "Trina, this is one of those things you work your way up to. Scott practiced with a single-tail for almost a year and still didn't feel comfortable using it on me, so he never did. Start with the flogger. Practice with that, and next week we'll have a lesson with the canes. Those are fun."

Amy had stopped loving on the deerskin, and now she gaped at the canes. "They don't look like fun. Don't they cane people in Singapore for littering? People get scars and are permanently disfigured."

"Or massages." Layla ran her hand over one of the thicker canes. "The thin ones sting, but the thicker ones can feel like deep-tissue massages. Very sexy—if you know what you're doing."

"And those"—Amy pointed at the single-tail—"break open the skin. They used those in slave days for brutally mistreating people. People have died from injuries from those whips."

Darcy exhaled loudly, evidence that her patience was wearing thin. "Amy, nobody should use any of this equipment without training and lots of practice. Yes, it can be dangerous. It can seriously hurt or injure a person. Why do you think Malcolm isn't comfortable letting anyone else flog me? He knows Layla's experienced, but he hasn't seen her in action."

The situation was getting tense. Katrina exchanged a look with Layla, but her cousin only mouthed, *Later*, and moved to stand between Darcy and Amy. "How about we try it out? Let's set the pillows up as a horizontal target first. Then you can practice vertical."

Katrina took the flogger Darcy handed her and followed Layla to the other side of the room. Her cousin explained the forward and backhand strokes, and then she showed them how to combine the moves for a figure eight. Katrina practiced on the pillow, watching the strike patterns in the suede fabric to make sure she was hitting where she was aiming. She found it easier to look at her target than to watch the falls trailing through the air, and she switched hands when her arm grew tired.

Amy wasn't having an easy go of it. She missed the pillow completely several times, and she'd accidentally hit her bare leg. Layla suggested jeans for the next practice session.

"You're good." Darcy sat on what looked like a leather-clad sawhorse with wings. Now that she was on it, Katrina could see the bondage and sex options present in the design. "Really good. You have a natural talent."

Katrina shrugged, but inside she beamed under the light of the praise. "It must run in the family."

Darcy let loose a short laugh. "It must." She nodded at her sister. Amy's face was twisted with frustration. Layla stood behind her, trying to help correct her swing. "I'm just as bad as Amy. It took almost six months for me to be accurate enough to practice on a person. You're ready today. Unfortunately you can't use me."

"That's okay. Learning a skill—any skill—takes time. I can be patient."

Holding out her hand for the flogger, Darcy smiled expectantly. "May I?"

It was her whip. Katrina handed it over, sorry to see it go.

"Some floggers are good for pinwheeling, which can deliver a variety of sensations from a light breeze to a constant sting." Using her wrist, she spun the falls in a constant circle. "Turn around and take your shirt off. You can leave your bra on."

This wasn't the first time a woman had invited Katrina to take off her shirt. No, it was the way Darcy's tone made the order gentle and authoritative that gave her pause. She'd definitely picked up a few Domme tricks over the years.

Katrina gestured to the spinning flogger. "Will it hurt?"

Darcy lifted a brow, and a mischievous light entered her eyes. "Do you want it to?"

She wanted to know the gamut of sensation for purely informational reasons. Part of her wanted to refuse, to ask Keith if he would introduce her to this different style because he was her Master. "You said you suck at this."

"I said it took me a while to get the hang of it." Darcy frowned and let the falls come to a halt. "You know what? You're right to be wary. You don't have permission. There's nothing worse than disappointing your Master. Here." She handed the flogger back to Katrina. "You're wearing shorts. Get a good spin going, and bring it closer to your thigh. You'll feel the breeze first, and then, when you actually hit skin, it starts as a biting sting. It progresses to a constant, broader sting. It's always stingy because you're not stimulating the muscles. Well, unless you have a heavier flogger and you're closer to your target."

Katrina twirled it in the air so that the spin was parallel to her body. Once she got a feel for it, she changed trajectory to bring it to a perpendicular orientation. As it came closer to her skin, she felt the breeze. Her skin tingled with electric anticipation. Just a smidge closer, and the small sting of the tips kissed her flesh. Closer still brought the sensation Darcy had described.

Without a doubt, she knew Keith was going to love this. She just didn't know how to tell him she wanted to practice flogging on him.

# Chapter Twelve

Stakeouts were notoriously boring. Hours of waiting in a small space with a partner might be followed by some kind of action. Even when they had their mark's itinerary, things rarely happened according to plan. More often than not, nothing at all happened.

Tonight was that night.

Of all the people he'd whiled away stakeout hours with, Keith usually preferred Malcolm for company. Usually. This time there was a tension in the air that wouldn't go away. Both of them were worried about Kat. She wasn't alone, which removed some of the immediacy of the concern, but it didn't erase it.

This would have been the perfect opportunity to talk to Malcolm about his relationship with Kat. Mal was essentially stuck with him. If he got mad, which was likely, he couldn't leave. He'd have to stay and talk it out. But Kat wanted to break the news together. She thought her presence would have a calming effect on Malcolm's temper, but Keith knew differently. If Mal was going to blow his top, he wasn't going to censor anything for his sister's ears, not where Keith was concerned.

"Jordan better beat the crap out of his snitch." Malcolm adjusted the focus on one of the IR cameras mounted on the exterior of the van. "Because we got nothing tonight. I'm pretty sure all the bad guys are in bed, sleeping."

"One hour left." Keith recorded another entry on his log. "Then you can go home to Darcy."

Malcolm shook his head. "We're close to Trina's. I want to go there and check out the surveillance. It worries me that nothing has happened in a week. Somebody broke into her house multiple times in the space of six days, and they stole her underwear. Only sick bastards do things like that."

The crime scene report had come back. Dustin had slipped copies to both of them. They'd found evidence of semen in her drawer. He'd checked it against Keith's DNA to rule him out. The weasel had ejaculated on her panties before stealing them. Perhaps he'd realized his mistake after he'd masturbated, and that was why he had stolen her underthings.

Keith only knew that if he got to the jackass first, the man was dead.

"How has she been holding up? My parents said you've been over there every night." Malcolm furrowed his brow. "I know she wants to stay at her place. We can take turns. I'm willing to sleep over there every other night. This has to be putting a serious cramp in your social life."

Striving for a neutral expression, Keith shook his head. "It's fine. We've been alternating whose house we're at." He really didn't want to get into the sleeping arrangements. Keith had a four-bedroom house, so it was reasonable for Mal to assume that Kat slept in one of the guest rooms. "Besides, if the Friedman brothers prove to be part of Snyder's organization, then you need to stay close to Darcy."

Though there had been no threats, Keith knew Malcolm wouldn't take chances. The memory stick he'd recovered from Darcy's dishwasher was still yielding helpful leads, albeit in a piecemeal fashion. They were finding that the documents on it were best when used in conjunction with other intelligence.

A key piece of information from one of Jordan Monaghan's contacts had given them perspective on several puzzling documents. It seemed that Snyder hadn't been the boss of the organization. He'd been high up in the hierarchy, but there were bigger fish to catch. If they could prove a link between the Friedmans and the Holbrook case, then the scope of the investigation would widen considerably, and they'd be able to use the evidence they had gathered in a more efficient fashion. To that end, Malcolm and Keith were stuck watching for a meeting that so far hadn't happened, but it had pulled him away from Kat for a whole night.

"I know. That's why I have Trina there. The girls can watch out for one another. It's not an ideal situation, but it's better than leaving any of them alone." Malcolm tapped his thigh. "Trina's keeping something from me. Every time I see her, she can't quite meet my eyes. I think she feels guilty. I don't want her to feel like this is her fault."

Keith nodded. He knew that, in addition to everything else, Kat felt like she was a burden. "She's doing okay. Not great. She's trying to keep it together for us. I told her she didn't have to do that, you know, that she can be angry or sad about it."

Mal pressed his lips together, holding it in the same way Kat did.

Keith resisted the urge to chuckle over the similarity. "You can get pissed too. I'm pissed."

"Really? Because bored and pissed look the same on you, so I couldn't tell."

In lieu of responding, he stared at Malcolm with his bored/pissed expression. "Attacking me won't help. Dustin is working his ass off to catch the bastard. You and I are protecting her in the meantime."

"Sorry." Malcolm glanced at his cell. His jaw was dark with stubble, and he looked beat. "As time passes and nothing happens, I just get worried that we're not going to close the case and she'll be living with this specter always looming over her shoulder. It's not like you can move in and protect her for the rest of her life."

Keith didn't see why he couldn't, but he kept his mouth shut.

"And I know you. After a week of no sex, you get bitchy. I'm surprised you're not ripping my head off right now."

This time he shrugged. "Kat is more important than sex." Then he changed the subject. "So what was up with that text from Darcy earlier? The girls wanted to flog one another instead of watch a movie?"

Malcolm's mouth opened and closed while his brow pinched in confusion. Finally he shook his head in resignation. "Apparently Amy and Trina want to learn to use the floggers. She wanted to let them practice on her. I said no because she's pregnant. One misplaced hit could cause problems."

"Not to mention that you should learn control and try it on yourself before you try it on another person." Keith strived for an extra dry tone, but he honestly didn't know what to think. Kat wanted to learn to wield a flogger? Why hadn't she said anything to him? They were going to have a talk very soon.

The last hour of their shift was uneventful, right up until the final five minutes when Keith noticed someone sneaking from the apartment building through a ground-floor window. He had the same height and build as their target, but Keith couldn't get a clear view of the face.

"Mal, we have movement. First floor, four windows from the left. He's wearing pants that are too small."

Malcolm leaned closer to the monitor screen. "That's giving skinny jeans a whole new meaning. Look up, fashion victim. Come on, let us see your face. Damn. Now his back is to us."

Neither of them wanted to move the van. This close to dawn, people in the neighborhood would assume it was vacant. When the target made it to the corner, he looked back long enough for them to make him.

"That's Rick. We need to follow the bastard."

As they watched, Rick Friedman got into a black Audi and drove away. Malcolm followed, leaving a good amount of distance between them. This early on a Sunday morning, there wasn't much traffic around to provide camouflage.

Keith radioed in to update their status. They followed Friedman to a quiet street in an older neighborhood. The houses, though small, had been kept up nicely. Friedman's car stopped across the street from the one run-down place on the

*Re/Paired*

entire block. Malcolm drove around the block and parked on a cross street that afforded them a view.

A tall man with a slim build got into the passenger side. He wore dark clothes and a hoodie, making it impossible to see what he looked like.

"I hate those fucking things." Malcolm leaned across the seat for a better look, crowding into Keith.

Keith rolled down the window and propped a night-vision camera on the edge. He snapped a series of pictures, zooming in as far as the technology would allow. "Personal space, dude. You look like you're about to give me a handjob."

"You wish." Malcolm didn't move. "I was right about you needing to get laid. Take today off. I'll keep Trina at my house."

Keith pushed Malcolm back and continued taking photos. The two men concluded their conversation, and the one in the hoodie got out. Keith adjusted his aim to try to capture this new player's face. Hoodie Man got into another vehicle, and both cars drove off.

"Go down that street. Get an address on the house Hoodie Man came out of."

Malcolm followed Keith's order without comment. Keith radioed Jordan and Dustin, both of whom were supposed to relieve them of their watch, and put them on Friedman's tail. Another pair of agents tailed Hoodie Man. This could end up being a break in the case, or it could just be another night of cat and mouse. None of them would know until it was all over.

---

Keith didn't end up having a chance to see Kat until Sunday evening. After checking the surveillance footage at her condo, he and Mal had crashed at Keith's house, not waking until nearly noon when they both were called in for a strategy session. Hoodie Man had lost his tail, and Dustin had reported nothing happening after he and Jordan tracked Friedman back to his house. Kat had texted him to say she'd left for home, but not to worry because she wouldn't be there alone.

He'd breathed a sigh of relief. If neither he nor Mal could be there, at least she would have her parents for protection. Papa L might be nearing his seventies, but the man was still formidable.

The strategy session had been taxing. Not only were they under pressure to make sure the Snyder case didn't unravel in the face of this new information about the Friedmans' involvement, but they now had a renewed focus on Katrina's case. The address that Friedman had led them to had turned out to belong to Erin Buttermore. From the general build of Hoodie Man, he could very well have been Aaron Buttermore, Kat's work friend.

At that pronouncement, Dustin had straightened in his chair and informed them about some files that Aaron had given to Kat, saying that she'd forgotten them on her desk. She'd told Dustin that the files weren't hers.

Then Jordan had let them know that someone was forging Kat's signature in the evidence logs, and that some of that evidence had eventually gone missing. It looked like someone—probably Aaron—was setting up Kat to take a pretty hard fall.

But they lacked hard evidence. Keith and Dustin had officially been charged with keeping a close eye on her. Jordan was to follow up with Buttermore. He'd already met with Chief Alder about the issue.

Afterward, Keith and Malcolm sat in Kat's parking lot, watching to see who came and went in the areas blocked from the cameras. Keith wanted to go in and sweep Kat off her feet. He hadn't seen her since Saturday morning when she'd refused to let him drive her to Darcy's house.

"Nothing's happening here either." Malcolm rubbed his eyes. "God, I'm tired. I have a bad feeling about this case. I know the Friedmans are up to no good, but I don't know what the hell they're doing with Buttermore. The guy's always struck me as somewhat of a dumbass."

Keith tapped his thigh impatiently. "Let's go inside. I'm hungry. Kat has to have dinner made by now."

Malcolm grinned as he reached for the latch to open the door. "Now I know why you don't mind hanging out with her so much. She is a pretty good cook."

Keith did his fair share of meal preparation, but once again he didn't say anything. Instead he called Kat to let her know they were both coming up. She answered the door wearing shorts, a loose shirt that she'd tied at one hip, and a weary smile. He felt like he had been away from home for far too long. He wanted to take her in his arms and just hold her, but they hadn't disclosed anything to Malcolm yet.

"Hi, guys. Come on up."

After securing the door, he followed Malcolm up the stairs to find nobody there. He wanted to ask, but Malcolm beat him to it.

"Where are Mom and Dad?"

Kat frowned at her brother. "At home? I don't know."

"Weren't they here?"

Keith did a visual sweep of the room, as did Malcolm. He spotted a strange briefcase and a laptop that wasn't Kat's. "You said you had company. We assumed your parents were going to be here."

"Oh." She went to the sink and poured a glass of water. "No. Aaron came over. We've been working all day."

"Where is he?" Malcolm peered down the hall.

"Bathroom. Want something to drink? I lost track of time, so I haven't made dinner. I was going to order out." She breathed that out in one huff and then downed her water.

"Water, thanks. I'm going to use the bathroom in your room." With that, Mal disappeared down the hall. Keith knew he was going to scope out the rest of the place. Keith's job was to keep Kat distracted. She didn't need to know they suspected Buttermore of collusion and tampering, or that they thought he was setting it up to make it look like she was the guilty party.

Keith closed the distance as soon as Malcolm was out of sight. He pulled her close and inhaled the scent of her hair. "You will explain your interest in learning to use a flogger as soon as they're gone."

She pushed against him and tilted her head back. "Did you have a nice time with Malcolm?" Her grin suggested that she knew he was going insane with curiosity. "Did you clean your guns and watch a karate movie?"

He couldn't help it, so he leaned down and planted a kiss on her inviting lips. It was a promise, nothing more. It couldn't be. He heard a noise in the hall that indicated somebody was coming. Reluctantly he released her just in time for Aaron to come into the kitchen.

"Hey, Agent Rossetti. How's it going?" Aaron held out his hand, and Keith shook it.

"Not bad. I hear you've been pressed into service cleaning out your parents' basement." He gave Aaron his best impression of a warm smile, which Mal had warned him wasn't much friendlier than his usual demeanor. Given the man's recent suspected activities, Keith congratulated himself for not responding with violence.

Aaron's expression tightened. "It's just my mom. My dad took off when I was little. I don't remember him at all. She's getting older now and can't navigate the stairs. I'm trying to convince her to get her hip replaced."

Since they'd profiled Aaron that afternoon, Keith already knew everything about Aaron's background that was part of his record. He used the opportunity to dig for information. "So you were over there cleaning last night? How long did that take you?"

Aaron frowned. "I didn't keep track. Not too late. Mom goes to bed early. Emphysema wipes her out."

Keith wanted to ask more questions, but he couldn't come off sounding like he was interrogating a witness. If Buttermore was working with the Friedman brothers, then he might not be as inept as he appeared.

Kat smiled indulgently. "Aaron went back over this morning to chip away at the mess, and then he came over to work with me after lunchtime. I was just about to call for carryout, Aaron. Did you want to look over a menu? I still owe you a meal."

Keith fervently hoped Aaron would refuse, and his wish was granted.

Aaron shook his head. "No, thanks. Your bodyguards are here now, so I was going to head out. I think we're in pretty good shape for next week's cases." He gathered up his things, his mind seemingly elsewhere.

"All right. Thanks for coming over, and I'm so sorry about yesterday." Kat hugged Aaron and saw him to the door.

Keith sent a text to Jordan and moved so that he could listen in on Kat and Aaron. His position put him seconds away if Buttermore should try anything physical. It didn't seem likely. If he was setting her up professionally, then he wouldn't risk doing anything that would tip her off or sour their personal relationship. He needed her trust in order to keep screwing her over.

Malcolm came strolling down the hall, a pensive expression on his face. "Bath and bedrooms are clear." He looked around. "Where's Trina?"

Inclining his head toward the stairs, Keith whispered, "Seeing Aaron out."

Mal stepped closer, his eyes scanning the open living and dining areas. "I found men's briefs in her laundry. Last night,

Darcy showed her how to use a flogger. I think Trina has a boyfriend. How the hell is she sneaking him past you?"

Ever the thorough agent, of course Mal had checked the laundry. He'd probably also gone through her drawers, not that he'd tell her he had invaded her privacy in the name of keeping her safe.

"She's not." Keith needed to talk to Kat. Darcy's deadline was looming closer, and he almost couldn't wait for it to arrive. "I've been here a lot, so she's been doing my clothes." He took his suits to the dry cleaner, which left his shirts, socks, and underwear. Kat had washed colors yesterday, and he'd promised to see to the whites today.

Malcolm mulled this over. "That aside, it occurs to me that her stalker could be strictly a personal thing. Maybe she turned down somebody recently who is having trouble taking no for an answer?"

"I don't get asked out nearly as often as you seem to think." Kat gave Mal a lopsided smile as she came up the stairs. "I've been turned down recently, but that's the extent of it."

Mal considered his sister affectionately. "Whoever turned you down is stupid, so it's better to just move on to someone intelligent enough to appreciate you."

Kat placed a kiss on her brother's cheek. "You're so sweet. Are you staying for dinner? I was going to order out."

"No." He smiled regretfully. "I'm going to leave you here with Keith. I haven't seen my wife-to-be since yesterday morning." He hugged Kat.

Keith hated the position in which he found himself. On one hand, he was lying to Malcolm about Katrina. From the other side of his mouth, he was keeping information from Kat about a man she considered a close friend. No matter how he sliced it, he was lying to the two people who meant the world to him.

He inched toward the stairwell. "I'll walk you out." Mostly he wanted to double-check the locks to make sure they were properly engaged. He trusted that Kat knew how to work her locks, but having visual confirmation would set his mind at ease.

When they got to the front walkway, Malcolm reached up to adjust a camera that had been nudged a little out of place. "You're right about her hiding the way this is affecting her. She's all jittery, talking fast, and looking a little flushed." Then his eyes widened. "Maybe she has a thing for Buttermore? Her taste has always run to men she thinks she can change for the better." He shook his head. "It's going to break her heart to find out what a noxious ass he is."

Sometimes Mal's conclusions were plain wrong, and sometimes they were close and still missed the mark. Keith coughed. "You think she has a thing for Buttermore? She's been friends with him for years, and nothing's happened. Plus, her taste isn't that bad." Only he could appreciate the irony of his statement. He was glad Kat was upstairs, because she'd probably blush down to her roots.

Malcolm shrugged. "I don't know. It'll be your job to find out. If that's the case, you're going to need to convince her otherwise. We can set her up with Owen Zaputo. He's a decent guy."

Owen Zaputo was a great agent, one of their best. He was a force in the field, and he had a quick, intelligent mind that could definitely keep up with Katrina. When Keith thought about it, he realized that Kat actually had a lot in common with Owen.

He did nothing to prevent the scowl from taking over his face. "Zaputo? Seriously? That guy is way too soft for her. She'd run right over him, and she's not the most forceful person."

"If she wants to be a Domme, she can start with Owen. He'd love to sub for her." Malcolm chewed his lip as he considered that theory.

Keith shoved him toward the parking lot. "Go home. You need sleep, because you're starting to sound ridiculous. Your sister is not Domme material."

Mal moved two steps, but then he turned back to Keith. "No, she's not. But if she wants to try out being a Domme, then we have to support her in that. She might be all sweetness to us, but she can be seriously tenacious when she decides she wants something. If we get in her way, then she'll just push us aside. Given the danger she's in, we can't afford to have her pissed off at either of us."

"Fine. Then I'll teach her how to use a flogger. She can practice with my equipment." Part of him wanted to see her wield it, to see if she could flog him and remain the feisty submissive he loved. "More weapons to use against an attacker."

Malcolm grinned as he backed away. "You could even let her practice on you. She could get out all her aggressions, and you can pretend you're doing it to be a good friend instead of admitting what a masochist you really are."

Without answering, Keith stepped back through the threshold and closed the door. When he got upstairs, Kat was just finishing up placing an order for pizza and salad. As she tossed her phone onto the counter, he gathered her in his arms, pressing the soft length of her body against his.

"Your brother thinks I'm a sex addict."

He thought she'd laugh, but she frowned as she considered it. "Well, I can't disagree. I think I've had more sex in the last week than I have in the past year." Then her expression morphed as she brought out that devious grin. "Dinner won't be here for twenty minutes. Want to feed your addiction first?"

He pretended to mull the offer. "Okay, but what do you want to do with the other nineteen minutes?"

She lifted a brow and slipped her hand between their bodies to cradle his cock through his pants. "I can think of ways to fill the time." With that, she squeezed him hard.

His breath caught in his chest until she eased her grip. Not wasting a moment, he tangled his hand in her hair and pulled. Tears wet the corners of her eyes, but she moaned. When she parted her lips, he claimed her mouth and didn't bother to temper the violence of his passion. She made a whimpering sound in the back of her throat, and that desperate noise nearly caused him to lose control. No, he wasn't addicted to sex. He was addicted to sex with her.

He broke suddenly, trailed kisses down her neck, and bit hard once he reached the curve of her shoulder. She cried out and gripped his head, but he was immovable.

"Mine." He licked a path up the side of her throat and took her earlobe between his teeth.

"Yes," she hissed, tearing at his clothes.

He bent his knees and banded his arm around her waist. Then he stood, lifting her from the floor, and he carried her down the hall. Throwing her to the bed, he gave an order. "Naked. Now."

He ripped off his shirt and pants, thankful they'd dispensed with condoms. Glancing up, he saw that she'd shed her clothes and centered her body on the bed with her legs spread in welcome. One finger moved over her clit, pressing and circling, enticing him closer.

He crawled over her and slid inside her waiting pussy in one smooth motion. Then he lifted his hips. "Close your legs."

When she was positioned the way he wanted, he hugged his thighs around her legs, pinning her in place. He flexed his hips, withdrawing nearly all the way before plunging deep inside. Yes, this was what he wanted. Her heat surrounded him, and her small cunt was even tighter than usual.

He wrapped his hands around her wrists and immobilized them on either side of her head. With his weight pressing her down, she could barely arch her back. She wiggled, testing the limits of this restraint. She was stuck.

He closed his eyes and concentrated on the feel of her velvet sheath. Beneath him, the sounds of pleasure grew more desperate with each thrust, and they only fed his passion. Soon he felt the fluttering of her internal muscles, and he increased his pace.

"Keith, please let me come."

"Yes," he whispered. This wasn't about denial or control. She'd submitted to him already, and that was all he needed. "Give it to me."

And she did. Her entire body trembled and shook, convulsing under him. He held her steady with his hips and arms, keeping her together as she came apart. Her surrender was a sweet balm for his soul, and he followed her over the precipice, grasping at stars as he fell.

The world spun. Slowly he became aware of her hand smoothing a path through his hair, a comforting and calming caress that made him never want to move. Well, that and he was still buried in her warmth.

The doorbell rang before he could say anything.

Beneath him, she heaved a sigh. "They're early. Move and let me throw on some clothes."

In a perfect world, he'd let his sub answer the door and bring the food to him. But it wasn't a perfect world, and she was in danger. He wasn't going to let her do it. "No. I'll go. You stay naked. Grab a towel and sit at the table."

She gave a long-suffering sigh. "Yes, Keith."

At her resigned tone, he glanced up to gauge her mood. She smiled widely as she ran her hand up her stomach and over one breast. He decided he liked her playfulness. He planted a kiss on the curve of her breast. "I'll get to those after we eat. You're going to need energy."

Five minutes later, she sat across from him with the contented expression of a woman who had been thoroughly sated. He didn't doubt her enjoyment, but they'd just fucked rather quickly. She couldn't possibly be that happy yet.

He loaded two plates with pizza and set one of them in front of her. "Explain why you want to learn to use a flogger."

She looked at the plate and then at the counter where a bag lay next to the pizza box. "I ordered salad. You want some?"

"Sure." He sat down and took a huge bite of pizza. She got up and opened the bag. "While you're doing that, answer my question."

"It wasn't a question, really. More like a demand." She got down two bowls and heaped them with lettuce, tomatoes, olives, and cucumbers. "But since you demanded to know, I thought I'd learn for you."

He blinked. "For me?"

"Yes. For you." She set down the salad and a packet of dressing. "It didn't take me all that long to figure out that you can be a Dominant and also a masochist. And that you're not really much of a sadist."

He narrowed his eyes, not sure where she was going with her accurate assessment.

The vixen smiled serenely as she stabbed her fork into the lettuce. "You know, after our little talk last Saturday, I noticed that you only do things I like now. Spanking, flogging, nipple clamps. Those kinds of things. If you were truly a sadist and you got off on my pain, you wouldn't limit yourself to things that make me hotter for you."

She was gloating, and he didn't have a problem with it. Perhaps he'd been selfish in the past, but he found that he truly wanted to engage in sensation play that increased her level of sexual pleasure.

"You can talk to me, you know. Tell me anything. I won't get upset or think less of you." The triumph had fled from her voice. Even her volume was low now. He had no idea what she meant.

He forced himself to meet her warm brown gaze. She'd bared her soul to him, given him everything. He'd warned her that he wouldn't give her anything in return, but he'd broken that promise already. He'd given her pieces of himself he thought didn't exist. Washing the salad down with water bought him a few moments.

"Okay. I'm a masochist. But I'm also a Dominant. I don't do submission."

She nodded and smiled encouragingly. "I had a long talk with Darcy after Layla and Amy fell asleep. She told me how you painsluts interpret sensation differently from other people. I might like a little sting or a light thud, but you want actual burning pain. You need it to provide a kind of release nothing else can."

That sounded about right. He'd gone so long without it, but that didn't mean he'd stopped yearning for it. Perhaps he'd taken to sadism out of jealousy. He was giving his subs something he really wanted for himself.

Still, he shook his head. He couldn't see how to get what he wanted without giving up the control he needed. "You're not listening to me, Kat."

She rose from her place on the other side of the square table and knelt next to him. "If you can order me to suck your cock, why can't you order me to flog you?"

The sight of her kneeling with perfect posture and her head bowed in a show of submission was at odds with her audacity. "You kneel at my feet and question my authority. That's some chance you're taking, Kitty Kat." He kept his voice soft, just firm enough to let her know that she was seriously testing his patience.

"I'm sorry," she said, and she sounded honestly contrite. "I just want to give you what you need so badly, and you're a very stubborn man."

He reached out to touch her hair, and he noticed his hand was trembling. "Fine. You can have what you want. I'll teach you how to use the implements I prefer. But I'll warn you now, being flogged doesn't take me to subspace, and I might end up treating you very roughly afterward."

She lifted her face, and he saw that she glowed with pleasure. "I'm okay with that."

# Chapter Thirteen

Katrina remembered to stop in the lobby to get coffee for Aaron. She'd felt like an ass when she'd checked her messages Saturday evening to find that he'd spent the morning waiting for her in the café where they frequently met on the weekends to get some work done. When she'd told him that she would pick up the coffee "tomorrow morning," she'd been thinking it was Thursday, not Friday.

He hadn't been upset, and when he had come over Sunday, he'd confessed that he was happy to have a reason to get away from his mother's basement, and he had been able to catch up on one of his cases.

Her shoulders and arms were sore today. Keith had helped her practice using the flogger he now kept in her hall closet. She'd beaten a throw pillow to death in less than thirty minutes. He had patiently corrected her form, and he had given many pointers about the mechanics of each type of swing.

Then he'd massaged her shoulders. That had turned into a full-body experience that had left them both sated and exhausted.

The elevator was out of order, so she climbed the stairs to the second floor. Aaron was already at his desk, mulling over his schedule. She set down the large, steaming-hot cup on his desk.

"Good morning."

He glanced up, frowning at her as if he smelled something bad. Then his expression cleared. He inclined his head toward the coffee, but he didn't smile. "Thanks. I need that. Alder is breathing down my throat about some evidence that's gone missing in the Holbrook case. First they kick me off; then they blame this screwup on me."

Because he muttered that last part, Katrina wasn't sure she'd heard him correctly. Not wanting to push on a sore issue, she said, "You're welcome. I might have some time this afternoon. Anything I can do to help?"

He ran his hand through his short blond hair. "Go find the files you said you put away. Those are the ones that are missing. If you can find those, that would help. I have to be in court in half an hour, and I need to meet with a witness first."

She reeled from the accusation in his voice. Though she didn't normally second-guess herself, she wondered if one of the files had fallen out in her trunk or if her mind had been on Keith and not her work. That could lead to a costly error. She felt bad, but at the same time, she remembered Jordan's oblique questions from a few weeks ago, and she wondered if this was related.

She spent her lunch in the file room, combing through the stacks until she found what she needed. Her mind boggled when she realized that Aaron had pulled files from cases related to open investigations. Keith and Malcolm had spent the weekend on the Friedman case, and that had been one of the misplaced files. As she riffled through it, she noticed that some of the pages were missing.

She was reasonably certain the Friedman file had been about twice as thick when she and Dustin had picked them up from the lobby floor. They'd been bulky when she'd filed them the next morning. With Jordan's concerns ringing in her ears, she decided to take the files directly to Chief Alder. The chief was busy, so Katrina left a message with Alder's administrative assistant.

An hour later, she sat at her desk, phone glued to her ear, pleading with a social services case manager for information about Angelina and Corey Shaw. "I just need information on their well-being. I'm not looking for names or addresses." Because she wasn't a caseworker or a family member, she was being completely stonewalled. She needed contacts in CFS.

The moment she hung up, Chief Alder's assistant called her into the chief's office. The chief had started as a trial lawyer and

Chief of Appeals at the Oakland County Prosecutor's Office in Pontiac. Like Katrina, she was an alumnus of the Detroit College of Law. The woman was sharp, and she had high expectations of those working under her.

She was ushered right into the office, and the door closed behind her. The chief's office overlooked the bustling traffic on West Congress, but Katrina wasn't looking out the window. She centered her attention on Chief Alder. If she had to guess, Katrina would place the chief in her late forties. She had a commanding presence and an air of confidence. Her lips were set in a firm line, softened by evidence of laugh lines around her eyes and mouth.

"Good afternoon, Chief. I know you don't have a lot of time, so I'll be brief."

Chief Alder held up her hand, halting Katrina before she could begin. "Ms. Legato, you took home confidential files containing key pieces of evidence from open investigations."

Cold fear raced through her system. All the files were labeled confidential. They contained legal information. Katrina had clearance for that file room. She had done nothing wrong, but Aaron certainly had. No, that wasn't entirely true. She should have put the files back immediately. Something didn't seem right. She wasn't sure what was going on. Loyalty wouldn't allow her to desert her friend, but taking a fall like this could ruin her career.

She opted to draw out the conversation by fishing for more information. "Aaron asked me to help him locate some missing files. I owed him a favor."

That answer didn't seem to defuse the chief's ire one bit, probably because she hadn't addressed the chief's concern. "I asked Mr. Buttermore to do that himself."

Katrina had no way of knowing that. "I'm sorry, Chief. He had to be in court, and I had some extra time."

"You made time." Chief Alder folded her hands on her desk. "I'm aware of your caseload, Ms. Legato. You don't have extra time."

"Yes, ma'am. I made time. Aaron helps me out when I need a hand. He's a good friend." She felt a little like she was on trial, but she didn't know the charges.

"Friend or not, I want you to stop writing his briefs and doing his work. This case"—she tapped a file on her desk—"is one that we've invested countless hours building. It's the culmination of two years of investigation. We can't be losing evidence or misplacing the logs. Carelessness is intolerable."

At least the file on the desk belonged to a case where charges had been filed. "I know, Chief. My brother and his best friend worked on that case. I'd hate to see their hard work destroyed almost as much as I'd hate to see a criminal set free." Lots of agents had worked that case. Some were still working it.

The chief sighed. "You haven't explained why you took those files home."

She truly didn't want to throw Aaron under the bus, but she couldn't lie for him. "I'm sorry, ma'am. I was leaving work, and Aaron handed them to me in the lobby. He thought I'd left them on my desk instead of taking them home. I don't know how they got on my desk. I put them in my briefcase because I was running late, and I took them home. Agent Brandt was with me. He can corroborate my story."

Chief Alder didn't move a muscle. "I admire your loyalty, Ms. Legato." After several moments, she shuffled some papers on her desk. Katrina had the feeling things were being left unsaid. She didn't know what she was missing.

Then the chief cleared her throat. "Due to an unexpected medical leave, there is an opening for a second chair on the Holbrook case. I want you working with me. This is your chance to show me what you're made of."

The world froze. Chances like this didn't come around very often. Many people in the office had more experience than she did. Sitting next to a prosecutor as talented as Elizabeth Alder could teach her more in one day than she could learn in the office in a year.

This was the chance Aaron had wanted. Anyone with ambition wanted it, and the chief had offered it to Katrina. Though she felt disloyal, she knew she couldn't turn down the chief. It hadn't been an offer as much as an order. "Thank you, Chief Alder. I won't let you down."

In lieu of an answer, the woman smiled in dismissal. As Katrina turned to leave, the chief spoke. "You'll get further with a social worker if you meet with them in person."

It seemed Chief Alder knew more about Katrina's business than she assumed, which was a little creepy. "Thank you, Chief. I'll do that."

She called Keith to let him know she would be out in the field and she'd meet him at his place for dinner. He didn't sound too happy about the change in plans, but last week had set an unrealistic precedent. He worked irregular hours, and she sometimes needed to work late.

Through sheer tenacity, she got in to see the social worker assigned to the Shaw children. The woman had strands of iron gray streaked through her coarse black hair. Her office was small, and her round frame took up most of the room. A half-filled cup of coffee sat at her elbow, and her desk was covered with papers. The nameplate on the door had fallen off, revealing the tarnished brass behind it.

"Mrs. Daley? I'm Katrina Legato. I'm an assistant prosecutor with the US Attorney General's office. Can I have a moment of your time?"

The woman eyed her with a steely look that said she'd seen it all. "If I tell you those kids are fine, will you go away?"

Katrina moved aside a stack of files and sat in the chair she'd uncovered. "No, I won't. I'm sure my situation is unusual."

She ignored Mrs. Daley's roll of the eyes. "The children belong to my friend's sister. He's estranged from the family. I don't think he even knows he has a niece and a nephew. I wanted to get all the information I could before I said anything to him."

Her eyes narrowed even more. "Estranged? I'm curious as to what it takes to become estranged from Mrs. Shaw."

Katrina guessed that Savannah was in the habit of using people, including her kids, to get what she wanted. "Well, Keith refused to associate with his parents and sisters unless they quit drinking. They wouldn't quit, so he moved on with his life. He's with the FBI now, and he's doing well. I don't want to rock the boat if I don't have to."

Mrs. Daley sighed. "And what is it you think you can do?"

"I don't know." She hadn't thought beyond passing the information to Keith. "I just want to make sure they're taken care of, I guess."

The woman lifted a brow. "Is your boyfriend interested in taking the kids? The state does prefer to place children with relatives when possible. The family they're with now only handles short-term placements. They're not interested in adoption."

Katrina hadn't seriously considered that possibility. She wasn't against kids, but she didn't see them occupying a prominent position in her life anytime soon. And Keith had been vehemently against having children of his own. "But they're young enough that somebody will adopt them, right?"

Mrs. Daley shook her head. "The baby, Corey, maybe. He's a cute little boy, with those golden curls and those green eyes. Good-natured too. But the three-year-old girl, Angelina, is a tougher case. She's biracial, and the mother has no clue which races those might be, and she's prone to temper tantrums. I'm not talking the regular kind, either. She can go for hours, and she can get pretty violent. I think she has some special needs, but I'm not sure what they are. Most people don't want to adopt outside their race, and they don't want special-needs kids. I'd prefer to keep them together if I can."

Katrina's heart jumped to her throat to hear that dire pronouncement. Just knowing what Savannah had done to her younger brother made her sick. But for the first time, she considered the fact that the woman hadn't treated her own kids much better.

"Can Keith meet them? I mean, if he wants to. I can't speak for him."

The social worker crossed her arms over her ample bosom. "If he's a relative, he can petition for visiting rights. You know where friend of the court is located."

Katrina picked up on the woman's changed attitude. "Did I say something to offend you?"

Mrs. Daley pursed her lips. "It's always the same story. Maybe you can't have kids and you're thinking you can raise these ones, but then you find out it's not all sunshine and roses. These kids have been through a lot in their short lives. I thought maybe you were the kind of person who cared about that, but now I'm not so sure."

She had no right to judge Katrina so harshly. She barely knew Katrina at all, though Katrina didn't feel the need to point that out. It was the perfect opening to end the conversation and kick Katrina out.

"I do care. It's a little overwhelming, that's all. I've known Keith for eleven years. He's an exceptional person. He served in Iraq, and when he returned home, he joined the FBI. He's dedicated his life to putting away bad people." She swallowed back unexpected tears and stopped thinking through what she wanted to say. The words poured out.

"He's never said much about his family. Savannah is eight years older than him, and she was horribly abusive. I don't know all the details, but I know that when he says he doesn't want kids, it's because he's afraid of reliving the horror of his childhood. After his mother approached me last week—he won't even talk to her—I went to see Savannah in jail. She seemed to want Keith to take the kids, but I didn't promise anything because I'm not sure he'll even consent to see them."

Mrs. Daley handed her a tissue.

"Thank you." Katrina dabbed at her eyes and blew her nose. She was more than a little appalled at her breakdown. Her heart broke for those kids as much as it did for Keith, though she knew he didn't want sympathy. "I honestly don't know what I'm doing here."

Mrs. Daley shook her head and blew out a stream of air, sounding like a pressure-release valve. "Honey, you're a mess. I'll set up a meeting, but you need to figure out what you want. I'm going to have to place those kids as soon as I can, and that might mean splitting them up and keeping Angelina in the system. Now give me your card and get out of my office. I have work to do."

---

That night at dinner, Kat was exceptionally quiet. Keith had arrived home first, and he'd downloaded an awesome tilapia recipe. It used capers and bacon, as well as all his favorite vegetables. He'd thought Kat would exclaim over it, and then he'd show her the surprise he had in the dungeon.

"What's wrong, Kitty Kat?"

She brightened at his use of her nickname, and she seemed to come to life a little. "Nothing. Chief Alder put me second chair on the Holbrook case."

That was a huge deal. Keith couldn't figure out how that would make her almost pensive. "And you don't want the responsibility?"

"No, I do." She focused her gaze on him, searching his face for something. "Aaron wanted second chair really badly. He was crushed when they refused his request. I came to the chief's notice when I found some files that had gone missing. It was a favor for Aaron. I don't want him to think I went behind his back."

This wasn't the first time Kat had mentioned Aaron's shortcomings. Keith had spent time with Jordan that morning, going over the evidence they had on Buttermore. The man was definitely setting up Kat in a way that could ruin her career. Thankfully Jordan was already gathering evidence.

He put his hand on her bare knee under the table. He'd allowed her to wear clothes, but he'd made her remove her panties and hose. "He'll be jealous at first, but if he's a true friend, he'll be happy for you."

Really he wanted to tell her that Buttermore was corrupt and that she should stay away from him, but Kat was a horrible actress. Her inherent honesty would inevitably lead her to slip up and say something to Buttermore, especially if she was feeling betrayed and her emotional guard was down. The elusive stalker provided enough stress for now.

She stretched toward him and kissed his cheek. "You're a very sweet man. And this is very good fish."

"I know." He slid his hand up her leg, scrunching the fabric of her skirt out of the way. "I have other good things planned for tonight."

She shifted her leg to let him have more access, and her expression turned downright flirty. "Really? Does it involve bondage?"

"Of course. And you'll get to call me 'Doctor.' Actually, you'll get to scream it." He pulled her onto his lap and slid her plate closer. Though she was sitting next to him, it was too far away. He plunged his tongue into her mouth until she clung to him and made those little kittenish moans in the back of her throat. Then he fed her the rest of her dinner.

When Keith had given her the folded garment and told her to change into it before knocking on the dungeon door, Katrina hadn't expected it to be one of those paper hospital exam gowns. She put it on with the opening in the front, frowned at her attire, and knocked on the door.

"This isn't sexy." She muttered it, but he opened the door just in time to hear her criticism.

His gaze traveled down her form and back up. "It isn't meant to be sexy, Ms. Legato. This is a doctor's office, not a sex clinic." He took her by the arm and led her into the room.

Maybe her gown wasn't sexy, but she had to admit that adding the lab coat over his shirt and tie did make him appear even more handsome.

Most of the dungeon had been hidden by strategically placed sheets that functioned as drapes. Only the corner with the exam table was open. It reclined like a chair, but it also had padded extensions on which to rest legs.

"Doctor, going to the gynecologist's office is never sexy."

"Of course not," he agreed somberly. "That would be unethical. Get on the table."

She sat on the center part of the table and leaned back.

"I'm going to lift your legs into the stirrups. Nothing to be alarmed about."

He lifted one leg, bending it at the knee and adjusting the stirrup part to fit her length. Then he saw to her other leg. She felt split open, exposed in a way that never happened with her real doctor. Analyzing the placement of her legs, she realized that her doctor never spread her this wide.

Then she felt the restraints being tightened into place. He secured her at the ankles and just above her knees. Next he tied her arms to the padded armrests, securing her at the wrists and elbows. Then he buckled a thicker leather band over her shoulders. An even thicker belt crossed her hips to hold them still.

He hovered over her, checking the fit of the restraints. "Comfortable?"

The exam table was surprisingly cozy. "What are you going to do to me?"

One corner of his mouth lifted with the suggestion of a smile. "Anything I want. We're alone in a soundproof room, and you're tied down." He ripped at her paper covering, shredding it as he pulled it from her body. "And now you're naked."

She tried to move, but it was a futile attempt. She could turn her head, but that was all.

He frowned at her, and then he disappeared behind the chair. She heard him rummaging around. When he returned, he secured yet another restraint across her forehead. Now she couldn't move at all.

"Now, Ms. Legato, what seems to be the problem this time?"

She was tied to a chair and trapped in a room with a sex addict, but she didn't consider that problematic. She searched for a plausible answer. "My pussy aches."

"Hmmm. Sounds like you need a full exam." He put on a headlamp and situated himself on a rolling stool between her legs.

She felt the heat of the light as it bathed her wet tissues. He probed her folds without any sense of urgency.

Abruptly he stood. "I can't see anything down there. I'm going to shave you."

Katrina wasn't sure she'd heard him right, but when he produced one of those rolling surgical carts with a bowl of warm water, a can of shaving cream, and a razor on it, she protested. It had been a few days since she'd groomed herself, but it wasn't that bad. She didn't object to being shaved, only to the fact of him doing it. "You're not really going to shave me."

He chuckled as he resumed his seat. "How are you going to stop me?"

She could call red, but she didn't want to stop the scene. She could see where this could get interesting. The heat of the lamp made her juices seep even faster, and the loss of control freed her to enjoy the process. He made quick work of it and cleaned her up with efficient movements. Then he produced his cell phone and took a picture, which he showed her. It looked downright pornographic.

"That's the prettiest pussy I've ever seen, Kitty Kat."

"You'd better delete that picture."

He chuckled as he slipped it back into his pocket. "Delete my screen saver?"

She wanted to rail at him, but he blew across her pussy. Sensations, wild and wanton, came to life. Then he ran his finger over her tender flesh.

"Now I can do a thorough exam. You do not have permission to orgasm."

That made her wary. She'd noticed that he often denied permission when he was going to make it difficult for her not to climax. Heat from the light came back, but it was quickly replaced by heat from his tongue. He licked her pussy lips, and she found out just how insidious he could be. The restraints let her go nowhere. The sensations on her bare pussy bordered on too much, and she couldn't lift her hips or wiggle back to ease the pressure. She was stuck in this position, completely at his mercy.

"Doctor, please."

He ignored her, exploring her folds with short and long licks. Soon he let his fingers join the party. He fucked them into her slick opening and found her sweet spot. She fought the heat coiling in her abdomen, but each tiny jerk of her arms or legs, even her shoulder and hips, against the straps only heightened the arousal. He buried his mouth in her cunt, and due to the inclined positioning of the chair, she could see the ecstasy on his face.

Her climax broke over her, and he moaned between her legs, lapping faster at her juices. When he sat back with a self-satisfied smirk lifting the corners of his mouth, she cursed him.

"Well, I can see that this naughty pussy needs to be taught a lesson."

Her body quivered with aftershocks. He used the flap of a crop to trace around her nipples. If he hit her with that in her newly exposed pussy, she didn't know if she could handle the pain.

"I'm sorry," she said. "I'll try harder next time."

"Yes," he said. "You will." With that, he brought the crop down on her leg.

The flap got her, but the plastic length of the implement did as well. It stung. It hurt. Heat radiated from the red line forming on her thigh. She mewed, a belated reaction, and he brought it down on her other thigh.

Back and forth, he alternated thighs and the force of his strikes. He peppered her inner and outer thighs. Dimly, she noted that he concentrated on the meaty areas and avoided the places where he might hit too close to the bone, strict guidelines he'd imparted at their practice session.

Sweat broke out on her brow, and the sting morphed into pure heat. Her thighs were a mess of red lines, and her pussy was thick with cream. Then he tapped the floppy leather flap on her clit, and she exploded. Colors burst behind her eyes, and she screamed with the force of another climax.

He didn't give her much time to recover before he turned his attention to her breasts. He was gentler there, tapping her swollen globes and pointy nipples. He varied the force as well. She never knew when he would bring the crop down hard or tap it lightly or just barely touch it down at all. When he stopped, heat spread over her breasts, stomach, and thighs. Her pussy craved the feel of him stretching her with his cock.

"How are you doing, Kitty Kat?"

She knew he wanted her color, but she played dumb. "My pussy still aches, Doctor."

He grinned. "I have just the thing."

This time, he disappeared on the other side of the sheet. When he returned, she recognized the bulky TENS unit he carried. He set it on the floor below the exam table.

"I'm going to clean you up first, Ms. Legato. You're quite wet."

She closed her eyes and enjoyed his ministrations. The pads felt sticky against her skin. He placed two where her butt muscle met her pussy, two on either side of her freshly shaved mons, and two on her lower stomach, just above the belt holding her hips in place.

He smacked her clit with the crop. "Let's see if we can't keep you from climaxing this way. Tell me when you feel it."

The tiny pricks grew in intensity until they felt like miniscule mallets thumping away at her. It felt good. "I feel it."

He turned the machine up a little more. "Tell me when it becomes unbearable."

The thumps came harder, which still felt good. Then they turned into something unpleasant. "There. Not that. Please not that."

He dialed it back. It was more than she wanted, but it didn't hurt.

"Doctor, please turn it down, just a tad. It felt so good a moment ago."

"No. You're not supposed to climax, Ms. Legato. We talked about this. It's inappropriate. I'm attempting to cure your ache, and you're behaving in a decidedly wanton fashion." He ran his hands over her flesh, exploring from the palms of her hands to the soles of her feet. That seemed inappropriate behavior for a doctor, but she was too busy trying to deal with the riot of sensations running rampant in her body to point out the hypocrisy.

When he got to her nipples, he rolled and pinched them. Then he clamped something on them that felt like it had spikes.

"Clover clamps, Ms. Legato. They'll help keep your mind on your treatment."

The TENS unit abruptly cut off, and her whole body relaxed. She hadn't realized how tense she'd become. She closed her eyes. He peeled off the sticky pads, but she could still feel the electricity stimulating her muscles. Every cell buzzed with anticipation.

When he pushed his cock inside her, she wasn't surprised. She was amazed he'd held out this long. She opened her eyes to find him watching her face. She felt like she'd run a marathon, and she hadn't moved an inch. Still that didn't dampen her brazen side. "Do you fuck all your patients, Doctor?"

"Internal massage." He winked and thrust hard. "There's a difference."

Because this was the part she'd been praying for, she didn't argue. "Yes, Doctor."

"No orgasms, Ms. Legato."

She wasn't in control anymore. If it happened, it happened. "Yes, Doctor."

She kept her gaze on him, though. He was sinfully handsome in that jacket. It gaped open at the bottom, revealing that he'd done nothing more than shove his pants out of the way before entering her. Seeing him clothed, looming over her as he pounded his cock into her, filled her with gentle powerlessness.

Pressure built, and she didn't bother fighting. Gazing into his emerald eyes, she surrendered to everything she felt. "I love you, Keith."

His eyes blazed brighter. He came, pulling out as he ejaculated and spraying her pussy with his seed. The hot mess seared her tenderized flesh. She whimpered at the sensation, but she didn't protest the way he marked her.

Leaning down, he captured her mouth with a hungry kiss. It overwhelmed her, as did his cock when she felt it elongating against her back entrance. Like a good patient, she hadn't climaxed. If he fucked her ass, she had no hope of controlling herself. Though, to be honest, if he had lasted a minute longer, she would have come with him.

She felt his fingers on her sphincter, rubbing in the lubrication. Then he eased his cock past the tight ring of muscle. "Now you're in trouble, Ms. Legato."

He moved at a leisurely pace, but it didn't matter. Molten heat tingled at the base of her spine. She panted and struggled to move—with him, against him, it didn't matter as long as she could release some of this energy.

Then he slid two fingers into her vagina, curving them to find her sweet spot, rubbing it to the slow slide of his cock, in and out, in and out. "Give it to me."

With a long, loud cry, she came. Her orgasm burst slowly and violently, like the birth of the heavens. He kept thrusting into her, making her ride that stardust to the crest of another orgasm. This time he removed the nipple clamps as she came. Heat radiated through every cell in her body, and her vision went black.

Keith loosened the straps binding her head and arms first, but she didn't open her eyes. He shook her shoulder. "Kitty Kat?"

No response. Her eyes weren't completely closed. He could see the whites peeking out where her lids didn't quite meet. Worried, he pried them open and checked her pupils. They responded to light appropriately, but she still didn't stir. He'd never driven a lover to this place before. They'd passed out, gone to sleep, whatever. But they always roused when he told them to.

He freed her shoulders and hips, but he kept her legs bound while he cleaned her up. As sensitive as he knew she was, she didn't flinch at all. When he finished, he wrapped her in a warm blanket and lifted her into his arms. He didn't have a sofa in his dungeon because he didn't want to encourage cuddling.

It looked like he was going to have to get one.

He carried her up two flights of stairs and into his bedroom. He had a very comfortable armchair there, so he settled in and held her in his arms.

Time passed. The digital display on his alarm clock changed fifteen times before she made a small whimpering noise that put him on high alert.

"Kat?"

Her cheek was against his shoulder. She stirred, shifting so that her nose touched his neck. Her hand came out of the flap in the front of the blanket, and she grasped at his shirt in a jerky, panicked twitch.

"I'm here, honey. I've got you."

She settled down and mumbled something, but he didn't catch what she said.

"What? Can you say that again, Kitty Kat?"

Seven more minutes passed. At least he knew she was all right. Then she stirred again. "I said I need to talk to you. I have to tell you something."

She sounded worried, so he smoothed his hand down her spine. "We have all night. I'm not going anywhere."

"It's serious." Now she was rousing. Her voice was stronger, but she didn't move a muscle. "And not about sex."

Iciness crept through his veins. "Okay. Do you want to get dressed?"

"No. I don't want you to let go. I feel like you're holding me together, like if you let go, I might break apart."

It had been a more intense scene than he'd originally planned, and it had left her vulnerable and emotionally wrung out. His ill-timed orgasm hadn't helped either. He'd heard her utter those three heartfelt words. He wanted to say them back, but the chance had passed him by, and his courage had gone with it. The least he could do was hold her.

Her voice was scratchy from all the yelling she'd done, and he didn't have water nearby to offer her a drink. Yep, he was going to have to tweak the setup in the dungeon to better meet her needs. A sofa and a small fridge went on his mental shopping list.

"Okay. I won't let go."

"You have to promise to listen to everything before you get mad at me."

That really didn't sound good. "What did you do?"

She tightened her grip on his shirt, her fist pressing against his stomach. "Promise first."

"I promise." He hated making a promise when he didn't know if he could keep it.

"Last Thursday, when I was late getting to the parking garage?"

He nodded, and he wished she would sit back so he could see her face. Right now, he only had a view of the top of her head.

"Your mom came to see me."

Fury boiled in his core. That bitch had no business going near Kat. "She what?"

"Keith, you promised."

He took a deep breath and slowed his temper to a simmer. "Go on."

"She told me that your sister was in jail and the state was going to put her kids up for adoption."

Though he'd known she was in prison, and he knew the conviction was triple manslaughter, he hadn't known that Savannah had kids. The fact he stayed silent was more a testament to shock.

"She really didn't say much more than that, so I did some digging. I looked up the charges. She's serving three consecutive eight-year sentences for manslaughter. The details don't matter that much. I went to see her, and she told me that she wanted me to make sure nothing bad happened to her kids."

Keith felt nothing but pity for those children. No doubt Savannah had been a shitty mother and they were better off with another family.

"So I looked up the social worker who is handling their case. Her name is Mrs. Daley. She wouldn't talk to me over the phone, so I went to go see her. That's where I was today. It's why I couldn't meet you in the parking garage."

Kat twisted her fist tighter in his shirt, and he heard the seams pop. More than that, he heard the distress in her voice. He wanted so badly to interrupt, but he'd promised, so he buried his questions and kept stroking his hand up and down her back.

"Mrs. Daley said that Corey stands a good chance of being adopted because he's eleven months old and has no health issues. But Angelina, who's three, has some behavioral problems. Mrs. Daley doesn't know if she'll be able to find a permanent home for Angelina, and she's pretty sure she's going to have to split them up."

She was crying now, her shoulders shaking with the weight of her sobs. He tightened his hold and rocked, tipping back her head so he could smooth kisses over her face.

"You're not mad?"

How could he get mad at her for doing something that was the essence of what he loved about her? "No. You have a soft heart. I can't imagine you not following through on finding them and making sure they're okay."

She searched his face the same way she had earlier. Finally she continued. "Mrs. Daley is going to set up a time for you to meet them, if you want."

He felt his eyes widen and his eyebrows lift, an outward manifestation of his shock. "Why would I want to meet them?"

"They're your niece and nephew. Your parents don't want them. This might be your only chance to be a part of their lives."

He didn't know whether to be stunned or angry. "Kat, they're strangers. They don't know me, and I don't know them. You said their caseworker was working on finding homes. Why would I interfere with that?"

She sat up and pushed away, not bothering to hide her disappointment. "I'm not asking if you want to interfere, you thickheaded man. I'm asking if you want to be part of their lives. You could be a positive influence. I'm sure whoever adopts them won't bar them from seeing you, not if you asked nicely."

With a scowl, she got to her feet and grabbed her overnight case. She shoved a nightgown over her head, which mollified him a bit because it meant she wasn't planning to leave in a huff.

"I can't believe you're not even curious. I know you hate your sister, but I don't see how that translates to innocent little children."

With that, she marched into the bathroom. He heard water running and decided to leave her alone. He didn't know what he'd say anyway. Was he curious about the kids? Not really. They were a foreign concept, and he was still stunned, both by the bombshell Kat had dropped and by her expectation of a different reaction from him.

He caught her as she exited the bathroom and headed toward the bed. Her body vibrated with fury. "Kat, I know you're angry, but you're being thoughtless about this. By my count, you've had five days to think this through. I've had five minutes."

Just like that, the tightness drained away. She threw her arms around him. "You're right. I'm sorry. I just... I think about those poor little kids out there in the big, bad world with no stability whatsoever."

"If they lived with my sister, then they never had it to begin with."

She looked at him with a wealth of sadness darkening her deep brown eyes. "At least think about it. I won't go against whatever decision you make."

# Chapter Fourteen

When Katrina started her period the next day, she understood the reason for her tears. She'd cried way too easily, both in Mrs. Daley's office and in front of Keith. It wasn't like she didn't know when to expect it. Those color-coded pills were pretty exact. She just hadn't been paying attention.

However, that wasn't the worst of her problems. Coming into contact with countless strangers each day put her at risk for any number of illnesses. In addition to her monthly visitor, her sinuses left her head feeling cottony. Because she didn't normally suffer from allergies, she figured on the flu. It had been going around in the Health Care Fraud Unit, and now it looked to be making a home in the WCCU.

Keith frowned at her when she had plain toast and weak tea for breakfast. "Kat, you can't survive on just that until lunch. At least have a bowl of cereal."

The idea of eating anything else made Katrina's stomach churn. "I'll be fine."

"You don't look fine. Was last night too much?"

Starting her period and getting the flu all in the same morning was too much, but she had a lot to do at work today. She couldn't let those problems get in her way. "No. Last night was wonderful. I started my period this morning, so I'm a little tired. Maybe we can just hang out tonight."

The calculating squint to his eyes didn't give her much hope that he completely bought her story, but he didn't say anything, so she let the matter drop.

An hour later, she reached her desk to find Aaron angrily packing his things into a cardboard box. Two security officers stood watch. Her jaw fell open. "What happened?"

He looked up briefly, long enough to deliver a glare. "I got suspended, thanks to you."

It felt like he'd punched her in the stomach, and that area of her body was already pretty battered. "Thanks to me? I don't understand."

"I asked you for one simple favor, and you turned me in for it."

Katrina shook her head. Chief Alder had known where she'd been and what she'd been doing the whole time. She'd been taken to task for it as well. "I still don't understand. You shouldn't be fired because I did some digging for you. When the chief called me into her office yesterday, I—"

Aaron held up his palm. "I don't care, Katrina. You got me suspended so you could take second chair on the Holbrook case. Don't think I don't know about that."

His aggressiveness didn't make sense on so many levels, but Katrina forced herself to let it go. She couldn't imagine how angry and hurt he must feel right now. She was going to schedule an appointment to talk to the chief. Then she would call Aaron and try to explain what happened. There had to be more to the story than either of them knew. Vaguely, she wondered if the person who was forging names in the evidence logs was targeting Aaron.

As she watched the officers escort him to the elevator, she bit back tears. It wasn't fair. Aaron had been a good, supportive friend. She felt horrible for him. And to top it off, she had to be in court in half an hour, so she couldn't do anything to help Aaron right that second. She fired off a text to Jordan as she headed to court, asking him to look into Aaron's suspension.

She didn't get a chance to talk to Chief Alder until her boss stopped by after lunch to assign work related to the Holbrook case. Even then, the chief dumped a series of tasks on Katrina's lap and walked away.

Katrina ran to catch up. "Chief Alder, I know I'm overstepping my bounds, but I wanted to ask about Aaron. It wasn't my intention to get him in trouble."

Half of Chief Alder's nose scrunched up. "I'm not at liberty to discuss the particulars."

She walked away, and Katrina knew better than to push the issue until she knew more about what had happened. She'd ask Keith if he knew what was going on. While he probably didn't, he'd have ideas. And contacts. The man had an amazing amount of contacts. This turn of events made no sense to Katrina.

When she spotted Dustin coming toward her with a tight expression on his face an hour before the end of the day, she almost ran for the door. She didn't want to deal with more stress, and with Dustin involved, the news couldn't be good.

"Hey, Trina." He stopped in front of her desk. "Is there somewhere private we can talk?"

Good news could be delivered with other people around. It was no secret that she had a stalker or that the FBI was investigating the case and all the ways it might be related to the DOJ. The sick feeling that had been simmering on the back burner all day became bothersome, and that did not mix well with the achiness in her limbs. Damn flu. Damn period. Damn stalker. Damn everything.

She rose from her chair and pointed toward the hall to the conference rooms. "Five is open."

He followed her across the room, past all the desks of people looking at her. She wondered what they were thinking about as they watched.

When they arrived—those fifteen yards seemed like a mile—Dustin reached around her to open the door, and he closed it behind them. "You look like I could knock you over with a feather. Have a seat, and breathe. I have some good news." Ever the gentleman, he pulled out a chair.

"Good news." She tried for a smile, but it wasn't forthcoming. She didn't want to get her hopes up too high. "I could use some of that."

"Someone broke into your condo today." He had to know full well that his delivery made her squirm, and his easy smile mitigated the butterflies somewhat. "Because your brother had the place wired with cameras, we have the crime on tape. We're running the pictures through facial recognition right now."

She stared at him as she processed what he'd said. Suddenly she felt much better. The effects of her flu seemed so paltry now, like she would wake up in the morning and be completely well. "So you don't know who it is, and you haven't made an arrest."

"We have a picture, Trina, of a woman. That's a lot. I know I'm jumping the gun on this a little. Nothing is official, and I'm still working on the case, but this is a major breakthrough." He closed his hands around the fists she'd made. Their warmth indicated exactly how cold her hands had become. "That, and I need to ask you not to go home today. The place was trashed. I have a team there now, gathering evidence. It's safest if you just go home with Rossetti."

Trashed. She closed her eyes and buried feelings of violation underneath the relief she felt at the imminent end of this ordeal. "Did you want me to look at the picture? Maybe I know her."

Dustin's pocket vibrated, and he checked his cell. "That's not necessary. We got a positive match."

From the expression on his face, she could only tell that the information he received hadn't made him happy. "Who is it?"

He shook his head. "This just got more complicated. I need to check this out before I say anything more, but I can tell you that I'll make an arrest in the next few hours." He stood up, pulling her to her feet with him because he didn't release her hand.

"Dustin, you have a name." She deserved to know the name of the person who had upended her life for the past two weeks.

Instead of answering, he hugged her close and kissed her cheek. "I'll let you deliver the news to Malcolm and Keith, and I'll call you once this is all over."

He left. Katrina spent the rest of the workday vacillating between bouts of manic productiveness and choking anxiety. She called and left voice mails for Malcolm and Keith. Her parents actually picked up the phone, and they both expressed relief.

Keith met her in the parking garage wearing a happy smile on his face. He opened his arms, and she stepped right into his embrace. "I'm still going to be sleeping over when you stay at home."

With his arms around her, the stress of the day melted away. She closed her eyes and realized how drained she was. "Dustin wants me to stay away from my house this evening. Let's go to your house. I want chocolate ice cream and a chick flick. You can paint my toenails."

He laughed and gave her one final squeeze. "I've never painted toenails before. You might come to regret that offer."

He released her and opened her car door. She slid into the driver's seat and looked up at him. "No resistance to a chick flick?"

He shrugged. "I can't remember ever watching one of those either."

"Wow. Two new experiences in one night. Are you sure you're up for it?" She was teasing, but her concern was real. Sex was off the table tonight. "Seriously, if you want to do your own thing while I veg on the sofa, I'll understand."

"As long as I get to be with you, I can handle the rest." He closed her door and headed to his SUV parked across the aisle.

Keith found himself shaking his head at random intervals for the entire drive home. He'd agreed to a romantic movie and possibly painting Kat's toenails. This was new territory for him in some ways. He'd watched plenty of movies with Kat, but they'd always been action-adventure or war themed or science fiction.

She'd been kidding about the toenails, but part of him wanted to try it. The act seemed so intimate, something a man would do for a woman he cherished. In the past, he would have nixed the idea purely because it seemed like a submissive thing to do, but the more he thought about it, the more it became a dominating action. It was like aftercare, only it didn't necessitate a scene beforehand.

He might actually enjoy it. He activated the voice controls for his cell and called Kat. If Dustin was making an arrest, then she'd be fine alone for a few minutes. "Honey, I'm going to stop at the store. You go to my place and figure out what movie you want to see."

"Okay." She didn't sound worried. "Can you pick up some ice cream with double fudge and brownie chunks? I am in serious need of chocolate."

He was pleased to see how much she'd perked up with this news. This morning, she'd been pale and lethargic, and he'd been gravely worried about her. He took his time at the store. The aisle with the nail polish was surprisingly huge, and just when he thought he'd looked through all the offerings, he noticed another display a few feet down the aisle.

Since he couldn't decide on one color, he chose several, and then he picked up a pedicure kit that contained toe spreaders. Painting her nails might be fun after all. The side trip turned out to take longer than he'd intended. Now he knew why Papa L always commented on how much time it took to shop for women. There were simply too many choices.

When he arrived home, Kat greeted him in the front hall by jumping into his arms. To catch her, he dropped the bag with her ice cream and nail polish. Her exuberance was definitely sexy.

"I should run to the store more often."

She giggled. "I got a voice mail from Dustin. They've made an arrest. I'm free, Keith. Nobody is hiding in the shadows anymore." She slathered kisses all over his face, forcing him to close his eyes and enjoy the attention.

But having Kat pressed against his body and wiggling her delectableness all over his front was fated to lead to a single place. Threading his fingers through her hair, he held her steady while he tasted the sweetness of her mouth. She moaned and rubbed against him. He let one of her legs slide to the floor, but he kept the other high on his hip so he could caress upward from her knee.

"Son of a bitch!"

His storm door slammed, jolting them both from the bliss they shared. Keith broke the kiss and slowly set Kat back on her feet. He'd dreaded this moment, but from the look on Kat's face, she'd dreaded it more. Malcolm stood in his entryway, fists clenched, chest heaving with pissed-off breathing.

Still, she didn't let that stop her from trying to protect him from her brother's wrath. "Malcolm, it's not what you think."

"Not what I— I'm not fucking blind, Trina." Malcolm's jaw tightened, and so did his fists. "Go wait in my car."

Kat's brows came down in hard slashes above her eyes. "I will not go wait in your car. I'm not leaving."

"You're not staying here where this bastard can prey on you." Malcolm stepped closer. His eyes contained more malice than Keith had ever seen on Malcolm. "You son of a bitch."

Keith knew his buddy's moves almost as well as he knew his own. Mal was going to ignore Kat's wishes and drag her from the house.

Keith snatched up the shopping bag from the floor and shoved Kat behind him. "Take the bag to the kitchen and put your ice cream in the freezer. Malcolm and I need to talk."

She eluded his attempts to keep her out of harm's way, probably because she didn't consider her brother a threat.

"Malcolm and you and I can all have a conversation like civilized people."

Malcolm growled. "I can't believe I trusted you with my sister. Of all the people in the world, she's the only one I forbade you from seeing. Thousands of women out there, but you had to have her."

And he'd readily agreed to the restriction. Kat had always been special to him, too good to be used and tossed aside by a man who didn't know how to do anything else. But he wasn't that man, not anymore. She'd changed him, shown him the delights he could have with her by his side, and it hadn't taken her long to work her magic. "I'm sorry that you feel betrayed right now, Mal. I didn't do this to piss you off. Kat means the world to me."

Mal moved one step closer. Keith knew Mal was getting ready to attack. He shoved the bag at Kat. "Kat, take this to the kitchen. Do not disobey me."

Giving her an order when Malcolm was ready to tear his head from his body probably wasn't the best way to get her out of the room. She took the bag from him, but instead of leaving them alone in the foyer, she stepped between them.

"Malcolm, be reasonable. I'm an adult, and so is Keith. If we want to be together, and we're happy, how can you honestly object to that?"

His heart broke a little, because he heard the anguish in her voice. It redirected some of the steam in Malcolm's sails as well.

"Trina." The growl was gone, replaced with a soft tone that left no doubt that Malcolm didn't blame her for this. "You have no idea what you're getting into. Whatever lies he's told you—"

"He hasn't lied to me." She squared her shoulders.

Malcolm closed his eyes, and Keith knew he was counting to control his temper. Kat had been right about one thing: having her here did make Mal more rational. If she had gone when either of them told her to, Mal would have thrown a punch by now. Keith wasn't afraid of fighting with Malcolm. The two of them had come to blows before. They were well matched.

"If I agree to sit down and discuss this, will you listen to me, Trina? I mean really listen?"

"Yes." She put up a hand when he stepped toward her. "But you have to agree to listen to both Keith and me as well."

Grudgingly Malcolm nodded.

"Rules." Kat moved so that she could see both of them. "No physical violence, and no name-calling."

They both peered at her curiously.

She pressed her lips together. "I've seen the way you two talk out your problems. It almost always involves bruising."

"No physical violence, and no name-calling." Keith would agree to anything right now as long as it made her happy.

Malcolm's face didn't move a muscle as he growled his agreement. Kat must have trusted them both, because she took the bag into the kitchen. She was stowing the ice cream as he entered the room and slid onto one of the high stools at his island counter. Mal took the one next to him. Strategically it blocked Kat's view if either of them felt like punching the other in the thigh.

The bag was on the counter between them. When she looked inside for more items to put away, her tense expression melted. She gazed at him with a tender smile that tugged at his heart. "Really?"

Malcolm snatched the plastic bag and peered inside. "Nail polish? What the hell kind of kink is that?" Then he appeared to rethink his question. "Never mind. I don't want to know. It doesn't matter, because it ends right now."

Kat extracted the bag from Mal's grasp. "You're such a pervert sometimes."

Normally one of them would make a joke about her "sometimes" qualification. This time nobody did.

"Listen, Mal, I know you're upset. Keith wanted to tell you right away, but you had just started speaking to him again, and I couldn't bear the thought of coming between you and your best friend." Her bottom lip trembled the tiniest bit, and Keith noticed that the tired circles under her eyes had darkened.

"So keeping this from me was your idea? When did you plan on letting me in on this little secret?" To his credit, Malcolm managed to keep his tone neutral.

"Thursday. I was going to invite you and Darcy over for dinner, and we were going to tell you then." She searched Malcolm's face anxiously. "I was going to tell Mom and Dad first. They like Keith."

Most of this was news to Keith, but he did like her plan. Darcy was a good influence on Malcolm, and Mama L and Papa L would probably approve of the relationship. Kat needed people on her side. At any rate, it would have been a good plan if Mal hadn't stopped by unexpectedly. Until now, that had never been an issue. Malcolm was always welcome at Keith's house no matter what else he had going on at the time. Lately, Mal hadn't dropped by. He was busy with Darcy, and Keith had been busy with Kat.

Malcolm turned to Keith. "Are you sure you want her here for this? What I have to say isn't exactly nice."

No, it wouldn't be. But Mal wouldn't say anything about his previous relationships that Kat didn't already know. Keith spread his hands. "You tried kicking her out. I knew better. Kat is her own woman. She does what she wants."

Mal's brows lifted in surprise. "And you're okay with that? Because I know how you like to control every little detail concerning your submissives when they're with you. What they wear, what they eat, when they eat, when they sleep, where and how they sleep, what they say, who they can talk to—"

"Enough." Kat parked her hands on her hips. "I knew he was a Dom going into this."

"But you don't know what that means, Trina. That's my point. He's not like me, or even Dustin or Jordan. For Keith, it's all about control. He could care less about what his submissives want. It's all about him. Why do you think none of his relationships last more than a week or two? It's not a healthy way to live."

"He treats his girlfriends like shit. I know." When Malcolm opened his mouth, Keith knew it was to drive home his point. She held her hand up to stop Mal. "I don't know why you think I would let him get away with treating me like that. It was hard at first, sure, but he adjusted quickly."

Keith chuckled at her characterization of events. She'd learned a lot, and she'd made a ton of changes, but she'd chosen to focus on him. It was so like her to minimize her role.

Mal punched him under the counter. "You think this is funny?"

"Kat makes me laugh." He spread his hands wide on top of the counter, making no move to retaliate. He'd get Mal back, but now wasn't the time. Kat would kill him if this degenerated into an actual fight. "That's just one of the things I adore about her."

"Adore? You have no respect for the women you date. The fact that they are willing to go out with you automatically makes you hate them. I love you, man, but I've known you for too long to think you can suddenly be the kind of man my sister deserves. And you know I'm right."

Keith scowled. He'd used that argument with Kat already, and she'd shown him how wrong he was. How could he prove to Malcolm that Kat made him a new man?

"That's mean, Mal. Keith has been good to me for eleven years. Sure, he tried to be a dickhead when we first got together, but I put a stop to that right away."

Malcolm narrowed his eyes. "A dickhead? What did he do to you?"

Kat blushed a little, bringing some color back to her face. She still looked tired, though. "Don't ask, Mal. Just trust me to keep him in line."

"You can't." Malcolm shook his head. "He's too messed up. Maybe you think he'll change for you, and he might do it for a week or two, but ultimately, he is who he is." Turning to face Keith, Malcolm looked tired too. "You're an alcoholic who doesn't trust a single woman. We talked about this years ago when you promised to leave my sister alone. She's liked you since the first time I brought you home. What's changed?"

In all the scenarios he'd run through his mind, Keith hadn't seriously thought that Malcolm would mention his addiction. He checked Kat to gauge her reaction. She was frowning, but he couldn't pin down the exact cause. The entire conversation had to be uncomfortable for her. She hated confrontation.

"I asked him to train me; that's what happened. Then when he turned me down, I asked Dustin. He turned me down too. I was going to ask Jordan next, but Keith got mad and agreed to train me. It grew from there." She ended with a flippant smile.

Malcolm looked like he was about to have a stroke. "You asked him to train you? Then you asked Darcy to show you how to use a flogger. Why? Keith doesn't switch. Unless... Oh." Shades of bafflement washed over Mal's face until he arrived at a conclusion that seemed to leave him with just as many questions. He nailed Keith with his most probing stare. "You're willing to let her flog you."

Keith nodded. "It was her idea, but yeah, when she's ready."

"You trust her?"

Kat punched Mal hard on his arm. Apparently only he and Mal were prohibited from violence. "Of course he trusts me."

Malcolm ignored it, though Keith knew she packed a wallop. He held Keith's gaze and waited for an answer.

"I trust her. And I respect her. I like her a lot, and I find her very attractive. It's not the same with her, Mal. You made me promise to stay away from the one woman who doesn't buy my bullshit. She makes me want to be a better man." His cheeks felt hot, and he hoped to hell he was coming down with a fever. He motioned to the plastic bag near Kat. "She asked me to paint her toenails and watch a chick flick, and I said yes."

For ten silent seconds, Malcolm stared at him, his hard expression etched on his face. Then he laughed and shook his head. "Holy shit. You're serious."

"Yeah. I am." His chest constricted a little. The people in this room were his whole world. "This is serious, the real thing. I wouldn't risk our friendship if it wasn't."

Malcolm nodded thoughtfully, his expression softening with acceptance.

Kat flew around the counter and threw herself at Malcolm. She hugged her brother tightly. "I knew I could get you to see reason."

Malcolm hugged her back. "I'm reserving judgment, Trina." That hardness was back as he nailed a warning to Keith's forehead with his stare. "I'm not completely convinced yet. You're a sweet, generous person, and if he takes advantage of that or breaks your heart, I will kill him."

If he broke her heart, Malcolm wouldn't have to worry about that. Keith would take care of that himself. He didn't take issue with the threat. "So, what brings you over on such a lovely afternoon? You never just stop by anymore."

Mal hugged Kat harder. "I came to tell you the person they arrested was not Trina's stalker, which I pointed out to Dustin the moment I got hold of him."

Kat pushed away and staggered back. Keith caught her before she could trip and drew her close to him. She stared at Malcolm, her wide eyes edged with panic. "What happened?"

"First, the person they picked up has no semen, which we found in trace amounts in your underwear drawer."

Her face twisted in horror. "Oh, ewww. That thing needs to get out of my house now."

Malcolm frowned. "It was Grandma's, and it's been cleaned. If you don't want it, you'd better give it back to Mom and Dad. Also, the woman Dustin arrested turned out to be Starr Rossetti."

That curveball puzzled Keith. His mother was a drunk, not a criminal. She'd never even gotten a DUI. She didn't drive at all; she used public transportation. "My mother? Why the hell was she breaking into Kat's house?"

"She claims she wasn't breaking in. She was just trying to see if Trina was home. Apparently she had some news to impart. She's not saying anything more unless it's to Trina. Interesting way to ask for a lawyer." Malcolm stood. "She's in the county lockup. I came over to see if Trina wanted to go down there and talk to her."

Kat looked to him for guidance. He could tell she wanted to find out what his mother wanted. She was thinking of his sister's kids, worry etched in the tiny lines around her pale mouth. He wondered when it would hit her that her stalker was still out there. From Dustin's description of the damage done to her condo, the stalker had definitely been there. He'd used her lipstick and eyeliner to scrawl "bitch" on every wall in her condo.

"We can go, but we're not staying long. You already look wiped out, Kitty Kat." He ran a light caress down her cheek. She closed her eyes and leaned into his palm.

"Give me a minute." She disappeared into the bathroom.

Malcolm regarded him with a strange expression on his face. "It's weird to hear you talk like that."

Keith had never before called a woman by a nickname. He pointed a warning finger at Malcolm. "Don't start."

"Good weird. Refreshing. I'd about given up on you." Mal chucked him on the shoulder. "Still, if you break her heart, they'll never find your body."

---

This was the strangest day in Katrina's life. Good and bad things had happened, and she didn't quite know how to feel about it overall. She entered the tiny interrogation room knowing that a team of special agents—including her brother and Keith—were watching. Keith had wanted to come with her, but Katrina had the feeling his mother wouldn't talk as freely if he was in the room.

Starr sat on the other side of the metal table, handcuffed to a rectangular bar that was welded to the tabletop. Her lip was curled in disgust, but other than that, she looked no different than she had five days ago when she'd stopped Katrina on the street.

"Hi, Starr. How are you?"

"In jail. I ain't never been in jail before. They think I was trying to break into your house."

Dustin had shown Katrina the evidence. Her door had been kicked in, and somebody had searched through her house. The mess was going to take some time to clean up, and the epithets on the walls made her stomach churn. Worse, the trajectory of the cameras outside her condo had been moved. It appeared that whoever had done this knew where the cameras were placed and how to approach them unseen in order to disable them.

For those reasons Katrina believed Starr. The woman didn't seem like much of a planner. "What were you doing in my house?

The recovered footage showed Starr skulking around the parking lot, glancing about furtively, and then she disappeared as she got closer to Katrina's place.

"Your door was open, but it was too quiet. It didn't look right." Her scratchy voice was laced with bafflement.

"So you went inside?" Dustin had been unable to get a clear accounting from Starr. Katrina was used to asking direct questions, but she was also used to knowing the answers beforehand.

"Yeah, but the place looked fine. A little messy, but nothin' too bad. My place looks worse on a good day." She laughed, but it turned into a nicotine cough. "Then the police come and arrest me like I was the one who did it."

It did explain Keith's fastidiousness. He was still rebelling against his childhood. Katrina managed a small smile. The reprieve from the flu had vanished. Her head pounded, her muscles ached, and she felt like she was going to fall over. "My place was broken into. The FBI is watching my house, and they're watching me."

"Oh." The light in Starr's eyes dimmed. "I didn't know. I was gonna ask you about those kids, and did you tell Keith yet."

Katrina's heart went out to Starr. "Yes. I talked to Keith."

"And you went and seen Savannah. She told me."

"Yes. I spoke with Savannah as well."

Starr grinned, and something in her smile reminded Katrina of the way Keith looked when he was about to get his way. "You want them kids, don'tcha?"

Katrina hadn't seriously considered that. Keith hadn't even agreed to meet them, to think about being part of their lives as an uncle. She couldn't honestly imagine taking on two kids. That was a feat for someone with a more generous heart than hers. People might think she was kind and had all those nice, ladylike attributes, but Katrina had limits. She wanted things in life, and she couldn't see how kids fit into the picture.

"I want them to be placed with a good family. I promised Savannah that I would look after them." She tried to couch it gently. She felt sorry for the kids, but their best bet would be to land with a family who wanted to build a life with them.

"I knew you was good people. Savannah'll give 'em to you, but she needs you to help her out."

Katrina felt like she'd lost track of the conversation. It seemed to have transformed into a negotiation. "She needs me to do what?"

Starr shrugged. "You know. Put in a good word with the parole board, maybe get Keith to say some nice things about her. And she's gonna need some help when she gets out, some money, and maybe when you move in with Keith, you can give her your place."

Katrina's mouth fell open. Starr had just proposed committing three separate federal offenses. "Starr, thank you, but I'm not interested in taking on the kids. I promised Savannah that I would make sure they were in a good home. I never specified my home. I met with their caseworker, and she assured me that they would be placed."

She didn't mention the complications or that she had planned to meet the children. Those issues had nothing to do with Starr.

Starr, for her part, gaped right back at Katrina. "Well, I was wrong about you. I thought you was one of those women who slobbers over babies everywhere you go."

Katrina shook her head. The older her nephews became, the more she liked them. She rose to her feet. "I won't press charges, but please call before you visit next time."

When she left the room, she found Keith waiting in the hallway. "Dustin will process the paperwork. I'm taking you home. We're stopping for food. You're going to eat, and then you're going straight to bed."

She didn't have the energy to argue with that.

# Chapter Fifteen

The next morning, her flu hit full force. She groaned the moment returning consciousness made her aware of the extent to which her body ached. She called the office to let them know she wouldn't be in, and then she called in some favors to cover the appointments she couldn't move.

When Keith emerged from the shower and found her still lying down, he approached with a frown marring his brow. "Kat? Are you okay?"

"I'm not going to work. I got someone to cover my cases, and I'm taking the day off." She pushed a stray strand of hair away from her face. It had been tickling her nose, and her strategy of trying to ignore it wasn't working.

He sat down next to her and pressed his palm to her forehead, a sure sign he had no experience feeling for a fever. "You're pale and warm. I'll take you to the doctor. Let me make a phone call."

She caught him as he went to get up, tugging on his arm to make him sit back down. "I'm warm because I'm still under the covers. I'm pale because I'm feeling achy and nauseated. I probably have the flu, and there's nothing a doctor can do about it. Mostly I'm staying home because yesterday was a phenomenally crappy day and I just want to sleep."

"It wasn't that bad. We came clean with Malcolm. He took it better than I thought he would. Banning violence was a brilliant call on your part. And my mother tried to sell my sister's kids to us. It wasn't the best engagement present, but I imagine she could come up with worse." He grinned in an attempt to cheer her up, but his heart wasn't in it.

She tried to laugh at his joke, but all she managed was a small smile. "We're not engaged."

Keith shrugged. "We told Malcolm we were dating. Same thing."

Katrina sobered. From somewhere she found the strength to sit up. "You're okay with that?"

"The moment you told me I couldn't ejaculate on your face, I began to realize my number was up." He kissed the tip of her nose. "I've had time to mull it over and accept it. I'm more than okay with spending the rest of my life with you."

"This doesn't count as a proposal. I don't think we're quite to that point yet. I'm in no rush." She brushed a kiss over his smooth cheek to soften that blow. "Now, you go to work, and let me spend all day in my pajamas. I promise to sleep a lot and drink at least one protein shake today."

Lying back down, she gave him a tired smile. He was wearing that enigmatic, stoic expression that made her feel like he was dissecting her. At last, he shook his head regretfully. "Honey, I can't leave you here alone."

Tears pricked her eyes, and he noticed, because he took her hand. She cursed her damn hormones and blamed the stress of not feeling well. "Don't make me go to work. The chief suspended Aaron yesterday. He accused me of betraying him and taking his job because I was appointed second chair on the Holbrook case. Then my place was broken into, and telling Malcolm was stressful, and then your mother... I truly can't believe she said those things in an FBI interrogation room to a federal prosecutor. It says right on the wall that the room is monitored."

"I've never been convinced she could read all that well." He heaved a sigh. "All right. You can stay home today. I can go in late, but I can't take the entire day off. I'll call your dad to come over and sit with you."

With victory on her side, she went back to sleep, getting up only when he made her come downstairs for breakfast. Then she crashed on his very comfortable recliner in the family room, a cooking show providing the background noise for her dreams.

She woke up to mild cramping, but she wasn't sure if it was from her period or her other malaise. Keith had gone, but her father occupied the other chair. He had the remote for the TV in his hand.

"Hey, Dad. Thanks for coming over."

He started and tore his attention from the commercial for cholesterol medication. "Sweetie, you're up. How are you feeling?"

"Okay."

With a grimace, he turned off the TV. "You don't look like you're feeling okay. Keith said you had the flu, and you look like you have the flu."

Only her father could get away with telling her she looked like crap and still make her remember what it was like to be his cherished little girl. "I'll be okay. I just need rest. And one of those powder flu therapy mixtures that has aspirin in it. I feel like somebody beat me up. I could go for some tea."

Her father raised a thoughtful brow. It struck her how much her brothers resembled their father. It wasn't just in their looks and build, but in the air of authority and the way they inspired people to have confidence in them. "I'll make you some tea, sweetheart."

She wanted more than plain tea. She wanted to take something that would knock her out until she woke up feeling a hell of a lot better. Keith never had anything like that on hand. Whenever he got sick, he relied on her and her mother to bring over soups and medications. In some ways, Keith was a very typical male. "Will you go to the pharmacy for me? I need some other things too. I'll make a list."

She needed feminine hygiene products. Her father had long ago established that he was willing to purchase those items as long as it was written on a list and not said aloud.

He chuckled. "You're just like your mother."

It was a compliment. Her father thought the sun and moon rose and set on her mother. "Thanks. I try."

Keith had put her phone on the side table next to the chair, probably so he could have instant access to her. She texted her list to her father's phone. That way he couldn't lose it.

"Honey, we need to talk about you and Keith."

The tone in her father's voice was the same one he'd used when he sat her down at the age of fifteen to tell her that her dog had died while she was at school. She'd been heartbroken. She had no idea what her parents knew and didn't know about Keith, though she assumed that Malcolm had given their parents an earful the night before.

"Daddy—"

He held up a hand, and she fell silent. Mario Legato was going to have his say, and she was going to be a good daughter and listen.

"Katrina Marie, I love you more than anything. I'd give my life for you. I know that Keith has had more than his share of problems, and he's worked really hard to overcome them. He didn't grow up in a good home. I know he used to be a drunk. When Malcolm first brought him around, your mother and I could smell the liquor on him a mile off. We've tried to shelter you from that, all of us, even Keith. He's a strong man, but he's got some pretty thick scars. I'm talking the emotional kind."

Mario took a breath, and Katrina tried to talk as fast as she could. "Daddy, I know all that. He has a good heart."

The look he gave her shut her up. "I know he has a good heart. Your mother and I wouldn't have let him into our home and welcomed him into our family if we couldn't see the good in him. He's the one who doesn't think he has a good heart. He's the one who doesn't think he's good enough to be loved. As much as I've treated him like my own son, he keeps all of us at a distance."

She was trembling now, not from the pain, but from the impending heartbreak. In her whole life, she'd never done a single thing to upset her father, but if he insisted she end things with Keith, she knew their relationship would become estranged. Nothing could make her give up Keith.

"Dad, I love him."

Sorrow gleamed in her father's dark eyes. "I know, sweetie. You always have, and he's always loved you, even if he didn't know what to do with those feelings. I knew this day would come eventually. I just don't want to see you get hurt. He's not whole inside. There's going to come a point when he can't give you the love you deserve."

"Stop it." She blinked rapidly, willing herself not to cry again. It was a weak and pointless act. "You don't know Keith as well as you think you do. I believe in him, and that's enough for me. I'm not breaking up with him."

Mario's stern exterior melted. "Aww hell. Trina, I didn't mean to upset you. I'm not telling you to break up with him. As long as he makes you happy, your mother and I will be supportive. I wanted to make sure you knew what you were getting into."

At least he hadn't brought up Keith's kinky side. Her parents had never shied away from frank discussions, but she really didn't want to talk about that with her father.

"I do, Daddy. You're going to have to trust me. I'm learning how to handle Keith, and he's learning how to be in a real relationship."

Mario chuckled. "Just like your mother."

Another wave of nausea struck. She closed her eyes against it.

Her father got to his feet. "Do you need a barf bucket?"

"No." That answer was going to be true no matter what. She had a strict policy about not tossing her cookies. Especially not in front of witnesses. "I'm okay, but I really, really need the things on that list. Keith doesn't keep extra tampons around the house."

That got him moving. He could talk about flu symptoms all day long, but mention tampons and he was out the door. It was a bit manipulative of her, but he left her with no other options.

Completely aware of her tactics, he scowled. "Ten minutes, Trina. I'll be back in ten minutes. You lock the door behind me, and don't let anyone in until I get back."

―――――

Keith studied the documents through the clear plastic of the evidence bag. Inwardly he fumed. His outward demeanor betrayed nothing, but he knew Dustin would read him correctly anyway.

The first was a love letter, found under the wiper blade of Katrina's parked car. Dustin had come by one evening the week before and found it on her windshield. The cameras he and Malcolm had set up covered her parking space. That particular day, her neighbors had extra guests who had parked in Katrina's spot, forcing her to park outside the range of the cameras. Keith had been with her, so he hadn't seen the need to have the car moved.

The tone of the second letter was vastly different. In it, the stalker sounded angry. Dustin had found it on her bed two days prior, when someone had broken into her condo and trashed it. The stalker had found out about her relationship with Keith, and he wasn't happy about it.

The third, delivered to her desk with the interdepartmental mail, simply read *Die, whore*. "Before you go off the deep end, I had a very good reason for keeping this information confidential."

Keith was hard-pressed to think that anything could justify this omission. "He's been leaving letters for her, and you thought it was a good idea to keep it from me?"

Dustin leaned casually against the side of his desk. The small office had a huge window, and right now Keith was considering that Dustin might well die by defenestration before the hour was over. Dustin pursed his lips. "You would have overreacted."

"Overreacted? *Overreacted?*" Keith wanted to seize Dustin and shake him, but they were evenly matched, and that was no way to treat a fellow agent.

Dustin's eyes glittered like frosted diamonds. "We had nothing. No definitive prints. No DNA. The paper and envelope are generic, as is the pen he used. And there was nothing on video anywhere. With the activity almost at a standstill, I figured there was a leak, that somehow her stalker had found out the precautions we've taken. Keeping key evidence from you meant keeping it from him."

That was a tough pill to swallow, but it made sense, so Keith forced himself to assimilate the new information. "What do you have now?"

Dustin tapped the shortest note. "On the day this one was delivered, we have witnesses putting Buttermore in the payroll department."

"That's it?" Keith pinched the bridge of his nose. Aaron could have been collecting his last check or changing his deduction elections.

"They saw him wearing gloves, and they can put him near the mail cart as it came through the room. Plus we now have a partial. Using interdepartmental mail was a mistake on his part. There were too many factors. He couldn't control for them all."

The urge to punch Dustin receded. "A fingerprint. You should have led with that."

"I should have results by tomorrow. I don't want you to say anything to Trina until we know for sure. Just make sure she's not alone for a second."

Keith nodded. He could do that.

The next morning, Katrina awoke completely refreshed. She'd begun feeling better the night before. Her mother had brought chicken noodle soup over for dinner. They'd all eaten together in Keith's kitchen.

Donna had taken news of Katrina's relationship with Keith in stride. She'd treated him the same way she always had, only she made herself a little more at home in his house. Several of her comments had been critical of his decor, but they'd been aimed at Katrina.

Keith had merely smirked when Katrina protested that the way his house was decorated was none of her business, but he'd also taken pity on her and changed the subject. All in all, it had been a pleasant dinner with her boyfriend and her parents. She spent her lunch break at her desk, catching up on work she'd missed the day before. Though she'd called and texted Aaron several times in the past two days, he hadn't returned her calls.

While part of her knew he was angry about losing his job, a larger part of her questioned why he had reacted so vehemently. His behavior didn't make sense, and she wanted an explanation. When her cell rang and she saw his name on the screen, she dropped what she was doing and picked it up immediately.

"Hey, you. How are you holding up?" Pangs hit her hard in the stomach. She knew his suspension wasn't her fault, but she couldn't help feeling bad for him.

Aaron released a stream of air on the other end, making the connection sound staticky. "Better. Are you alone? Can you talk for a minute?"

"I'm at my desk. People are around, but nobody is listening." The office was never deserted until the workday was over. Many people worked through lunch.

"Listen carefully, and don't say my name."

Katrina frowned, but she figured Aaron wanted to confide in her, so she was determined to be a good friend. "Okay."

"A little while ago, I found out that somebody has been setting me up, signing my name to evidence logs, and then that evidence would go missing. Those... Shit. This line isn't secure. Can you meet me? I think they're going after you next."

"I can come now."

Katrina knew somebody had been doing the same thing to her. Though none of them had said anything, she knew Jordan, and probably others, suspected Aaron. To her dying day, she couldn't believe he was capable of such a betrayal. It looked like they were both being targeted. She'd hate to think that if she ended up in Aaron's shoes—and there was no telling where this was headed—she might find herself in need of a friend.

If nothing else, she wanted to hear his side of the story. She owed it to him to hear him out.

Besides, she knew how to hedge her bets. Even though she could handle herself and she didn't fear Aaron, Keith or Dustin would have tried to stop her. She fired up her computer and accessed the phone logs. Starr's number had to be in there, and Katrina needed to have a conversation with that woman.

---

People in dark blue jackets with the bright yellow FBI logo swarmed the building. Dustin was closeted in a room, watching footage from the parking garage. Katrina's car was missing. She'd assured Dustin that she had no plans to leave the building. She'd developed a habit of texting Dustin to let him know her whereabouts at all times. It made it easier to keep tabs on her.

Keith tried her cell one more time. As it had the last fifteen times, it went right to voice mail. In the past hour, he'd called every single one of her friends. Darcy and Layla had joined Donna and Mario at his house. They were stationed there in case Kat showed up.

Nobody had seen or heard from her in four hours.

Dustin entered the large, open office area, stopping to speak with Chief Alder. Keith crossed the room, his long strides eating the distance.

"What did you find?"

Dustin shook his head. "She entered the parking garage alone, got in her car, and left. I found footage of her getting on I-75 heading south. That's all."

Rage clouded his vision red. Keith saw nothing but that and the blazing blue of Dustin's irises. He grabbed his friend by the shirt with the intention of shoving him against the wall behind him, but Dustin's reflexes were every bit as fast. He countered Keith's move. Arms threaded underneath his, and he felt Malcolm pulling him backward.

"Easy, buddy. Losing it on Dustin won't bring her back. Save it for the motherfucker who took her."

Chief Alder straightened the jacket of her power suit. She held her head high and ignored Keith's display of emotion. "Gentlemen, I just got word that her cell records have arrived. Your efforts might be better served looking at those."

———

Katrina opened her eyes, but she couldn't see much. Faint light filtered through a grating in the wall. She guessed it was a vent of some kind. Her head felt worse than it did when her nephews "played" the piano at her parents' house for two hours straight.

She tried to move, but her arms and legs were stuck. The floor beneath her cheek was cold and hard. It smelled like grease and dirt. Panic stole her focus for a minute as she struggled against her bonds. Using the techniques Keith had taught her, she breathed until she had herself back under control.

The last thing she remembered was Aaron's smile. He'd been dressed in jeans and a cotton shirt that brought out the mossy green of his eyes. It had thrown her off to see him dressed so casually. Even when they got together outside of work, he always wore khakis and a button-down shirt.

The tenseness she'd heard in his voice during their hurried phone conversation didn't seem to be present in his relaxed stance. He'd held out his hand, as if he wanted to give her a hug. His smile had been tinged with regret and sadness.

Three steps from him, the world had gone black. Judging from the pain in her head, someone had hit her hard enough to knock her out. She probably had a concussion. This confirmed her worst suspicion and made her realize that Keith or Dustin would have been right to halt her plan. In retrospect, it hadn't been a good one.

It made sense, now that she was forced to stop rationalizing Aaron's intentions. In various circumstances, he'd enjoyed access to her things. It would be a small matter to copy her keys during lunch when she'd excused herself to use the restroom.

And he'd been in the perfect position to hear about all the security precautions Malcolm and Keith had installed at her house. When he'd visited her, he would have had time to discern the location of each camera, find their blind spots, and move them. She had no doubt that he'd broken into her apartment.

The back of a liquor store on the corner of Inkster and Eureka seemed like an out-of-the-way meeting place, but Katrina knew someone living nearby. Of course, Katrina didn't know how much she could trust...

Voices carried through the grating, intruding on her thoughts. She'd never imagined that this farce would go this far. She'd meant to trap the person setting up her and Aaron. In a million years, she wouldn't have thought him capable of arranging for her to be kidnapped. It seemed she really hadn't known him at all. She concentrated to try to make out the words she was hearing, but that only caused her head to throb harder. Breathing helped. It didn't banish the pain, but it reminded her that Keith, Malcolm, and probably half the FBI were out there, searching for her.

She'd left a trail. They were clever enough to find it.

"Move a shipment next month. We got orders from Lansing all the way to Tampa." The speaker was male. His voice vibrated through the air.

He was answered by another male. This one's voice was higher pitched, though still masculine. "We need merchandise. Snyder's arrest put a serious cramp in that side of the business. We gotta get it going again. It brings in more money than guns, and it's a hell of a lot easier to procure."

The two men chuckled for a moment. Then papers rustled.

The first voice spoke. "Buttermore better come through for us."

"If not, I have a plan for his lady friend. That's one we can't afford to have traced back to us."

Higher Voice grunted in agreement. "Did my homework. Bitch has connections to the Fed who took down Vic. Getting rid of her will win us big points with the boss."

Katrina realized that her kidnappers were not only working with Aaron, they were part of the larger Snyder syndicate the FBI had theorized existed. Now she had evidence of the connection. If only she could get free.

---

"She went to meet your mother."

Keith looked up from the list of numbers in his hand, evidence from the fastest cell phone dump in bureau history.

Malcolm fingered a sticky note. "I found this underneath her laptop. Good thing I picked it up to move it."

The small, yellow paper contained a clear message: *Starr R. Ink and Eur.* There was no telling how old it was. Katrina had been researching his family in order to find information about his niece and nephew.

Keith tapped the list in front of him. "The last call she made was to Starr Rossetti, whose last known address is in a trailer park near Inkster and Eureka."

Malcolm narrowed his eyes at Keith. "You think your mom is involved?"

Keith shook his head and stood up. He grabbed his jacket and checked for his guns. "Starr isn't that deep or intelligent. She doesn't have an interest in committing crimes on purpose, just in staying drunk. I don't know why Katrina called her, but I'm going to find out."

Running a hand through his hair in an anxious gesture, Malcolm rose to his feet. "You think your mom is still trying to make some kind of deal with her concerning your sister's kids?"

"Don't know. I wouldn't put it past her. She's a stubborn bitch, even when she's wasted." The pair headed for the elevator. Keith pressed the button.

"Well, you get it from somewhere." Mal delivered the joke with a grimace, and Keith knew his heart wasn't in it. Both of them were desperate to find Kat.

They stepped into the elevator. The doors shut them in that tiny steel room. Keith closed his eyes and, for the first time in his life, prayed to whatever deities were out there.

"We'll find her." Malcolm put a reassuring hand on Keith's shoulder.

Keith stared at his best friend's hand. Mal's olive skin was the exact same shade as Kat's. "I kissed Kat when she turned eighteen. I was drunk at the time. I was always drunk. It kept me numb, and that's how I needed to be. But she made me feel. She made me realize that I could handle some emotions. She made me want to be sober. I think I've always been in love with her."

Malcolm stared at him. Keith expected his hand to drop away, or for Mal to punch him—something violent and retaliatory. Instead, Mal squeezed his shoulder affectionately. "My sister is pretty damn special."

"I'm going to marry her."

Mal nodded. "I know."

"First I'm going to kill the bastard who took her."

Mal's lips thinned into a grim slash. "I got your back."

He didn't mention that she'd definitely earned a punishment for this. He couldn't even envision punishing her when all he wanted to do was hold her in his arms. The punishment might involve being chained to him at all times. He'd think about it later, when he had her back with him, safe and sound.

The elevator doors opened to reveal Dustin. He leveled a stoic stare at them as he stepped back to let them exit the car. "I was just coming up to see you."

Keith ignored Dustin. Standing next to him was a woman who had a lot of explaining to do. "Mom. Where the hell is Kat?"

She looked like hell, and that was saying a lot. Her gray-streaked blonde hair was pulled back into a ponytail. Half the strands hung free, as if she'd forgotten it was up, and she'd run her fingers through it repeatedly. Ghosts showed in her sunken eyes, and she smelled like a cigarette factory had exploded in her mouth. She shook so hard it was a wonder she was still on her feet.

She darted forward and gripped his jacket. Fear deepened the lines around her mouth and eyes. "Keith, they took her. She called me, said she wanted to talk about them kids. I was waiting out back, like she told me to, and they took her."

Hope surged through Keith's body. Kat hadn't disappeared without a trace. "Who? Mom, think. I need to know exactly what you saw."

She bit her lip. "First I need a promise from you."

"I'll get you a drink as soon as you tell me what you know." He'd gladly give her a lifetime supply of vodka and wine if she could help him find Kat.

"No. I want you to promise to see Savannah's kids. You're the only kid I got who ain't drunk or in jail. You take care of them. You make sure they're okay."

He'd do anything to get Kat back. "I promise." He pushed his mother away from the elevator and deposited her in an alcove. Dustin and Malcolm stood behind him, both of them poised to act on any new information.

Starr nodded. "I took pictures."

---

Katrina worked the ropes binding her arms behind her. It took some time, but she was able to loosen them enough to slip one hand free. These men either didn't have much experience with knots and rigging, or they didn't come across people who tried to escape them.

The reasons a captive might not try to escape were ones Katrina didn't want to consider. She kept her thoughts positive and untied her ankles. The voices in the next room had vanished, and from the opening and closing of doors, she thought they either had left or they were in another room.

She'd been unconscious when they'd brought her here, and she truly had no idea how much time had passed. Her head felt cottony, and her thought processes were not working quite as fast as normal.

The one thing she knew for sure was that she was pissed at Aaron. In her whole life, she couldn't remember being this angry. Part of the haze she saw had to have come from the blow to her head, but the rest of it came from her fury. Why on earth would he do those horrible things? Was he threatened by her competence? Jealous because she'd never shown an interest in him? She'd loved Aaron as a friend, worked with him, leaned on him, confided in him—and he'd reciprocated by stalking her. He'd violated her home, defiled her furniture and clothes, and stripped away her sense of safety and security.

And she'd proofread his fucking briefs. She'd covered for him, advocated for him to keep his job. Keith had indicated he wanted to kill her stalker, but now he was going to have to get in line. When the bastard had been a nameless, faceless entity, Katrina had been happy to let Keith have him. Things had changed. This was personal, and she wanted retribution.

Now that she was free, she felt around, exploring her new, dark environment. The scant light showing through the grating wasn't very helpful. She crashed into a metal shelf unit, which brought footsteps pounding down the hall.

Frantic, she grabbed a section of brackets that had come loose. When the door to her prison opened, she swung. No thinking—she acted purely on instinct. The blow took the man in front by surprise. He fell to the ground, a heavy lump whose head cracked against the cement floor.

The second man stood back. He aimed his gun at her chest. "Put it down, bitch."

Katrina took exception to being called a bitch, especially when her behavior was completely warranted. Again, she went with her instincts. She swung again, aiming for the man's wrist.

With a loud *bang*, the gun went off. Katrina hefted her makeshift club back and whacked the second man in the face. Blood poured from a gash, and he screamed. She'd never heard a man scream before. The sound shook some of the cobwebs loose inside her brain.

She backed away, slowly making her way down the hall in the direction she'd seen the gun fly. It wasn't as easy to look for a gun as television shows made it out to be. There was no close-up shot of the gun lying under a pile of debris. The hallway was fairly clear. Orangey-yellow paint covered most of the walls.

Piles of industrial plastic sheeting were pushed against the walls in several places.

Taking her gaze from the groaning gunman wasn't an option. It was a good thing she stepped on the gun. Unfortunately, she twisted her ankle in the process and fell on her ass.

The second man, blood dripping down his face and onto his shirt, lunged for her. She scrambled for the gun and pulled the trigger without aiming. In a perfect world, she would have shot him in the chest. As it was, she was thankful not to have hit herself.

A small spot of blood appeared on his arm. He screamed again, a high-pitched, girlie sound that matched his skinny-boy exterior. "Bitch! You're not going to get out of here alive!"

Thick arms banded around her, pinning her arms to her sides. She bowed out her body, flinging her head back and kicking with her heels at the same time. A sickening crunch and another scream told her she'd hit her target.

The sharp pain in the back of her skull sent waves of nausea through her system. She threw up a little in her mouth, but she just spat it out. The arms around her loosened. With a screech, she used her head and jabbed backward with her elbows.

The man dropped her. She fell to the floor, twisting as she did so. She made no attempt to catch herself. She brought the gun up, aimed, and shot.

Behind her, the sounds of people moving reached her ears. The woolly feeling in her head grew thicker. She turned around to find nobody there. Black dots danced in her field of vision.

"I came here to save you." That voice had laughed with her and lent her emotional support for nearly two years. Now it was laced with disbelief. "I thought we were friends."

Friends didn't kidnap one another. Aaron had only kept her close to screw her over. She moved slowly and regarded Aaron with pure hatred. "You stalked me, set me up to lose my job, and had me kidnapped. You are *not* my friend."

Blood seeped from a hole in his side and spread in a circle, staining his clothes. She watched the growing flower bloom, her finger on the trigger of the gun and her back against the wall. She motioned toward his pocket.

"Give me your cell. I'll call an ambulance."

———

Keith let Malcolm drive. Mal's little silver sports car went fast and cornered well.

The video on his mother's phone hadn't lasted that long, and it had been fuzzy, but he'd been able to make out Kat greeting Aaron. Then two men came out from behind a large metal trash bin, knocked her over the head, and carted her off.

His mother had hidden behind a line of bushes and trash separating the store from the houses next to it. She'd only been able to get a partial plate for the car that had taken Kat, but she'd been able to get everything they needed to put Buttermore away for a long time.

Dustin had cursed under his breath. None of them had thought Buttermore capable of this. They'd pegged him as a low-level patsy. Jordan had led a team to wait outside Buttermore's house. Another team watched Buttermore's mother's house.

Dustin had crowded his large body into Malcolm's backseat. He wore a headset and consulted a tablet. "Take the next left. Buttermore is making a call right now."

Keith kept his eyes on the road. He knew the area. This was where they'd tracked Friedman the weekend before. They'd been hunting for reasons to get a search warrant for these warehouses. He exchanged a glance with Malcolm. Both of them were thinking the same thing. If the Friedman brothers were involved, then Kat's life was truly at stake. They wouldn't leave her as a loose end.

"Fuck me. Trina's calling an ambulance." Dustin sputtered, his voice growing louder with excitement. "Turn right. Take another quick right. Here. We're here."

Malcolm slammed on the brakes. The three of them sprang from the car, pulling their guns as they hustled to the building. Keith led the charge, using the hand signals they all knew so well.

In the back of the warehouse, he found Kat, sitting with her back against a wall and a gun trained on a wounded Aaron Buttermore. She looked up at him, a wan smile on her face. "Check me out. I saved myself. Don't touch that metal bracket. I whacked both the guys who kidnapped me with it. I'm thinking hair and blood samples."

Then her eyelids closed, and she passed out.

# Chapter Sixteen

Keith couldn't believe how much Kat perked up once she'd had some plasma and her family was gathered around her. Aaron had confessed to kidnapping and a host of other crimes. He'd negotiated a plea that involved a lesser charge in exchange for his cooperation. It turned out he knew a lot about the Snyder-Friedman syndicate.

Keith stood by the window in her hospital room as her parents flanked her, delivering regular hugs and a smattering of tears. Every once in a while, Mama L would brush her fingers over Kat's cheek, shaking as she avoided touching the area of Kat's head wrapped in white bandages. Kat had sustained one hell of a concussion. For the first time in his life, Keith almost cried with relief. Almost.

When visiting hours ended and everybody had gone, he glowered at the nurse who told him it was time to leave. He flashed his badge. She gave him a skeptical look and shrugged. "We let spouses stay the night. That chair over there converts into a sleeper."

Kat smiled at him as he sat on the edge of her bed. He'd spent the last two hours pacing her room, afraid to come closer because he might shake her if he did.

She didn't seem to be afraid, though. She placed her hand on his cheek. "Those self-defense lessons you and Malcolm gave me sure came in handy."

"I have the urge to take you home and lock you in the dungeon just because I know you'll be safe down there."

A little bit of the forced cheer faded from her eyes. "I had no idea Aaron was mentally unhinged. He was such a good friend to me."

Keith shook his head. "You should have called me, Kat."

"You wouldn't have let me go."

No, he wouldn't have. "I would have put together a sting operation. We could have nabbed the Friedman brothers too."

She had identified the brothers from photographs, but the DNA evidence would take a little more time to come back.

Tears rolled down her cheeks, fat ones that showed no signs it would be a short shower. He folded his arms around her, and she buried her face in his shoulder. She'd kept it together for her parents and brothers, but now that it was just the two of them, she could let it all out.

---

When the nurse came in the next morning, she didn't bother being quiet about it. Katrina opened her eyes to find Keith in the narrow hospital bed with her, cradling her in his arms. No wonder she'd slept so well. He gave her a sleepy smile and kissed her forehead. It amazed her that he could spend the night crammed sideways in a hospital bed and still wake up looking like sex incarnate.

She smiled at the black-haired nurse, who frowned back at her and pointed at Keith. "Sir, you can't be in that bed."

He sat up slowly, stretching muscles that had to be sore. "Good morning, ladies."

The nurse rolled her eyes and checked the machines hooked up to Katrina. "I'm Brenda, and you're going home. The doctor will stop by in an hour or so to talk to you. I'll process your paperwork so you can leave once he gives the okay."

That was good news to Katrina. She hadn't wanted to stay overnight, much less for the day. They'd gathered evidence from her body and run her through a battery of tests. The concussion could take months to heal, and she was more than ready to go home now.

"Do I have time for a shower?"

Brenda pumped the blood pressure cuff full of air. "Yep. Doctor starts rounds at eight. You have a couple hours."

Keith frowned. "Are you sure she should get out of bed? She was too weak to walk yesterday."

"She's fine. Probably still weak, so don't overdo it." Brenda gave Keith a tolerant smile. "Can you step out for a minute?"

He muttered something about getting coffee and left the room. After the nurse finished her exam, Katrina took a shower. She emerged fully dressed to find Keith lounging on the chair he was supposed to have folded out and slept in. His large frame dwarfed the piece of furniture. There was no way he would have been able to sleep on that thing.

He motioned to a cardboard cup. "It might be cold by now. I can get you more. Your mother brought a change of clothes. She's at your condo with Darcy and Layla. They're packing your things and moving them to my house. Malcolm and your dad are replacing your front door and reinforcing the frame. New locks again."

She wrapped her hospital gown tighter around her body and sipped the coffee. It was cool, but it hit the spot. "Thank you. I didn't want to wear those dirty clothes home."

"They're in evidence. You won't get them back."

"Mom didn't want to stay?" She was a little hurt to have missed her mother.

Keith lifted her and put her on his lap. With his arms around her, she felt safe. "She said you were in good hands. She's making chocolate ice cream with brownie chunks to go with lunch."

That was one of Katrina's favorite flavors, a figurative hug from her mother. She snuggled into Keith's embrace. "What happened to Aaron?"

He stroked her hair and pressed his cheek to her head. "He's in a secure wing recovering from a GSW to the stomach and a broken nose. He was surprised to see us and fell backward. Broke some bones and smashed his face."

Katrina knew better than to ask more. The shot she'd delivered to Aaron had been nonfatal, leaving clear entrance and exit wounds. No doubt some of the other injuries had been inflicted by her brother and Keith. "I'm glad he survived. He's not right in the head. He needs help."

From the way Keith snorted, she gathered he didn't agree with her assessment. "Kat, there's something I've neglected to say to you."

At the gravity in his tone, she peeled herself away from him so she could see his face. "Go on."

A brief smile flashed across his lips. "I love you."

It was a momentous occasion. She knew he'd never said those words out loud before, not to anybody. He probably wouldn't say them to her very often, but she could live with that. She cupped his cheek. "I know. I love you too."

"I want you to move in with me. We'll get married, and I'll take care of you for the rest of my life."

She laughed. "That wasn't quite the romantic proposal I expected."

His brows drew together, and he frowned. "What were you expecting? I don't know how to be romantic, and that whole kneeling thing just isn't me."

"Hmm." She pretended to consider. "I think we'll have to work on the romance part. I like romantic. It makes me feel loved and appreciated."

He sighed. "I can't promise anything but that I'll try."

That was all she wanted. The fact he was willing to make the effort meant the world. Perhaps he wasn't well versed in romance, but he was intelligent and a fast learner. He'd get the hang of it eventually. She rewarded him with a kiss.

"I have something else to tell you." He leaned back in his seat and rested his head against the cushion. Tension stiffened his body, and some of the color had left his face.

She rubbed her hand up and down his chest. "I'm listening."

He sighed. "For my nineteenth birthday, I bought myself a vasectomy. I've never told that to anyone before. I can't get you pregnant. If you want kids in a few years, we can talk about adoption."

"Why would you do that?" She'd always thought that kind of surgery was something a woman had to talk a man into, not something he did voluntarily. And part of her wondered about his reluctance to meet his niece and nephew.

"I never thought I'd be in a position to think about having kids around. But with you, things seem somehow possible. I'd never deny you anything, Kitty Kat, but if you want kids, then that's the only way it's going to happen."

She smacked his shoulder as hard as she could. He didn't flinch. "I mean, why would a healthy young man voluntarily get a vasectomy? You said I'm the only woman you haven't used a condom with."

Some of the stiffness left him, and that ever-present self-confidence wavered. "I'm not sure if you were paying attention when Malcolm was arguing against you dating me, but I'm an alcoholic. I've been sober for nine years, four months, and twenty-seven days. It's not something I tell people or talk about. My sisters and parents are alcoholics. Even my grandparents were heavy drinkers. I think I have an uncle somewhere who is also a drunk. Somebody like me has no business having kids."

She had no business feeling betrayed or upset. At the core of this was a sacrifice by a man she loved, one that probably took a lot of courage and self-loathing to make. Her heart broke for the person he'd been, even though that heartache created the man she loved.

She took his hand in hers. "I'll still marry you. It doesn't change the fact that I love you."

He looked at her, fathoms of sadness swimming behind his eyes. "I never planned to fall in love, especially with you. I always thought you deserved better. I still do. But now I'm not willing to let you go, so you're stuck with me, for better or for worse."

She planted a subdued kiss on his lips. "Sounds good to me."

# Epilogue
*Three Months Later*

Katrina checked the thick leather belt encircling his midsection. He wore nothing else on his magnificent body. "Is it loose enough?"

Keith smiled patiently. It was the third time she'd asked that question. "It's fine. Too loose and it'll fall off." When she reached to check it again, he grabbed her wrists, halting her action. "If I say you're ready, then you're ready. Stop stalling, Kitty Kat."

He'd made her practice with the flogger for two weeks, but he hadn't let her start until he felt she was sufficiently healed from her ordeal. She'd vented some of her pent-up energy on pillows, and then he'd propped a futon mattress against the wall with pieces of colored tape marking various targets. She'd become pretty good at hitting the target, which had led Keith to consent to this step.

As they were preparing to come down to the dungeon, he'd carelessly dropped a bombshell on her. He'd never allowed a submissive to flog him. The people he usually saw for this kind of thing weren't dominant either. They were pure sadists, interested only in the delivery of pain.

Though he'd given her the opportunity to chicken out, she hadn't chosen that avenue. She wanted to do this for him. It was just jitters. She wasn't sure if the jitters came from the fact that she'd never done this or from Keith's warning that he might not be all that gentle afterward.

He turned around, and she snapped his wrist cuffs to the Saint Andrew's cross. While he wasn't keen on putting her up there, she was very familiar with how to secure the snaps. He liked to tie her to the Y-table, the brand-new spanking bench, and the exam chair. She'd come to realize that the cross was for him, a fantasy he kept that proved he wasn't as jaded as he'd originally thought. When she'd pointed that observation out to him, he'd just smiled and continued painting her toenails, an activity it turned out he very much enjoyed.

"I'm going to start slow and warm you up."

"Don't push it, Kitty Kat. Stop when you get tired. Stamina will come with time and practice."

The wrist cuffs were to remind him not to move. They in no way indicated that she was in charge of the scene. He trusted her to do right by him.

She targeted the upper left section of his back first. Today she wasn't going to do anything fancy like move around to hit unexpected areas or vary the intensity of her swing. Keith was quite skilled with those nuances. While she enjoyed them, he'd been clear that she couldn't expect to have that level of skill in just a few weeks. He'd been at this for years.

On his torso, his skin was still bronzed from working in the yard, but his ass was lily-white. When she got to those knee-weakening, sculpted muscles, she enjoyed the pattern of emerging marks. As she played over that area, she lost herself in the darkening shades of red that layered one on top of the other.

Her head buzzed, and she realized that she'd been at it far longer than she'd intended. She placed the flogger on a table at the side of the room and released his cuffs. Immediately he pushed her to her knees. She'd forgotten his first condition. After the flogging, she was to kneel and thank him for letting her pleasure him this way.

"Thank you for allowing me to flog you, Keith. You have a very nice ass."

He didn't say anything, but the long, hard length of his cock pointed eagerly in her direction. Finally, he gathered her hair in one hand. "It's a rush, isn't it, Kitty Kat?"

A rush? Yes. That was a good way to describe it. It was almost like subspace except that she was the one responsible for the action of the scene. "Yes, it was."

"You need to be careful to stay in the present. Dommes who go too far often do so when they're completely unaware of what's happening with the sub. They're lost in the feel of the swing or the snap of the whip or the way the lines and welts make pretty designs. They forget there's a living, breathing person on the other end. That's how accidents happen." His voice was soft, not at all the feral monster he'd predicted. She wondered if she'd disappointed him.

"I'm sorry, Keith. Did I hurt you too much?" Her heart was heavy with dread. She hadn't wanted to hurt him. No part of her was a sadist. She wanted to give him this in order to please him.

"No, Kitty Kat. But it's one of the reasons I'm not letting you use the heavier floggers yet." With his free hand, he cupped her chin and ran his thumb along her lip. "That was pretty good for your first time. I am pleased with you, and I'm going to reward you."

She wanted to ask how, but she knew better than to speak. Using the tangle of her hair as a guide, he helped her to her feet. Then he hooked his arm under her knees and swept her off the floor. The firm mattress they'd used for target practice now sat on a frame in the corner of the dungeon.

He set her down gently and settled himself on top of her. The kiss began sweetly, with the worshipping of her cheeks and eyelids. Then he explored her lips leisurely. She opened to him on a breathless sigh, luxuriating in his expert attention. The man kissed like a god, and he was all hers.

With tiny, teasing forays, he deepened the kiss. By the time he ravaged her with his tongue, she was lost in the sweetest bliss. Then he positioned his cock at her entrance and thrust inside, claiming her swiftly. Given the pace he'd set so far, she expected him to make love to her slowly, but Keith had other ideas. The frenzy took him, and he pumped his hips, taking her with long, hard strokes that filled her completely and then left her empty and pining for more.

She whimpered as the fire grew. She became a cinder, a hot ember floating through the air, and she held on to his shoulders to keep from drifting away. She whispered his name, but it evolved into a scream and a desperate request for orgasm.

"Please let me come, Master. Please, oh please!"

With a growling purr, he bit her earlobe. "Yes, Kitty Kat. Come for me."

The bomb inside exploded, and she forgot how to move. Her arms dropped down on either side of her head, and the legs she'd been unaware were wrapped around his hips also fell with a dull thud. Keith's body jerked as he came, and then he collapsed next to her.

"Thank you, Master."

He gave her a satisfied smile. When she felt it to the core of her heart, she used his title, and she was okay with that.

---

Later they went upstairs, hand in hand, to take a shower. Her parents expected them to be on time for Thanksgiving dinner. On the way to the master suite, they passed one of the guest bedrooms that Keith had converted into a child's room. He'd arranged a crib along one wall. Perpendicular to it was a pink-and-white toddler's bed, complete with side rails. A dresser, a low set of shelves, and a huge toy bin rounded out the furniture.

Mrs. Daley was still working on a permanent placement for Angelina and Corey, but Keith had been granted regular visiting privileges, which he exercised at least twice each week. The kids hadn't stayed overnight, but they'd napped in that room quite often.

Katrina bit her bottom lip as they passed. Keith might protest now that having children wasn't a priority, but she'd seen him with Corey, a little blond boy who greatly resembled his uncle. And Angelina had wrapped him completely around her tiny finger. She had only to smile up at him with those big brown eyes, and he would scoop her into his arms and swing her around.

They'd dealt with one full-out tantrum. Keith had kept his calm as he wrapped her in his embrace, which had helped Angelina normalize. Since then, they'd been working on appropriate ways to express anger and frustration. It wasn't easy, but Mrs. Daley had been helpful in providing names of counselors. While they hadn't discussed the idea of the children becoming a more permanent part of their lives, the possibility remained out there, with Mrs. Daley giving them stronger and less veiled suggestions every time they met.

Keith and Katrina stepped into the shower together, and he drew her into his arms. He kissed her lips and whispered in her ear, "Touch yourself for me."

Katrina reclined on the shower seat, one of her favorite features in the house they now shared, and lifted one foot to let it rest on the edge. Across from her, Keith stroked his cock as he watched her through his half-closed lids.

"I love you, Kat."

She smiled at the man of her dreams. "I love you too, Keith."

# Michele Zurlo

I'm Michele Zurlo, author of over 20 romance novels. During the day, I teach English, and in the evenings, romantic tales flow from my fingertips.

I'm not half as interesting as my characters. My childhood dreams tended to stretch no further than the next book in my to-be-read pile, and I aspired to be a librarian so I could read all day. I'm pretty impulsive when it comes to big decisions, especially when it's something I've never done before. Writing is just one in a long line of impulsive decisions that turned out to showcase my great instincts. Find out more at www.michelezurloauthor.com or @MZurloAuthor.

# Excerpt from Re/Claimed

Dustin wanted to be her boyfriend. He wanted to date her. Go steady. Be an item. It seemed both juvenile and momentous.

After Brodie, the man she'd thought would fill the roles of friend, lover, and Master, had proven to be not at all the person she'd thought he was, she had sworn off dating a Dom. The liberties he'd taken—and forced her to consent to—still gave her nightmares. Memories snuck up on her at the oddest times, battering her with intense waves of humiliation that stole her confidence and sense of self.

Yes, Dustin was a good man—much too good for her. Once he found out about the things she'd allowed Brodie to make her do, he would gently break her heart and run as far as he could go.

Dustin's palm pressed against hers, warm and firm, tangible proof that she was about to take a step forward. Right now, she had paused in a figurative half-step, her foot hovering uncertainly in the air. Once she put her foot down and shifted her weight, the ground behind her would fall away, leaving her forever teetering on the precipice.

Full disclosure. She should warn him of the consequences to his actions.

"Dustin, if you're serious about this, I think you should know that I date vanilla."

He didn't move. She lifted her gaze from the floor to find him staring at her curiously. Was she nervous? Utterly. She stared back, her manner appropriately sober.

"Why?"

No need to go into the details or give voice to uncomfortable memories. "BDSM scenes are fun, but they're not what I'm looking for in a long-term relationship. If I ever settle down, I want a husband, not a Master." Nobody was ever going to order or coerce her into doing anything she didn't want to do. Not again.

He brushed his thumb back and forth over her wrist, evidence that he was both considering and bothered by her assertion. "Can't you have both?"

Once she'd thought it possible. Brodie had proven her theory wrong. "No. A husband is a partner. A Master is the boss. That's exciting, but impractical for the long haul. I just think you should know my views on the issue before you decide to change lanes." Silence fell in a heavy, oppressive blanket, but she didn't attempt to alleviate it with mindless chatter, further explanation, or false assurances.

Finally his head bobbed a brief nod, indicating he'd arrived at a conclusion. "So you're thinking that we'll eventually get married?"

# Lost Goddess Publishing

Visit www.lostgoddesspublishing.com for information about our other titles.

## Lost Goddess Publishing Anthologies

BDSM Anthology/Club Alegria #1-3
New Adult Anthology/Lovin' U #1-4
Menage Anthology/Club Alegria #4-7

## Lost Goddess Publishing Novels

Re/Bound (Doms of the FBI 1) by Michele Zurlo
Re/Paired (Doms of the FBI 2) by Michele Zurlo
Re/Claimed (Doms of the FBI 3) by Michele Zurlo
Blade's Ghost by Michele Zurlo
Nexus #1: Tristan's Lover by Nicoline Tiernan
Tessa by Ali Baran
Dragon Kisses 1 by Michele Zurlo
Dragon Kisses 2 by Michele Zurlo
Dragon Kisses 3 by Michele Zurlo

*Re/Paired*

Made in the USA
Middletown, DE
09 September 2016